the rebel

the
rebel

SPADE
HOTEL

USA TODAY BESTSELLING AUTHOR

MARNI MANN

Entangled Publishing, LLC
644 Shrewsbury Commons Ave., STE 181
Shrewsbury, PA 17361
rights@entangledpublishing.com

Amara is an imprint of Entangled Publishing, LLC.

Visit our website at www.entangledpublishing.com.

Edited by Jovana Shirley/Unforeseen Editing
Cover art and design by Hang Le/By Hang Le
Interior design by Britt Marczak

ISBN 978-1-64937-738-8

First Edition February 2024

P1

ALSO BY MARNI MANN

The Spade Hotel series

The Playboy
The Rebel
The Sinner

The Dalton Family series

The Lawyer
The Billionaire
The Single Dad
The Intern
The Bachelor

The Agency series

Signed
Endorsed
Contracted
Negotiated
Dominated

Some women like heroes.
But this is for all the women who prefer The Rebels, the naughty
men who deliver in every deliciously dirty way.
Ways you can only dream of…

Playlist

"South Dakota"—Chris Stapleton

"The Fire"—Chris Stapleton

"Wildflowers and Wild Horses"—Lainey Wilson

"Part II"—Jay-Z, featuring Beyoncé

"What Ifs"—Kane Brown, featuring Lauren Alaina

"Take Me to the Bottom"—The Cadillac Three

"Lose Control"—Teddy Swims

"Like You Mean It"—Steven Rodriguez

"The One That You Call"—Mackenzy Mackay

"What You Waiting On"—Hueston

"Porch Light"—Josh Meloy

"Angel"—Toby Mai

"Save Me"—Jelly Roll

Prologue

COOPER

"Don't fuck this up," my uncle, Walter Spade, hissed from the head of the conference room table, his salt-and-pepper hair glistening from the fluorescent lights above.

As he looked at me, squinting, the lines around his eyes deepened. His hands gripped the back of his chair as he stood behind it, refusing to sit.

When Walter was disconnected from work, he was the nicest guy in the world.

When it came to anything related to Spade Hotels—the company he had founded with my father, where my brothers and I worked—he was one nasty motherfucker.

Today was certainly no exception.

"You have nothing to worry about," I replied. "The land will be ours as soon as I see it, assuming I deem it worthy enough to add to our collection."

"You'd better act fast," Macon, my youngest brother, said from the seat next to mine. His dark brown beard was coming in thick, longer than I'd ever seen him grow it. Since spending all those months in Hawaii building one of our latest properties, he'd developed a more relaxed, surfer-like appearance. He'd also come home with a woman—something I never anticipated. "Since you know we're not the only ones looking at it, right?"

The land he was referring to was supposedly a slice of paradise along the shoreline of Lake Louise—a lake within Banff National Park, nestled in the Canadian Rockies.

Until I saw it in person, I wouldn't be able to confirm just how perfect it was.

"I bet all the big names are eyeing it," Brady, my oldest brother, said from the other side of me. His hair was freshly spiked, like he'd just stepped out of the shower. If I had to guess, he'd probably fucked a woman in the backseat while his driver brought him to work this morning, then showered in his en suite once he arrived in his office. That man wasn't just a player. When it came to women, he was a goddamn sinner. "If the realtor reached out to us, then she reached out to everyone. That means all our competitors will be viewing that property tomorrow."

"I fully expect a bidding war," Jo, my cousin, said with a smile, clasping her hands and aligning each finger before she tapped them together. Her white nail polish caught the light above, reflecting the illumination and shining like a mirror. "This is going to be fun."

Walter's daughter thrived on the anticipation of the fight and the win.

Even though she was a Dalton now—her wedding to Jenner, my best friend, who happened to be sitting beside her, was less than a month ago—she was full of Spade blood.

And the Spades always won.

"Let's not get ahead of ourselves, honey," Walter said to Jo. "Cooper will arrive before any of the others, and the offer that Jenner's going to submit will be more than fair."

"And contingent on an immediate decision," Jenner added, completely relaxed in his seat, unfazed by Walter's orders. "We're not giving the others time to counter."

Jenner's family owned one of the largest, most successful law firms in the country. The Daltons—Jenner and his two brothers, Dominick and Ford, along with their twin cousins, Hannah and Camden—represented all different fields of law.

Jenner had been working with the Spades long before he became part of our family and was a wild bachelor prior to settling down with my cousin.

Confident. Cocky. And a hell of a good time.

That was Jenner Dalton.

He also happened to be one of the richest, most successful people I knew.

"Which means, again, Cooper, you can't fuck this up." Walter wiped his mouth, like he'd just spit. "Timing is the only thing we have on our side."

I'd been working for my uncle since I'd graduated from the University of Southern California, following in my father's footsteps. He'd retired from Spade Hotels about ten years ago, preferring a life on the beach with my mom rather than reporting to his office every day. Walter had bought him out, and part of the deal was that when the three of us had enough years under our belt and put in our time, we would be equal owners, along with our cousin, Jo. The transition hadn't happened yet. Walter wasn't ready to retire.

But in the seven years I'd been employed with Spade Hotels, I'd done some remarkable things for our brand. I'd established levels of luxury that our competitors hadn't even thought of launching. I'd hired some of the most competent, efficient general managers.

But this—this property, this acquisition, if it went through the way I hoped it would—would be my biggest accomplishment to date.

"Don't stress. I've got this," I said to Walter. "I fly out in the morning. Since the following day is Christmas Eve, I'm not staying the night. I'll call Jenner from the property and have him process the offer, so it hits right before the holiday. We'll have things signed and sealed before the new year."

Walter's knuckles turned white before he released the chair and crossed his arms over his chest.

I knew the gesture well.

We were about to get another earful.

"One day, I'll hand over the reins to the four of you—Jenner, I'm not leaving you out. I just know I'll never be able to drag you over to our side." Walter offered a rare smile. "And when you all run this business, you'll know exactly the kind of pressure that's involved on a daily basis. In the meantime, don't tell me not to stress—stressing is my fucking job." As he exhaled, his nostrils flared. "If I want the company to stay on top, I have to continue growing it, but it has to be the right kind of advancement, for the right dollar amount, and I need the right people running the operation." He nodded toward the monitor in the back of the room, which showed aerial footage of the land in Alberta. "You all know Canada has been on my radar for a long time, but the land and price were never right."

His stare returned to me. "I'm counting on you, Cooper. Don't fucking let me down."

I nodded.

Walter then glanced around the room. "Anyone else have anything to contribute?"

There was silence.

Until Jo said, "There's something I need to discuss with you. I'll walk you to your office." As she got up from her chair, she clasped Jenner's shoulder, waving at me and my brothers before she followed her father out of the room.

The moment the door shut, Jenner said, "Don't fuck this up," in a voice that was meant to sound like Walter's. He placed his hands behind his head, his elbows bent, leaning back in his chair like he was in a goddamn recliner.

"Come on, my man. Everyone in this room knows I've got this. This is what I'm good at." I circled the air, pointing at my brothers. "What we're all good at."

Macon had done the same thing in Hawaii, and Brady, in Florida.

My brothers and I weren't meant to sit behind a desk and push paperwork. The three of us needed to be out in the field, overseeing the design, build, and changeover of our properties, making sure things ran according to our standards.

The Spade standards.

We didn't do it for higher titles—we were already part of the executive team. We did it because we loved it, because this was what we had been born to do.

And when situations like this occurred, it came with a rush.

A surge of adrenaline.

A level of control that we all strived for.

Like laying a woman on her back and thrusting into her cunt.

Fuck, there was nothing better.

"You know I'm just giving you shit," Jenner said. "You're going to crush this, and then I'll take care of things on my end."

"And then we're all going to celebrate on Christmas," Brady added.

Jenner chuckled. "Another Dalton and Spade celebration." His arms dropped, and he shook his head. "You should see the amount of wine and booze Jo had delivered to the house last night in preparation for the party. Do you know the mayhem that's about to ensue?"

Since our families had melded, the Spades now spent the

holidays with the Daltons. Birthdays were celebrated together.

This year, the newlyweds had requested to host Christmas, and no one had put up a fight.

"All I know is that I won't be the first one to pass out," Macon said.

We all laughed.

Macon had fallen asleep at the last get-together after drinking way too much, and Ford's daughter, Everly, had drawn all over his face with a marker.

Of course, she hadn't come up with the idea on her own. Camden and I'd had a little something to do with it.

Still, he'd never live it down.

"I ordered three bottles of tequila just for you, brother," Jenner joked.

"Tequila and I broke up after that night." Macon shoved his hands through the sides of his hair. "Never again, do you hear me?"

"No one told you to have that many shots on an empty stomach, asshole," Brady said.

"Listen, I was missing my girl, all right?" He paused while we remembered the ordeal—when Brooklyn had gone back to Hawaii to visit her family, leaving Macon like a puppy chained to a fucking stake. All sad eyes and mopey. "Besides, I can hold my liquor, and I guarantee I can outdrink all you fools."

Jenner smiled at him. "I don't know about that, but what you *can* guarantee is that you are an expert at getting Sharpie off your skin."

Macon flipped him off. "Fucker."

Jenner chuckled as he stood. "I need to get back to the office." He looked at me. "Have a safe trip to Canada tomorrow. Call me the second you're ready to submit that offer."

"I will," I replied.

Chapter One

Cooper

"Talk to me," Walter said as he answered my call.

I climbed into the backseat of the SUV, wiping the snowy wetness off my hair. "It's exceptional. Everything we're looking for in a property. We need to make an offer immediately."

Even with the heat blasting through the vents, my cheeks feeling the warmth, my hands starting to thaw, I shivered.

Winter was a temperature I couldn't handle.

"Were you the only one there? Or were others viewing the property too?"

As the driver pulled out of the gravel lot, the tires crunching over the accumulated snow, I glanced behind me. Just as I'd expected, the realtor's car was still the only one in the lot.

"It was just me, and now, the conditions outside are fucking brutal. The snow is coming in thick and heavy, and it's not supposed to let up. The pilot even delayed my return flight by three hours, hoping the runway will be cleared by then." Now that we were on the road, I looked through the windshield, where the visibility was diminishing and not a single car was on either side. "No one is going to view the property until it stops snowing. I don't know if that'll be today or tomorrow."

"Get in touch with Jenner. I want the ball rolling. Now."

"Sure thing."

Walter disconnected the call, and I pulled up the last text I'd sent to my best friend when I flew out this morning—a TikTok that reminded me of Macon and the masterpiece Everly had created on his face.

Me: *Make the offer. That property needs to be ours.*

Jenner: *It will be. I'm on it.*

I'd caught up on emails while the driver carefully maneuvered the icy roads, slowly making his way toward Lake Louise's highest-rated hotel, where I'd be killing time until my flight. There was no sense in waiting at the private airport. I'd rather check out the competition and get myself a drink in their bar.

It turned out that the competition was less than a mile down the road with an entrance that lacked appeal, trees that needed trimming, a driveway that should have already been plowed, and bellhops whose uniforms were mismatched. The hotel's ranking, which varied depending on the website, fluctuated between four and five stars.

From the exterior alone, I could tell this was no five-star resort.

Once our hotel was complete, we'd show the visitors of this town what luxury, ambiance and class really looked like.

The SUV came to a stop by the front door, under a canopy that was just long enough to cover the length of the car—far too short for a Spade entrance—and I said to the driver, "Are you planning on coming in and joining me?"

"No, sir." He looked at me through the rearview mirror. "I'm going to wait for you in the car."

"Are you sure?" We were supposed to be on the way to the airport, where he'd drop me off and then probably go on to his next gig. He hadn't anticipated these three extra hours, so I added, "Lunch is on me."

"I appreciate that, but I brought a cooler full of food, and my granddaughter is on Christmas break. I plan on FaceTiming with her."

"If you change your mind, meet me in the bar," I told him.

A bellhop opened the back door, and I climbed out of the backseat and walked into the lobby.

Every hotel, especially if it was part of a brand, had a distinct smell. Since I was hypersensitive to scents, that was one of the first things I noticed whenever I walked inside a lobby.

The aroma that met me in the doorway was as important as the interior of the hotel.

If the smell was insipid, uninviting, I was immediately turned off.

And here, I was definitely underwhelmed. A mix of leather, like an accumulation of briefcases, and coffee. Not scents that were piped and vented through the ducts—something we did at all our hotels—but rather what a man would smell like after returning from a long day at a job he hated.

I quickly scanned the interior on my way to the bar, bored by the brown and gold accents, unimpressed that they hid the view of the lake behind short windows and heavy drapery, and I took a seat at one of the barstools. My ass wasn't even settled on the hard surface when the scent came over me.

Not one that came from the hotel.

This was the perfume of a woman.

A smell that reminded me of late summer sunsets and the anticipation of cool fall nights.

A perfect combination of Granny Smith apples and cedarwood with a heavy dose of lust.

I looked to my right, scanning the faces of the people sitting nearby. None seemed to fit the fragrance. Just as I looked to my left, a woman sat beside me, sending me a stronger whiff of what I'd smelled before.

An essence that matched her exceptionally.

Her long, mocha-colored hair hung in curls. Her profile—a balance of soft lines, a small and sloped nose, and a jaw that outlined thick, pouty lips—was stunning. As I looked down, I noticed her sweater hung to the bottom of her thighs, where there was a hint of creamy skin before the start of her knee-high boots.

My eyes weren't satisfied.

I wanted more.

No.

I fucking needed more.

My gaze slowly lifted, and that was when our stares connected, hers a bright and beautiful emerald.

Goddamn it.

The side view of this woman was breathtaking.

Straight on, and I was practically speechless.

Especially when she smiled, her straight white teeth piercing her bottom lip before she let out a soft, quiet laugh. "Hi."

One thought instantly nagged at me, demanding my full attention.

It churned through my body, giving most of its focus on my cock.

I fucking need her.

"Hello," I replied.

"What can I get you to drink?" I heard.

Reluctantly, I turned my head toward the bartender. "Bourbon. The oldest one you have."

"On the rocks?"

"Never," I responded.

"And for you?" he asked the lady.

"*Hmm*." I felt her eyes on me. "I like the sound of that. I'll have the same."

Even her voice was enticing, a tone that wasn't whiny or demanding. Just smooth and alluring.

"Do you want to start a tab or charge the drinks to your room?"

"Tab," I replied, but my voice was almost cut off when, at the same time, she said, "My room."

The bartender had figured we were together.

I chuckled at that thought and reached for my wallet, handing him a card from inside. "Tab," I repeated. "And the first round"—I nodded toward the gorgeous woman beside me—"is on me."

He swiped the card and gave it back to me.

"Thank you," she said the moment we were alone. "You didn't have to do that." She tucked a chunk of hair behind her ear, revealing a lobe with a good-sized diamond earring in the center. "I suppose with that, you've earned yourself an introduction." With the same hand, she reached across the air between us. "Rowan."

Rowan, I repeated in my head.

A name as unique as her.

"Cooper Spade," I replied, clasping our fingers together, the warmth of her hand a welcome temperature. "A pleasure to meet you."

"And you."

Questions filled my head at a speed I wasn't accustomed to.

Normally, in scenarios like this, when I found the woman next to me completely irresistible, I asked very little and didn't absorb much of what was replied. I didn't care enough to. What I wanted, what I desired, was skin on skin. The scent of latex and sweat filling my nose. The sound of moans in my ears.

I wasn't sure why Rowan's answers felt relevant.

Maybe I just wanted to hear more of her voice.

Yes. That had to be the reason.

"What brings you to Lake Louise?" she asked before I had a chance to say anything.

"What makes you think I'm not a local?"

I licked across my lip, and her eyes followed my tongue, her legs uncrossing and recrossing.

She was paying attention.

Her thoughts were going exactly where I wanted them to.

Where mine were, which was fucking dreaming of her pussy and what it would taste like if my tongue was swiping her clit.

Goddamn it, I wished I weren't flying out soon.

"I assume, if you lived here, you'd be at home or at work, but certainly not on the roads, where a foot of snow per hour has been accumulating."

I laughed. "Good assumption." I stretched my arm across the bar, carefully avoiding where she was leaning against it. "I'm here on business. Flying out in a couple of hours."

Her brows rose. "You're sure about that?"

I liked how she wasn't cocky when she challenged me. She had a more teasing nature.

"I'm supposed to be heading to the airport now. The flight has only been delayed by three hours."

"I think your airline is being a little too hopeful." She pulled out her phone, showing me the radar on the Weather app. "They're expecting over forty inches. We're going to be snowed in." She gave me a hesitant smile. "For days."

"They'll clear the runway."

"Maybe, out of protocol, but they've already canceled all the flights for today."

I assumed she was talking about the commercial flights, but private was a whole different animal.

She didn't need to know how I was flying, so I replied, "Aren't you just the bearer of bad news?"

Still, I thought it was a good idea to check in with the pilot, given what she'd just told me, so I pulled out my phone, and there was a text from him on the screen. "Fuck."

"I take it you just heard from the airline. And now, you finally believe me." She gave me a smile, then laughter.

I liked them both.

Equally.

And far too much.

Which was something that shocked the hell out of me.

"Yes." I shoved my phone in my pocket. "You were right."

"I know, but look at it this way." She paused to take the bourbon the bartender was handing to her. "Maybe you needed an unexpected vacation, and why not do it somewhere as beautiful as Lake Louise?"

I lifted my drink from the bar top, where it had been placed. "Aside from the fact that tomorrow is Christmas Eve and I have somewhere I need to be, I suppose you're right." I clinked my glass against hers. "Cheers."

"To new holiday traditions." She grinned. "Cheers."

I watched her take a sip, the way her throat bobbed as she swallowed, picturing the way it would move if my dick was between her lips. A warmth immediately filled her cheeks once the booze hit her, a color that looked exceptional on her.

So much so that I forced myself to look away and waited for the bartender to get close enough again before I said to him, "Do you mind sending over someone from the front desk?"

There was no chance I was getting up from this stool, risking Rowan leaving or someone trying to steal my spot.

He voiced, "No problem."

Rowan held the glass near her mouth, the liquid sloshing against the sides as she circled the tumbler. "Something fun planned for the holiday?" She grimaced. "Please don't tell me you're about to miss a trip to Curaçao or Tahiti or somewhere tropical. Because that sounds positively magical right now." She glanced toward the windows, where the small amount of glass was already snow-covered, and she turned back toward me. "Winter and I aren't friends."

"We're not friends either unless I'm on a snowboard at the top of a mountain."

She grinned. "Agreed."

"No, I don't have anything tropical planned for this holiday. Just a big family party that I've really been looking forward to." I rubbed my fingers around the rim of the glass, the motion catching her attention.

First my lips.

Now my hand.

And it appeared she really enjoyed both.

"How about you?" I inquired.

"Same." She sighed. "Siblings. Extended family. And *alll* of their kids."

I glanced at her left hand. "I'm assuming there's no spouse… or boyfriend?"

Her lips pulled wide. "Why would you assume that?"

Because from the moment we'd connected stares, I could tell she liked what she saw.

I could tell she was turned the fuck on by my appearance.

I could tell she was fantasizing about what my lips, my tongue, my hands could do to her body.

And when you combined those with her expression, I knew she was single.

But I wouldn't say that to her yet. That was far too forward.

I ran my thumb past my day-old scruff, stopping at the side of my mouth. "Let's just say it's a feeling I have."

"Your feeling is right."

Before I could respond, a hotel employee moved in next to me and said, "What can I help you with?"

The front-desk clerk.

I'd been so entertained that I almost forgot I'd requested to speak to one.

I turned to fully face him. "I need to book a suite for the night." I reached for my wallet again and tried to hand him my credit card.

He wouldn't accept it and said, "I apologize, sir, but we're completely sold out."

My heart began to pound. "Sold out?"

"Unfortunately." He nodded. "I don't even have a regular room available until after the New Year."

"There's a blizzard outside." I pointed toward the lake for emphasis. "I'm stranded in this town until at least tomorrow. You're saying there isn't a single goddamn room in this entire hotel that you can put me in?"

He nodded. "Again, I apologize, sir. But there's a hotel about two miles down the road. They might have an opening, but I honestly doubt it. Lake Louise gets pretty busy around the holidays." He paused. "Is there anything else I can help you with?"

It was a standard response—the staff had been trained to ask that question, even when they couldn't fulfill the initial request.

What I wanted was to tell him to go fuck himself because I knew there were rooms held for emergencies—employees who couldn't get home for the night and needed a place to stay, executives who came in at the last minute. A hotel was never technically sold out. They just weren't willing to give me one of those rooms.

It wouldn't matter if I told him who I was. In fact, it would probably make matters worse.

I would get back at them in another way.

I would build a hotel less than a mile down the road that would fucking bury theirs.

I muttered, "No, thanks," and I turned back toward the bar, downing what was left in my glass. I called the bartender over as I set the empty down. "Keep these coming." I chuckled even though not a single word I'd uttered was funny. "I need to be drunk enough that I'll be able to pass out on the couch in the lobby."

Rowan requested a second round as well and then said to me, "There must be an assistant in your life who's about to get your wrath for not booking you a hotel." She winced.

"Another assumption." I narrowed my gaze as I looked at her.

"Well, it is my turn. You assumed last...no?"

The spouse comment. She was right.

"Yes," I replied. "But it's not my assistant's fault. I knew the weather when I scheduled this trip, and I insisted on flying home today. In my mind, a backup plan wasn't needed. I was returning to LA, no matter what."

I hissed out some air, wishing I'd done things differently, and took out my phone again, sending my assistant a text that told her to find me a hotel in the area. The moment the message went through, I shot off a text to the driver who was waiting for me out front, letting him know he could go home. I wasn't going to make him stick around while my assistant found me a place to sleep. I'd rather him be home and safely off the roads since they were getting worse by the minute. If she happened to secure a room for me, I'd somehow find a ride there.

"Let's see if she can score me a hotel nearby." I placed my phone on the bar so I would see my assistant's message the second it came through.

"That might take some serious magic."

"If anyone can do it, it's her," I said. "She's good."

The bartender delivered two more drinks and placed them in front of us.

Rowan handed me mine. "There's one plus side to this." She clinked our glasses together.

"And that is?"

I stared at her mouth as she said, "Me."

It only took that one word for my dick to grow into the stiffest hard-on. My hand gripped the glass with so much strength that I was positive it was going to shatter.

"You...huh?"

"Well, we wouldn't have met if your flight hadn't been delayed." She took a drink. "Things have a way of working out the way they're supposed to."

I mashed my lips together, my stare taking a slow dip down her body. "Tell me, how are things going to work out for me? Or even better, how are they going to work out for us?"

The redness that moved through her face was a sight I couldn't get enough of. The color had deepened to a dark crimson, and it matched the gloss on her lips.

"Us?" Her laugh was a beat my ears appreciated. "I wasn't exactly referring to that."

"What were you referring to, then?"

Her stare changed. It almost pulled back, taking in the entire picture. "You're direct, aren't you, Cooper Spade?"

"When I want something, I go after it. I don't believe in waiting. Time only allows other things to interfere."

"Like..."

"Another man taking my seat. A meeting that you must suddenly get to. A phone call that takes you away and you don't return."

"All possibilities, I suppose." She turned her body a little toward mine. "What exactly do you want, and what are you going after?"

"Not what, but who." I leaned across the small space between us, getting closer to her. From here, I took deep breaths of her perfume as it wafted off her neck. All that did was make me wonder what the skin around her navel smelled like. If her pussy held an aroma that was as sweet as I imagined. "And that who is you," I whispered just above her ear.

Chapter Two

Rowan

"Not what, but who…and that who is you."

Even though Cooper had just spoken those words, they continued to echo through my ears, vibrating across my chest, purring through my entire body.

He wanted me.

An interesting admission, to say the least.

Except I knew his type, my two older brothers, Ridge and Rhett, were just like him. They would walk into any room—whether it be a business meeting, a bar, or even a place as unexpected as the dentist—and it was like the women could smell them the second their toes crossed the entrance. Those immediate connections were just based on their good looks, but when they spoke, revealing their charm, the ladies were even more captivated. They would compete for my brothers' attention, doing absolutely anything to gain it.

Ridge and Rhett would then have their pick of which woman they wanted to bring home.

Or women.

Depending on how they decided to roll for the night.

As much as I wished I didn't know about my brothers' sexual escapades, I'd witnessed it more times than I could count.

So, I knew how this worked. I wasn't naive.

It only took one glance at Cooper Spade—the way his stare devoured me, the way his smile was so charismatic, the way he emphasized his movements with his hands and mouth to ensure I was paying attention—to know he wasn't any different from my siblings.

He certainly had the handsome factor going on.

He had dark blue eyes that didn't just look at you, but saw right through you. A shadow across his cheeks that was several days' worth of scruff. Golden-brown hair that was the right kind of messy. Thick lips and a square jaw, a neck that would take both hands to wrap around. Broad shoulders that led to the most muscular frame, where I could only imagine the depth of the muscles hiding beneath his clothes. And then there was his scent, a cologne that was a mix of earthy sage and burnt orange, a combination that was incredibly seductive.

To add to the attraction, Cooper had the sexiest hands I'd ever seen. Long, thin fingers and short, trimmed nails that stirred every sensation within me. Along with a tongue that expertly swiped the outside of his mouth in a pattern that was designed to trigger every naughty thought.

Any woman with a pulse would have her curiosity piqued.

Including mine.

I just couldn't help myself, especially since the circumstances surrounding us weren't typical. We were in the middle of a snowstorm, stranded at this hotel. Something told me, if the accumulation continued—and it was supposed to—that tomorrow's flight would be canceled as well.

So, maybe, just maybe, it was time to explore a side that I'd never unleashed. The side that hooked up with men I'd just met versus waiting the usual time frame of a couple of dates when I was pretty sure things were progressing.

But with this man, I had a feeling he would do things to my body that I'd never experienced before.

Was I stupid to consider this?

Was I playing with fire?

Would I regret this decision?

Does it matter right now?

Before I let my brain fantasize even a second more, I had questions.

Like, "Cooper, I've been sitting next to you for less than ten minutes. How do you know I'm what you want?"

"I like that question."

My brows rose while I tried to ignore the aroma that wouldn't stop wafting from him. "Why?"

"Because I get to be straightforward and cut out all the bullshit."

I laughed. "You're telling me you haven't been that way from the start?"

"No, I haven't."

The fact that he could be even more direct caused me to take a long drink of my bourbon. "All right. I'm ready to hear it."

"The truth is, Rowan, before you even sat down, I got a whiff of you in the air. You know what that did to me?"

I shook my head, trying to remember which perfume I'd packed in my suitcase.

"It turned me the fuck on." He stroked the pad of his thumb across his lips. "But that was nothing compared to what happened when I actually laid my eyes on you."

I squeezed my legs together, my clit already tingling. "Yeah?" I took a deep breath. "What did you feel then?"

"Feel?" He chuckled. "I'm not sure you're ready for that kind of description. But what I will say is that I was blown away by how gorgeous you are."

It wasn't that I didn't believe him.

I could just see right through him.

The game, the flattery—guys like Cooper came at you from every angle.

A sly smile pulled at my lips. "Tell me more."

"I've had to force myself not to touch you. You know, to not accidentally graze my hand across your arm"—his fingers landed on the outside of my bicep, stroking across the thickness of my sweater dress—"and for my knee not to drag over the side of your thigh every time you recrossed your legs." He closed in the space between our knees. The softness of his pants touching the bareness of my skin felt like little bolts of electricity bursting right through me. "All I've thought about is putting my hands on you, using my fingers to make you scream." He pulled his leg away, along with his hand, and sipped his drink. "Aside from being beyond beautiful, there's more, Rowan."

"More than just wanting to get me naked?"

He nipped his lip, the bottom one, the fatter of the two. The one that would be the perfect size to suck on. "Getting you naked has consumed me, yes, but it does go deeper than that."

I couldn't wait to hear this, so I stayed silent.

Waiting.

Anticipating.

He returned his drink to the bar top. "There's something about your personality that I can't get enough of."

"You mean...conversation?"

"Answers. Knowledge. Small talk. Fuck, you could look around this room and tell me every detail you see—I wouldn't care. I just want to hear more of your voice."

A response that I hadn't expected.

My brothers always said they didn't care about getting to know any of the women they slept with. For them, it was only about how quickly they could strip off their clothes and hers.

Was Cooper different?

"Tell me what you want to know," I whispered.

"Everything."

I let out a small laugh, shifting in the narrow seat. "You need to be more specific than that."

And I needed to be careful with my replies. There were things I just couldn't say.

At least not yet.

We were facing each other, our sides pressed against the bar top, which he stretched his hand across, the hint of his fingers now teasing my back. "Why don't you start with where you live?"

"LA, like you."

His head tilted in a way that made his stare deepen. "What brought you to Alberta, then? It certainly wasn't the weather if you and winter aren't friends. Unless you came to ski?"

"I planned on doing some skiing today. That got canceled."

"So, you're here for pleasure?"

I laughed, this time much harder. "All you've done is talk about pleasure, so if that's what you're referring to, then, no, I didn't come here for *that* kind of pleasure. You're just…an unexpected surprise." I smiled. "Why are you here?"

"Business."

I'd suspected as much. "Is that all you're going to say about it? Business?"

He glanced around the bar before his eyes came back and locked with mine. "I don't want to bore you with the logistics of my visit. I flew in this morning with all plans to fly out several hours later. That obviously didn't work out." His tongue swiped the corner of his mouth. "But it's a cancellation I'm quite fond of at the moment."

I grinned. "Next question."

"What do you do for work?"

"I don't want to bore you with the logistics." I winked. "So, I'll say I work for the family business. In a new role. I just joined only a few months ago. Which is funny because I told myself I'd never get sucked into the family politics, and yet, here I am, sucked into the family politics."

The lines on his forehead became more pronounced. "What did you do before?"

"I owned several boutiques in LA." I pulled at the bottom hem of my dress, trying to lengthen it past my knees. "I had been a design major in college. Not long after I graduated, I realized it was easier to sell the clothes than make them myself. I started with one shop in West Hollywood, and by the time I sold the business, I had four locations."

"Amazing."

"What would have been much more amazing was if I had grown the brand internationally, like I'd intended. But, no, I got persuaded to join the family business, and now, I know they'll never let me go."

"I can understand why."

I focused on his eyes, trying to read them. "Why do you say that?"

"Because if you worked for me, I wouldn't let you go either."

I laughed. "Cooper, are you offering me a job?"

His grin was so tantalizing; it made me smile.

"That's not what I'm offering you."

"What is it for you, then? The promise of the most mind-blowing orgasms? A tryst in Canada that I'll never forget?"

"Yes, and fuck yes." He eyed me down, so slowly. "I'll have

that dress off you within a second of walking through your door."

"Yes, that." I rubbed my thumb over the glass. "You make things sound so easy."

"Aren't they?"

I adjusted my position, turning more toward the bar. "I suppose…if I was ready to say yes."

"And you're not?"

Before I could reply, his phone vibrated on the bar top.

I pointed at it even though I couldn't see the screen. "You'd better get that. Something tells me it's important."

"It can wait."

"Even if it's your assistant, wanting to see if she should book you a hotel she found?"

He lifted his cell into his hand and read the message on the screen.

Since his stare was finally elsewhere, I took the moment to really study what he had on. The richness of his dark gray jacket with its collar popped high and the light-gray sweater he wore underneath. The contrast of colors worked so well with his skin tone, and the texture of both fabrics was the sexiest combination.

His gaze gradually lifted to mine. One that, after a few seconds passed, was even more powerful than before.

"She found one, didn't she?" I inquired.

"Did you want her to?"

I laughed.

God, he was good with words.

"Did *you* want her to?" I shot back.

"I think you know the answer to that."

He returned the phone to the bar and crossed his arms over his chest, the pull of the fabric showing just how large those arms were.

I couldn't imagine sinking my fingers into those muscles.

To have them wrapped around me.

To have them lift me into the air.

"You have two options, Rowan. You can invite me up to your room, or you can tell me to book the hotel my assistant found."

I felt myself wet my lips.

Inhale and fill my lungs.

Hold the air in and not release it.

"What are you going to choose?"

Chapter Three

COOPER

Watching Rowan squirm was one of the hottest things I'd ever fucking seen. Although I knew which option she was going to pick, I could still see the fight in her. The way her body couldn't sit still. How she was on the verge of panting. How the heat moving across her cheeks told me she was already turned on.

She wasn't about one-night stands. That was obvious. I could tell just by the way she'd responded.

But there was something about me she couldn't resist.

She was intrigued.

Her body was tuned in.

I could feel it.

See it.

And I felt the same way, unable to resist her.

I wasn't leaving this bar unless I knew I was going to taste her, whether that be a parting kiss or her fingers looped through mine while I walked her up to her room, where we were going to stay for the night.

There were some things in life that just had to go down.

Fucking Rowan was one.

I adjusted the way I was sitting. Removing my arm from the bar top, I placed it over the back of her barstool, molding it around her.

She didn't move away.

She didn't straighten her spine.

She almost leaned into me.

"What am I going to choose?" She sighed.

"Yes, Rowan, what do you want?" The hard-on in my pants was fucking aching to be released. "Do you want to return to your room alone? Or do you want to spend the next twenty-four or so hours with me? Where I plan to pour a few of these"—I held up my bourbon—"over your naked body and lick them off your skin, giving you orgasms until you can't physically come anymore."

The smile that crossed her mouth wasn't one that was built with confidence. I could see the nervousness that fluttered through her.

"I know you don't usually do this," I said, my lips not far from her ear. "Picking up a stranger at a bar, spending the night with him, giving him your body—not typical. I get that."

"You're right. This isn't typical at all."

I pulled back far enough so she could see my lips. "But I'm not a stranger anymore."

She took a breath that was long and deep. "No?"

"You know my first and last name. You know what I like to drink. Where I live. That I'm here on business. That I prefer suites to regular rooms." I swiped my thumb, rubbing just under her shoulder blade. "You know my scent, a cologne that has notes of burnt orange and a woody sage."

"Funny, that's almost exactly how I described it in my head."

"And when I touch you"—I continued to stroke the same spot,

but I lowered the tempo—"goose bumps rise over your skin."

"How would you know that?"

I chewed the corner of my lip, pleased that she'd asked. "There." I pointed at the small sliver of flesh that peeked out from the bottom of her dress, the inch or so before her boots began. A section she'd tried to hide earlier by tugging on the fabric, but it had ridden right back up. "Look."

"I don't have to." She shivered. "I can feel them all over my body."

"Can you imagine how it will feel when I'm tracing those bumps with my lips?" My voice lowered when I added, "And tongue?"

She'd moved the drink onto her lap and lifted it to take the final sip. "What are you doing to me, Cooper?"

"What do you want me to do?" When she went to respond, I continued, "What are your fantasies? What are the dreams that come through your mind when you close your eyes at night and lower your fingers to your pussy?" I slid my hand under her soft hair and skimmed the tips of my fingers across the back of her neck. "I want to fulfill them."

"Tonight?"

"Yes."

As she inhaled, her chest rose, lifting a set of tits that I was fucking dying to flick with my tongue. "And all of this is going to go down in my room?"

"Unless you have a better location."

Her teeth ground over her lip. "And that's where you want to go right now?"

I nodded, the hunger making my mouth part. "Fuck yes."

But after I'd told her she had a choice, I'd read her initial hesitation. For someone who didn't do this often, I could understand how it could be a lot. I didn't want her to feel like I was rushing things even though my need for her was growing. I wanted her to be comfortable and content with the fact that she wanted to fuck me as badly as I wanted to fuck her.

So, I added, "How about we have another drink first?"

She glanced down at her glass. "I like that idea."

"Except it doesn't have to be a bourbon. Get water, soda, whatever you want."

She turned toward the bartender, who was making his way over to us. "I'll have another one of these"—she pointed at her glass—"and can you charge all of mine to my room? Eleven twenty-six."

"Put all the drinks on my tab," I insisted. "And I'll have another one as well."

My eyes locked with hers as the bartender's hand tapped on the computer screen, entering our orders.

"Dominant and chivalrous." She placed her hand on my chest, a brief look of shock in her eyes, like she was surprised by how muscular I was. "I feel like I just found myself a unicorn."

"And giving," I growled. "You're soon going to experience that part of me as well." I moaned as I took her in. "You have no idea what I'm going to do to you."

When she put her lips close to my ear, I didn't know what she was going to say.

Whether she had all of a sudden changed her mind or she was going to ask for more time or tell me her fantasy.

But when she whispered, "I'm already so wet," I swore my dick got even harder.

"*Mmm*, yes." My eyes closed as I thought about how that wetness would taste. "I take it you've made your choice, then."

"I have."

I wanted to hear it.

The words would be like foreplay.

"Why don't you tell me what it is?"

A color entered her cheeks, one that was deeper than any of the previous times she'd flushed. "I want to take you back to my room."

"Tell me more."

"More?"

"Yes, Rowan. Tell me what you want me to do to you. Tell me what you're going to do to me." I moved her hair away from her ear to make sure nothing came between her and my voice. "Tell me how many times you want to come tonight."

She huffed air through her lips, the sound like a low, almost-shy laugh. "I want you to do things to my body that I've never felt before." She pulled back a few inches, locking our eyes and lifting her hand until her finger was resting vertically across my lips. "I want you to show me what you can do with this mouth." She sucked on her bottom lip. "Something tells me, when it comes to business, this mouth dominates. But what about outside of business? What can it do then?"

Just as she started to pull her finger away, I caught it. I brought it back to my mouth, and I sucked on the tip, rolling my tongue around her nail. But the whole time I was licking it, I stared at her, using my eyes to tell her that this was exactly what I was going to do to her clit.

After a few rotations, I dropped her finger and handed her the glass the bartender had just placed down. "Drink up."

Breathlessly, she lifted her bourbon and swallowed a sip.

"I'll take the bill," I said to the bartender.

He handed me a leather billfold. "Sign your name across the bottom of the receipt, and then you're all set."

I grabbed the pen from inside, giving him a hundred-dollar tip, totaled the numbers, and signed my name.

I didn't know how long it took us to finish our drinks, but during that time—full of more small talk and flirting and a quick text to my assistant, letting her know I didn't need a room—I lost myself in her eyes.

Her lips.

The apple and cedarwood scents that drifted off her body.

And when I shot back the last bit of my bourbon, she was standing by the time I set my glass down. The same fingers I'd used to hold the tumbler were now finding their way to her side. With her upright and next to me, I discovered she was the best height, the top of her head hitting the highest part of my chest. What this new position also gave me was a full, better view of her body. I allowed my eyes to wander, viewing the way the sweater dress hugged her curves and narrow waist, revealing her perfect-sized tits. Her boots were just tight enough that I could see the shape of her lean legs. But it was that hint of skin between the top of her boots and the bottom of her dress that sent me right over the fucking edge.

Because when I looked at it, all I saw was an entrance that would grant me access to her body, and I was fucking dying to run my hands underneath it.

"Rowan"—my head shook as I held her close—"you're flawless."

"You haven't even seen me naked yet."

I was mid-dip, but that response caused me to look into her eyes again. "Jesus," I groaned, unable to pause my admiring. "And you called me a goddamn unicorn. Nah, I don't think so."

Her lips spread wide. "Stop."

"Stop?" Both hands now surrounded her waist. "Do you know how incredible your body is? And you're right, that's just in clothes. I'm guessing what I'm about to see when we get to your room is going to blow me the fuck away."

"Luckily, for you, you don't have to wait long."

"Thank fucking God for that."

I positioned my palm on her lower back, and we walked through the bar and past the bland lobby, halting in front of the bank of elevators.

We weren't alone. There were multiple people waiting to get on as well.

Once the door slid open, allowing us to enter, Rowan hit the button for the highest floor, and we moved to the back, the rest of the parties filling in the front.

I shifted myself behind her, and as the chamber became more crowded, she had to get closer.

And closer.

The back of her pressed against my front.

There was no doubt that she could feel my raging erection. I wanted her to. I wanted her to know what she was doing to me. That the words I'd expressed while we were in the bar weren't meaningless, that the desire to have her was driving me fucking wild.

As the elevator rose, pausing at different floors to let people off, it became less cramped inside.

But Rowan didn't separate us.

She stayed pressed against me, my long, hard shaft grinding into the back of her.

She didn't just take it.

She moved with me.

Her hands gripped the sides of my thighs. Her head rested against my chest. Her back arched, like I was already thrusting into her.

God, I didn't know if I could wait until we reached the top floor.

I wanted her stripped bare, kissing every part of her body.

Slowly moving my lips lower until they were buried within her wetness while my fingers explored every angle and arc of her.

I slid my hand across her navel, feeling the flatness, the heat from her skin that penetrated through the sweater, and my lips moved to the top of her ear, the softness of her hair tickling me. "Should I reach under your dress and make you moan in here?" My voice was so low that only she could hear.

"You could, but we're only two floors away."

"Are you assuming I can't make you come that quickly?"

"I'm past assuming." She'd been giving me her profile but turned her head to face me. "I can't even think at this point."

I smiled.

Fuck yes, she was as worked up as me.

We finally reached her floor, the doors sliding open, and a couple stepped out before us, heading to the hallway on the right. But Rowan, whose hand was linked with mine, led me to the left. The key card was already in her free hand, and fortunately, she was only a few doors down. The second she had it open and we stepped inside, my arms surrounded her, and I led her toward the wall, holding her back against it while my mouth fucking devoured hers.

She tasted of lust and bourbon—two flavors I couldn't get enough of.

"I'm going to fucking tear this dress off you."

With my lips still on hers, my tongue circling the inside of her mouth, I tugged the material up past her stomach and chest, waiting for her to pull her arms through once I lifted it over her head.

I dropped the dress onto the floor, followed by her boots, and I leaned back to take in the view.

She'd positioned herself against the wall with her legs spread, her arms hanging at her sides, her expression feral and passionate. And while she stood there, I took in her black lace bra and panties, coverings that hid nothing, aside from her nipples and the center of her pussy.

She had a body that I would fucking dream about the second my eyes closed.

"Damn it," I hissed. "I knew once I got that dress off you that you were going to look incredible." My gaze gradually dropped to her feet, taking its time to climb back up to her face. "But what I didn't expect was this…" I hissed out a mouthful of air while I took another dip. "Rowan, I've never seen anything like you."

"I'm glad you like."

"Like?" I briefly locked eyes with her. "That word doesn't apply here."

She had just the right amount of curves and tightness, hips that I could grab, an ass that I could squeeze, like I was doing now.

"I didn't think it was possible, but you're even more gorgeous than I envisioned." I kissed her. "I need you naked. On the bed." I reached for her thighs and lifted her into the air, wrapping her legs around me while I carried her to the mattress, placing her on the edge.

With my hands free, I got to work on my clothes, first the jacket before I lifted the sweater over my head, letting the heavy fabric fall to the floor, and moving on to my belt.

She eyed me and said, "Allow me."

She busied herself with my belt and button and zipper and pulled my pants down. I slid out of my shoes, socks, and stood before her in just my boxer briefs.

"Like you can talk." She was grinning. "You have the best body I've ever seen, which I sensed while we were in the bar, but I didn't expect this." She ran her hand over my abs. "I could get lost in these."

"Yeah?" I moved in between her legs. "And what exactly do you want to do to this body?"

"First, I want you to lose those." She nodded toward my waist.

Before she had a chance to help me take them off, I reached behind her and, with one hand, unclasped her bra. I pulled the cups from her tits, and the lace dropped from my fingers.

Her breasts bounced from the freedom, nipples hardening to small peaks.

"Fuck me." I flicked one with my thumb. "My tongue is dying to lick you."

She stared up at me from the bed, leaving my abs to slip her fingers into the waist of my boxers, lowering the cotton down my thighs. My cock sprang out, and I watched her take in the size and girth, our stares locking again as I stepped out of the leg holes.

"Cooper..."

I knew that tone, the deep breath that followed, that specific look in her eyes.

Because this wasn't the first time I'd heard and seen it from a woman.

"Don't worry. I'll go slow."

I didn't give her a chance to touch my dick, to wrap her plump lips around the tip. Not that I didn't want her to—I just couldn't wait to taste her.

My hands landed on the bed on each side of her, and I used my body to lean her back against the mattress. Starting at her neck, I kissed across her collarbone, inhaling the apple and cedarwood scents from her skin.

"*Yesss*," she moaned.

Her perfume wasn't just on her clothes.

It was here too.

Subtle.

Delicious.

I lowered until her nipple was in front of me, and I breathed against it, teasing it with my nose, using that part of my face to swipe it back and forth.

"Oh God." She held my shoulders, bearing the tension in her fingers. "Yes."

I'd given her nothing, yet my ears were full of her satisfaction.

I looked up from her chest, and she gazed into my eyes, her breath hitching as my tongue came out of my mouth and circled around the center of her tit.

That was when her eyes closed.

When her lips parted.

When the back of her head returned to the mattress.

"*Fuuuck*," she cried.

I sucked on her nipple, rubbing the very end with my tongue, pulling it with my lips. And while I was giving her breast all the attention, my fingers slithered down her navel until they hit lace.

"I can feel how wet you are, even through these panties."

I was stroking her clit, cupping her pussy underneath.

There was too much separating us.

I needed these panties gone.

I yanked the sides down her thighs, leaving them at a place where she could kick them off, and my hand resumed its position between her legs.

But this time, I could feel her wetness as it soaked into my skin.

Her warmth.

The way her pussy concaved around my finger the moment I slid it into her.

"So fucking tight," I roared. "I can't wait to sink my dick into you."

"I want it." She gasped, and she did it again when I bit her nipple. "I want you."

Before she got me, there was something I had to do first.

Something I needed for myself.

I gave her other tit a quick lick, and I lowered down her stomach, leaving my finger inside her, but rather than pressing my thumb to her clit, I used my tongue.

Her hand was in my hair. Pulling. Fucking tugging on my strands.

"This…"

I glanced up, my tongue stalled at the very top of her, waiting for her to continue.

"The question you asked earlier? Here's your answer. This right here is my fantasy."

I grazed my nose over her clit, breathing in the sweetness, and then I rubbed my scruff between her lips.

I wanted to be covered in her.

I wanted to be able to smell her cunt while I was fucking her.

"You've never had a man lick your pussy before?"

"I have." The hunger had grown in her eyes. "But no man has ever made me come this way."

"That's going to change. In about one minute."

"There's no way—" Her voice cut off as soon as I started licking. Each of her exhales ended in a moan, and within just a few inhales, she shouted, "Cooper!"

She wasn't coming yet.

She was just shocked at what my tongue could do to her.

At how well I already knew her body.

But it wasn't only about knowing.

It was about listening too.

And when it came to pleasure, I was all fucking ears.

I added another finger, twisting my wrist as I plunged in and again as I pulled out, hitting every angle, giving her the friction she needed. And while my hand had a specific job, my mouth did too. When I flattened my tongue, I swiped it from side to side and pointed it to add more pressure.

Alternating.

Back and forth.

"Oh my *Gooood*."

Hearing the way she reacted, sensing when she got wetter, observing the movements of her body as her hips began to rock with me—that was how I determined what she needed.

What more I had to give.

How fast, how hard I needed to lick.

And even though Rowan thought this was for her, that I was satisfying her fantasy, this was every bit for me as well.

I wanted her taste.

I wanted her scent.

I wanted her screams filling my ears.

And with my face in this position, I wanted to watch her come.

It only took a few more strikes across her clit before that happened.

When her body was wriggling, shudders rippling across her stomach.

And she was panting, "Yes," while straining to keep her legs open. Her nails stabbed my skull. "Cooper! Fuck!"

I licked.

I didn't stop.

Neither did my fingers as they drove in and out of her.

I used both parts of me to send her toward that edge, and once I sensed she'd reached it, I didn't let up.

I went even faster.

"*Ahhh*!"

Fuck me, she was a sight.

A vision of pleasure that made me ache as I watched her.

She was practically a stranger—despite my telling her that she knew multiple things about me—so why did I want her this badly?

Why was there this need to see her come again?

Why was I already thinking about the next time I was going to put my tongue here?

My movements slowed when her sounds began to quiet and when her stomach stilled, and I gently pulled my fingers out. Rather than leave her pussy altogether, I kept my lips on her, kissing her folds.

Swallowing some of the wetness and spreading what was left.

Her nails pulled back from stabbing me, and she raked her fingers through my strands, her breathing still loud but steady. "I had no idea it could be like that…"

"Do you want it again?" When I didn't receive a response, my gaze taking her in, I said, "I have no problem staying here for the rest of the afternoon and into the evening, licking you until you can't come anymore."

Her head shook, like she was in awe. "Yes. I want that. But I want you first."

She hooked her feet under my armpits and attempted to pull me up.

Of course, she couldn't. I was far too strong and weighed more than she could handle.

But the gesture was adorable.

Before I hovered over her body, I found my pants on the floor and grabbed my wallet from the pocket, taking out one of the condoms I kept in there. I tore off the corner of the metal packet and rolled the latex over my shaft.

"You're going to break me," she said as I moved onto the bed.

I placed her on her side and positioned myself behind her, holding her back against my chest.

"I promise that's not going to happen…unless you want me to." I chuckled as I wrapped her leg over both of mine, giving me more access to her pussy, and backed her ass up until my tip was poking her entrance. "I give you about three minutes until you're coming again."

As I inched my way in, going slow, moving with the wetness, I rubbed her clit.

"Jesus, you're huge."

She needed both spots touched. The combination would keep her mind off the invasion because—*goddamn it*—she was so tight that this had to feel like a lot for her.

That was why I continued to gradually stroke my way in, pausing once I was fully buried so she could get used to me.

"Rowan..." I swallowed, forcing myself to stay still. "You have no idea how good you feel."

"Show me."

Only someone ready to be fucking pounded would request something like that.

And just as I was about to confirm, she wrapped her arm around the back of my neck, pulling our faces closer, and begged, "Make me come again."

The sexiest order I'd ever heard.

I tilted my hips back and ground my way forward, her slickness letting me slip right in. But with each plunge, she became narrower. Her pussy clutched me from the inside.

With her hand now on my ass, squeezing it, like she was urging me to fuck her harder, I caved.

My speed increased.

So did my pressure.

And all that did was earn me moans.

Lots of them.

Loud ones.

Filling my ears and mouth as I turned her head and slammed our lips together.

This woman.

Fuck.

While I fondled her clit, feeling it get harder, knowing her orgasm wasn't far, I upped the intensity again.

This position was gentle.

Forgiving.

It wasn't like doggy style, where I could drive in the deepest and it would feel like my dick was hitting the back of her throat.

Here, she could move and adjust herself, stopping me from reaching the end of her.

That was why I stayed just like this.

For now.

Until it was time for round two.

"I have one more request."

Her voice was something I was beginning to crave.

"What's that?"

"I want you to come with me. I want my body to make you feel so amazing that you can't hold your orgasm in for another second."

The truth was, I wasn't far. Within a few thrusts, I could easily make that happen. I just hadn't planned on coming so soon. I had intended to go slow, shift us into another position, drag this out for as long as I could.

"That's what you want?" I questioned.

"Yes." She looked at me over her shoulder. "Seeing you vulnerable is going to be so fucking hot."

"Then, I'll give you a better view."

I moved on top of her, straddling her legs around my waist, and bucked my hips forward to show her not only what this position would allow her to see, but also how it would make her feel.

"Oh!" She drew in some air. "Yes!"

I got on my knees, pulling her ass off the bed to guide her toward me, and she sat up halfway, putting her weight on her elbows. I held her lower half against me with one of my arms, and

I sank into her cunt, twisting my hips before I pulled out.

As I repeated that motion, I used my other hand to graze her clit.

Her head fell back; her mouth opened. "*Daaamn.*"

"I want to hear it," I told her. "I want to hear you scream so loud that the fucking neighbors call the front desk."

Her next move surprised me. She reached under our legs and cupped my balls, bouncing them against her fingers.

I was already there.

This sent me straight to the peak.

"*Fuuuck!*" I growled. "Rowan!"

She was coming with me, the crests swaying across her navel, her mouth releasing sounds that I was beginning to know well. "*Ahhh!*"

The tingles were already through my sac and churning in my shaft, and I was shooting my first load into the condom. As the second wave worked its way through me, her pussy began to tighten around me.

"*Daaamn,*" I hissed, emptying more of myself into the rubber.

She was moving with me, her hips surging up, screaming, "Cooper," as though she was about to lose her voice.

And just when my body turned sensitive, hers became still, and I slowed completely, keeping myself buried after I came to a halt.

A smile crossed her mouth, and she pushed herself up even higher, climbing until her arms were resting on my shoulders and our faces were together. She was straddling my lap, and not once during any of the movement had she let me slip out of her.

"I told you I wasn't going to break you." I chuckled. "I also told you how fast you were going to come. I like being right."

She gave me a soft kiss. "You were easy on me."

"Maybe."

"What exactly would it look like if you were being hard on me?"

I dropped my hands down her body until they were squeezing what had become my favorite part of her—the lowest section of her ass that could handle a hard, rough grip. "You're not ready for that yet."

"No?"

I shook my head. "I need to prep you a little more first."

"And how will you do that?"

"By eating your pussy." I pressed my lips to her ear, watching the goose bumps rise over her skin as I whispered, "Again and again."

Chapter Four

Rowan

"I"—I swallowed, shaking my head over the pillow—"can't breathe."

I was gripping the covering that lay over me, squeezing the soft material, waiting for my lungs to fill with more air so I wouldn't suffocate from pleasure.

Because, at the moment, it felt that way.

My entire body was numb.

Tingly.

Coming down from the most intense orgasm.

And every time I let my knees fall inward, I felt the deliciously coarse scruff of Cooper's face.

He gave my clit a few final kisses and surfaced from underneath the comforter, where he'd been for the last several minutes. As he moved over me, hovering above my body, a smile dragged across his handsome face. "Does that mean you don't want me to make you come again?"

Again.

A word that had been on repeat since we'd entered my suite.

I'd lost count of the number of times he'd gotten me off. It seemed that almost every hour, starting when we'd taken the elevator up here yesterday afternoon all the way until this morning, he got me to scream.

As for the count, that had to put me in the double digits at least.

And what I'd learned during that time, what I'd suspected before he even touched me, was that Cooper Spade wasn't just the most gorgeous man.

Dominant.

Confident.

He was a sex god.

A kind that, in my twenty-nine years, I'd never experienced.

And now that I had, that I'd been given a double-digit taste, I didn't know how I would ever go back to pre-Cooper sex. The future men I dated would pale in comparison to what I'd experienced here.

But the reality of this situation was that the moment we left this hotel, there would be no Cooper and me.

There would be no more sex between us.

And I was reminded of that every time I gazed into his eyes, like I was currently doing.

"Come *again*…" I sighed. "Can my body even handle it?"

He chuckled, a sound so gritty and masculine. "How about I give you a little break and get some food into you first, and then I'll repeat that question?" The kiss he gave me wasn't soft or gentle.

It was passionate.

Slightly rough.

Needy.

And I loved it.

He separated us and climbed off the bed, walking naked toward the large living room area. The sight of him was something

I could stare at endlessly, full of hard, corded muscle and smooth, perfect skin.

He picked up the phone from the desk, hit a few buttons, and held the receiver against his ear. "I'd like to order some room service. To drink, a bottle of champagne and some cranberry juice. To eat, why don't you bring a mix of sandwiches—turkey, roast beef, salami, and ham? Condiments to go with them. Some fries and potato salad." He gazed at me as he spoke. "And for dessert, a mix of chocolate and vanilla—ice cream, cookies, cake, whatever you have, I just want some in both flavors." When he hung up, he slowly walked back to the bed.

He knew I was taking him in, and the cockiness in his expression told me he was quite satisfied with that.

Of course, any man who looked like Cooper with a dick as large as his would walk with just as much arrogance in his step.

"You know...most men would have asked what I wanted to eat and drink." I adjusted the pillow behind me, rising into a seated position, resting my back into the fluff.

"Would you rather have most men in this room? Or me?"

Although I shrugged, we both knew my answer to that question. "What if I'm gluten-free?"

"I was told the sandwiches come with lettuce. I'll toss the bread and wrap it in one of the leaves for you."

There had been no hesitation; he'd had an answer waiting. He was that good.

"And if I'm vegetarian?"

"I'll call back and have them make you a caprese sandwich." He crossed his arms over his chest, the light catching the golden-brown hair on his forearms. "I'm a problem solver, Rowan. Keep going. I can do this all day."

I smiled. "I'm a fan of strawberry."

His eyes narrowed. "Maybe. But it's not your go-to. Chocolate is. You tolerate vanilla. But if I'm wrong, which I hardly ever am, I wanted you to have another option in case the chocolate sucked."

I laughed. "God, you're cocky as fuck."

His smile only reinforced that. "You're not going to ask why I didn't get you orange juice and opted for cranberry instead?"

"I was getting there."

He scratched his scruff, the sound filling the silent room. "You don't like orange juice."

I stared at him, engrossed and wildly entertained. "Why would you think that?"

He shifted over to the nightstand, where his phone had been charging, plugged into my cord since his battery charger had died, and he brought the cell into bed with him. "When I went to grab a drink from the fridge last night, there were bottles of cran stocked by the bar. They're not randomly sitting there. They're there because you requested them, which tells me you prefer that over orange." He reached across the space between us to run his fingers over my chin. "Cran happens to be my favorite too."

He watched.

He paid attention.

Two things I hadn't suspected from him.

I turned to my side the moment his hand was gone. "Since you're the alpha in here, why don't you tell me what tonight's going to look like? You know, how we're going to celebrate Christmas Eve."

He looked at the screen of his phone, tapping it several times, eventually aiming it toward me. "The snow isn't stopping. It's supposed to continue through today, tonight, all of tomorrow, and finally let up the day after Christmas."

I knew the weather. I'd checked this morning before he woke up. The storm had strengthened overnight, the accumulation far more than what they had predicted. Officials were urging people to stay off the roads, and the airport would reassess things on Christmas morning, but if conditions stayed the same, we probably weren't going to get out of here until the day after Christmas.

Three total nights together.

Including a holiday.

With an infinite number of orgasms to come.

This was certainly going to be a time in my life that I would never forget.

"You didn't happen to bring any mistletoe in your messenger bag, did you?" I joked, knowing a messenger bag was the only thing he had with him. The hotel had even provided toiletries since he hadn't had any. "Or a tree? Or some lights? It's going to be a very interesting Christmas."

He hit a button on the tablet next to him, and the shades began to lift, showing the whiteout, the visibility so poor that I couldn't even see the falling flakes. "We'll be spending it right here."

"Yes, we will."

"You're good with that?" he asked. "I know you're missing out on some family plans." His eyes left the window and focused on me.

"I'm good with it."

"Then, you have me for two more nights." He licked across his bottom lip. "Assuming you're good with that, too, and you're not going to kick me out."

"And why would I do that? You feed me. You make me scream. I can't think of a better scenario."

I could though. But that scenario would be impossible.

And I'd be an idiot to bring it up.

"You're happy... I like that."

Although the screen was mostly hidden, I figured his thumbs were typing out a text, and when he finished, he placed the phone on the nightstand and crossed his arms under his head. The position caused his abs to flex, the blanket falling to the bottom of his happy trail.

A trail that was so incredibly sexy that I was wet again.

"And that's going to continue until the airport reopens." He exhaled a long breath. "You've got all this time with me, so what are you going to do with me, Rowan?"

"Nice try, but I've already asked you what tonight's going to look like, so it's on you, not me." I pushed the hair out of my face. "Besides, you wouldn't give up the control long enough for me to make a decision for us."

"A few things." He cleared his throat. "One, I asked what you were going to do with me—my body, my dick. It was a sexual question. I didn't ask what *we* were going to do. And two, you like being dominated."

"You're assuming that."

He untucked his hand from behind his head, and it shot beneath the blanket and went straight between my legs. "No, I know that," he growled. When he lifted his fingers out, the ones that had just swiped me from clit to pussy, he made sure to show me how wet they were. "This proves that to me." He licked the wetness off before his hand returned to its original spot.

My God.

He was untamed.

Unhinged.

And everything I wanted in a man.

An admission that would, the day after Christmas, make this departure even more difficult.

"So, I'm going to ask you again, Rowan. What are you going to do with me?" He paused. "You have about twenty or so minutes before the food gets delivered. Why don't you start with your mouth?"

Chapter Five

COOPER

Me: *How'd the party at Jenner's go last night?*

Macon: *I didn't get shit-faced on tequila if that's what you're asking.*

Me: *I wasn't, but good to know you handled your booze, brother.*

Macon: *Who said I handled my booze? I just said, for once, it wasn't the tequila's fault.*

Me: *LOL…motherfucker.*

Brady: *It was a sick party, my man. We're sorry that you missed it.*

Brady: *I still can't believe you're stranded there. Didn't you check the weather before you left?*

Me: *Don't get me fucking started. My phone has been blowing up with texts from the Daltons, Mom and Dad, Walter—everyone. You're all asking the same question. But if it was supposed to be that bad out, why didn't the pilot say anything before we left LA?*

Brady: *Maybe he just assumed there would be enough of a window to fly back. Whatever the reason is, it's fucked up.*

Macon: *What's even more fucked up is that we don't have the land yet in Lake Louise.*

Me: *I was positive our offer would be enough, that the seller would immediately bite, especially with the contingencies we set.*

Brady: *Jenner said the realtor informed him that the seller is away for the holiday and unable to be reached.*

Me: *Bullshit. You don't fall off the grid when you know a buyer is flying in to look at your land. They either don't want to be found or they're buying themselves some time for a backup offer.*

Macon: *Latter.*

Me: *Agreed.*

Brady: *For sure.*

I looked toward the bathroom, thinking I'd heard the sound of Rowan coming out from her shower. I was curious what she'd put on when she eventually walked out, knowing within minutes of joining me, I'd have her naked again. But as I really tuned into the noise, I could still hear the water, which told me that the door I'd heard open came from the room next to hers.

Macon: *You'll be home tomorrow?*

Me: *Flight is scheduled for 10 a.m. Weather looks clear, so it won't be canceled. And when I get back, I want a Christmas redo. Klark's cooking. A big-ass bash at Mom and Dad's, like you're all having tonight.*

I closed my eyes for a second, seeing the whole setup, how my family would be gathered in Mom and Dad's living room, the way I was positive they all were right now. Macon and his girl, Brooklyn. Brady would be alone—a player like him didn't bring a one-night stand to a holiday dinner. Walter and his girlfriend, Gloria. All the Daltons.

Every year, my mom's interior designer decorated every square inch of the downstairs of their house, making you feel like you'd stepped into Christmas. Festive music played. Klark, our personal chef, tore shit up in the kitchen, as usual. A roaring fire lit up the whole room even though it was gas.

Not that the table and spread that I'd ordered for Rowan's suite was bad. I was sure she was going to be surprised as hell whenever she came out of the bathroom. I'd done the best I could, given the little resources I had, and my time with her had been far better than I'd ever expected. There was just something about spending holidays with family that felt so right.

Macon: *Klark's making enough food to feed the entire neighborhood. Don't worry, there will be plenty of leftovers when you get here. As for the celebration, I'm not sure if the Daltons can make it over—I'll ask them—but Brady and I will be here. Probably Walter too.*

Brady: *What Macon said.*

Me: *You guys have a good time tonight.*

Macon: *What do you have planned? Hotel bar? A bottle of bourbon?*

Me: *Something a little hotter than that.*

Brady: *Of course my brother found a chick for the night. I'd have been disappointed if you hadn't.*

Me: *For the last two nights and tonight.*

Macon: *Fuck yeah! Is she Canadian or there on vacation?*

Me: *Why? Are you hoping she's based in LA?*

Macon: *That shit should be obvious.*

Me: *Jesus, little brother. Are you trying to get me settled down, like you?*

Macon: *You say that like it's a bad thing.*

Brady: *It is.*

Brady: *And there's no need for your head to even go there. Just have fun, Cooper, and return home a single man, so we can keep playing the field, like we've always done.*

Me: *See you guys tomorrow…and merry Christmas.*

Brady: *Merry Christmas, brother.*
Macon: *Merry Christmas.*

I was just setting my phone on the table when the creak of the bathroom door finally opening caused me to look up, immediately catching Rowan's expression. The look on her face only deepened when she processed what she was actually seeing.

Her hand went over her mouth, her eyes widening. "You did all this for me?"

I nodded toward the seat across from me. "Join me."

She was in a pair of jeans and a tight black cotton top that ended mid-arm and just below her waist. It was a plain shirt, yet nothing, so far, looked simple on Rowan's body.

Not when it was covering a body like hers. Everything hugged her in the right place, showing off her gorgeous curves and dips.

Fuck, that woman was hot.

I waited until she sat and leaned my arms on the small table, her face illuminated by the flickering candles. "Merry Christmas."

Last night, we'd eaten our Christmas Eve dinner at the restaurant inside the hotel. Because none of the guests could really leave, the dining room was overpacked, the service lacked, and the quality of food was just above mediocre.

I didn't want that for tonight.

So, while Rowan had stepped into the hallway a few hours ago to take a call, I'd ordered this meal. Room service wasn't operating with a full menu since the storm prevented them from getting any food deliveries in, causing the options to be slim. After speaking with the kitchen, I'd settled on an appetizer of shrimp cocktail. Cheeseburgers, fries, and a Parmesan risotto. Cheesecake was for dessert. As for creating an ambiance, the best they could offer were candles and an expensive bottle of red wine.

A combination I certainly wouldn't have chosen for a date or a holiday dinner, but it would do.

From the expression still growing across Rowan's face, she was more than pleased.

"Merry Christmas." Her cheeks glowed as she placed her napkin on her lap, wrapping her fingers around the stem of her wineglass. "A cheeseburger for Christmas. Aren't you a rebel?" She winked. "This is beautiful, Cooper."

"Beautiful would be a tender, succulent steak and a Maine lobster tail with a forty-year-old bourbon to wash it down. A private room with our own waitstaff and rose petals and candles covering every surface. This here is adequate for the circumstances." I smiled. "You know, since I don't have any mistletoe, a tree, or lights."

"Tis the damn season." She returned the grin. "But seriously, it's more than enough. In my eyes, it's perfect." She held up her glass. "To a Christmas neither of us will ever forget."

I clinked my glass against hers and took a long drink. When I set the wine down, I reached under the table toward the floor, where I'd stashed the present. "For you." I set the large clump of toilet paper in the center of the table, far enough away from the candles so it wouldn't set on fire. "Excuse the TP. It was the only pliable wrapping paper I could find in the room."

"You got me a gift." She sounded almost breathless.

"Rowan, let's make one thing very clear. You are my gift," I growled. "This is just something small, and with limited resources, it was the best I could do."

"I love it already."

Her face proved that as she began to unweave the layers of toilet paper that I'd wrapped around my creations, the small designs falling onto her hand. "You made these?"

"Yes."

The two paper cranes were sitting on her palm, along with the flower, and she traced her fingers across the sharp folds and steep points. The colorful paper was from the magazines I'd found on the coffee table.

"Cooper, these are incredible."

"Our nanny, growing up, was an origami wiz. It'd been a long time since I'd applied the skills she'd taught my brothers and me."

"I really, really love them." She took her time looking at each of the cranes, both slightly different, and the flower, which had taken the longest because I didn't have any scissors. "I'm blown away."

I laughed. "Put me in the outside world, and I can do a hell of a lot better than some bent paper."

"But I don't need you to. This was so thoughtful." She held up a finger. "I'll be right back." She took the origami with her and disappeared into the bedroom, returning less than a minute later with just a small bag in her hand. "I was going to give this to you later, but now feels like the right time."

"You didn't have to do this."

"I wanted to." She smiled again. "When you were in the shower, I wandered into the gift shop downstairs. At that point, they were pretty much sold out of everything, except this. When I saw it, it made me giggle and immediately think of you."

I took the bag from her and pulled out a small wooden bear from inside, just big enough to fit in my palm, the etchings and markings done by someone who was outstanding at woodworking.

"According to the salesclerk, Banff is known for its grizzlies and black bears, so this will be the perfect memorabilia from your trip here." Her smile grew. "But why it made me giggle and think of you is because, until you, I'd never met a man who roars."

"I roar?"

"Oh, yes." Her eyes widened. "When you're teasing my body. When you're inside it. And it's loud."

I was surprised by what she was telling me. She was the first woman who had ever mentioned anything like that, which made me think that sound was just for her.

"You did good, Rowan." I set the bear on the side of the table. "This little guy is going on my desk at home."

She laughed, her expression so fucking beautiful.

"Now that the gifts are out of the way, I want to know more about you." I took one of the shrimps from the metal bowl of ice and dipped it in the cocktail sauce. "Tell me something. Something everyone in your life knows but me. Something I'd never guess. And something no one knows about you."

She nodded toward the appetizer. "I don't eat shrimp."

I laughed. "My first wrong guess."

She bit half of a fry and chewed. "My family would tell you I'm sensitive. That my heart is the reason why I ended up selling my business. The weight of carrying employees and angry customers was too heavy on me. That I took it all in and it became too much. That's not the truth." She lifted her knife and cut her burger in half. "The truth is, I saw a hole in their company, and I knew what I could bring and how I could fill it. My family needed me, and that's why I sold. Because honestly, I could have dealt with bashing customers and difficult employees for the rest of my career, and it wouldn't have bothered me."

"Most people wouldn't give up their dreams to help someone else. That's admirable, and it says a lot about your character."

"Or it's extremely stupid."

"Only you can decide that."

"At this very moment, I'm going to say I don't know." She chewed off the corner of her burger, moaning a little. "This is better than it looks."

"Yeah?" I glanced down at the plate, the juice from the burger oozing out. "Because it doesn't look very good."

"It's going to surprise you. The swiss cheese and mushrooms

really make it." She wiped her mouth. "Just like I've surprised you."

I glanced back up at her. "You have." I paused. "In ways I wasn't expecting."

"You want to elaborate?"

And talk about how this woman was making me crave her. That her voice was something I was after as much as her pussy. That even though I was missing the celebration at home, this was where I wanted to be.

Right in this chair, feet away from her, gazing into her beautiful green eyes.

Macon had sworn off women until he met one who changed his whole world. Brady never wanted to settle down; he wanted to live the single life until the day he died.

I was always open to the possibility of a relationship. If a woman could hold my attention, if she could give me what I needed and wanted, I was down.

But the women I'd dated in the past weren't right, and I learned that pretty quickly, bailing within a few months. In LA, that had earned me the reputation of being a rebel, a title far more unruly than serving a cheeseburger for Christmas. Women assumed I didn't like the restraints and commitment.

That wasn't it.

I'd just learned over a short period of time that I didn't like them.

Really, it was that simple.

But there was something about Rowan that intrigued me. How there was a side of her that was so soft and caring, and on the flip, there was this fierce, independent, badass woman.

I wanted to soak myself in the middle.

I wanted the snow to keep fucking falling.

Rather than elaborating on the details I was sure she was after,

I said, "Let's just say that we're entering our third night together and this is the longest amount of time I've spent with a woman in months. Shit, maybe even over a year. I usually find something that immediately turns me off."

"A flaw?" Her brows rose.

"Nah, we all have flaws. I find them hot as hell."

"Then what? Give me an example."

I picked off a mushroom and chewed it. "The last woman I was with wanted to know where I was at all times. She wanted to put a goddamn tracker on my phone. And when she asked for my location, she wouldn't believe my answer. I didn't lie. I had no reason to. But because of her past, she didn't trust what I said, and inevitably, it would turn into a fight." I chomped on another shrimp. "A few weeks in, the good times should have outweighed the bad. Because they didn't, it was time for me to go."

"So, you don't think a lack of trust was her flaw?"

I shook my head. "It wasn't a fault, it was her belief. The way she lived her life. And I sure as hell couldn't spend one more second caught up in a web that thick." Once I finished a stack of fries, I added, "Are you avoiding your last question?"

She smiled. "Maybe."

I finally took my first bite of burger, my groan letting her know I agreed with her mushroom and swiss assessment.

"The thing no one knows…" She sighed.

I wiped my mouth. "I'm looking forward to this one the most."

"Why?"

I dipped a fry in some ketchup. "I suspect you have a bestie you tell everything to, yeah?"

"Sky. We've been friends since college."

"If you haven't told Sky this, then, shit, it has to be deep."

She let out a huff of air and instantly brought her wineglass to her lips, swallowing several sips' worth. "I've never been in love. I told my ex I loved him. I think I even said it to my first boyfriend. But it wasn't love with those guys. I even knew that then."

"How are you so sure?"

As she stared at me, her breathing began to speed up. "Because I don't know what love is." She pulled her glass closer, holding it in front of her chest. "I didn't grow up seeing it. My parents hated each other. Eventually, Dad cheated and got caught, and they got divorced. My brothers have always been about sleeping with as many women as possible, so they're not exactly shining mentors." She stared at the top of her glass. "What I learned from my family was work ethic. Accountability. To be a woman of my word. But love? No." She took another long drink. "And because I never experienced it in my last relationship, I felt this overwhelming disappointment. It didn't matter what he did, it wasn't enough."

I'd never had a conversation like this before. Although I'd had relationships, none of them had been long-term, so love was never said or brought up.

But I was intrigued.

Hell, I was captivated.

"Do you think it's something you feel immediately?" I asked.

"That's attraction, not love."

I crossed my arms over my chest, fascinated by another one of her descriptions. "What is it, then?"

"In my previous business, when I worked the floor, I'd watch people. The way they interacted with their husbands and wives. I consider myself an expert observer. But during those times was when I actually got to see firsthand what love looked like."

I lifted another fry and dragged it through the ketchup. "Tell me what you saw."

"Not just saw, but heard." She set down her drink, freeing her hand, placing both on her lap. "Words that caused a smile. A look of complete contentment and security. The comfort in certain acts—easy ones, like holding someone's hand." She rested her voice for a second. "I learned that it's more than just a statement and a feeling. It's a fulfillment. Everyone has different needs, but when yours are met, that's love."

Points I'd never considered.

But she was right because had these women fulfilled me, I was sure I would have loved them.

They just didn't.

And within a few weeks, I hadn't wanted them to.

"Your ex," I started, taking a drink, "why didn't he fill you?"

"Easiest question you've asked all night." She laughed. "He was too immature. He didn't view the world with eyes of a thirty-two-year-old, he acted more like a twenty-two-year-old. If I was only looking for someone to have fun with, he would have been perfect."

"But you are looking—that's what it sounds like you're saying."

She shook her head. "I haven't been, no. I've actually been single for a while, getting acclimated to this new job, navigating all of these life challenges and changes before I hit the big three-oh in a couple of months." She winced. "It's wild to me that I'm this age. Where did the time go?"

I chuckled. "We're the same age." Done with the burger, I moved the plate to the side and leaned over the table. "Yet...you said yes to me." I let those words churn. "Why?"

"Why not?"

"No, no." I crossed my hands. "That's not your answer, that's a placeholder." When she didn't immediately respond, I surrounded the wine stem, swirling the dark liquid before I took a sip. "You let me into your room. You let me into your body. And you've let me into your life for the last two nights, going on three. There's a reason for that, Rowan. What is it?"

She glanced down at her lap, and when her head slowly rose,

her hands came with it, gripping the sides of her plate. "Have you ever looked at someone and just knew they were going to be an amazing fuck?" Her eyes narrowed. "I saw that in you. I wanted it. And for once, I let myself have it."

"That's the only reason?"

She nodded. "Yes."

"And now?"

Her teeth found her lip, running across it, sinking into the soft flesh. "I'm ready for the next round."

Chapter Six

Rowan

"You have my number now," Cooper said as he gripped the armrests of the living room chair that I was sitting in, leaning down so his face was inches from mine. "If you need someone to go to dinner with or to make you fucking scream again"—he let out a short, deep laugh, which I knew had everything to do with our conversation last night over dinner—"call me."

It had been days since he'd used cologne—he didn't have any with him—yet I could still smell it, like the scent permanently lived on his skin. "It's funny, you didn't ask for my number."

"It's funny, you didn't offer it."

He closed the distance between us, his lips pressing against mine. He kept them there, and I sensed that he was breathing me in, his hands suddenly holding my cheeks, keeping us together even though I wasn't going anywhere.

Because, oh God, I liked the feel of Cooper's mouth.

And I loved the way my body reacted to him.

There was a small slip of his tongue; it only lasted a few seconds before he pulled it back in, pecking my lips until those parted from mine too.

Before I could respond, he said, "I've got to catch my flight."

I nodded.

This was a goodbye I hadn't mentally prepared for. I'd pushed it far from my mind, planning on dealing with it when the time came.

Now that it was here, I didn't like the feeling inside me.

But I pushed that away too.

"Thank you for a perfect Christmas."

"Perfect?" I challenged.

"Yes." His hand went to the back of my neck, clasping it hard enough that I felt it everywhere. "I needed nothing but you."

How could words make me breathless?

I didn't know.

But his did.

I set my fingers on top of his, attempting to ground myself despite the fact that I was sitting with my feet on the floor, and whispered, "Thank you for making mine so memorable." I tried to take a deep breath. "Safe travels back to LA."

I scanned his face one last time.

Those dark blue eyes.

Lips.

Scruff.

"You as well."

The chair felt too confined, so I stood, and I found myself closing the small distance between us and wrapping my arms around his neck. My eyes closed as I inhaled, as the sage and burnt orange took ahold of me. As thoughts from our last three nights together moved through my brain like a movie reel.

I didn't know why I had such an urge to hold him tighter. Why I wanted just one more moment with him and then instantly questioned whether that would be enough.

But what I realized fairly quickly was that I had to force myself to unravel my arms from around him and take a few steps back, ignoring the pounding in my heart and the aching in my stomach and the desperate need pulsing through my fingers to reach for his.

This was—this had to be—enough.

"See ya, Cooper." My voice was quiet and gentle.

He gave me a smile that was so incredibly sexy, and then he picked up his messenger bag from the table and walked toward the door, giving me a low, "You'd better," just before he opened it and disappeared.

As soon as I was alone, my arms wrapped around my stomach, holding the air in my lungs as I stared at the closed door, listening to the silence in the room. A sinking feeling was filling me. One that had completely come out of nowhere.

It had been inevitable that we both had to leave. Lake Louise wasn't home. I was the one who hadn't given him my number, a move that had been strategic, which was why I didn't understand where these emotions were coming from.

Regardless of whether I wanted him or not, I couldn't be with Cooper Spade.

So, what the hell is wrong with me?

Knowing there was only one person who could get me out of this mood, I went into the bedroom and grabbed my phone from inside my purse. I found Sky's contact in my Favorites and called her.

"Finally," she said as she answered. "I thought you were never going to call. How was your Christmas?"

"Interesting." I sucked in air. "Really, really interesting. How was yours?"

"Not nearly as eventful as yours. I know things didn't go as planned—I got that much from your texts. Spill the beans, girl."

As I walked back into the living room and took a seat on the couch, the grin was there, tugging its way to the surface of my mouth. "I met someone." I squeezed my thighs together, feeling the ache that Cooper had caused this morning when he ravaged me before he got in the shower. "And I had the most incredible sex of my life."

"You little dirty bird." She laughed. "Seriously, I'm screaming for you right now. Who was the guy? It couldn't have been some stranger you picked up. My girl doesn't roll like that."

"He wasn't a stranger per se. I mean, I was to him—I'm positive he had no idea who I was." I wrapped my free arm around the edge of the couch and tucked my legs beneath me. "But I certainly knew who he was." I paused, anticipating her reaction. "It was Cooper Spade."

"Wait...wait...*wait*." She gasped. "Cooper Spade, as in Spade Hotels?"

I sighed, "Yes."

"Rowan, holy shit." I could hear the shock in her tone. "And you said he didn't know who you were? How is that even possible?"

I stared at the door he'd walked through just a few minutes ago. "I never gave him my last name, and he never asked for it."

"My mind is officially blown."

I pushed the back of my head against the cushion behind me. "Honestly, me, too, now that I'm processing the three nights we spent together." My eyes closed; my throat tightened. "He was sweet, Sky. Not in a way that was too much, more like a thoughtful way. He surprised me with a big Christmas dinner and gifted me the cutest origami that he'd made, he said it was the best he could do, given his lack of resources, but I loved it." A swoony expression was growing over my face.

"He was constantly getting food delivered to the room, ordering what he thought I wanted, and most of the time, he got it right. He showered with me one night, drew us a bath another night. And the dirty talk that came out of that man? My God, it was straight-up fire." I knew my cheeks were blazing red. "I don't know... I guess with his reputation, I had envisioned something completely different than what I experienced."

"You know, he sounds kinda dreamy."

As I swallowed, my chest burned. "He was."

"And now, he's gone?"

I quickly scanned the room, where there wasn't even a trace of him. "He's headed to the airport now. I'm sure the Spade jet came to pick him up." I laughed. "Can you imagine if the Cole jet had come for me at the same time? Now, that would have made things even more interesting."

"Good Lord." She snorted. "How did you leave things with him?"

I squeezed the phone between my fingers. "I got his number and intentionally didn't give him mine. We kissed, hugged, and he left. There was no promise of any kind of future, although it sounded like he wants me to call him."

"Seriously, you're just full of surprises." She went quiet for a moment. "This isn't you, Row. I don't even know who I'm talking to right now."

"I know." I lifted my head, my heart pounding. "But we can't be together—even you know that."

"I'm sure you left a lasting impression and Cooper is going to do everything in his power to get in touch with you."

"You really think so? I doubt that."

"You mean to tell me that he's not going to hunt for the woman who rocked his world in Canada? Come on, babe." I could see her rolling her eyes.

"He has so many women flocking to him on a daily basis. I highly doubt that he's even going to remember me."

"But let's say he does. Then what?"

I got up and paced toward the windows, seeing the grounds crew shoveling the snow into banks that were far taller than Cooper. "He won't find me, nor will he run into me. You know I'm not like my brothers. I don't hit up the LA party scene, so he's definitely not going to see me shaking my ass at some club."

"Your paths might not cross *that* way, but there are plenty of other ways you two could run into each other. Like his assistant, who's probably an Instagram genius and can find you in seconds. Or the PI he can hire. Girl, there are endless ways for him to track you down."

I put my back to the window, the cold glass not even touching my body temperature.

I was burning up.

On the outside and on the inside.

"If he finds me...that's not going to change anything."

"Except how pissed he'll be—that'll change all right. He'll go from the happiest man alive to the angriest."

She was right.

"But, Sky, Cooper and I aren't going to be friends after this. We're not going to date. What happened in Lake Louise is going to stay in Lake Louise. It was three nights of fucking earth-shattering, scorching steam. And now, it's over, and I've already moved on."

She hummed, "But have you?"

My head shook even though I said, "Yes."

"I don't believe you."

"Then, believe this—some couples can smooth out all the logistics and roadblocks and find their happily ever after. But getting into a relationship with a Spade—my family's number one enemy—is a scenario that will never ever work."

Chapter Seven

Cooper

"Looks like you got everything you wanted," Brady said as he took a seat beside me on the couch. "You happy?"

With my legs extended across the ottoman and no plans to move anytime soon, I rubbed my stomach, full from all the food Klark had served tonight.

My mother had come through in a hard way and re-created Christmas. No matter how old we were, she treated the holiday like we were kids again, and I wasn't complaining. The lights, scents, music, the whole meal—everything was the way I wanted it to be.

"Very," I replied to my older brother. Except I could tell he felt the opposite. "Don't tell me you're about to complain that you had to eat turkey and prime rib two days in a row. I could eat that meal all week and never grow tired of it."

"Same," Macon moaned from the other side of the sectional. "But I'm so stuffed, I want to die."

"That makes two of us." Brooklyn rested her head on Macon's shoulder. "Coop, tell us about your trip"—she glanced behind the couch into the kitchen—"you know, the juicy stuff before your parents come in here and join us."

Before I could say a word, Brady barked, "Who gives a shit about the juicy stuff? The more pressing matter is that we don't have the land yet." He looked at his watch. "Isn't Jenner supposed to be here by now to give us an update?"

"I just spoke to him," Macon responded. "He's on his way over. Relax."

Brady chuckled. "I know you didn't just tell me to relax." He sipped his scotch.

"Hey, Mom," Macon yelled toward the kitchen. "When you come in, can you bring Brady a refill?"

"Sure, honey," Mom replied.

Macon then glared at Brady. "Unless you prefer the whole bottle...you know, to help you relax." He laughed.

"It might take that to get this one in a good mood." I nodded toward Brady and then looked at Brooklyn—the best thing that had ever happened to my little brother. "The details are juicy, but I'm not going to share those. I will say this woman isn't like any others I've ever met, and we had one hell of a time together."

"What? You're suddenly not going to kiss and tell? Normally, I can't get you to shut up about the women you fuck," Brady said, shaking his head. "I don't know what's gotten into you."

"I do," Brooklyn said. "He likes her. That's what has gotten into him."

"Jesus..." Brady rested his elbows on his knees, holding his drink between his legs. "Spare me the part where you confess your love. I don't want to hear it. I want the goddamn juice."

"Which you're not getting," I told him.

He stared at me, his dark-blue eyes narrowing. "Do you really like her?"

I laid out his question in my mind.

A question I'd pondered since I'd left Lake Louise this morning.

Rowan wasn't a one-night stand—that was for sure. She felt far more than a weekend fling too.

The time we'd spent together wasn't just hours upon hours of devouring each other's body, although there had been plenty of that. We talked. We shared.

We spent fucking Christmas together.

And we built a small foundation.

Since I'd left Canada, I hadn't been able to get her out of my mind.

I was obsessing over her pussy.

Her voice.

Scent.

The way I'd felt when I was in her presence.

A feeling that I couldn't get enough of.

What is it about this woman that makes me want so much more of her?

I wondered how long it was going to take for her to reach out. I knew I should have gotten her number before I departed. I just didn't understand why she hadn't offered it to me, even after I called her out on it.

There was a reason.

And if that reason was because she wanted to be in control of the communication, then I was good with that.

But I wasn't going to wait forever.

There were ways to find everyone's number—and I'd have no problem finding hers.

Do I like her?

I inhaled a deep breath and turned to look at Brady. "Yeah, I do."

"*Fuuuck*," Brady moaned. "Another one down. I can't handle

this shit."

"I wouldn't describe it that way," I told him. "We're not in a relationship. We're not even dating. Hell, I don't even know her last name, so it's nothing like that."

"Ignore him," Brooklyn said, "and tell us what it is like."

Macon patted her cheek. "God, I fucking love that you fit right in."

She certainly did, starting from the moment I'd interviewed her for a role at Spade Hotels—she was already Macon's girlfriend at that point. And since then, she'd grown to know Brady and me quite well, never afraid to give either of us shit.

I ran my hand over the top of my hair. "Unlike you," I said, focusing on Brady before I glanced at Brooklyn and Macon, "I've never been one to shy away from a woman, knowing she's more interested in a relationship than a one-night stand. I've always been open to the idea. I've just never found anyone who's held my interest. Who I could really see myself falling in love with."

"And then…you met her."

Brooklyn had only spoken a handful of words, but they were a powerful combination.

I ran my thumb across my lips. "You're going to ask me what it is about her, and I don't have that answer." A view of her profile was in my head. The slope of her nose. The pout of her lips. How her head tilted back a few inches every time she laughed. "I just like her. I like to be around her. I like the way she views things. I like the way her quick, short answers challenge me. I like—"

"Her pussy," Brady said.

I nodded. "I certainly like that, too, but it's not all about that."

Macon stretched his arm across Brooklyn's shoulders. "We're ready for double dates."

"Exactly what Macon just said." Brooklyn smiled.

Brady shook his head. "I'm melting. Really. The cuteness—I

just can't fucking handle it."

I laughed. "But in order for that double date to happen—or any date for that matter—Rowan needs to call. All the power is in her hands."

"Hold up," Macon said. "Why is it up to her? You can't text her?"

"I don't have her number," I admitted.

Macon looked at Brooklyn. "Rule one, which I learned the hard way, is that you always get the number, brother."

Feeling the heat from the fire, I rolled up the sleeves of my shirt. "It wasn't that I didn't want it, it was that she didn't offer it. So, I gave her mine."

"And you haven't heard from her yet?" Brooklyn asked.

I pulled out my phone, scrolling through the notifications that had come in since I'd last checked, not a single one from a number I didn't recognize. "Nah, nothing." I returned my cell to my pocket. "She was flying back to LA today too. I'm sure she's with her family. She missed the whole holiday, like me."

But the truth was, I had no idea what her plans were. She never discussed them.

I was assuming—something I'd done a shit ton of during our time together.

"I don't know how to handle this not-in-control thing." I sat up, dropping my feet to the floor. "In the past, I've always dictated the communication—when we speak, when we make plans. Yet here I am, waiting, like a fucking—"

"Pussy."

I looked at Brady. "I've had about enough of you."

"But it's the truth. If you hadn't gotten any feelings involved, you wouldn't be whimpering on the couch, like someone just took away your goddamn puppy."

"You"—Brooklyn pointed at Brady—"need to zip it." She

then looked at me. "Let me tell you from personal experience, we don't always reach out as quickly as you think we're going to." She gave Macon a quick smile. "Sometimes, it takes us time to process things and come to terms with it. I didn't text Macon the same day or even the next day."

"Or ever," Macon clarified. "I had to hunt her ass down and find her myself."

"I get that." I adjusted the pillow behind my back. "I don't mind hunting if that's what it takes, but I also don't want to chase someone who doesn't want to be found."

"I don't think that'll be the case," Brooklyn said softly.

I smiled at the woman who I figured, one day soon, would be my sister-in-law. "What makes you think that?"

She shrugged, but her expression was confident. "Obviously, I don't know her at all, but it's just a hunch I have."

"Because?"

She turned toward me, leaning her elbow on the back of the couch, her hand holding her face. "It sounds like Rowan and I might be a little similar. If it were me, there's absolutely no way I'd spend three nights with a guy, including Christmas Eve and Christmas, if I didn't feel something. I would have kicked him out after one night and spent the rest of the time alone."

"Maybe she hates being lonely," Brady offered.

"She has a phone, she could call her bestie," Brooklyn countered. "She could hang out in the hotel bar. It's not like she'd have to sit in her room and be by herself the whole time." She grinned at him. "Nice try though." She then grinned at me. "I guess what I'm trying to say is, be patient. And if you still don't hear from her, which I'm sure you will, then make the effort." She dropped her elbow to grab Macon's hand. "It'll be well worth it in the end."

Before I could comment, there was the sound of heels clicking on the hardwood floor, and I turned toward the entryway of the living room, where Jo and Jenner were walking in.

"About fucking time," Brady moaned.

I pointed my thumb at Brady. "He's on fire tonight. Don't pay any attention to him."

"We normally don't," Jo offered, laughing.

I got up and hugged Jo before I man-hugged Jenner. "Welcome, you guys. Thanks for coming over."

Jo took a seat on the other side of Brooklyn and Jenner stood in front of the couch, addressing us all. "I've been on the phone with Walter—that's why I was late. I wanted to speak to him before I talked to any of you."

"I don't like the sound of this," Macon said.

Brady didn't either by the looks of it, throwing back the rest of his drink.

Jenner's hands went into his pockets. "Based on every number I pulled and the research I put into this purchase, I was positive our offer and the contingencies we laid out would send us straight into escrow."

"Don't even fucking tell me..." Brady fumed.

"That's why I nurture my relationships with my network of realtors—so I can score us these pocket listings." Jenner crossed his arms. "But, fuck me, the last couple of years, things haven't gone as smoothly as I wanted, and it's been one complication after another."

"It's the seller. He fucked us," Macon said. "He went MIA on some holiday trip, which is the most bogus thing I've heard in my life. You don't disappear when you're selling land. You just fucking don't."

"It's bullshit," I snapped. "You can't tell me that wasn't intentional. I won't believe it."

"Agreed." Jenner shifted his stance.

"I don't know why...but something tells me that wasn't a coincidence." Brady moved his ass to the end of the couch cushion. "The seller's agent—someone got to her, didn't they?"

Jenner let out a long breath. "Well, she finally got back to me a few hours ago."

"And?" I clasped my hands on my knees.

"And"—Jenner shook his head—"during the holiday, like I'm sure you're all suspecting, the whole fucking environment changed."

Chapter Eight

ROWAN

"I left the fob in the center console," I said to the valet attendant as I climbed out of the driver's seat, standing in the parking garage attached to our office.

"Do you need your SUV parked or kept out front?"

Since I often came and went several times a day, it wasn't an inappropriate question.

"Park it, please. I'll be here until this evening." I handed him a twenty-dollar bill. "Thank you so much."

"Thank you," he replied, climbing into the driver's seat.

I headed for the back entrance of the building, waving my key card across the reader. When the lock clicked open, I let myself in, rounding the corner to the elevator. While I waited for it to open, I took out my phone, thumbing through the texts that had come in during my morning commute.

Sky: *Tell me you've texted him.*

I laughed as I read my best friend's words.

Words that didn't surprise me one bit.

Me: *And say what? Hi, you're gonna hate me, buuut…*

Sky: *Invite him to dinner—start there. Ease your way into it. He's going to understand as long as you're honest with him.*

Me: *I think we're beyond that, no?*

Sky: *You mean the easing part? Or the being honest part?*

Me: *Both. LOL.*

Sky: *Girl, I will strangle you if you give up this opportunity because you're afraid to tell him the truth.*

I stepped into the elevator as the doors slid open. Just as they were about to close, one of our employees rushed inside, hitting a button to a lower floor than mine.

"Morning, Miss Cole."

A title I'd never get used to. But things were so much fancier and formal here compared to the boutiques I used to own. So was the dress code, my toes already aching from the way these four-inch heels pinched them.

I smiled at him. "Good morning."

Me: *It's not just about being afraid to tell him. There's also the issue that Cooper Spade is the last man on the planet I can date. Things would have to be kept a secret and—just no.*

Sky: *There are ways around it.*

Me: *Like what? Moving to Antarctica? I've seen TikToks that take place there, trust me when I say, that wouldn't even be far enough.*

Sky: *So, what are you going to do? Ignore your feelings and everything that happened and hope you never run into him?*

The elevator stopped, the doors opening to let the gentleman off. Feeling his eyes on me, I lifted my face and gave him a grin.

"Have a good day," he said as he walked out.

"You too."

Me: *For the moment, yes. I've been home for, like, 5 seconds. I haven't even unpacked yet. I need time to figure this all out.*

Sky: *Suuure.*

Me: *You're relentless.*

Sky: *And you're being stubborn.*

Me: *Love you, mean it.*

Sky: *You're going to be the death of me, woman.*

Me: *Sounds like I owe you a drink. Tonight?*

Sky: *Yes. My apartment. Bring all the wine.*

Me: *Done. <3*

"Rowan, I'm so glad you're finally here," our assistant said, standing from her desk on the executive-level floor. "Your brothers are waiting for you."

I'm finally here?

Still holding my phone, I quickly checked the time. It was ten minutes before eight, and my first meeting wasn't until ten. "Why are they waiting for me?"

"Your father called an executive meeting for eight o'clock."

I stood frozen in front of her desk. "Really? Why didn't anyone tell me?"

"When I called Rhett this morning to tell him, he said he'd text you and let you know."

I sighed, shaking my head. "Rhett was probably in some woman's bed at the time, and he very well could have been sleeping off a hangover." My hand went to her arm the second a look of concern came across her face. "Always feel free to call me directly."

I understood I was new; processes were still being implemented with me in mind. But I wasn't any lower in rank than my brothers.

When it came to Cole International, we were all equals.

Except for my father. He was the boss.

Her voice was soft when she said, "I'll never make that mistake again."

I gently squeezed her. "It wasn't a mistake at all. Anyone would assume that my oldest brother would be the most responsible out of the three of us, right?" I winked as I released her.

She laughed. "Can I get you a coffee? Juice?"

"A coffee would be wonderful, thank you."

"I'll bring it into the conference room."

I left her desk and walked down the long hallway, quickly dropping my bag in my office, and continued until I reached the conference room, opening the door to find my brothers sitting on opposite sides of the long oval table.

"Thanks for calling, asshole," I said to Rhett, who was holding his coffee cup with both hands, resting it against the outside of his mouth.

His expression told me I'd guessed right. He was hungover as hell.

He'd at least attempted to throw himself together by combing his black hair flat and putting on a suit. As I walked around him toward the other side of the table, I could smell the booze.

"Call you?" he uttered.

I took a seat next to Ridge, the scent of his cologne masking the waft of Rhett's alcohol. "Yeah. Call me. Because when our assistant called you this morning, you told her you were going to tell me about this meeting."

His icy-blue eyes widened. "Shit."

"You're lucky I'm always early, or I would have missed this." I leaned my arms on the table, feeling the pull of my blazer. "Did you leave any liquor at the bar last night?"

"Barely." He took a sip and set the cup down. "But I did find myself a nice piece of ass—"

"I don't want to hear it," I told him, knowing he was about to describe that piece of ass in great detail.

My brothers often forgot that I was a woman. My whole life, they treated me like I was one of the guys. Which was fine—I didn't hate it; I actually loved it—but that didn't mean I needed a play-by-play of their sex life.

"Fair enough." Rhett laughed and then held the side of his head, instantly regretting the chuckle. "Jesus, I wish I were in bed right now. Do any of you know what this is about? And how long it's going to take? I need to get the fuck out of here and sleep this off."

"I know nothing," Ridge replied. He looked at me. "You?"

When it came to women, my brothers were the same person.

When it came to anything else, they couldn't be more different.

That was because Ridge was a single dad to the most perfect, beautiful, playful, sweet little girl who owned my entire heart.

Daisy was about to be five, going on twenty-five.

"Dad said nothing to me," I responded. I took in his eyes, a foolproof way to know how either of my siblings was always feeling, their emotions coming straight through the blue of their irises. "Are you okay?"

He nodded. "I'm exhausted."

"Is it because of Daisy?"

He folded his fingers together, the metal of his cuff links scratching against the wooden table. "The past few weeks, she's been having issues with the dark. It doesn't matter what I try—Christmas lights, per her request, a night-light, a glowing unicorn, nothing works. She wakes up, she's scared, she comes into my room. And then throughout the night, we go back and forth between my bedroom and hers. Over and over until it's morning."

"Why don't you let her sleep with you?" Rhett asked. "Brother, you look like a walking fucking zombie."

"If I open that door, it'll never close." Ridge rubbed the sides of his face, his scruff thicker than normal. "But something's gotta give, man. I need sleep."

I circled my hand around the center of his back. "She'll get there. Don't worry. I know this is tough."

He slowly turned his face toward me, the light catching the dark circles under his eyes. "She was gutted you weren't at Christmas."

"Gutted?" Rhett hollered. "It was all she fucking talked about. *Where's Auntie Row? When is Auntie Row coming? Why hasn't Auntie Row arrived yet? What do you mean Auntie Row isn't going to be here for Christmas?*"

"*Awww*," I sang, "that's cute."

"She told Dad she was taking his plane to go pick you up," Ridge said. "She made a whole production about it, she even tried to go pack her suitcase."

I laughed. "My girl has my back. I love her for that."

"What the fuck did you do for the three nights you were stranded in Canada?" Rhett asked, running his hand over the sides of his beard, the color and thickness the same as the dark locks on his head.

I sighed, buying myself some time.

Even though I'd spoken to my family while I was there and we texted frequently, we hadn't really discussed the three nights thoroughly or how I'd occupied my time.

And we certainly weren't going to discuss it now.

"I drank, ate, watched TV—all things you'd suspect I'd do when being alone in a hotel room."

"But it was Christmas," Rhett said.

I moved in my seat, unsure why he was still on the topic. "So?"

"So, you didn't go down to the bar and hang with the guests? Or find yourself someone to cozy up to?"

"Cozy up to?" I looked at Ridge for help, but he was just smiling. "What does that even mean?"

Except I knew what it meant. I just couldn't believe my brother was asking.

Just because he was an open book when it came to this part of his life didn't mean that I was.

But when it came to the two of them, nothing was off-limits. They would always ask. Whether I replied was an entirely different thing.

"Come on, Rowan. Don't play coy." He leaned back in his chair. "I know what the hell I'd do if I was stranded at a hotel for that long with nothing but time and booze on my hands."

"We all know what you'd do," I responded. "But we all know that I'm not you."

I wasn't him. I didn't sleep around. I didn't have one-night stands.

I had relationships, searching for this thing called love that I'd never felt before.

Still, it pinched to say those words.

Because in Lake Louise, I had been him.

I'd taken Cooper back to my room, knowing that the moment I checked out of the hotel, I'd also be checking out of his life.

That was something Rhett would do.

I hated myself for that.

And I hated myself even more for allowing it to happen because since I'd left Lake Louise, there was a feeling inside me that I couldn't shake.

A pulse that vibrated throughout my entire body.

A beat in my chest that quickened every time I thought of Cooper.

And I found myself constantly thinking of him.

What that did was cause a nagging, burning question to come over me.

To haunt me.

To make me repeat, multiple times through the day and night, the same words over and over.

If Cooper weren't a Spade, would he be the man I fell in love with?

"So, you're going to tell me you didn't do shit the whole time you were there besides look at the property and work?" Rhett said. "You were a total angel?" His eyelids narrowed as he looked at me.

I wasn't the only one who could read the eyes of my siblings.

They could also do the same to me.

And just as I started to say, "Yes—"

He cut me off with a chuckle and said, "I can see that's what you want me to believe, Row. We'll end it at that."

Maybe it was because the three of us had been inseparable as kids.

Maybe it was because when my parents had fought—and they'd fought a lot—the only thing we had was each other.

Maybe it was because as we'd gotten older, we were more than just family; we were best friends.

But Rhett was looking right through me.

And there was nothing I could do to stop him.

"I—" My voice cut off once again, this time from the sound of the door opening, my father walking in with our assistant.

She placed my coffee in front of me while my father took a seat at the head of the table, the door then closing behind her as she left.

Dad's hands landed on the wood with a sharp, almost-startling bang. "We have a problem."

He looked at Rhett, then Ridge before his eyes landed on mine.

They didn't move on.

They stayed locked.

And as the silence thickened in the room, so did his stare.

It grew more intense.

He wasn't looking through me, like my brothers. He didn't have that ability.

What he was doing was letting everyone in this room know that the problem—somehow, someway—lay within me.

It felt like an eternity before the wrinkles around his eyes deepened, the ends of his fingers turned white, and his lips finally parted. "And it's a big fucking problem."

Chapter Nine

Cooper

"Do you want to talk about it?" Ford asked the second I answered my phone, his calm voice coming through my speakers as I weaved my way through the thick LA traffic.

Talk about it, talk about it, I silently repeated in my head.

"I have no idea what the hell you mean," I told him.

"You told me you were going to call me back seven hours ago. You're normally a one-hour-tops kind of guy"—he laughed—"and since it's been so long, I figured I'd give you a call and see if you were alive and if you were all right and if you wanted to talk about it."

The youngest Dalton brother was one of my closest friends and golfing partner. There was just something about Ford that I really dug. He had this cool, chill demeanor. He wasn't hotheaded or conceited, which I appreciated, given how successful he was. He knew his worth and what he could bring to the table, and he felt no need to broadcast it.

"*Fuuuck*," I groaned. "I sent that text seven hours ago? I honestly just forgot." I sighed. "Yeah, it's been a hell of a day." I turned at the light. "But it was my first day back at the office after my trip, so I assumed it was going to be a bitch, and I was proven right." I flipped on my blinker and switched lanes. "Things good with you, my man? What did you want to discuss anyway?"

"All is good. I called to see how you were doing now that you're back. I was disappointed you weren't at Jenner's on Christmas Eve. So was Everly—she loves having all her uncles around. And I know we texted a bit while you were in Canada, but I wanted to see how things went since we didn't get to discuss it in detail."

Ford worked with Jenner at The Dalton Group, but each brother—along with their cousins, Hannah and Camden—focused on a different kind of law. Ford was an estate attorney, and he managed my will and trust. And even though he saw Jenner multiple times a day at the office and was in with the Spades, that didn't mean he was privy to what was going on in our professional world.

When it came to the Spades, Jenner said nothing to his family unless it was absolutely necessary.

"On a personal front, things went well," I told him, pausing. "Ford, I met a woman."

"You're shitting me?"

I laughed. "Nah, man. She's great. Actually, she's perfect."

What would have made her even more perfect was if she had fucking called me.

This was the end of our second day home, and she still hadn't reached out. I'd heard everything Brooklyn had said to me last night about Rowan processing what had gone down between us and taking her time to contact me.

For some women, that made sense.

But for Rowan, who hadn't taken long at all to decide she wanted me to come up to her room, I didn't buy Brooklyn's theory.

There was a reason I hadn't heard from Rowan. For the fucking life of me, I couldn't figure out what it was.

"It's about time you settled down, old man." He laughed again. "That makes me happy as hell to hear."

"Old man? You're older than me." I hissed out a whole mouthful of air. "I don't know if I'll be settling down anytime soon or if anything is really going to happen between us, but I like where your head is at." I cleared my throat. "On the flip side of things, Lake Louise is causing us a bit of agony at the moment. We haven't been able to get the seller to agree on our price."

"Hold on...didn't that happen last time?"

"Yes." I groaned. "And the time before." I slowed as I reached the red light. "There's only one reason it keeps happening, and it's bullshit. I'm tired of it."

It wasn't just me; my whole family felt that way. Every goddamn deal causing us nothing but fucking stress.

And since I'd returned from Canada, it was all we had talked about and the fact that there was no end in sight.

"I hear you," Ford said. "I wish there were something we could do. Or something you could do."

I could drink.

That was the only thing that would help this feeling of rage.

Although I had quite an extensive bar at home, there was a specific kind of bourbon I was craving that I happened to be all out of. Knowing that, I'd gone a different way home, so I could stop at the liquor store that I knew carried it.

"There are things that can be done." Right before the light turned green, I ran my hand over my head, returning to the gearshift. "But until Spade Hotels is ours, it's all in Walter's hands. We've given him our opinion, but he's the one who makes the final decision."

"If it makes you feel any better, it's the same over here. Not that I want my parents to fully retire—I want them to be happy with whatever they do—but when the firm is ours, we're going to run things differently."

"You get it." I sped through two more intersections and pulled into the liquor store, parking out front. "Life's going to be different when we're in command, isn't it?"

"Fuck," he moaned, "you can say that again."

I smiled. "Listen, I've got to run. Text me some dates you're available—I know it's hard to break away from that little girl, but I can make myself free whenever you can get out."

"Will do, bud."

I hung up and slid my phone into the pocket of my suit, walking inside the store. I'd been here many times before; I knew exactly where the bourbon was located, and I went to that aisle, scanning the bottles until I found the one I wanted. It was located on the top shelf, and I grabbed two.

As I was headed for the register, rounding the endcap of the aisle, I heard a familiar voice say, "Are you in the mood for red or white?"

If her voice hadn't caught my attention, her scent would have.

Rowan's was unique, and the mix of apple and cedarwood that instantly flew up my nose caused me to halt halfway to the register. While I stood in that spot, frozen, watching her talk on the phone, I took in the sight of her.

A sight that was professional, which was a side I hadn't seen during our time together in Lake Louise and one I simply couldn't get enough of.

She had on a black skirt that showed off her incredible legs, an emerald-colored blouse that was tucked in, and a black blazer. Heels that were fucking sky-high and sexy. Her long hair was down and a little messy, like she'd been tugging on it during a day just as stressful as mine.

Fuck me.

I wanted that hair to slap against my chest and slither down my abs as her mouth worked its way to my cock.

And those fucking lips—I had so many plans for them.

As she stepped toward the front of the aisles, she finally looked up.

Our eyes slowly connected.

And I gradually witnessed the recognition pass through her as she saw me standing here, the shock as she realized it was me, and the layers of emotion that moved through her.

Eventually, she said into the phone, "Sky, I-I have to go," and tossed her cell into her purse.

She stopped only a few feet from me, her eyes widening even more as she took in my face. Her lips flexing, like she was breathing heavy. Her cheeks fully flushed.

"Cooper...hi."

I nodded. "Rowan..."

"It's nice to see you." She smiled.

I knew that was the appropriate response, but that didn't mean I was going to let her get away with it.

I was going to call her ass out, and I gave zero fucks about it.

My brows furrowed; my lips pulled wide. I let the silence eat at her until I replied, "Is it really nice to see me?"

She laughed. I could tell it was out of nerves. "Why would you say that?"

I could beat around the bush, dragging this out, possibly never getting a real answer.

Or I could be honest.

I shifted my stance, adjusting the bottles under my arm, and decided on the latter. "It's just an interesting comment, given that I haven't heard from you. If things had been so nice, why did you ghost me?"

Her chest rose, staying high as she replied, "Ghost? No, that's not it."

"Then, what is it?"

She finally let out the air she had been holding in, her chest deflating. "I just…" She turned quiet. "I didn't know…" She took a breath. "I don't know."

She was flustered.

I'd solve that.

"Listen, I'm not the kind of guy who needs to hear an excuse. I understand how this works. Fuck, I'm one of the inventors of it." I turned, giving her my profile, disappointed that we were here when I'd had a gut feeling that we'd be more. And, hell, I really did want more. "We had a good time, Rowan. But it wasn't good enough for you to reach out. No more needs to be said."

I was out of words.

Looking at her, for even a second longer, would only make my dick harder, so I went to take a step toward the cashier.

But out of nowhere, her fingers clamped my forearm, stopping me from moving.

"Cooper, that's not it." Her nails dug in, in a way that I remembered well. "That's not even close to being it." She waited, and when I said nothing, she added, "It's not that I don't want you. I do. God, I really do. It's that… I shouldn't want you." She paused again. "And that's what I've been fighting with."

I wasn't facing her anymore.

So, I turned my head, first to look at her hand and then her eyes.

They had changed since I'd last gazed at them.

The emotion was thicker.

Heavier even.

Like there was a war happening inside her.

But why?

"Shouldn't want me…" I repeated.

Despite what I'd just said, I knew that feeling. There had been women in the past who I knew I shouldn't fuck with. I'd tasted because I couldn't help myself and ghosted them right after, knowing that was the safest route.

But to hear that she felt that way about me…now, that was interesting.

"Yes," she whispered. "I shouldn't want you."

Was she assuming I was a player? That I'd never settle down? That I'd used her during our time in Lake Louise?

Had she, somehow, heard about my reputation?

I'd thought I'd made myself clear in Canada, so there wouldn't be any surprises when she got home. But I'd also thought that where we'd left things, she could tell I wanted more.

Whatever it was, I needed to hear it.

"Tell me why," I demanded.

She filled her lungs, her expression softening but the emotion stayed. "That's going to be a long conversation. One that won't be easy for me to have." She continued to hold my arm, squeezing even tighter. "I have some explaining to do."

A reply I hadn't anticipated.

She was single—she'd confirmed that in Canada. She hadn't been able to get enough of me. She hadn't been in a rush for the snow to stop.

So, what the hell was this about?

My mind couldn't piece it together.

"But I want you to know—I want to make myself really clear—that since the second you left my hotel room, I've thought of nothing but you." Her head dropped, her eyes no longer on me. "I shouldn't have said that…shit."

Ignoring her hand, I raised my arm and placed my fingers under her chin, lifting until her eyes returned and locked with mine. "I'm happy you did."

"This is messy, Cooper." Her voice was breathy and low.

"It doesn't need to be."

Her head shook. "That's not a choice either of us has." She swallowed. "It just is."

I was getting more confused every time she spoke.

What I knew was that standing here, in the middle of this liquor store, wasn't going to solve anything, so I offered, "Why don't we go back to my place? I'll open one of these bottles, and you can tell me everything over some bourbon."

Her head shook again. "I don't have time tonight. I'm going to Sky's apartment to see her." She looked around the store. "That's why I'm here. I'm buying wine to bring with me."

I didn't want to let her out of my sight.

The last time I had done that, it hadn't worked in my favor.

Besides, there was a reason we'd run into each other here when I was positive I'd never run into her anywhere in LA before—I would have remembered. Rowan's face was one I could never forget.

I wasn't going to let this become a coincidence. I was going to turn this into a memory she'd never fucking forget.

I dragged my thumb across her lips.

I needed the contact, the softness.

I needed her to remember what my mouth and fingers were capable of.

If Lake Louise hadn't scored me a text or phone call, tonight would.

I was sure of that.

My hand left her chin and moved down her shoulder, arm, slipping around to the inside, where it traveled down until I reached her hip. From there, I pulled her a few inches closer. "What do you have time for?"

A different kind of red filled her cheeks as she processed what I'd said. "You mean—"

"Yes." My eyes narrowed as I pressed my hard-on against her. I didn't care who was looking—if they even were. I didn't care if we had an entire damn audience. As far as I was concerned, Rowan and I were the only ones in this store. "That's exactly what I mean."

The base of her throat hollowed as she inhaled. "You're not kidding, are you?"

"I would never kid when it comes to fucking you."

She searched my eyes. "But here? In this liquor store?"

Her questions confirmed one thing. She wanted to; she just couldn't wrap her brain around the location.

Shit, that was the easy part.

"And let the motherfuckers in here see you naked? Fuck no. No one has that privilege but me, Rowan."

A heat moved into her eyes.

"We both have cars outside," I said. "At least, I'm assuming you drove here." My hand lowered to her ass. "We don't even have to leave the parking lot."

My sports car was tiny, but the windows were tinted. No one would see a thing.

"That's what you want from me right now?" She was hiding a smile. "Not an explanation. Just my pussy?"

I wanted an explanation too.

Hell, my brain was still focused on sliding those pieces together.

But I'd take whatever I could get.

"Do you know how fucking amazing your pussy is?" I leaned into her ear, and when I didn't get a response, I continued, "It sounds like you need the reminder, so let me tell you. It's the hottest, tightest, wettest cunt I've ever felt and tasted. I've done nothing but dream about it since I left Lake Louise." I pulled back to look into her eyes. "So, yeah, I want your pussy. I want an explanation, too, but it sounds like I'm not going to score that tonight." I placed my hand on the back of her neck, feeling her pulse hammer against my fingers.

"Why do you always make it so hard to breathe?"

"Because I own your body. Because I know just what to do to make you wet." I nodded toward her pussy. "She is, isn't she?"

She let out a small laugh. "You are...something else."

And she fucking loved that about me.

I turned my wrist, placing my palm on her cheek to tilt her face fully toward mine. "What do you say, Rowan? Are you going to let me taste you? Or are you going to go to Sky's apartment, all wet and turned on, wishing I had made you scream? You know just how good I am at that." I dipped my face closer, hovering my lips above hers. "So, tell me...what do you want?"

Chapter Ten

Rowan

What do I want?

That was an easy question to answer when the star of last night's dream was standing directly in front of me, looking hotter than I'd ever seen him.

It was the suit—it had to be. The dark gray with the silver tie that made me want to ravish him.

Or maybe it was that a tiny bit of time had passed since we'd seen each other, and during that distance, I'd forgotten how incredibly sexy this man was.

Could I forget? Was that even possible?

Whatever the reason was, my body was losing its battle at staying calm and unbothered.

And even though we were no longer on the phone, I swore I could hear Sky singing, *I told you you'd somehow run into him.*

She was right.

Damn it.

And now, I had to make a decision, the seconds ticking away as he waited to hear what it was.

To buy myself a few more seconds, I took in what looked like days' worth of scruff on his cheeks. I processed his dark-blue gaze as it pierced mine. A gaze that, without a doubt, was seeing beneath the clothes I had on. I inhaled his cologne, the sage and burnt orange blend, which wasn't just filling my nose, but also wrapping around me and holding me.

What I wanted was clear.

But what I should want was something entirely different.

Because it shouldn't be him.

Cooper Spade was off-limits.

Especially to me.

But why wasn't my body following those rules? Why was the spot between my legs pulsing for him?

Why wasn't I backing away a few inches and separating us? Why did I want to bring us even closer instead?

As I held his stare, I felt the weight of the decision I needed to make.

I prided myself in almost always doing the right thing. I was a rule follower. I would never hurt anyone intentionally.

This was completely out of character for me—and it had been since the beginning.

Yet here I was.

Again.

Doing more wrong.

Despite how upset my family would be if they knew I was with him.

Despite the fact that Cooper was looking at me as if I were just Rowan Someone and not Rowan Cole.

I filled my lungs with as much air as I could hold, the war of wrong versus right like bolts of electricity shocking every one of my muscles as I whispered, "I want you."

He leaned down to the floor, where I heard the click of the

glass, the two bottles free from his arm when he rose. Both of his hands went to my face, holding my cheeks. "What do you drive?"

What do I drive?

Why was I having such a hard time thinking?

Or connecting any dots that didn't involve him?

"A Range Rover," I finally replied.

"Perfect. The windows—are they tinted?"

It took another moment for me to consider that question.

"The backseat are, yes."

A smile adorned his face.

A face that I'd woken up gasping to because, in my dream, it had been buried between my legs, his tongue wiggling over my clit, my body high from the most intense orgasm.

God, that tongue and the things it could do to my body.

And then there was his smile and the magical things it was capable of. The way it induced these wavelike shivers that went all the way to my toes and shot back to my chest.

I didn't know how he made it happen.

But it was lethal.

"Take me there, Rowan."

I would eventually purchase the wine and make my way to Sky's apartment, where I'd probably end up crashing for the night because I knew, after this, I'd be too drunk to drive home.

But right this second, I needed this.

His hand was suddenly clasped around mine, and I was walking with him toward the entrance of the liquor store and into the parking lot, where my SUV was in the second row. There weren't any cars around mine—they were mostly in the first row—and the lot was in the back, hidden from the main road. The area wasn't exactly private, but it was as private as we could get in a public space.

I unlocked the doors, and Cooper opened the one to the backseat.

I looked at him as I stood between the seat and door, his expression reinforcing what was about to go down.

Not that I'd questioned it.

Not that I hadn't believed it.

But if there was ever a doubt of how much he was about to devour me, the look in his eyes told me there wasn't a place on my body that was going to go untasted.

"After you," he growled.

I found myself holding my breath as I climbed into the backseat, moving toward the far side, and just as I turned to place my butt down, he was already behind me.

The door was closed.

And his arms were surrounding me. "Get over here."

Cooper was an expert, his mouth seamlessly finding mine as though we weren't in a semi-tight space and there weren't logistics to maneuver, especially given how tall and broad and muscular he was.

But he made it seem like we were on a king-size bed.

And without even realizing it, I was being lifted into his arms and placed onto his lap, like I weighed nothing. From there, my skirt was unzipped so that my legs could spread, my knees pressed into the soft leather on either side of his thighs.

My button-down was no longer tucked in.

My jacket was gone.

And all of this was happening while our lips were locked, his tongue slowly sliding into my mouth, his air heavily scented with his cologne.

"Cooper..." It was a sigh that left me the second our lips parted.

"*Mmm*," he moaned. "I know you want more." He glanced

toward his lap. "Show me."

My arms had been balancing on his shoulders. They left that spot to lower down his chest, my fingers immediately meeting the definition of his pecs. Etched muscle that was harder than steel. My hands continued to drop past the ridges of his abs until I reached his belt, pulling at the leather to unhook it, unclasping his suit pants, and reaching inside.

I fed his cock through the hole of his boxer briefs, releasing every inch of his hardness.

I remembered so clearly the way his dick had made me scream. Moan.

Cry out for more.

How it had given me the most mind-bending, body-shuddering orgasms.

Two miserable nights had passed since it had been in me, yet it felt like so much more.

"Have you missed it?"

I slowly glanced up from his waist. "How are you inside my head?"

He reached up my shirt and flicked my nipple over my bra. "It was an easy guess based on how you're looking at my cock." He rolled the hard peak between his fingers, tugging it through the thin lace. "You don't have to deprive yourself of my dick, Rowan. If you've wanted it, you knew where to find it."

"I—"

"You don't have to explain yourself right now. In fact, you don't have to talk at all. All you have to do is focus on how good I'm about to make you feel." With my skirt high on my waist, his hand went underneath the hem and landed on my panties. "It's too bad these are in the way. I hope they're not your favorites."

His other hand joined, and I gasped as he ripped the lace apart, pulling it from both sides to create the hole he needed.

And when there was nothing separating us, he gave me the softness of his fingers. "Fuck me, you're so wet."

He was using just the pads of those fingers, rubbing from the top of my clit to the bottom, spreading my wetness.

"*Fuuuck*," I hissed.

My head fell back, exposing my whole throat, my body arching from each of his swipes.

It was just a simple touch with hardly any pressure.

But it was enough.

More than enough.

"Cooper..." My nails were somewhere on him—his chest, I thought—and they dug through the fabric, bearing some of this pleasure.

Because I couldn't take it.

Because I wanted more.

"Your pussy likes that, huh?"

I couldn't even fathom that feeling at the moment. This was already so much. And when he began to play with my nipple again, tugging it, pinching, the word, "*Yesss*," echoed through my ears and lips.

"What's it going to do when I fill it with my dick?"

"Oh God." I quivered. "I'm going to come."

It wasn't going to take much more for that to happen.

Just a few more seconds, and I'd lose it.

His hand resumed, and the first stroke came in horizontally across my clit, dragging back and forth, and then his thumb was gone.

I waited for it to return, for a second stroke, for any kind of touch at all, but I got nothing.

My head straightened, and I rose a few inches to circle my arms around his neck, drawing our faces closer. We were breaths away from kissing.

"Are you punishing me?"

"No, Rowan, I'm reminding you. There's a big difference."

"Reminding me of what?"

He slammed our lips together, and while we made out, he replaced his finger with the tip of his dick, rubbing his head over me. His skin, although silky, gave me the friction I needed.

"How much power I have over your cunt," he roared against my mouth.

My hips were moving forward and back, sliding him around me.

"Look at you." His fingers bit into my ass. "Look at how badly you fucking need me."

Air was huffing through my mouth as the tingles started in my clit. They came through hard and fast, swirling toward my stomach. And as they built and peaked, all I could do was hold on.

Take them.

Let them work their way through me.

But while they did, I screamed, "Cooper," and I pulled our bodies together, feeling the heat of his skin through his shirt and mine.

He didn't stay silent while I moaned; he breathed with me.

Held me.

And the second my voice quieted, my body still shaking, even though I was coming down, I heard, "Your pussy is making my cock so fucking wet." He gripped my ass even harder. "You know, there isn't anything more beautiful in this world than watching you come."

Our eyes were suddenly locked.

I was still.

But he wasn't; he was lowering the tip that had just gotten me off and was rubbing it toward my entrance. "Now, I get to watch it again, but this time, you're going to be riding me." He lifted me higher until there was only about an inch between my head and the ceiling, and he positioned me directly over his tip. "Take it when you're ready, Rowan." His mouth was on my neck, kissing around the loose collar. "You're so fucking wet, I'm going to slip right in."

I could tell.

Because it took no more than a slight bounce, and I was opening to fit him in.

I would think that with how much sex we'd had in Canada, my body would remember his size and automatically be ready for him.

That wasn't the case.

So, I took my time—testing his patience, I assumed—while I slowly filled myself with his shaft, eventually sinking all the way to his base. Once I was there, I paused, allowing my body to recall the way he felt.

To really take him in.

To get used to this all over again.

His hands rose to my face; his thumbs pressed against the sides of my lips. "That tightness, fuck, I'll never get used to it."

"I can say the same about the size of your dick."

He let out a small, short chuckle. "I'm in no rush, you can take your time. We can do this all fucking night as far as I'm concerned."

He released my face, and I, almost instantly, felt his thumb on my clit again.

"*Ohhhh*, that."

"Yes, that. I want to feel your pussy squeeze my dick when you come."

I still hadn't moved.

So, I shouldn't be anywhere close to that happening, considering I was still sensitive from my last orgasm.

But as I rose toward his tip, the pressure from the way he was hitting me on the inside and the way his thumb was rubbing me on the outside was a naughty combination.

"What are you doing to me, Cooper?"

There was that sound again. The chuckle. The one that was full of ego and confidence, the tone deep and raspy. "You know exactly what I'm doing to you." He flicked me as I bucked. "And you're giving it to me...right now."

The moment the last word left his mouth, I was shuddering.

The orgasm came out of nowhere. I couldn't control it, even now as the sensations were churning through me, and I realized I couldn't stop it either.

Here I was, on top of this man, barely beginning to ride him, essentially holding all the power when, in actuality, I held no power at all.

He was doing this to me.

He was causing these feelings.

And I loved it.

"Cooper!"

"Let me fucking hear it." With our eyes locked, he exhaled against my mouth. "Yes, that's just what I want."

He watched while I breathed out his name again.

He watched as my lips stayed open and my chest rose.

He watched as I paused mid-climb, unable to move another inch because the pleasure became too much.

And that was when he took over, thrusting his dick upward, sliding into me, circling, and pulling out, and each time he repeated that pattern, I screamed louder.

I sank my fingers into the back of his hair, tugging the strands that were long enough to grip. "Oh God..."

"That was beautiful." His voice was still so masculine, but this time, it came out soft and whispery. "You're giving me everything

I want, Rowan."

The moment my body hushed, I was unable to keep his gaze for even a second longer, and I collapsed around him, feeling like I'd just run several miles.

And while I hugged us together, he left my clit and wrapped an arm across my back, holding me in the most protective way. "Don't get sensitive on me. We're not even close to being done."

I leaned back and cupped his face. "You're"—I searched for the right word—"insatiable."

"I just love making you come."

"Cooper, I don't think I can again—"

The laugh entered my ears at the same time he pumped up, his thumb grazing that spot that he'd just finished playing with. "You're going to say that to me? When I know better? Come on, Rowan. You're forgetting how many times I've done this to you before."

My head shook, but there was a smile on my lips.

"One more time. For me," he demanded.

"For the both of us."

His teeth nipped his bottom lip before he licked across it. "Then, show me what you've got, baby." His gaze traveled down my chest. "Make me come."

I wanted that.

The challenge.

The satisfaction that I could make him feel as good as he was making me feel.

And I wanted to achieve that smile that would happen right after, the one I saw every time we had sex.

So, slowly, I began to give him what he wanted, and within a few dips, the tingles subsided, and a scorching heat started to build between us.

A heat that I didn't just feel in temperature, but I also heard in moans.

In taste, by the flavor of his tongue against mine.

In movement, by the way our bodies joined together, meeting in the middle.

I didn't know how I was getting there again, how my body could return to that place, but I was here.

"You don't have to tell me." His thumb slid over my clit. "I know. I can feel it. You're getting so fucking tight."

"I want you to—"

"I'm already there, Rowan."

It was those words that changed the pace. That had his hips thrusting even harder.

Faster.

Deeper.

That had me screaming, "Cooper!"

"Rowan, *yesss!*" His arm, as it held my back, urged the movements out of me. "That's it. Give it to me."

I didn't have to give it; he already had it.

But I let out more screams.

More moans.

And there was a wetness that even I could feel as my pussy took in his dick, releasing it just enough for him to dive back in.

"Your cunt—it's sucking the cum out of me."

The power that he used, the sharpness of each plunge, that told me just what my body was doing to him.

"*Ahhh*, yes, Rowan."

That was the last thing he said before his lips found mine, and we kissed through the rest of our orgasms.

But even though our voices were quiet, our bodies weren't. The shudders plowed through me so relentlessly, the tingles so fierce, I couldn't stop wriggling.

Cooper used those movements to pull me against him, our

bodies staying in sync, our lips still melded. He held us that way until the last burst began to die down, until there was only stillness left.

Even then, I left my mouth on his. There was just something about his taste that I couldn't get enough of.

That I wanted more of.

Maybe it was the sweetness of his tongue.

Maybe it was the calmness of his breath.

But when I finally separated us, I instantly regretted it, and I pressed my forehead to his.

"I didn't expect this to happen tonight." I didn't know what to say, but what came out of me was total honesty.

"Agreed, but I'm happy as hell that it did." With his hands now on my face, he positioned me a few inches away, where he searched my eyes. "You're something...you know that? You have me thinking about you. Wanting you"—he exhaled loudly—"in ways I didn't know was possible."

Same. So much the same.

Fuck.

I smiled. "We have a lot to talk about."

"When is that going to happen?"

I took a deep breath. "Soon. Very soon."

"Does that mean I get your number?"

I wasn't surprised by his question. I'd expected it. But that didn't make it any easier to hear, and as soon as I did, my heart began to pound.

"Cooper—"

"I just came inside you, Rowan. That isn't the first time I've done that either. So, are you really going to tell me you're not going to give me your number?"

· · ·

Me: *I'm so sorry. I'm on my way.*

Sky: *Good, you're alive. I thought work swallowed you.*

Me: *I did get swallowed…but not by work.*

Sky: *Huh? You lost me.*

Me: *I ran into Cooper at the liquor store when I went there to buy us wine.*

Sky: *WHAT?!*

Me: *I know what you're dying to say, but you can save it. Because I know. I knooow.*

Sky: *Never mind that. What the hell happened when you saw him? And if you got swallowed, does that mean what I think it does???*

Me: *I'll tell you everything when I get there.*

Sky: *You had liquor-store restroom sex, didn't you?*

Me: *LOL. Close…*

Chapter Eleven

COOPER

Me: *I want to taste you again.*

Rowan: *Good morning to you too.*

Me: *It would have been a much better morning had I woken up to you in my bed. There's nothing better than a wet dream that comes true.*

Rowan: *And what was your dream last night?*

Me: *Getting to eat your pussy the second I opened my eyes.*

Rowan: *You get right to the point, don't you?*

Me: *I don't believe in fucking around.*

Rowan: *You don't? ;)*

Me: *I see what you did there.*

Me: *When can I see you? Say tonight. Please.*

Rowan: *Can I get back to you? I'm walking into work right now, and I have a feeling it could be a very long night of meetings.*

Me: *Don't make me wait long.*

• • •

Rowan: *I was right. It's going to be a very long night. Ugh, I'm sorry.*

Me: *Tomorrow?*

Me: *Scratch that. Fuck. I can't do tomorrow night. I'll be tied up.*

Rowan: *The day after tomorrow, I'm traveling for work. I'll be gone for the weekend and the first three days of next week.*

Me: *Thursday then.*

Rowan: *The day after I return home from a weeklong trip? Ick. The chances of me canceling will be high. You know it's hell to return to work after being gone for so long. How about Friday?*

Me: *That's 10 days from now. You're fucking killing me, Rowan.*

Rowan: *Is that a no?*

Me: *It's a yes. But I'm not happy about it.*

Me: *And for the record, 10 days is a goddamn eternity. Expect to be punished for that.*

Rowan: *Isn't the 10 days already a big enough punishment for the both of us?*

Me: *You haven't experienced what I can do…*

Rowan: *Now, you're the one killing me.*

· · ·

Me: *I just parked at the liquor store, and I've got to say, the last time I was here, this parking lot was much more entertaining than it is now.*

Rowan: *Sounds like you're missing me.*

Me: *It does sound that way, doesn't it?*

Rowan: *If it makes you feel any better, I'm sitting in a hotel room, bored out of my mind.*

Me: *Sounds like you're missing me too.*

Rowan: *It does sound that way, doesn't it? LOL.*

Me: *If I wasn't heading out, I'd FaceTime you, and I'd take that boredom away.*

Rowan: *Ohhh. Does that mean…SexTime? You've done that?*

Me: *You haven't?*

Rowan: *No.*

Me: *I'd be your first. I like the thought of that.*

Me: *You're going to be in that hotel for several more nights. We have plenty of time to pop that cherry.*

Rowan: *You're one relentless man, Cooper Spade.*

Me: *When it comes to you, fuck yes.*

• • •

Me: *Will you be at your hotel in about an hour?*

Rowan: *Yes. Why?*

Me: *I'm going to FaceTime you. Make sure to answer.*

Rowan: *And if I don't?*

Me: *You're going to miss out on SexTime, where I plan to make you come so fucking hard.*

Rowan: *You mean, I'm going to make myself come.*

Me: *But I'm going to tell you everything I want you to do, and I'm going to watch while you do it. When I want you to go faster, I'll command it. Slower, that'll be my call. So, yes, it'll be your fingers and my orders.*

Rowan: *What about you?*

Me: *What about me?*

Rowan: *Will I get to watch you touch yourself?*

Me: *Is that what you want, Rowan? You want to see me stroke my dick…*

Rowan: *Yes.*

Me: *Then, I'll make that happen too.*

Me: *One hour—have your phone nearby. I won't call back and track you down.*

• • •

Rowan: *I…still can't breathe.*

Me: *And when you picked up, you weren't sure if you were going to like SexTime and if we should do it. I don't know why you doubt me, Rowan.*

Rowan: *I doubt you because I'm afraid.*

Me: *Of what?*

Rowan: *You.*

Me: *In what way?*

Rowan: *In the way where I can't get you out of my mind.*

Rowan: *And remember when I said I shouldn't want you? That hasn't changed.*

Rowan: *I shouldn't. Yet I still do.*

• • •

Me: *Another day of waking up, wishing I were eating you for fucking breakfast.*

Rowan: *I wish you were too.*

Me: *One night until you're home.*

Rowan: *And only a few until I see you…*

Me: *I know you said we need to talk, but I'd much rather move straight to the screaming. My mind is filled with all the things I want to do to you.*

Me: *There will be plenty of time to talk after. I promise.*

Rowan: *Cooper…*

Me: *My place or yours?*

Rowan: *Yours.*

Me: *I'll text you my address.*

• • •

Me: *Did you make it back to LA safely?*

• • •

I picked up my office line that was ringing on top of my desk and held the receiver to my ear. "This is Cooper."

"Walter would like to see you," our assistant, Kathleen, said.

My hand moved to the mouse, clicking on the calendar to see if I'd missed something when I checked my schedule earlier this morning. There were zero executive-level meetings for today, just like I'd thought.

"He wants to see me now?" I asked.

"Jo was first on my list to call. Then Macon, you, and Brady will be next. I know it's last minute, but all your schedules are clear, and somehow, luckily, everyone is in the office today."

But my schedule wasn't clear. I was in the middle of a report that I'd been working on since I'd arrived at the office two hours ago. One that needed to be submitted by this afternoon, and it was going to take me all goddamn day to finish.

Meeting with Walter wasn't part of my plan.

"I'll be right there," I told her and hung up.

I quickly checked my phone to see if Rowan had replied to my last message. She didn't have Read receipts on for her texts. That was something I didn't have either, but, man, I would love it if she did.

Because, right now, I was curious as fuck if she'd read the one I'd sent an hour ago and was ignoring me or if she was really busy since it was her first full day back.

Since I didn't have that answer, I tucked my phone into my suit pocket and got up from my desk. As I approached Macon's office, on my way to the conference room, he was just walking through his doorway.

I put my arm around his shoulders. "What the fuck is this about? Do you know?"

"I don't know anything. But I wish like hell Walter had waited until the end of the day to get us all together. I have to prep for this trip to Hawaii, and I don't have time for this."

"It's a good thing Walter isn't long-winded."

He looked at me and chuckled. "But he's demanding as hell, and I can only imagine that whatever he's about to tell us is going to turn into more work for us."

"Let's fucking hope that's not the case."

We walked into the conference room, where Jo was already sitting along one of the sides of the table. I took the spot next to her while Macon sat across from us.

"You have to know what this is about," I said to my cousin.

She took a deep breath and slowly turned toward me.

And as she continued to stare at me, she stayed completely silent.

There were very few women I knew well, who I could peek into their eyes and know just what they were thinking.

Jo was one.

And as I stared into hers, my damn hands began to sweat.

"Shit," I groaned. "I don't like that look at all."

She smiled, but it wasn't out of happiness. "You're not going to like hearing what's about to come out of my father's mouth either."

I glanced from her to Macon—who I knew was listening to us—to the door that Brady was just coming through and back to Jo. "What do you mean?"

"My husband's here this morning," she said softly.

Jenner was here all the time.

That told me nothing.

Besides, he should be here. We were in the thick of the Lake Louise deal, as far as I knew, and Jenner was the only one who could make that shit happen.

"Jo, what the hell are you saying?" I growled.

"I'm saying—"

But her voice cut off as Walter and Jenner came in.

I scanned their faces, trying to piece this mystery together, and when I couldn't, I locked eyes with Brady. I knew by my older brother's expression that he was as clueless and annoyed as Macon and me.

Walter took a seat at the head, and Jenner took the foot, a pile of folders in both of their hands that they placed in front of them.

"Tell me we're in escrow," Brady declared. "That within thirty days, Lake Louise will be ours."

Walter gradually looked around the table, connecting eyes with each of us before he focused solely on Jenner. "We're in escrow, yes."

I released a mouthful of air I hadn't realized I'd been holding. "Finally."

"Don't get excited," Walter said. "It's not exactly the deal you had in mind, Cooper."

"What are you talking about?" I said.

Walter's pose was relaxed, especially as he leaned back in his chair and crossed his hands. "Let's get right to it." He cleared his throat. "You know that I've been waiting for the right time to retire. For as long as I can remember, I thought that would be at a certain age. That I'd reach a milestone and be ready to hand over the throne."

As he looked at Jenner, my heart began to pound. He'd teased us with the word *retirement* before, but we'd never been given a date. A time frame. Or even a hint that he was moving forward with it.

"But as that age came and went, the urge wasn't there. I'd then set another deadline, and I'd blow right through it. It took me some time to realize it wasn't about an age, it was about leaving a legacy to my heirs."

"And it's quite a legacy," Macon said. "Now that we have Hawaii and it sounds like Lake Louise is in the bag, we have some of the most exclusive resorts in North America and Europe. We've changed the landscape of what luxurious hotels look like, and that's all because of your vision, Walter."

"But it's not enough." Walter's voice was sharp. "I've wanted more—you all know that. We've fought for more. We've gotten tips and pocket listings. We've been alerted when other hotels are selling, giving us the option to buy them and turn them into our own." He shook his head. "And still, more times than not, we end up with nothing."

"That's the nature of the market," I offered. "Just like residential real estate. You win some, you lose some."

Walter's gaze intensified on mine. "We both know that's not the case here. There's a clear reason why those properties didn't become ours."

I nodded.

Because he was right.

And everyone at this table knew what that reason was.

"I've been thinking long and hard about the future of Spade Hotels," Walter continued. "How I can grow this company and hand you a fleet that's far larger than what exists now."

I didn't know why, but there was an ache that followed every pound in my chest.

Something was off about this conversation, and I couldn't put my fucking finger on it.

"I've come to a conclusion." Walter's voice echoed throughout the entire room. "I've slept on it. I've discussed the ramifications with Jenner and our in-house accounting team. I've weighed the pros and cons. For the last week, I've done nothing but think about that conclusion, and I'm happy to tell you all, it's settled." He paused. "I have no doubt that it's the right decision." He gazed around the table. "For all of us." He set his hands on top of the folders. "This will be my final legacy, and once it's complete"—

he tapped the folders—"this is the paperwork that will make the four of you equal partners, solidifying my retirement and handing Spade Hotels over to you."

My mind was exploding with questions.

But more importantly, with plans.

Spade Hotels was officially going to become ours. The four of us would be partners with equal shares—something we'd talked about for as long as I could remember.

We'd finally get to do everything we'd always dreamed of.

Except there was a *but*.

"What's your final legacy?" Brady asked.

The room turned silent, and I stole a quick glance at Jo.

She'd been quiet since her father had walked into the room. She'd made no comments and asked no questions.

Which told me that whatever news he was about to drop on us, she already knew.

Her arms were crossed over her chest, a chest that was rising and falling much faster than normal.

Fuck me.

"Jenner," Walter said, "would you like to do the honors? Since you're the man who made this all possible, who negotiated a deal that's more than fair for everyone."

A deal?

That's fair?

For everyone?

"I think it's only right if the news comes from you," Jenner said.

And when that news hit my ears less than ten seconds later, my fucking stomach dropped, and my entire world...came crashing down.

Chapter Twelve

Rowan

I gripped both sides of the sink, staring at myself in the reflection of the mirror above it, positive that I was going to be sick. The little I'd put in my stomach this morning, which was just a small cup of black coffee, was threatening to rise at any second, the acid burning the back of my throat.

I couldn't stand this feeling.

I'd rather have the flu than be nauseous.

And the most recent bout had lasted much longer than it ever had before, starting yesterday afternoon, when I'd gotten back to LA, the driver taking me straight to the office instead of my house, where I immediately stepped into a meeting that lasted far into the night.

A meeting that triggered a level of anxiety I hadn't anticipated.

When I finally got home, I didn't touch any wine.

I didn't order the Thai food, like I'd planned to while I was on the plane, prior to knowing about the meeting.

I drew myself a bath instead and tried to find some Zen, unsuccessfully, followed by a night of tossing and turning until I gave up on sleep altogether and returned to the office.

It was there, a few hours ago, that I received Cooper's text.

Cooper: *Did you make it back to LA safely?*

I had known he was going to reach out at some point. After all, we'd made plans to see each other tomorrow. Given the way he'd been communicating since I'd given him my number, I wasn't surprised that I'd heard from him first thing.

But I just didn't have it in me to respond.

Even though, periodically, I stared at his words a few times an hour. Each time, my heart rate increased, my throat tightened, and the nausea kicked up a gear.

What have I done?

I'd played with fire.

That was what I'd done.

I had known that from the moment I'd met him in the bar, his name instantly resonating the first time he'd said it. His face identical to the pictures I'd seen of him online at Spade Hotel openings and movie premieres, interacting with celebrities at galas and tournaments, always looking every bit the hotel royal that he was. But if I was being honest with myself, he was even handsomer in person, something that felt nearly impossible because he was sexy as hell on social media.

Cooper Spade.

What was I even thinking?

I released the sink and reached into my purse, digging around until my phone was in my hand, and after I unlocked the screen, I read his words again.

This wasn't right.

None of it was.

What the hell am I going to do?

Another wave of sickness hurled through me as I dropped the phone back in my bag. My mouth watered and my inhales were short and far too breathy.

I needed this anxiety to leave my body, so I could survive the rest of the day.

A day that wasn't going to be easy on me.

And I knew I certainly couldn't run back into this restroom and hug the porcelain bowl.

I needed to be present. I needed to keep everything inside my body until I left this building.

I needed to keep these feelings masked.

Because there was absolutely no way that I could let on to Ridge, Rhett, or my father that I was a mess inside this designer suit. That my muscles were shaking. That my skin was hot and clammy.

The only thing I wanted them to see when they looked at me was that I was a fucking rock star.

I repeated that in my head while I took in my reflection again.

While I released the sides of the sink.

While I forced the bile back down to my stomach, where it was going to stay.

My family was outside the restroom door, waiting for me. I'd told them I was only going to be a minute, and I was sure I'd taken at least a few.

I couldn't hold things up any longer.

So, I finger-curled the pieces of hair that framed my face, and I swiped the skin around my lips, making sure my lip gloss stayed within the liner that I'd drawn on before we drove over here, and I walked out of the restroom.

Rhett must have heard the door because he looked up from his phone. "You good?" he asked me.

I nodded, wishing my mouth would stop watering.

"Then, let's go," my father announced.

I moved in next to Ridge while my father and Rhett took the

lead, and we entered the narrow hallway, the sound of my heels filling the silence until I heard Rhett say, "This is the longest walk of my fucking life."

"Agreed," Ridge replied.

I thirded that.

But I was afraid to speak, not quite trusting my stomach yet.

To keep my brain busy and my mind off the obvious, I focused on the name plaques outside each door we passed. Some were familiar since we were here so often. People who had helped us with our normal business dealings.

But people who wouldn't be participating in today's ordeal.

Because today was hardly normal.

And the sirens going off in my body only emphasized that.

We rounded the corner of the hallway where the conference room was at the end.

We knew the location well.

Each time we came, we sat at that table.

But none of those occasions felt anything like this.

This was…too much.

Oh shit.

Now, I really couldn't breathe.

I left Ridge's side and moved into fourth position, doing everything I could to fill my lungs, to calm the storm exploding within me, to ignore the churning that had amplified during this walk.

But nothing helped.

Nothing soothed these sensations.

If anything, they increased.

The jitters. The nausea. The discomfort.

Once we reached the door, my father turned and faced us. "Remember, I've made my decision. There's nothing any of you can do to change what's about to happen." The pause that followed reinforced his statement. "So, what I need is for each of you to go in there and act like a Cole. I need you to represent our brand and family name and not do anything to embarrass me or yourselves." His stare moved to Rhett. "I mean it, Rhett. We will not have the police called on us. You will not raise your fists. This is a business meeting. I expect you to treat it like one."

"*Fuuuck*," Rhett growled quietly.

"I'm doing this for the three of you," my father continued. "I know you don't see that now, but you will."

The talk.

We'd gotten the same one yesterday.

This morning.

And now, here—again.

But it was needed because my father's assessment was right; the three of us didn't believe this meeting was for us.

It was for him.

And the reason behind that was something we couldn't understand.

As his words sank in, I could feel my brothers' emotions bubbling through their suits.

"Nod your head and tell me you're going to comply," my father hissed to my oldest brother.

Rhett reluctantly gave my father the gesture he'd demanded from him.

Ridge did as well.

Dad's eyes eventually landed on me.

"Of course," I whispered, the movement in my throat reminding me that my stomach was far from settled.

My father's stare circled our small group. "Then, let's go show them the power of the Coles."

Before any of us could respond, he opened the door, and my anxiety lifted to a peak I hadn't anticipated. While I watched my father step inside the conference room, my knees weakened. My heart clutched as Rhett moved in directly behind him, my stomach clenching into a ball as Ridge proceeded.

I gazed at their profiles.

Their reactions.

Their breathing.

And with fisted hands, palms that were filling with sweat, knowing I couldn't stay in this hallway despite how much I wanted to, I took two paces inside.

Even with my eyes on the oval table, I could feel all the stares hit my face.

I could sense the combination of personalities overflowing in this large room.

I could smell the mixture of perfume and cologne.

They could identify this room with whatever title they wanted, but it was a battleground.

And within these walls, a war was brewing.

Still not looking up, I balanced on my four-inch heels, straightened my shoulders, held in the bile threatening to make an entrance, and moved past the threshold. I quickly scanned the empty chairs on the near side of the table, and I sat in the one that Ridge had pulled out for me.

Seated wasn't any better than standing. This position only made my stomach pains more prominent.

And it deepened the realization that I was here—and couldn't escape.

That I would have to endure every moment of this meeting.

I'd never felt silence as thick as it was in here, like a dense fog that clouded the air, making it even harder to inhale.

That lasted for several more seconds before our attorney, who sat two seats away from me, finished shaking our hands and said, "Ray," as he addressed my father, "and Ridge, Rhett, and Rowan,

I suspect you already know everyone in here?"

"Sure do," my father replied.

"And do you know Jenner Dalton, one of the partners of The Dalton Group?" our attorney then asked.

My father reached his hand toward Jenner. "I've heard all about you. It's nice to meet you."

"And you, Mr. Cole," Jenner said.

Jenner shook my hand as well as my brothers and said, "We're here for one reason. To get everyone in this room on the same page. We realize there are decades of history between—"

"Three decades, to be exact," my father clarified.

"Yes, three," Jenner said. "That's certainly a long time and a time frame that's allowed opinions and assumptions to form. We're not going to address any of that today. That's not what this meeting is about. The past is in the past, and as competitors within an extremely lucrative market, tension is bound to form. But it's tension that no longer needs to exist." He folded his hands on top of the wooden table.

Except my brothers didn't agree with him.

Because that tension was an extremely sore subject in our family.

For as long as I could remember, this wasn't a competition.

This was a match that the Coles intended to win.

"Our purpose for today," Jenner went on, "is to finally bring the two families together. To start things with a completely clean and fresh slate. Because as of next week, when Walter and Ray sign the paperwork, Spade Hotels and Cole International, the two largest hotel brands in the world, are going to become one."

"The merger of the century," our attorney added.

A merger that my brothers and I had never expected.

Until my father had dropped the news on us yesterday when I returned to LA.

And now, as we sat in this battlefield, on the executive floor of The Dalton Group, I could feel a set of eyes boring through my body.

I could smell the sage and burnt orange as though my nose were pressed against his neck.

I could practically feel his hands on my skin.

A blend that was so powerful, so overwhelming, so consuming that it forced me to look up.

To gaze across the table.

And lock eyes with the man whose stare I'd been avoiding since I'd walked into this room.

Cooper's expression was easily readable.

It was the same look Rhett had worn when my father dropped the merger on us.

But Cooper's face took things one level deeper.

Because he wasn't just looking at the woman who hadn't been honest about her identity.

Or a woman who bore the last name of his family's biggest enemy.

Or a woman who was employed by his largest competitor.

He was looking at a woman who, as of next week, would be his business partner.

Chapter Thirteen

COOPER

You have to be fucking kidding me.

From the moment Rowan had walked into The Dalton Group's conference room, that was the thought that continued to repeat in my head.

But it wasn't the only thought.

I had plenty of others.

Like, *Why the hell didn't she tell me she was a Cole? Why did she continue to string me along, goad me, fucking work me, if she knew I was a Spade?*

I was assuming she had known who I was based on some of the things she'd said that I was now piecing together, which meant the three nights we'd spent in her suite, the run-in at the liquor store, the text conversations, the SexTime—it was all lies.

Lies that had been calculated.

Lies that made not a single second of what had gone down between us real.

But why?

Was it to get information out of me?

An attempt to bury Spade Hotels?

Because I couldn't think of any other reasons, not when she had known that the two of us could never be more than a one-night stand.

Not when the Coles were our biggest competitors.

But they weren't just opponents.

When it came to business, they were our archnemeses, a name that had been spoken with disdain for as long as I could remember.

Because Ray had been my father and Walter's rival since day one.

The Coles were the reason we had lost so many properties, the reason deals slipped through our hands, the reason opportunities dissolved into thin air.

It wasn't that they fought harder; it was that they played dirtier.

We weren't innocent. We got tips; we made unethical offers. We did what we needed to do to secure what we had.

But they went after land, knowing we wanted it.

That was why Rowan had been in Lake Louise—I was sure of it. Somehow, they'd been alerted that we wanted that property, and they attempted to lock it down.

The seller wasn't on holiday. He had been contemplating both offers or waiting for theirs to come in before he made a decision.

From the start, it was a piece of land that should have been ours.

And now, it was...all of ours.

This was fucked.

And what made it even worse was that I'd spent the entire holiday with our enemy.

I knew all about her brothers, the day Rhett had joined the business, along with Ridge. But Rowan was a name I hadn't heard before. Of course, I had known Ray had a daughter, but my family had always been under the impression that she had nothing to do with their company. I remembered her telling me that she was recently employed by her family business, which explained why hearing her name in Canada hadn't raised any red flags.

Now, she sat on the other side of the table. Her expression aloof. Her posture stiff. With an entirely different look in her eyes than she'd had in Lake Louise.

A look that told me one thing.

She had zero regrets.

Fuck that.

And fuck her.

"In regard to this merger," Jenner said, his voice breaking my concentration and capturing my attention for the first time since Rowan had walked in, "I'd like to reiterate that once the papers are signed, Walter and Ray are going to relinquish their CEO roles, and the seven of you are going to become equal partners. Spade Hotels and Cole International will now be Cole and Spade Hotels. As for your corporate offices, Walter and Ray have decided that it's only fair to purchase a new space and sell your existing buildings." Jenner mashed his lips together, knowing that extra bit of information was going to send all of us over the edge. "There are many, many logistics to work out, but I want to address your immediate questions if you have any."

Silence spread throughout the room.

There weren't immediate questions, just a lot of fucking opinions and I could see them on everyone's face.

And none, on either side, were positive.

"We understand there are some strong feelings between both parties," the Coles' attorney said, "but we're determined to find a way for everyone to work together."

This wasn't kindergarten. We weren't in the sandbox, taking turns with the shovel.

We were grown-ass men and women.

Who fucking hated each other.

And Brady, who I knew agreed, couldn't contain his sarcasm, chuckling loud enough for all to hear. "That's a big ask."

"But a necessary one if this merger is going to be successful," Jenner countered, adjusting his navy tie. "And success is what we're all after. The last thing anyone wants is an in-house implosion that'll take down a company the size that Cole and Spade Hotels is about to be."

"A merger that still doesn't make any sense to me," Rhett said. He crossed his arms, stretching the top of his suit jacket, like he was flexing. "The two of us becoming one? I think it's bullshit. What's the point?"

His muscles, his opinion, meant nothing to me.

But I had to agree with him, so I said, "I second that."

"The point," Ray started, "is that Walter and I are tired of fighting for the same thing. Growth, profitability, stability in a market that's constantly changing and, more often than not, volatile—that's what we should be focused on. And in the recent years, those sights have been lost in a sea of competition that's unneeded and unnecessary. There's strength in numbers, and when you combine our strategies, we're a force to be reckoned with."

"In addition, if we keep up the current trend," Walter voiced, swinging his chair toward Ray to look at him while he spoke, "the competition between our families will only worsen. We don't need to spend another day in a war that doesn't need to be fought. Not when we all want the same thing. So, we come together, and we own the hospitality industry."

I didn't know what the fuck Ray and Walter were smoking.

Where this sudden camaraderie had come from.

Why, out of nowhere, they were both singing the same tune.

But I'd had enough.

"We're just supposed to forget everything that's happened?" I asked. A fire was burning through me, and it wasn't just from having to compromise on Lake Louise. It was the gorgeous face staring back at me that had manipulated me. It was the two motherfuckers next to her that I couldn't fathom working with. "We're supposed to shake hands with men and"—I looked at Rowan, and my chest pounded—"women who have trashed our business, our name, who have stolen our properties, who have done everything in their power to make our practices and deals a living hell." I tore my eyes away from her and glared at my uncle. "Because I don't see how that's possible."

"You will in time," Walter replied.

Ray then voiced, "I don't need to tell you what my feelings were for Walter. I think it's clear how we felt about each other." He ran his hand over his salt-and-pepper hair. "But when I reached out to Walter and we met, we discussed the options and came up with this conclusion, and I found it in myself to move on." He paused. "We both did."

Rhett's hand landed on the table, the sound a full-on smack. "That's easy for you to say, you won't have to work with Walter after the transition. You get to watch the merger and wipe your hands of the whole fucking mess."

"I wouldn't call it a mess," Ray said to his son.

"No?" Macon hissed. "Then, what would you call two different groups of people who have been bred to hate each other now forced to own a company together?"

"Listen," Walter demanded, his voice the sharpest it had been all day. "Ray and I aren't looking to hash this out right now. We're—"

"What are you looking for, then?" Rhett asked, cutting Walter off. "To coach us into a giant group hug? For the seven of us to become fucking besties or whatever that shit is called?" His fingers that were spread wide on the wood tightened into a fist. "You've given us no choice. You've forced something on us when this isn't what any of us wants." He glanced around the table. "I can tell you with certainty there isn't a goddamn person in here who disagrees with me, except the two of you"—he pointed at his father and Walter—"and the two lawyers who are paid to be attached to your nipples."

Walter looked at Ray.

What the fuck had they expected?

A quiet, peaceful treaty?

If that was the case, they didn't know us at all.

"We didn't think you'd all come here today and immediately form a bond," Ray said. "But we expect that, over time, the seven of you will find a way to resolve the animosity and work together respectfully."

Walter put his hand on Ray's shoulder. "I don't know the Cole family as well as my own, but what I do know is that everyone in this room is exceptional at their job." He took his time gazing around the table, making eye contact with each of us. "Every one of you brings a strong, individual talent that when combined will be a collaboration neither company has ever seen or experienced. I'm excited to see what the seven of you can do. The way you can build the brand and grow it in ways that Ray and I weren't able to achieve."

I hissed out the air I'd been holding in, reaching my quota of bullshit for the day.

And just as I was about to express that, Brady beat me to it and said, "What you've done is create a giant shitstorm." He gripped the edge of the table. "You should have had a discussion with us. We should have been able to voice our concerns. But instead, we were told this was happening. That doesn't sit right with me. I've given ten years to this company, Walter. I even spent my summers in college working for you. I've poured my life into Spade Hotels—all of us have." His hand traced the air where Jo, Macon, and I were sitting. "And for what? To be told that the empire we were growing isn't even going to have the same name anymore. That we're going to have to compromise on our beliefs and values. No. Fuck no."

"I promise, in time, this is something you'll accept and even grow to appreciate."

Walter's standard answer.

I was fucking tired of hearing it.

He didn't know shit.

And he especially didn't know what the outcome of this was going to look like when it involved a family like the Coles.

"I want you all to remember that this is just an introduction," Jenner's voice boomed across the room. "The first of many meetings, where you'll get a chance to come together to discuss the business and how the seven of you intend on running it." He lifted the folder resting in front of him and banged the bottom of it on the table as though he were aligning the papers inside. "In the next few days, your assistants are going to schedule a time for you all to meet with a realtor who will begin showing you properties. Once you've agreed on one, both of your buildings will hit the MLS immediately. That'll be the first step of the merger."

"Just like that?" Jo said softly. Her chest rose the same way it had when I sat next to her in our conference room minutes before the bomb was dropped. "This is…a lot."

Jo wasn't one to normally hold in her feelings, but I could tell by what little she'd said that she was in the thick of processing all of this and what it meant.

"I agree with you," Rowan replied. She tucked a chunk of her long, dark locks behind her ear. "I'm not even going to attempt to play peacemaker even though that's a role I normally take on with my family." She completely avoided my eyes as she spoke.

"But I want you to know that since I found out the news from my father, I've spent some time researching all of you." She shifted her gaze between my brothers and Jo, but still didn't look my way. "Your achievements individually are extremely impressive. Your list of accolades, the standards you've set, and how, in some ways, you've changed the hospitality industry with a level of excellence that didn't exist before you." She stalled for a moment.

"I'm looking forward to learning from each of you. And I hope that, in time, you'll be able to see the value our side will bring to this merger." She shifted in her seat, a movement that was slow and almost looked like it pained her.

"I believe in our brand. That's why I sold my business and joined the family company. I believe in the talent of my brothers. I get the impression our similarities are far greater than you think— our drive, our work ethic, our dedication. I see no reason why we can't all find a common ground." She offered the smallest hint of a smile. "That's what I want anyway."

"Thank you," Ray said to his daughter.

You have to be fucking kidding me.

There were those words again, repeating non-fucking-stop in my head.

Sure, it was easy for Rowan to believe this—she was new to this world. She hadn't spent her entire career hating our side, losing deals because of our practices, constantly battling my family.

Peacemaker?

How about fucking liar and manipulator? That was what she was.

"I've heard enough for one day," Brady said when the room had been silent for at least a minute. "Are we done here?"

Jenner and the Coles' attorney exchanged a look, and then both men glanced toward Ray and Walter.

When they received a nod, Jenner said, "Yes. We're done."

The silence was instantly replaced with the sound of chairs moving back and the swishing of suits. There was even a dull chatter as we shuffled into the hallway.

But I didn't say a goddamn word.

Because anything that came out of my mouth was going to be nothing but hate.

My hands clenched as I walked, my fingers tight in a fist. My weight heavy in my feet every time I stepped.

I needed to get the hell out of this building before I exploded.

It looked like I wasn't alone in thinking that; the pace while we headed toward the elevator was much faster than when we'd entered. And because the Coles had been the closest to the door, they had fled the conference room first and reached the bank of elevators before us.

Fortunately, there were several, so the Coles and the Spades didn't have to enter together.

And we didn't.

My family waited for the one on the right; the Coles stayed to the left.

While we waited, I noticed Rowan from the corner of my eye, briefly saying something to Ridge and then leaving his side to head down a different hallway.

A hallway that would bring her to the restroom, assuming that was where she was going.

I forced myself to look at the doors as they slid open, the left side doing the same, both families beginning to fill the elevators.

I should have been following suit.

I should have moved in right behind Brady, leaning against the back wall, fuming my opinion to my brothers and cousin, ignoring the presence of my uncle, who was endlessly pissing me off.

But I wasn't.

I was standing feet away, reaching into my pocket to pull out my phone, checking the dark, non-ringing screen prior to holding it to my ear.

I have to take this call, I mouthed to Macon, the only one looking at me. "I'll meet you downstairs in a second," I added.

Macon nodded, and the elevator shut.

You have to be fucking kidding me, I thought, except this time it was about myself.

About what I wanted to do.

Something I shouldn't even care enough to do.

But I wanted answers.

No, I needed answers.

Damn it.

I rushed down the hallway, dropping my phone into my pocket. As I approached the ladies' restroom, I didn't stop to knock, nor did I give a shit if anyone aside from Rowan was inside. I just opened the door and walked in.

"Cooper..." Rowan whispered, looking at me through the mirror above the sink, holding the porcelain like it was a toilet bowl and she was about to be sick. When I didn't immediately answer, her hands dropped to her sides, and she turned to face me. "You shouldn't be in here."

I practically laughed. "How can you even say that to me after what you did?"

Her arms went around her stomach. "I told you I needed to talk to you." Her throat moved as she swallowed. "This was why."

"You also told me you shouldn't want me. Because you knew the whole fucking time who I was, who my family was...didn't you?"

She nodded. "If I'd told you the truth, I don't know what would have happened at the bar."

"I do." I glared down her body, wishing the situation were

different. That I could have just one more taste. But, goddamn it, everything was different now. "I would have walked the fuck away and stopped talking to you."

She shook her head. "I didn't want that to happen."

"That wasn't your choice to make!" My voice was full of rage. I forced myself to calm down and ran my hand over my scruff, whiskers I hadn't bothered to shave off even though I'd been up all night, unable to sleep, and I had plenty of time to. "But instead, you manipulated me. Lied to me. You spent the entire fucking holiday in my arms, goading me into—"

"Let's not be ridiculous, Cooper." She mashed her lips together. "In that bar, it wouldn't have mattered if I were a Cole or an electrical outlet, you were cranked up and ready to fuck."

When my mouth opened, only air came out.

"Did I omit my last name? Yes," she continued. "I'm sorry for that. Because of it, I've been sick to my stomach since I left Canada. I wanted to tell you tomorrow night during our date, and that had been my plan all along. But then I returned from my work trip, and my father threw the merger on us, and there was no way I could tell you in time."

"That doesn't make the situation any better."

"I know. I just want you to know that I had good intentions about tomorrow." Her voice turned soft. "And I just want to be honest with you."

This time, I did chuckle. "Now, you feel like being honest. Isn't that ironic?"

Her arm left her stomach, like she wanted to reach toward me, but she let it drop to her side. "I want to talk about this. I want to break it all down, and I want you to give me a chance to explain myself, but I don't want to do that here, in the restroom, at the Daltons' law firm."

Was that what I wanted?

Did I even care enough to hear her side?

She was a fucking Cole, a soon-to-be partner. Why did what happened between us even matter when it could never happen again?

I gave her body one final visual swoop, remembering the tightness, the wetness, as though I wanted to torture myself again. Fuck me, she was a good one. "Nah, there's nothing to talk about. I'll see you around, Rowan—"

"Don't do this." She grabbed my arm just as I began to turn, and she took a few steps around my side until she was facing me. "Hear me out, Cooper. Give me that opportunity." She shook my arm. "Please."

"Why?" I paused. "And for what?"

"Because I care." Her other hand touched my abs. "Because I know you care." Her fingers pressed down harder. "Because I felt it in your touch every time we were together and I heard it in your voice each time you spoke. And that alone is a reason to discuss this."

It didn't matter if she was right.

It didn't matter how good her hand felt.

It didn't matter if I wanted that hand to lower until she was cupping my dick.

The truth was that what I wanted, what I hoped for, couldn't happen.

My teeth bared as I growled, "*This* doesn't exist, Rowan."

"Maybe." She held me tighter. "But let's talk about what happened and why it happened."

I said nothing.

I just stared into her emerald eyes and remembered those nights we had spent in Lake Louise.

And while I did that, I felt the anger bubble inside me as her last name echoed in my ears.

Out of all the fucking names, why did hers have to be Cole?

"I'm going to text you my address," she said. "I'd like you to come over tomorrow night. Seven o'clock. Even if you only stay for a couple of minutes, I just want you to give me a chance to explain myself."

I sucked my bottom lip into my mouth, biting the inside with my teeth.

Why was it so hard to keep my hands off her?

To not walk her into one of the stalls and lift her into my arms and fuck her against the side wall?

Why was there an ache inside me that went beyond a physical sensation?

You have to be fucking kidding me.

"What do you say?" she whispered. "Can I expect to see you tomorrow night?"

I pulled my arm from her grip and kicked open the restroom door, and I walked my ass out.

Chapter Fourteen

Rowan

One glass of wine. That was all I was allowing myself while I waited for Cooper to arrive at my house. Just enough sauvignon blanc to melt away the edge I was feeling and hopefully calm the nerves in my chest.

Of course, I had no idea if he was actually going to show. When I'd invited him, he'd stormed out of the restroom without confirming, and hadn't replied to my text when I sent him my address.

Maybe, during the short amount of time we'd spoken in the restroom, I'd handled things all wrong.

Maybe he'd wanted me to grovel a bit more.

Maybe he truly wanted nothing to do with me.

I wasn't sure what the case was.

But what I was sure about was the competition between the Spades and the Coles. I'd always heard my father and brothers groaning about them. And since I'd joined the family business, it had only gotten worse.

The thing was, as someone who had owned four boutiques in

an extremely competitive industry, where there were stores just like mine on the same block, I couldn't understand why there was so much hate between the families.

Was that what happened when a group of confident, cocky, ego-fueled alphas all wanted to be the best and most profitable in the business?

Because, on paper, according to my father's attorney, the two companies were about equal when it came to the number of hotels they owned and yearly revenue. And for the most part, there wasn't an overlap in locations, aside from a few large markets, so it wasn't that we were fighting for their guests and they were after ours.

Something must have happened between my father and Walter years ago that had caused this much hate.

I had no idea what it was.

All I knew was that the second I'd walked into that conference room and Cooper realized I was a Cole, a look came over his face that was unlike anything I'd seen from him before.

He wasn't gazing at me like I was the woman he wanted, the way he had while we were in Canada and again when we ran into each other at the liquor store.

He had glared at me like I was his enemy.

I couldn't handle it.

Not when we'd be working so closely together.

Not when I'd probably see him every day.

And especially not because Cooper Spade was all I thought about.

A man I tried to push out of my thoughts, and every time I attempted, he somehow slid right back in. I couldn't express my feelings to him while he didn't know about my identity. It hadn't felt right. Not when I was withholding something so vital. But things felt entirely different now that my name was out in the open.

In every way.

The biggest difference was that I hadn't expected my feelings to grow.

And they had.

They had burrowed in my chest and refused to go anywhere.

I knew what it was like to care about someone. I'd cared for the men I'd dated in the past.

But this already felt unlike those other times.

This was heavy.

Consuming.

Just thinking about Cooper had the power to completely change my mood. The expression on my face. My desire for the future.

He wasn't someone I had been looking for.

I hadn't been looking for anyone.

But he was something I wanted.

And I hoped, more than anything, that tonight he would give me the chance—

My thoughts came to a halt when I heard a beep, the tablet on the coffee table letting me know that someone was at my gate.

I quickly lifted it off the glass and pulled up the camera system, where the live feed showed footage of his car, the driver's-side window rolled down and his handsome face looking directly at me.

With eyes that were so aloof that I had no idea what he was thinking.

But he had come.

I pressed the button that would open the gate, and I returned the tablet to the table, the weighted glass in my hand reminding me that I'd barely even taken a sip.

I'd been far too lost in my thoughts.

Thoughts that had consumed me to the point where I didn't even realize it was nearing seven thirty. Almost thirty minutes past the time I'd told him to come over.

At least he'd shown.

I carried the glass to the front door, sipping it with each step. I still felt the edge that I had hoped to alleviate by drinking this— failing on both accounts—and now, the sensation was peaking as I opened the door, watching him walk up to the front of my house and stop a step below me.

Why did he have to look so delicious tonight?

The dark jeans, the black button-down, the golden-brown hair that was currently just the right kind of messy, the dark-blue eyes that were so fixed on me that I couldn't breathe.

I squeezed the glass, feeling the coolness of the wine under my sweaty fingers, and joked, "You're very late."

"You're lucky I came at all."

So, he was in *that* kind of mood.

Damn.

I attempted to fill my lungs, my entire body a tight, nervous ball, and I shifted to the side so my back was resting against the door, moving out of the way for him to walk in. "What can I get you to drink?"

"I won't be here long enough for that."

Well, I'm not taking no for an answer…dick.

Once he was in the foyer, the movement sending me a full breeze of his cologne, I shut the door and headed straight for my bar. I'd picked up a bottle of bourbon just for tonight from the liquor store we both shopped at, the salesclerk helping me choose one of the best from their inventory. I unscrewed the top and poured several fingers' worth in a small tumbler, and when I turned around, he was in the entryway of the living room, about ten feet behind me, his shoulder pressed against the corner of the wall with his arms crossed.

A position that, under any other circumstance, would have

been so incredibly sexy.

But the scowl on his face ruined it.

"Come on." I nodded toward the couch, and after I walked there, taking a seat toward the center, I added, "Join me." I dangled the glass in the air to entice him.

"I knew this was a fucking bad idea."

"Why?"

His exhale was long and loud. His hand then shot up to his head, his palm flat against his hair, rubbing toward his forehead and back to his neck. "Because there's nothing for us to talk about. There's no reason for me to even be here. Nothing that you can say will—"

"I have a lot to say, Cooper." My heart was pounding. "Come sit." When he didn't budge, I slid toward the right side of the couch, hoping that would encourage him. "Please."

Hesitation and anger moved across his expression in waves, but he eventually took the spot on the opposite side of the couch, putting as much distance as possible between us. His fingers grazed mine as I reached forward and gave him the glass, my breath hitching from the contact.

It was just a touch.

It hadn't even lasted a second.

But it was enough to shoot a round of tingles through my body.

His fingers were just that powerful. I had known that from the moment he touched me at the bar in the lobby of the hotel.

Because every day since, I'd thought about those fingers. I'd recalled each time they'd touched my body.

And I'd yearned for them.

I took a drink of my wine, swallowing to say, "I understand why you're mad at me."

"You couldn't possibly." The tumbler sat on his thigh, untouched, his posture as cold and uninviting as his words.

"No. I do." I pushed up the sleeve of my sweater, instantly regretting it, and pulled it back down. "I've been thinking about your side of things and how it could look from your point of view. How you could have taken my actions and processed them, and I want to make a few things clear." I took another sip, holding the gaze of his dark-blue eyes. "I didn't know your family was looking at the land in Lake Louise. I didn't assume we were the only ones viewing it, but I certainly had no idea you were going to be in Canada. And when I arrived at the bar and sat down, I didn't know it was you at first. I mean, I figured it out before you introduced yourself, connecting you with the photos that I'd seen of you online, but I didn't take that seat to intentionally put myself next to you."

I glanced toward the top of my glass, remembering the moment it had hit me that Cooper Spade was the man sitting on the barstool to my right and how connecting those photos to the real thing was this overwhelming swish of electricity that didn't just shock me, but practically choked me too.

He was just far too hot for his own good.

I wiped the sides of my mouth with my sleeve. "So, if you think I was there to get information out of you or that I had a motive or that my family had sent me there to talk to you, that's not the case at all. Please don't let any of that even cross your mind."

"That changes nothing." He finally lifted his drink to his lips, and as he pulled the glass away, he looked at the liquor that was left inside, like he was surprised by how good it was.

"Cooper—"

"Like I was saying before you interrupted me, not a goddamn thing you tell me tonight will make this situation any different."

I shook my head, discouraged that he wouldn't give even a little. "Because?"

"You're a Cole."

"So?"

He chuckled as if he was shocked by my response. "I don't fuck with Coles. Especially ones who are about to be my business partner." Another exhale left his mouth, this one full of angst. "A scenario I still can't wrap my head around."

"Hold on." I put up my hand. "Let's go back for a second." I turned my body to face his a bit more. "I know I should have told you who I was before we went up to my suite. I intentionally left out my last name during our introduction, and that was so wrong of me. I'm sorry. I really am."

He mashed his lips together. "You're sorry... Jesus Christ, Rowan." Instead of patting his hair, he tugged on it. "I can't, for the life of me, figure out why you created this fucking mess." His gaze strengthened. "Now that I'm putting it all together, it makes sense why I didn't immediately hear from you when we got back to LA. I'm sure you were shitting your pants over how I was going to react when you told me. But then you texted me for days after our little run-in. You could have told me at any point. You didn't have to see me in person, you could have called."

"I could have, yes. But I didn't feel right about that. It was something I wanted to say to your face."

"But what if I hadn't run into you? Were you planning on never reaching out? Were you just going to ghost me, hoping I'd never learn the truth?"

I shook my head. "I honestly don't know."

"Of course you don't."

"It's not like that, Cooper. It's just that this all happened so unexpectedly. Sure, my plan wasn't a good one, and there were holes and wrong turns in everything I did. I take full accountability for that. But I also didn't expect our families to merge—that definitely altered the course of everything."

"Because now, you can't avoid me. All those ghosting plans

went to hell."

"No." I put my hand on his leg, removing it once the furiousness crossed his eyes. "That's not why at all." I guzzled half the glass of wine. "I wanted to tell you—I did—but I wanted to do it on my terms. I had every intention of having that conversation tonight, and then the Daltons' conference room happened, and it was too late." I wrapped an arm around my stomach. "Seeing your expression when I walked into that room—that's something I'll never forget."

"You're fucking unbelievable, Rowan." His nostrils flared. "Every bit of this conversation has been about you. What you wanted. When you wanted to do it. What about me?" He moved to the end of the couch, holding the glass between his legs so it hung toward the area rug. "Did you ever once consider how this would make me feel? How fucked up this would be for me?" Before I could respond, he continued, "I know you didn't."

"You're right. Every word you just said…is right. I thought about myself, not you, and I fucked up. I'm sorry. I can't say that enough."

He ran his teeth over his bottom lip. "If it were only a few hours together, even a one-night stand, that would be one thing. But three fucking nights and a liquor store run-in? Shit."

"I disagree with you because I felt something for you from the moment we connected eyes, so whether it was five minutes or three nights, I still should have told you who I was. I owed that to the person I care about."

His eyes left me, and he hung his head. "Don't tell me that."

"It's the truth."

"Don't fucking tell me that. I don't want to hear it." His voice rose at the same time his head did. "I don't want to hear about your feelings. They no longer matter. This—whatever this was—is over. It should never have happened to begin with."

"Because I'm a Cole…" I knew we'd already discussed this, but I just couldn't understand why it mattered.

He had to turn his neck to look at me, the angle giving me the perfect view of his square jaw and stubble and the hump of his Adam's apple. "And because of all the shit your family has put mine through over the years."

"Which I had nothing to do with."

"It doesn't matter."

I inched forward; the jitters running through me were making it hard to sit still. "You do know how ridiculous that sounds, don't you?" I drained the rest of my wine. "You're punishing me for something I had no part in. I'm basically guilty for having my last name."

"You're guilty for lying. For manipulating me. For stirring this feeling—whatever the fuck it was—inside me and then letting a goddamn bomb drop. That's all on you. And now, we're going to be working together, and that's just the icing on the fucking cake."

"It doesn't have to be."

He finished his glass and set the empty on the table in front of him. "So, your plan for tonight was to come clean, apologize, and confess you have feelings for me?" His jaw moved as he ground his teeth together.

I nodded.

"No. Fuck no. This is"—he got up and began to head for the door—"bullshit."

I placed my glass next to his and followed him. When I caught up, I pulled on his arm, positioning myself between him and the door. "Don't go. We're not through here. There's still so much to say."

"Oh, we're fucking done. There's nothing to say."

I tried to look past his eyes, to a spot deep inside, where I knew he was holding the truth. "My feelings aren't nothing, Cooper."

My voice was only a little above a whisper, but I knew he heard me.

Because I watched the words hit his face.

I watched him process.

I watched his expression intensify.

"This"—he traced the air between us—"cannot and will not happen. The two largest hotel brands in the country are merging. Even if I forgave you for the lying and manipulation, I can't even think about dating a goddamn partner, Rowan. Not now, not ever. Do you have any idea how my family would react? Walter just started to like your father again, but this would send him into a spiral I don't want to experience."

There was a mask he was holding up; I could see it perfectly.

But I also saw something else.

A touch of softness around the outside of his eyes that told a far different story.

"But you want to."

His brows shot up. "Are you listening to what I'm saying?"

"Yes." My voice was the opposite of his. "I'm hearing every word. And what you're telling me is that you can't. But what you haven't said is that you don't want to."

"I don't have to say it, it's a given," he roared.

"But is it?" Still holding his arm, I lowered my grip to his hand. "It doesn't feel that way." The edge returned to his eyes, making sure I saw nothing inside him. "And before I walked into the Daltons' conference room, I was positive that something was happening between us. You can't make me believe that it wasn't."

He scanned my eyes. "What are you doing?"

I knew I had limited time.

Limited words.

Limited chances to convince him.

Nothing I could say would take away his anger. That was eventually something that would die down. The only thing I could concentrate on was what existed between Cooper and me that extended far past Canada.

"I'm telling you that I don't care what our last names are or our families' past or that we're about to be partners. This feeling I have for you, I can't make it go away, Cooper. I don't want it to go away. And now that you know the truth about me, I can finally be honest about how I feel."

He pulled his hand away from mine. "Do you realize what you're saying? What you're asking?"

"Yes."

He gazed up at the ceiling, like his patience was dripping through his body and going out his toes. "I didn't come here to start something with you. I came here to end it."

"I'm asking you not to." I put my hand on his chest. "Don't shut us off." I waited until his eyes met mine again and then said, "If you need time, fine. If you need to keep us a secret until this all blows over with our families, I'm okay with that too. But don't end us when there's a chance we could turn into something amazing." My head tilted as I recalled that special conversation we'd had at the bar. "Something both of us have always wanted and never had."

"How dare you." His chest rose several times. "You have no idea what you're even asking for."

I nodded. "I do."

"If you knew me, if you knew anything about my loyalty, then you wouldn't have uttered those words to me."

"You're not a stranger to me anymore." My hand lowered to his abs, feeling their hardness through the thin fabric of his shirt. "I'm not asking you to make this decision now, but I'm asking you not to leave." My hand tightened around the top of his belt. "Come back into the living room. We can talk, sit there in silence—I don't care. I can even make us something for dinner. But please, Cooper, don't go."

He was quiet for several moments, his breathing the only thing I could hear. "You're playing with fucking fire."

That was how my body felt.

A burning sensation that traveled all the way through me.

"I just...don't want to say goodbye. Not yet. Not like this."

His eyelids narrowed, his shoulders broadening. When his lips parted, he made them wet. "There's only one thing you're going to get from me right now."

I held in all the air I could, hoping this was going to be the answer I was after. "And that is?"

"My fucking dick."

Chapter Fifteen

COOPER

My hands went to Rowan's face, holding her cheeks, aiming her gaze at mine. She needed to understand what this meant. What I was offering. How it was only a onetime deal.

"I'll give you my dick right now, and I'll fuck you until you're screaming so loud that you lose your voice. But that's all you're getting from me—forever." I traced her bottom lip with my thumb. "Is that what you want?"

What she wanted was to believe everything would be all right between us.

But it wouldn't.

To believe we were going to have a future together.

But we couldn't.

To believe I was the man of her dreams.

But I wasn't.

If she wanted something, I would give her this.

My cock.

Until we were both shuddering from orgasms.

Because after everything she'd just confessed to while we were sitting on her couch, my dick was the only thing I could think with at the moment.

It didn't matter that she hadn't groveled enough.

She wasn't going to get anything more than this.

Neither was I.

But if she agreed, at least I would have tonight.

One evening.

Of fucking.

Of earning the wetness and tightness of her cunt.

Of coming inside her.

And then I was done.

I had to be done.

This goddamn merger was just too much.

Tonight, at her house, was too fucking much.

So was Canada and our liquor store run-in.

And the fact that Rowan had lied and was now going to be my business partner.

But Walter and Ray hadn't signed the contract, so technically, she wasn't my partner yet. That meant that every sinful, unprofessional thing I wanted to do to her body was still allowed.

Until our companies became one.

"I just want you." Words I wanted to hear despite my anger toward her. "And right now, I'll take you however I can get you."

As she clung to the top of my belt buckle, her hand lifted and flattened on my abs. A place she'd already touched tonight. The placement wasn't what had caused my dick to harden. That had happened from the closeness of her body when she grabbed my arm and blocked me from exiting.

What was it about this woman that I couldn't resist, even when I was mad at her for withholding the truth?

What was it about her that I constantly wanted more of?

Even her voice was a kind of satisfaction I'd never experienced before.

I growled, "I know just how to satisfy that pussy. I promise I'm going to give you even more than you want."

I reached around her back, lowering to her ass, which I grabbed and squeezed, using it to lift her into the air. While those green eyes gazed at me, the movement sent me her apple and cedarwood scents.

Why did she have to be so perfect for me?

I held her gaze, teasing myself.

Antagonizing every inch of my body, knowing I was more than ready to rip off her jeans and plunge inside her pussy.

But if this was the last time I was ever going to get to taste her, I needed to take my time.

I needed to savor.

Sample.

And worship.

Because whenever she walked by my future office, or we rode in the same elevator in our new building, or we sat around the conference table for a meeting, this was what I would remember.

I walked her over to a wall that wasn't covered in art, and as I held her against it, I devoured her lips, spreading them with my tongue, dipping between them, where I was instantly met with the flavor of the wine she'd been drinking.

Her tongue circled mine.

And she began to moan with each exhale.

It was as if those sounds had been generated in my own chest, as if they were coming through my throat—that was how much I felt them.

And, fuck, it was enough to make my hips thrust forward, pressing my hard-on against her pussy, as I fantasized about the heat that was waiting for me in there. The way Rowan was going to be so turned on by the time my tip slid in that it would slip right into her snugness.

"Cooper!"

"You want to know something?" My mouth went to her throat, where I slowly kissed to her collarbone. "I'll take you however I can get you right now too."

"Have me, then. Don't make me wait for it."

I leaned back to take in her eyes. "You know what's so sexy?"

"That I want you as badly as you want me?"

Damn it.

She was fucking right.

"Yes," I hissed. And because of that, I slammed my mouth to hers, holding her ass so hard—a part of her I loved—that I was locking her into my palms. "Where's your bedroom?"

"On the other side of the living room. The doorway by the giant plant."

I carried her to where we'd been sitting earlier, rounding the corner of the couch, toward the entryway she'd mentioned. It was easy to spot the plant, even while my lips were on hers, a quick peek ensuring I was headed in the correct direction.

"Right," she said as soon as we entered the arch.

I realized there was a left option as well, but I followed her instruction, tossing her on the bed once we reached it. I waited for her to settle before I demanded, "Get me naked."

As her hands returned to my belt buckle, I busied mine with the buttons of my shirt, the collar becoming loose enough that I could lift the long-sleeved shirt over my head. By the time it hit the floor, Rowan had my jeans and boxer briefs around my ankles, and I stepped out of my shoes, socks, jeans, and boxer briefs. By the time I straightened my body, her fist was around my shaft, pumping it, her thumb rubbing over the bead of pre-cum that had leaked out just for her.

"Yes!" I shouted.

A hand job wasn't something I particularly cared for—I could do it better myself—but even her palm felt slick and soft against me.

"Rowan Cole, I'm going to fucking ravish you." I gifted her a couple more strokes before I took the control back and aimed my tip at her mouth. "Suck this first."

"God, yes, Cooper."

Her lips surrounded my crown, her fingers moving to my sac, and while she took in as much of my dick as she could handle, she gave my balls a gentle tickle.

"*Ahhh*." My hand shot into her hair, gripping the strands, urging her to take in more. "Do not stop, whatever you do."

The friction was everything, and so was the way she was swirling her tongue, positioning her free hand around my base, rotating across it to cover every spot.

My head fell back, my mouth opening. "Fuck *yesss*."

I could come right now. That was the kind of blow job she was giving me.

But I just wasn't ready to end this night.

I allowed her a few more bobs, hitting the back of her throat every time she sucked me in, and when I popped out, I got straight to work on her clothes. She was wearing as many layers as I'd had on. I lifted the sweater over her head while she unbuttoned her jeans, freeing her legs completely once she took off her slippers.

I wanted nothing separating us.

I wanted full access to her body.

And once I had her bra and panties off—a set that was white and lace and too angelic for this insatiable woman—I hovered over her torso.

"*Mmm*." She held the back of my head and spread her legs. "Yes!"

I brushed my tip across her hairless folds while my mouth landed on her neck, kissing my way to her tits.

God, they were something else. Handfuls of smoothness with nipples just large enough that I could pull.

Bite.

And I did both, circling my tongue around each one, grazing my teeth over the ends.

"Cooper!" The heels of her feet dug into my back.

"You want more?"

"*Yesss.*"

"Beg for it, Rowan." I flicked a nipple. "Tell me just how much more you want."

"Please." She gasped in some air. "Please give it to me."

"Give you what?" I glanced up as I reached her belly button.

"Your tongue."

A smile pulled at my mouth.

Fuck, that was one sexy request.

But since I was already headed there, it was easy to fulfill, my kisses stopping when I reached the top of her cunt.

That spot.

The one at the beginning of her pussy that was the most sensitive place on her body.

Before my mouth got near it, I pressed my nose against her clit, and I took the longest, deepest inhale.

I could smell her trademark scents down here, but those weren't the only aromas.

There was another.

Sweetness.

And I wanted to fucking bathe myself in it. To cover my face and leave it there, so whenever I was missing this woman, I could just breathe her in.

"Is this where you want my tongue?" I gave her a quick swipe.

She was looking down her body at me, her lips parted and pouted. "Yes."

"And you want me to lick you?"

She nodded.

"Say it, Rowan. I want to hear the words."

Both of her hands found their way into my hair. "Lick me, Cooper. Use your tongue to make me come."

Fuck.

I couldn't deny that want.

Not when I needed it as badly as her.

I didn't hesitate. I didn't make her wait. I stuck my tongue out and glided it horizontally across her clit. And while I focused on that one spot, I dipped my finger into her pussy.

"Oh God!" she screamed.

I wasn't going to tease her endlessly, build her up, and edge her toward an orgasm, only to let her fall.

The reason my mouth was on her cunt was to make her come.

So, I did what I knew would get her there, dragging the long wetness across her clit, massaging the top, circling until I felt it harden—the sign that she was close.

Along with the, "Cooper," that she exhaled every few breaths.

I wanted to feel her come.

I wanted to hear it.

I increased the speed in which I licked, the pressure in which I pressed, and I added a second finger, twisting my wrist, aiming the point toward her G-spot.

It took seconds.

Just like I had known it would.

"*Fuuuck!*" she shouted across her bedroom.

Her knees bent.

Her back arched.

Her nails dug into the top of my head.

"*Ohhh, yesss,*" she added right before the shudders pounded through her stomach, causing a rippling that I felt in my tongue. "Cooper! Fuck! Me!"

Her legs threatened to cave in, and I held them apart, her nails stabbing me so hard I was sure she was drawing blood.

I didn't care.

I needed her to feel good.

I needed to taste her cum.

I lapped even harder, sending her past that cliff, not letting up until she stilled.

When she did, she purred, "*Mmm.*" There was a moment of silence before, "That was...well, I don't know that I even have words for what that was."

I kissed the spot I'd been licking and carefully pulled my fingers out, moving up her body until I was hovering over her again. "That was the beginning, Rowan."

"The beginning," she sighed, like she couldn't believe it.

Using her waist, I turned her onto her stomach, positioning her ass and legs so that I was able to poke at her entrance. And while my cock worked its way in, I kissed across her shoulders and down her back.

Taking in her scent.

Her skin.

Her sounds as she moaned, "Cooper."

I didn't need to be gentle. We were beyond that. She welcomed my size, and by now, her pussy knew just what to do with me.

So every inch that I stroked in, she hugged me.

She became tighter.

Wetter.

And the deeper I went, the narrower she became.

"God, you're fucking perfect." My forehead pressed against the center of her spine.

I couldn't imagine sex that was better than this.

That could top what I was feeling right now.

I'd certainly never experienced it before.

But I would have to.

Because...fuck.

"Harder," she pleaded.

I was all the way in, my hands on the bed, holding my weight, her body beneath mine, my dick fully swallowed and still because I just wanted to take this all in.

A sight that was beyond fucking beautiful.

A feeling insanely overwhelming.

And I finally said, "You want to come again?"

"Yes."

"So fucking greedy."

She reached underneath her ass, her fingers disappearing until I felt them on my sac.

"What are you doing, Rowan?"

"I'm making sure we both come."

That was going to happen regardless. But the second I moved, she went in the opposite direction, allowing me to pull back to my tip, and then she met me in the middle.

There was nothing slow or tame about her motion.

Or mine.

We were hungry.

Feral.

Desperate with our thrusts.

And with each one, I grew closer.

I didn't know if she understood what this night meant for us or what it signified, but I'd never felt this kind of need from her before.

The way she clutched me.

Held me.

Encouraged me to drive toward the deepest part of her.

"Rowan…"

"*Yesss.*"

"What the fuck are you doing to me?"

"I'm taking what I want."

An orgasm.

One I wasn't quite ready for yet.

I pulled out and flipped her over, wrapping her legs around my waist and taunting my tip, giving her short, shallow dips. "You want to come, huh?"

"I want both of us to come."

I lifted her off the bed and moved us to the edge, placing my feet on the ground and Rowan across my lap, her knees balancing on the mattress on either side of me. "Show me. Ride the cum out of me."

She smirked. "With pleasure." She circled her arms around my neck and bounced over my shaft, grinding as she reached the base, rocking her hips forward and back, and then rising again to my crown.

The friction came from every angle.

But it wasn't just that.

It was the look of her as she straddled my dick.

Her tits bouncing in my face.

Her gorgeous features lit from the lamps in her room.

A mouth that I fucking dreamed about kissing that was only inches from mine.

"Give me your cum, Cooper. Fill my pussy with it."

"That fucking mouth." I grasped her ass, trying to control her movements. But they were getting faster. She was bucking to the point of no return. "Do you know what you're asking for?"

"I'm not asking. I'm telling you what I want."

I couldn't fight her on this.

I was too far gone.

My balls were tightening; the wave of tingles was moving through my shaft.

So, instead of trying to dominate what was happening between us, slowing her down or stopping her completely, I joined her. I held those fucking ass cheeks that I loved and closed the space between our mouths, so when she came, I could feel her moan, and I could taste it on my tongue.

It only took seconds for me to reach that place.

And a few more for her to join me.

I knew she was there because of how wet she got, how loud she was breathing, how she took my lip and began to bite it.

I couldn't scream her name, not with the way her teeth were launched into me, but the pleasure was just as intense without it, rushing straight through me, taking hold of me, sucking the cum out of me.

"*Ahhh*!" The first shot projected from my tip. "*Yesss*!"

She was just as loud as me, her hips as fierce as mine as they circled and pumped.

And when she pulled her mouth back, she screamed, "Cooper," from the top of her lungs.

She was starting to lose momentum, which told me she'd reached her peak, so I took over the movements, striking my cock through her tightness, feeling each stream as she milked it from me.

"Goddamn it, yes, Rowan!"

I was positive I'd never feel a cunt like hers again.

That it would be years—if ever—that I'd get to do this without a condom, something we'd decided on in Canada because I'd run out and so had the small store in the lobby.

It was that realization that had me squeezing her until she drained every drop out of me.

Until her body stopped shuddering.

Until her screams died down.

Fuck me.

This was it.

The end.

A moment I wasn't ready for and a moment I wanted to fucking run from.

This hurt.

More than I wanted to admit, even to myself.

I gave her a final quick kiss, and I lifted her off my lap, setting her on the bed before I got up and reached for my clothes, pulling them onto my body as fast as I could.

"What are you doing?" she asked from the edge of the mattress, where she sat.

As she watched me, she pulled her knees to her chest and wrapped her arms around them, eyes wide, breathing heavy, as her body started to come down.

I didn't reply.

I hurried through the motions, and when everything was zippered and tied and buttoned, I slipped my hands into my pockets. That was the safest place for them.

"I'm out of here," I told her.

Those words fucking burned, but I couldn't take them back.

"You're...*what*?"

I wasn't going to let her know what tonight meant to me. What it was going to symbolize. How often I would think of it.

Because it didn't matter.

Not when everything was about to change between us, and this—this thing I'd grown to really like—would be long over.

"I'm leaving," I said.

"But I thought—"

I gazed at her from the doorway of her bedroom, a place I'd

paused to cut her off from speaking, and said, "You thought that us fucking would change the outcome. Not a good plan, Rowan. You knew what this was. Nothing more than a taste, and it was the last one. From here on out, we're business partners. Aside from that, we're done."

Business partners.

Goddamn it.

And a woman I'd have to spend almost every day with.

All of those hours obsessing over how badly I'd want her.

How much I'd fucking need her.

Only seconds had passed since I'd last tasted her, and I was already angry at the idea of not being able to touch her. In a few days or even weeks or—*fuck me*—months, I was going to be like that bear that sat on my desk in my home office.

If she'd thought I roared before, she'd heard nothing yet.

"We're what? No." She shook her head, her legs dropping, like she was going to stand. "You're not seriously leaving right now. You can't…"

I released the doorway, and before I walked into the hallway, I said, "And I don't plan on ever coming back."

Chapter Sixteen

Rowan

Me: *I think we should talk about last night. What happened… why you left. All of it.*

. . .

Me: *Silence, really? Okay. Then, I think we should just talk in general.*

. . .

Me: *I know you're not ignoring me. You wouldn't do that. You're not that kind of guy. I KNOW you're not.*

. . .

Me: *Cooper, what the fuck?*

. . .

Cooper: *There's nothing to talk about. Don't make me say it again.*
Me: *You are that guy.*
Me: *And you're an asshole.*

• • •

Rhett couldn't take his eyes off our realtor. He was more focused on her body than any of the buildings we'd looked at today. A mission that the seven of us hoped would result in finding a location we could convert into our corporate headquarters. Ridge, based on his expression, was impressed with the one we were viewing now, unlike the six others we'd toured. I had to agree with him. This was the most spacious and practical for the amount of people we were about to combine into one office.

As for me, I was fuming.

And I had been since we'd all met this morning at Spades' corporate office, where we'd climbed into a van rented for today's showings.

Because being in Cooper's presence made me want to scream.

The same had been true for yesterday and the day before.

Three days had passed since he'd been at my house. After the one line of text that he'd finally replied with, he hadn't spoken or messaged another word to me.

But I was the only one he wasn't speaking to. He responded to all the emails we were both copied on. He contributed to yesterday's meeting when both lawyers wanted to discuss more of the logistics of the merger.

With me, all I got was silence.

Not just with words, but also from his eyes—they wouldn't look anywhere near me.

Why?

All because he wanted to stay professional now that the Spades and Coles were becoming one? Because I hadn't told him who I was?

Funny though because he'd had no problem having sex with me.

When I broke it down in my head, when I really tried to make sense of everything, it seemed like he was really overreacting. Especially considering what had gone down in Canada and at the liquor store, both before either of us knew about the business deal. If he was worried about how his family was going to react, all he had to do was explain the timeline of events. They would understand that we'd had no knowledge of the merger when all of that took place, that the acts were innocent. That we were just two people who had met in an unexpected way and our explosive chemistry prevented us from wanting to be apart.

If that was even the case for him.

But that still meant that two partners would be involved.

Jo and Jenner seemed to pull it off. Of course, they didn't work for the same company, but Jenner was their corporate attorney, which gave them plenty of crossover.

So, what the hell was Cooper's problem?

That was what I wanted to ask him. I just needed to find the chance.

Because this building was twenty-six stories tall, and although we hadn't viewed each floor, the realtor had taken us through the first few, pointing out how departments like accounting and HR could construct their layouts. That didn't give me an opportunity to discuss anything with him. And now, we were on the executive level, a completely open, rectangular floor plan that had no privacy, aside from the offices that were built into the perimeter. Since this was where we'd all be working, the seven of us had scattered once we got off the elevator, passing each of the doorways, taking in the possible spaces we could claim.

As I made my way around, I noticed Cooper checking out the corner office. None of our other siblings or Jo were nearby, giving me, what I hoped, would be a few minutes to confront him. Even if they were close, there was no reason I shouldn't be speaking to one of my soon-to-be partners.

Granted, between our families, it would raise every alarm for every reason.

I just had to make sure I kept my voice down.

So, I did, whispering as I approached, "I'll make sure to request the office right next to this one," and stopped directly behind him. "You know…so I can torture you."

One of his hands dropped from the framework, where he'd been gripping the top of the doorway, the muscles in his cheek moving, which made me think he was flexing his jaw. A gesture that emphasized today's amount of scruff and how sexy it looked on him.

God, I didn't care how angry I was; Cooper Spade was still the most gorgeous man on the planet.

But he didn't look at me. His eyes stayed pointed at the interior of the office.

"What do you want, Rowan?"

I laughed.

Because I couldn't believe what I'd just heard.

"What do I want? Answers. How about we start there?"

He turned his head just enough to give me side-eye. "You know exactly why I left your house. You know why this can't become a thing. And you know you shouldn't be bringing this up when there are so many fucking ears around us."

My hands began to shake, and I tucked them into the pockets of my suit jacket. "I wouldn't have brought it up at all if you'd just written me back something that was even remotely respectful."

He shook his head, sighing. "I told you once. I don't know why you keep making me repeat it. There's nothing for us to talk about."

"And I heard you loud and very clear, but that doesn't mean I agree."

"This isn't a debate."

The anger was rising so fast and so hard; my fingers clenched into fists. "You owe me a conversation. I don't care how dominant and controlling you are, this isn't just about you." I leaned into the wall by the doorway, bringing us even closer. "You got all hot and bothered that I'd only thought about myself and I hadn't told you who I was. Don't you see that's what you're doing now? You're only thinking about yourself. But what about me? What I want?"

A smile.

That was what he gave me.

And despite the wrath I was feeling—that look, his face—it sent tingles straight through me.

"I am thinking of you, Rowan." He glanced straight ahead again, leaving a coldness in his wake. "That's why I'm telling you, there's nothing to talk about."

What?

My head shook, like a fly had just hit my forehead, hoping the movement would piece together what he'd just said.

But it didn't.

"I don't understand."

"It's not difficult to comprehend."

The arm that had originally dropped joined the other at the top of the door. When it did, I felt like I was stepping into his cologne.

That was how hard it hit me.

A scent that I now constantly craved.

"Well, it is for me." I took a deep breath, which only punished me even more. "So, please explain."

"The more we talk, the more time we spend together, the more you try to negotiate—or whatever the hell you attempted to do at your house and what you're doing right now—it keeps you attached." He gave a quick glance in my direction as he said, "Let me go, Rowan. Move on. Once you cut the cord and realize we're never going to be anything, you can set your sights on someone else. It'll be like we never happened."

How could it be that easy for him?

My feelings weren't simple at all.

And neither were his—I could feel that as deep as my soul.

Everything Cooper was saying right now was bullshit.

And I was going to call him out on it.

I ducked under his arms and moved inside the office, so I could look at him while I said, "You know what's funny? There were moments the other night—you know, when we were naked and fucking in my bedroom—when you were so soft. Even softer than you had been in Canada." I shifted my weight as I placed my hands on my hips. "It was the way you kissed me. The way you looked at me when your face was between my legs. Moments when I was thinking to myself, *This man wants me. Needs me*." I paused as his expression began to harden. "Are you going to tell me that was all in my head? That none of it ever existed? That I was seeing things? Feeling things that weren't real?"

"Rowan"—he glanced behind him, assuming to make sure no one was close or listening—"I can look around this floor and mentally convert the entire space into a restaurant. But you might look around here and just see offices. It's all how a person wants to perceive something."

I returned the smile. In fact, I grinned so hard that my cheeks hurt. "You're precious—you know that? A precious fucking asshole."

His teeth flicked his lip. "You're looking for me to say something that I won't."

"Because?"

I knew that question was causing us to circle.

I didn't care.

Everything he was saying was sending me straight over the edge.

"Because there's no reason to," he snapped. "I've already told you—"

"Do you have a fucking problem?" Rhett shouted, his tone so loud that it cut Cooper off mid-sentence. "We can have it out right here. I give zero fucks."

Cooper released the doorframe and turned around, immediately walking toward the center of the room, where my brother was squaring off with Cooper's brother. As I made my way closer, I observed Rhett, the way he was almost chest to chest with Brady.

The look on my brother's face terrified me.

He was going to explode.

I saw it in his eyes, his hands, his posture.

My oldest brother had no fear. He didn't care who he pissed off. He didn't filter his words. He wasn't afraid to draw his fists in any situation.

He was the German shepherd of our family.

And if his frustration and attention were aimed at Brady, then something told me this wasn't going to end well.

"Yeah, I do have a fucking problem!" Brady yelled back while Macon and Cooper joined him. "You've been on me since we walked into this building. I don't fucking like it. You have some smart-ass reply to everything I say. I don't want to hear it. Keep your goddamn words to yourself."

Ridge rushed over, standing next to Rhett, attempting to calm him down.

It seemed Macon and Cooper were trying to do the same to Brady.

But among all the chaos, Rhett countered, "That's because I don't fucking like you. I keep hearing you chirp in my ear, and I can't stand it. I don't give a shit what you think about this building or any of the others we've looked at. I don't give a shit what you think about anything—"

"All right, fellas," Jenner said as he moved in between them, "we're going to settle down. Right now. There's not going to be a brawl in this building, not on my watch."

Rhett's lips were wet and flaring, and as I put my hand on his back, he spit, "Fuck you," into the air.

I didn't know if he was speaking to Jenner or Brady or any of the other Spade brothers.

But what I did know was that it was time to separate the families before things got even worse.

"How about I call a car for my family and we end things for today?" I suggested.

"Good idea," Jenner agreed. "But first"—he held a hand toward Brady and another toward Rhett, as though he were playing referee—"let's make a decision. I know there's tension and a lot of strong personalities under this roof, but we need to put that all aside and come together as a company." His gaze shifted between Brady and Rhett. "We've looked at the best buildings in LA today. Unless you want to relocate outside the city, you've seen all there is to offer within your criteria." His fingers pointed at both men. "Regardless of how badly you want to kill each other, this merger is happening, a building needs to be purchased, and there's nothing either of you can do to stop it."

"There's plenty I can do," Rhett threatened.

I grabbed his arm, circling mine around it, and whispered, "Relax. We're almost done. Let's just get through this."

He glared at me and then at Jenner. "My vote is this building."

"Mine too," I offered.

Jenner looked around the room, collecting all the nods and approvals, and finally said, "It's unanimous, then. I'll have the paperwork drawn up as soon as I get back to my office. I'll let everyone know once I hear from the seller's agent." He looked at me. "I assume you'll be in charge of getting the Coles back to the office and the Spades will take the van?"

I nodded, partly humiliated and partly disgusted.

We were all adults.

Why couldn't they act like it?

"The Spades, come with me," Jenner said, and his arm went around Brady's shoulders, walking him toward the elevator.

Jo and Macon were behind them.

Cooper went last.

But this time, it was me that avoided his eyes.

That didn't even attempt to look at his face.

That wanted nothing more than for this whole day to be over.

Chapter Seventeen

Cooper

I couldn't look at Rowan. Because if I even glanced at her for the briefest of seconds, I'd end up dragging her into my arms the moment we walked out of this conference room and then pull her into my office, ravishing her on top of my desk.

She was that addictive.

My body, my hands, desperate to have her.

Touch her.

Slide into her tight, warm pussy.

So, I forced myself to avoid her.

Conversation, glances—I didn't fuck with either.

Except, as the days passed since our last chat at the real estate showing, we seemed to be in each other's presence nonstop. Meeting after fucking meeting. And she'd sit at either her conference room table or ours or the Daltons', dressed in a suit or a dress, the outfits hugging her perfect body and delicious curves. Taunting me from the other side of the room, where I'd always plant my ass, not wanting to be close enough that I'd smell her with every inhale.

I didn't look at her during any of those times.

Fuck me.

But I searched the air for her perfume.

And I caught glimpses in my peripheral vision, little hints as I was speaking to someone next to her or when she'd walk in or when she'd stand to leave. Details that would peek their way through, like the shine from her goddamn lips or the way she'd whip her hair off her shoulders, how her neck and collarbone would catch some kind of overhead light, highlighting that even that part of her body was exceptional.

She was nothing but a fucking cocktease.

Rowan probably assumed I was making a rash decision when it came to us.

But I thought about her a lot, whether I was doing the right thing.

If I should keep up this wall, not even allowing my eyes near her.

It wasn't just the way my uncle would react. Shit, at this point, Walter probably wouldn't be pissed; he was climbing into bed with the Coles after all and gave zero fucks about it. It was that my brothers would lose their shit if they found out. It was that partners, whose actions would affect the future of our company, shouldn't be fucking. It was that her last name had been cursed by my family for as long as I could remember.

She knew that.

That was why she hadn't told me the truth in Canada.

And that was what really ate me up because I wouldn't have tasted her if I'd known.

Without a taste, I wouldn't have developed this addiction.

So, this was all her fucking fault.

And that was what I wanted to growl in her face as she sat at the other end of the large oval, waiting for Jenner to arrive and give us the latest update on this bullshit merger.

I was just about to get out of my chair and head to my office, tired of waiting for this damn Dalton to arrive, when the door to the conference room opened and the motherfucker walked in.

Behind him were Walter and Ray and the Coles' attorney.

They took up an entire side of the table, holding folders that they placed down on the wood, the grins on their faces telling me the deed was done.

We were one.

I had known it was supposed to go down today—my brothers and I had started a countdown in our group text. But seeing the proof didn't make it any easier to accept.

The realization hit me straight in the gut, causing my breakfast to churn.

Fuck this.

And fuck them.

I looked at Brady, Macon, and Jo. Their faces told me they felt the same way.

The biggest moment of our career was a disappointment instead of a victory.

"The paperwork has been signed," Jenner said, tapping the folder in front of him. "It's official, Cole International and Spade Hotels are now Cole and Spade Hotels."

The room went silent.

There wasn't a single word of congratulations spoken.

Or a smile, aside from the assholes grinning at the head of the table, the only ones who benefited from this catastrophe.

"Does anyone have anything to say about this?" Walter asked. "And if you do, keep it positive."

He was met with more quietness.

Until Jo said, "Good God, Dad. I want you to be happy, but I don't like this at all."

"Let me say what Jo is too nice to voice to you," Brady started. "You know how the hell we feel about this. The fact that no one in this room has even clapped their fucking hands shouldn't come as a surprise to you."

Walter crossed his arms, peering down at each one of us. "What I find ironic is that you all got what you wanted. I'm out. Ray's out. The company is now in your hands. There shouldn't be any reason for disappointment, but when I look at all your faces, that's what I see."

I laughed. Most of those words couldn't be further from the truth. "I don't know how you can even say that. When I look around this table"—I tried to skip Rowan during my scan, and, fuck, my eyes landed right on her, stopping on her face for longer than they should have, and what I saw made every part of me ache—"there's an entire section of people who shouldn't even be here."

"Is that really how you all think?" Walter pointed at the four of us and the three of them, receiving nods from everyone. "My God." He sighed. "You're one group of ungrateful sons of bitches."

"Who just inherited billions' worth of assets," Ray added, the room turning mute again. "Most people who work for large corporations, like ours, aren't even given a goddamn retirement package. They're sent home with a coffee mug and a card that's signed by HR. What we should be hearing is a collective thank-you. Words of appreciation." He shook his head. "This isn't how we raised you."

"And this isn't a side of you that Ray or I want to see. I'm ashamed of the bunch of you."

I was about to freak the fuck out.

Why was it so impossible for them to see things the way we did? Why were the two of them having such a hard time wrapping their heads around this sudden explosion?

"We don't deserve to be scolded for having an opinion,"

Macon voiced. "You don't have to like our opinion, but we're allowed to have one." He turned his head toward the elders. "Or are you going to take that away from us too?"

"Regardless, you need to come to terms with this," Walter replied, ignoring Macon's last statement. "To stop fighting us on every step and to stop, for Christ's sake, fighting each other." He eyed up Brady. "This can't be reversed, you need to accept that."

Even though Walter hadn't been at the showing, I was shocked to hear he'd found out.

Ray moved his chair back and crossed his legs. "Now that Walter and I are finally on the same side, I can tell you with absolute certainty that it's a much better place to be than where you all are right now."

"Agreed." Walter gripped Ray's arm. "And to hand our legacy to a team who can not only handle this company, but also grow it, well, there's nothing better." He fully turned toward Ray. "I think it's time the two of us took a long vacation together. What do you say? How do France and Germany sound?"

"Will we be staying at your hotel or mine?" Ray joked.

I looked at my brothers and Jo, trying to understand what the hell I was hearing. Where this new friendship had suddenly come from.

How they had gone from being enemies to wanting to merge and travel together.

This was some shit I just couldn't fathom.

And by the look of it, my brothers and Jo couldn't either.

Because we had been raised to hate the Coles. To do everything in our goddamn power to make our hotels better than theirs. If we heard they were going to open in a new location, we scouted for land nearby. I knew they did the same to us. But the only thing we had ever been told about their history was that Walter and Ray despised each other.

And now, we were supposed to share an office? With a family we couldn't stand?

What the fuck?

"Before the two of you start a bonfire in the middle of the table and cook some fucking s'mores like one big happy family," Rhett groaned, "is there any other information you need to share, Jenner? Or can I return to my office—an office that was earned with blood, sweat, and tears, but that's going to be taken away from me too."

Ridge's hand was in a fist, resting on the table like a gavel.

"Amen," I exhaled. "One of the few things I'll ever agree with you about."

I felt eyes on me. Eyes that I knew belonged to Rowan.

But I couldn't look.

Not now.

Not...ever.

Jenner flipped folders, taking one from the bottom of his pile to move it on top, and said, "A great segue into our next order of business." He lifted the top of the folder and took out several pieces of paper. "The offer to your new corporate headquarters was accepted."

"Of course it was," Brady said. "Had the Spades made the offer, the seller would have suddenly gone MIA or asked for our best and highest because we'd be in a bidding war with the Coles."

"Are you done?" Walter glared at him.

"Are you done?" Brady said to Jenner. "Or is there more business to discuss? Because I'd like to get the hell out of here."

"Same," I offered.

"I think we all feel that way," Ridge countered.

"I'm not done," Jenner said professionally, but I could tell he'd had enough of everyone's shit today. "The building is going to take approximately sixty days to close. After the merger is announced to both of your teams of employees, I need you to discuss with them the plans for the new office space. As soon as the building is yours, the contractor will go in and complete the changes you want, assuming within thirty days, and as long as the build-out isn't extensive, you'll be moving into the new space."

This wasn't just a property merger; this was a corporate merger.

Two HR departments, two accounting departments, two extremely large customer service departments and IT departments. Processes that would change at each of the hotels to combine both of our requirements.

Moving office spaces was the easiest part of all.

The rest was going to be a fucking nightmare.

"Whose contractor will we use?" Jo asked. "We have one we've employed for years. I assume the Coles do as well."

"That's a good question," Jenner said. He looked at Walter and Ray. "Do either of you have a preference?"

"Shouldn't that question be directed at us?" Rhett shot back with. "As of today, they're not the ones making the decisions anymore." He smoothed down the whiskers of his black beard. "Am I right?"

Jenner nodded. "I stand corrected. You are right."

The seven of us looked at each other and said nothing.

Except, in my eyes, there were only six of us at the table.

Still, we had to make a decision, and the first time we'd attempted to make one together—regarding purchasing the building—it hadn't gone well at all.

"You have time to decide," Jenner added. "The important part, for now, is that the merger is handled well from a PR standpoint, that guests from both of your brands see the benefit, and that bookings continue to rise, and you start the long, daunting process of changing everything into the new name. That should be your main focus at the moment, along with the Lake Louise property."

My hand was rising toward my head, but stopped midair. "What about that property?"

"Since this will be the first hotel constructed under the new name, it's an extremely important kickoff. That's something Ray and Walter emphasized to me before they signed the merger contract. They want this new hotel to incorporate the style and taste of both brands—not just one." Jenner's cuff links hit the table. "It's going to set the precedent going forward, showing guests and travel critics, along with what's left of your competition, that this new brand is not one to be fucked with."

Jenner's words had been carefully crafted.

But I sensed there was something he hadn't said.

Something that was going to make my anger fucking boil.

"What does that mean?" I inquired.

Jenner's eyes locked with mine, and then he slowly looked toward the opposite end of the table, where the Coles were sitting.

Why was he glancing at them?

As his stare returned, he said, "It means that a Spade can't spearhead this project alone. If that happens, it'll end up having a Spade feel and design. So, you're going to have to partner with a Cole on this one to ensure both brands are represented."

"No." I gripped the edge of the table. "Fuck no."

"This was decided before the merger took place, Cooper." Walter's voice was caustic, assuming that was so he'd get his point across. "It was one of the major elements that Ray and I discussed in great depth before we signed on that dotted line." He leaned forward as though he were trying to get closer to me. "This build-out holds more weight than you can imagine"—he moved back, resting against his seat—"than any of you can imagine."

My uncle wasn't doing this to me.

He wouldn't make me share when he knew this project was mine.

I ground my teeth together. "I'll get it done the way both brands want me to. But I'm not working with Ridge or Rhett—"

"Then, it's a good thing you'll be working with Rowan." Walter linked his fingers on top of the table. "And there will be zero negotiation on that."

Chapter Eighteen

Rowan

"No," Cooper barked at me as he looked at the blueprints I held in my hand, "we're absolutely not going with your idea." He shook his head as though he needed to emphasize his opinion even more. "Fuck no."

I didn't get easily frustrated. That was one of the traits my father appreciated about me the most and always complimented me on, which was a big deal for a man who didn't give compliments. It was also one of the reasons he'd asked me to join his company since the moment I'd graduated college, hoping I'd, one day, cave and become part of the team. Cole International needed a balance due to all the hotheads who worked there.

That balance, in the short time I'd been employed, had become me.

And that was the reason, I assumed, I'd been partnered with Cooper for the Lake Louise build-out, along with the fact that Lake Louise was going to be the first property I'd be responsible for on my own.

But that was prior to the merger.

Everything was different now.

And as the two of us stood on the slice of land the newly joined company had purchased, facing the most magnificent body of water, a view I couldn't stop admiring, I was beginning to lose my damn patience.

I didn't care how incredibly handsome he looked in his dark gray peacoat, the collar high and framing today's scruff that I swore had grown while we flew here, or how deep and gritty and enticing his voice was every time he snapped a reply.

Cooper looked ravishing, no matter where we were.

But returning here—at the place we'd met, almost the exact location, and the spot where all the feelings had started—there was something full circle and extra emotional about this specific visit.

I just wished he was making this a little easier on me.

I sighed. "Why?" I released a side of the poster-sized paper and traced the entire lot with my finger. "Because look right here. If we just maximize the space from the east, erecting the main building here, then we can—"

"You're not listening. I said no."

No.

A word he'd been repeating since we'd climbed out of the backseat of the SUV and toured the land. It was during that walk-through, just moments ago, that I'd attempted to point out my ideas on design and layout, and every single one had been met with a negative reaction.

He didn't want to listen to me.

He didn't want to hear my plans.

He didn't even want me around.

He'd made that very clear.

I didn't think all these noes had anything to do with Cooper hating the concepts I had been coming up with—ideas that were actually brilliant. It had everything to do with him having to share this project.

With me.

I needed to take a different approach.

"So, in your opinion, if we build the tower on the west—"

"That's the only place to put the tower. For you to think it should be on the east is the dumbest idea I've ever heard. You clearly know nothing about construction or the importance of the layout of a hotel." His eyes narrowed. "The fucking east. You have to be kidding me."

I smiled as I took in his face, something I was positive would annoy him, so I grew my grin even wider.

I understood Cooper much better than he realized. Because despite how much it would pain him to hear this, he was very similar to my brothers. And I'd mastered the two of them.

That didn't mean he wasn't a giant asshole. That just meant that I understood his kind of asshole-ness.

I folded the blueprints and tucked the heavy paper under my arm, my fingers gently landing on his bicep once they were free. "Come with me for a moment, will you?"

"Rowan…" My name came out like a roar. "I don't have the fucking patience for this. There's nothing to discuss. We're going with a west build-out—"

"Except there is something to discuss, Cooper. In fact, everything is up for discussion." I was going to make this man learn to compromise even if it drained every bit of endurance I had. "What you're forgetting or maybe what you're ignoring is that this isn't just your project. That means, when it comes to anything—like the build-out, the design, the processes that are implemented within the hotel—you have to consult with me." I straightened my shoulders, facing off as I felt a battle begin to erupt. "You don't have the authority to tell me which side of the lot the high-rise will be constructed. That's something we'll decide together whether you like it or not. So, stop chirping and come with me."

His nose flared as he exhaled, the air so hot that it looked like steam as it hit the coldness outside. "You have balls."

He was right.

But it was also necessary to bring him down because the place he was perched on right now was far too high for his own good.

"And there's nothing I fucking like about that."

My grin grew wider. "I know." I tightened my grip on him, surprised that he hadn't thrown my fingers off. "Come on. There's something I want to show you, and you're wasting time."

It took a few seconds before he broke eye contact and started walking. But when he did, our feet crunched across the pressed snow as I led him toward the road.

"Does it ever stop snowing here?" I said mostly to myself, glancing up as the little flurries touched down on my eyelashes. "I can't wait to experience summer here."

"Why?"

I turned my head just enough to look at his profile, wishing I didn't remember what it'd felt like when I was kissing that cheek. "The water sports on the lake are going to be so fun."

"Fun?" The annoyance was etched into his face now. "Who the fuck is going to have time for fun? When the two of us move to Lake Louise for this build-out—something I'll never come to terms with—it's going to be a twenty-four/seven job. Fun won't be on the agenda, sweetheart."

He could take his *sweetheart* and shove it.

Because he was wrong.

Again.

"The first two months of construction will only hold us up six days a week...*sweetheart*," I countered. "After the first two months, when we start concentrating on the details, yes, the hours will be grueling. But during my time off, however much that ends up being, I have every intention of spending some time on that water."

"You do you, Rowan."

"And what are you going to do?"

As his eyes locked with mine, a flicker came across them. I couldn't tell if it was heat or anger, but the change came with a wave of emotion even if it was brief.

"Not spend it with you."

Dick.

"You know, you're such a gift, Cooper."

He laughed.

He actually let that sound leave his lips, and it felt like a rubber band snapping against bare skin.

"Even with the patience of a saint, I don't know how I'm going to deal with your grumpy ass during the, what, four or five months that we'll be living here."

"First, you need to survive the next few months of planning. And that's before we'll be living in the same hotel, seeing each other on the jobsite every minute of every goddamn day. We'll be meeting with the architect and contractor and interior designer, going over every inch of the hotel. Decision after decision." He looked at me again. "Sounds like hell, doesn't it."

He wasn't asking.

He was letting me know that it would be hell.

"And I'm not fucking grumpy."

It hurt to fill my lungs, and that wasn't because of the freezing temperature outside.

"If you're not grumpy, what are you, then? Because you're certainly not the sweet, charming, captivating man I met in the bar down the street from here. That man is long gone."

He shoved his hands into the pockets of his coat. "You just

didn't know me well enough back then. I haven't changed one fucking bit."

"I think we both know what's causing this. I just hope that the more we continue to work together, you'll learn to drop the attitude because it'll—"

"Don't count on it, Rowan."

He'd even used my name.

Now, it was my turn to laugh. I was just positive that our reasons for laughing weren't the same. "Figures." Although I'd long since released him, I tapped his arm, signaling for him to stop. "We're here."

He halted and glanced in both directions. "You dragged me all the way up to the road to show me what? How well they plow in Lake Louise?"

God, he loved to throw digs in every direction.

"No, I brought you here to show you this." I moved behind him, held both of his muscular arms, and did my best to turn his rock-hard body around to face our piece of land. And even though winter was my enemy and I despised the cold, the snow, my smile was currently at its largest. "Just look at this view."

"What about it?"

I moved to his side and pointed toward the road. "This is the direction that guests will be coming in from the airport. I also pulled traffic reports, and more than seventy-five percent of the traffic on this road comes from that direction."

A furrow dug between his brows. "Get to the point, Rowan."

"The point is"—I raised my hand in the air, flattening my palm and spreading my fingers wide—"if we build the building to the east, like I suggested, anyone coming from that direction—which is the most popular direction—will get to see a view of the water prior to seeing the hotel. Think of it like a tease. The most perfect sliver of paradise—something they don't currently have sight of due to the number of buildings that hug the lake. But if we go with my idea, they'll get that tease, and it'll be just enough to entice them to want to see more, which they will because the next structure will be our gorgeous hotel."

"That's your point?" He shook his head. "It's weak."

My hands dropped. "Federico Bodega, the most famous commercial architect in the world—"

"I know who he is."

"Then, I'm sure you read his most recent interview, where he discussed his opinion on buildings that are constructed on the water." I was met with silence. Something that didn't surprise me, but pleased me immensely. "When asked about his most successful design element, he discussed a property he'd built in Italy that was constructed along the Mediterranean."

"I know you're not comparing countries that are nothing alike."

"And in that interview," I continued, ignoring him, "he said that out of all the properties he had built over his long tenure, the design he chose for that particular one was the most successful because he teased the water view, just like I want to do here, prior to the building, so the line of sight would be the same as I'm suggesting."

My hands rose again. "Cooper, I want them to take in the grandness of the lake as the focal point during their drive. And while they do, I want them to envision what it would be like to swim in that water or boat or Jet Ski—whatever their poison is— and then I want them to cast their eyes on the beauty of the hotel. To dream about the fluffiness of the bed and the dark roast they'll sip in the morning while they sit on their balconies, admiring the color of the water and the magic of the mountains that surround us. I want them to fantasize about our spa and the different cuisines from our restaurants and—"

"Rowan…"

My hands went to my hips, holding them through my puffy jacket. "If we follow through with your idea, hotel and then lake, they won't have those same dreams. There's a chance they won't even connect our hotel with the view. In fact, they could pair the view with the wrong building, which"—I pointed again, this time to the structure that existed beside us—"is far from dreamy."

I knew Cooper was going to give me a hard time about my proposition. That was why I'd silently rehearsed this exact conversation during the plane ride this morning. And in my head, I'd overcome every objection I could possibly think of him giving me.

It was a good thing he was as predictable as I'd anticipated.

But as I stood here, waiting for him to hit me with another, I was met with only silence, along with the most tempting view of him as he stared at the lake.

That jawline.

Those lips.

The broadness of his chest.

Man.

"It's not just a good idea because Federico would say so," I offered, taking another stab at persuading him. "It's a good idea because it makes sense, and this is one of the many things this property needs to set us apart from our competition."

"We have no competition anymore." His tone was a reminder of how unpleased he was about the merger. "Besides, our name alone will do that."

"But the amount we're going to charge per room, depending on the state of the market, could really depend on whether a guest books our hotel or the one we're staying in tonight." I paused. "Giving guests everything they need is as important as showing them precisely what they're going to get, which is all I'm trying to do with the build-out."

"You won't let it go, will you?"

My lungs loosened as I drew in some air. "Admit it…I'm right."

"Fuck that."

"Admit you're considering an east build." I adjusted my position so I had more than just his profile. "I know you are. I can see it all over your face."

His eyes left the water and moved to mine, where he slowly took me in.

But they didn't just admire me.

They dug into me.

And the look that crossed him was one of the reasons I'd been so attracted to him since the first glance I'd taken at the bar.

Why I had an ache inside me, a need so immense that I would do almost anything to have him wrap his arms around me right now.

For him to tell me he cared.

For him to voice how much he wanted us.

It was the look that told me he'd never seen anyone as beautiful as me or wanted anyone as badly as he wanted me.

"What you're seeing is annoyance. Impatience. And a desire to get the fuck out of here." He reached inside his jacket and pulled at the collar of his shirt.

"I don't believe you."

"What you should believe is that if I knew you were anything like this, I would have walked away long before I even learned your first name."

I smiled. This time as sexy and flirty as I could make it. "Ditto."

"Except you knew my first name…"

I couldn't win.

So, instead of telling him I was leaving, I gave him a view of my ass, and I headed toward the SUV that was parked and waiting for us. Once I heard him walking behind me, within a few paces, I looked over my shoulder, his eyes exactly where I wanted them, below the hem of my crop jacket, and I said, "The east build is eating you up, isn't it?"

His gaze rose to mine. "No, it's not."

I reached the door to the SUV and said, "I know it's going to kill you to admit it's what you want. Don't worry, I won't make you. I'll just wait until we meet with our architect and contractor and it's three against one."

"Jesus Christ."

I climbed into the backseat, moving all the way in so he could get in behind me.

"Back to the hotel," Cooper growled to the driver the moment the door was shut.

He took out his phone, and although I couldn't see the screen from here, the movement of his thumbs told me he was attempting to keep himself busy.

"I think we need to—"

He cut me off with, "Tomorrow."

Tomorrow?

"Excuse me?" I asked.

"Tomorrow, you can chirp all you want. But right fucking now, I need silence and a cocktail."

· · ·

My hands froze on the keyboard of my laptop as my stare darted toward the door of my hotel room.

What is that sound?

The noise was a creak in the floor, like a person was standing over a particular spot, shifting their weight back and forth so the ground beneath gave off a light squeak in both directions. A sound just loud enough to come through my door and cause me to stare at the wooden barrier that blocked me from seeing whoever was on the other side.

I heard it again.

And again.

Even my door was making a noise, almost like there was pressure being forced against it.

I set my laptop beside me and silently got out of bed, tiptoeing to the door until I was close enough that I could align my eye with the peephole.

I saw nothing.

Not even a flash of clothing from someone running away or the door on the other side of the hallway closing. All I saw was the carpet, wallpaper, and the sconces that hung on the opposite wall.

Assuming I was just overtired and on edge, I walked back to my bed. Instead of grabbing my laptop, I lifted my phone off the nightstand and typed out a message to Sky.

Me: *I swear someone was just outside my room, and when I checked, no one was there. Why am I hearing things? WTF is wrong with me?*

Sky: *It's Cooper. He's making you wild.*

Me: *Ugh.*

Sky: *And you're sex-deprived. All you want to do is jump his bones, and the asshole is making it painful to even be around him.*

Me: *You're right.*

Me: *And the rage I feel toward him isn't like me at all. Why is he being so mean to me?*

Sky: *Because he's in love with you. And he thinks he can't have you. And it's making him a grumpy motherfucker.*

Me: *You're...kidding?*

Sky: *Not even close.*

Sky: *You know he likes you, babe. Like turns to love pretty quickly when you have a connection with someone as strong as you have with him and chemistry that's literally explosive.*

Me: *But he's full of excuses. When will those go away? Or they won't...and we were just never meant to be.*

Sky: *Oh, they will. When he can't fight it anymore. It being you.*

Me: *God, he's just been so spicy.*

Sky: *Trust me when I say, this is messing with both of your brains—not just yours.*

Me: *Sigh.*

Me: *Tell me something good. Tell me you're going out on a date tonight. Or tell me you're cooking something amazing for dinner so I can be jealous I'm not there to eat it with you.*

Sky: *Girl dinner, which is popcorn and wine while I plow through my client's books, trying to figure out how the hell he's created such a mess with his month-end.*

Sky: *Back to you—nice try though. This is your second night in Lake Louise. Have you guys at least talked about things? Eaten together? Done anything other than discuss the upcoming construction?*

Me: *No. The second we get back to the hotel, we go our separate ways. We don't eat together. We don't talk, aside from the hotel stuff. He wants nothing to do with me.*

Sky: *So, where have you been eating?*

Me: *Room service.*

Sky: *What about tonight? Room service again?*

Me: *I haven't eaten yet.*

Sky: *Do me a favor—get out of your room. Go to the bar and eat there. Girl, you need a change of scenery and a stiff cocktail.*

The last thing you need is to stay in your room with all those thoughts, doing work that can wait until tomorrow.

Me: *You really think so?*

Sky: *Text me when you get back to your room for the night, and it'd better include a pic of the burger and fries you slammed down, along with your third glass of something extra strong. You'll thank me, trust me.*

Me: *An extra-dirty martini does sound delicious right now.*

Sky: *GO.*

She was right.

I needed to get the hell out of this suite. I needed to sip some vodka and eat something hearty and be around noise and people instead of this lonely room with the silence broken every few seconds by the ping of a new email coming in or by a person standing outside my door who wasn't really standing there.

I shut my laptop and grabbed a sweater from my suitcase, letting it hang to the sides of my tank, and I slid into a pair of UGGs that fit perfectly over my leggings. I made sure I had my phone, key, and wallet, and I hurried out of my room. Once I arrived at the elevator, I hit the button for the lobby and reopened Sky's last text.

Me: *I took your advice.*

The doors slid open as I arrived at the bottom floor, and I stepped out, walking toward the lobby, watching the bubbles bounce as Sky typed her reply. I rounded the corner where the two sections split—the bar and the front desk—and as I headed for the bar, her reply came in.

Sky: *Good. ;) Now go enjoy that cocktail.*

As my thumbs hit the screen to respond, I quickly glanced up to check out the empty seats and where I should sit, and it was during that scan that I saw him.

That our eyes locked.

That I took in the sight of him as he was parked on the left side of the bar, his hands surrounding a small tumbler that I knew was bourbon, wearing a USC sweatshirt and a backward hat.

Oh God.

Casual and athletic was a look I'd never seen on him before, but it was one that completely took my breath away.

How could a man be that hot in a backward hat?

But then there were his eyes that only added to it.

His lips.

The way he stared me down as though I was his prey.

I stood frozen, halfway between the bend in the lobby and the bar, unsure what to do.

I could turn around, although that would make me look foolish, like I couldn't stand the thought of sharing the bar with him, his presence enough to send me back to the elevator. I could sit on the opposite side of the bar and show him I was unbothered and uninterested.

Or I could plant my ass directly next to him and make him even grumpier.

Chapter Nineteen

COOPER

There were only two things I wanted: to breathe in air that didn't have her scent and to sit and drink in a bar that showed no signs of her.

Five minutes. That was how long I had gotten to soak in both, enjoying my freedom, until it was suddenly taken away from me.

Why the fuck couldn't she have gotten room service?

There was no way she could have heard me outside the door to her room. I had been silent the whole time I was standing there, my hand pressed against the smooth, painted surface, forcing myself not to knock. I didn't know why I'd stopped at her door or what had possessed me to even get close to it. But after I had passed her suite, I'd backtracked. I got near it, and then I practically pressed my whole damn body against it. Of course, while I was there, doing everything in my fucking power not to bang my fist on the wood, the floor decided to creak.

It was that noise that brought me back to reality.

That had sent me straight here, where I downed a bourbon

and quickly ordered a second.

And instead of relaxing in the quietness and a Rowan-free space, I was looking into the eyes of my enemy.

The woman who was making me question my loyalty to my family.

Who was making me want things that I'd never wanted before.

Who was testing the very little patience I had.

When she was within ten feet, I caught a whiff of her apple and cedarwood scents, and a bolt of anger shot straight through me. But it was also there, within that distance, that I allowed my eyes to dip down her body.

The second I reached her chest, I knew it was a bad idea.

She didn't have on a bra, so her tits were loose in the tight tank, her nipples hard, the ribbed top showing the start of her cleavage and the perfect curves of her waist.

Goddamn it.

I should have stopped there. I shouldn't have looked even an inch lower.

But I couldn't help myself.

Her black leggings forked at her pussy, hugging her gorgeous thighs until they met her boots, which only hid her cute toes that I'd only ever seen painted white.

As she reached the spot beside me, she sat in the empty stool, flicking her hair to my side so I was hit with even more of her perfume.

My eyes closed as I took it in, squeezing the glass into my palms. "There are at least ten open seats around this bar. Why in the fuck would you choose this one?"

She turned to me, her lips wide in the most beautiful smile. "To make you say those exact words."

"You succeeded. Congratulations."

"Order me a drink, Cooper. The hell you've put me through

the last two days, it's the least you could do."

I huffed all the air from my lungs, dragging my stare away from her, and focused on the bartender, waiting for him to approach before I said, "The lady will have a bourbon."

"I'm a lady now, huh?"

I faced her, wishing I hadn't, so I turned my attention to the bottles that were stacked on the shelves behind the bar. "Would you rather me have called you a pain in my ass?"

She laughed, and I fucking hated how much I loved that sound. "Do you ever get tired of being cranky? Of holding so much frustration inside, everything that comes out of you is Negative Nancy?"

I took a long drink, swirling the liquor around my mouth while I pondered her question. "I say it like it is. Some people would rather lie. I don't."

"Look at me, Cooper."

I didn't want to. Looking at her would do nothing but increase the need pulsing through my body and amp up the thoughts already dominating my mind.

"Look at me—"

Her voice cut off as I did what she'd asked, and the second her eyes landed on mine, she took her time analyzing my face. Not just my eyes. She studied my nose, lips. Cheeks. Hell, even my chin.

"Just what I thought," she said with far too much confidence.

"What the fuck does that mean?"

She shrugged. "I had an interesting conversation with Sky tonight, and she was telling me some things about you. I wanted to see if they were true."

"She knows nothing about me."

"But she knows men, and you happen to be one. She was dead on—about everything."

I eyed her down, gradually lifting my gaze. "And you know

that just by looking at me?"

She nodded. "I see it all over you."

I shook my head, hissing instead of huffing this time.

My reaction seemed to only make her smile harder.

"And the best part: I questioned what she said, unsure if she was right. But she was—I'm positive—and now, everything she said makes perfect sense."

The furrow between my brows was so deep that it could be a permanent etch on my face. "It terrifies me that you're a partner of our company, and you're going to be speaking to our clients and vendors, and you don't make a fucking bit of sense. They're not going to be able to decipher a single word that you say."

"*Ohhh*, you have nothing to worry about." She waved her hand in the air. "I'm great in front of clients. Remember, I worked in retail. Pretty much all I did was charm my customers."

"Charm?" I laughed.

As she was about to respond, the bartender set the bourbon in front of her and said, "Can I get you a menu?"

"Please, I'm starving." She looked at me. "Have you eaten?"

I wanted nothing more than to toss her over my shoulder, carry her to my room, and feast on her cunt.

But I held up my glass instead. "This is my dinner."

"No, it's not." She glanced back at the bartender just as he was getting her the menu. "I'm sure you have cheeseburgers?"

"We do," he replied.

"How about with caramelized onions, mushrooms, and swiss cheese? For the fries, if you have truffle oil, go heavy on the drizzle." She held up her pointer and middle finger, spreading them into the peace sign. "All of that times two."

"Got it," he responded.

She looked at me once we were alone again. "How'd I do?"

It sounded like fucking heaven—I couldn't lie.

But instead, I said, "I told you I was drinking my dinner."

Her hand went to my shoulder. "Then, don't eat it. Or take it to go." She left her fingers there for only a few seconds, just long enough to cause a damn tornado inside my body, and then lifted her glass and held it near her lips as she continued to gaze at me. "Why aren't you hungry tonight, Cooper? You're a foodie, it's not like you to skip out on a meal. Is something causing a little disruption in your world? Or maybe a certain someone?"

Fuck yes.

She was turning everything about me upside down.

But I wasn't going there. Because I knew Rowan, and the moment I admitted anything, we would be neck-deep in that conversation, and there would be no way out.

It was best and easiest to avoid that topic altogether.

"Yeah, this project." I took a long drink and signaled to the bartender that I needed a refill. "You heard what the architect said today about the soil. Do you know what's going to happen if the shoreline erodes due to the weight of the hotel and it turns out that we can't build here and this entire purchase is for nothing?"

"Then, we'll just find another lot of land to buy."

I stared at her as though she'd suddenly grown two heads. "I'm not surprised you say it like that. Because you don't know the business and how long Walter has dreamed for a hotel on this lake. And how difficult it'll be to unload a piece of land this size when we'll have to disclose that the lot can't hold a certain amount of weight, which means it's going to take a particular buyer—basically a buyer who doesn't fucking exist."

She turned her body fully toward me. "I'm surprised *you* say things like *that*. Because I've spent twenty-nine years of my life hearing my father speak nonstop about this business, and it's monopolized every conversation I've ever had with him regardless of how old I was or how involved I was with the business. Every waking hour that I was with Dad after my parents got divorced was spent at the office. We didn't go to the park, we went to the mailroom. We didn't go to Disney, we went to the copy machine. I napped as a child on the couch in the break room. From my earliest memory, my entire life revolved around Cole International, it never revolved around us kids." Her teeth stabbed the very bottom of her lower lip until she pulled it free. "Please, Cooper, take your assumptions elsewhere. I know hotels as well as I know clothes, and for you to even doubt that is insulting."

I nodded—that was all I could do.

Because the fire inside that stunning woman had rendered me fucking speechless.

"Listen, you can dig me all you want for soil and erosion. Admittedly, what's beneath the ground and what laps the shoreline are not my strong suits. But don't question my work ethic or love for this company in any roundabout way. You won't find anyone more loyal or dedicated than me."

I wasn't going to bring it up.

I fucking wasn't.

But her last comment was the perfect introduction, and I just couldn't stop myself.

"You call yourself loyal," I started. "But what would Ridge and Rhett think about what happened between us?" I held my glass in the air, needing it closer to my lips than when it was sitting on the bar. "And Ray? What the hell would he say?" Before she could even think of replying, I added, "Put yourself in their shoes, Rowan. Consider the past our families have had and the current relationship between the seven of us. The Coles and Spades aren't hanging on by a string, we fucking despise each other. Anything, even something minor, would implode our entire organization." I paused, letting those pieces settle. "So, what would it do to your side if they knew I'd fucked their sister?"

"You say it like it was dirty."

My eyes narrowed in on her lips. "What we did in this hotel and what I did to your body for three consecutive nights—it was fucking dirty."

She glanced away, nursing her drink, looking as though she was deep in thought. "I'm the peacemaker. I'd make it right."

"You're saying they'd have a problem with it?"

"I don't know." Her voice was so quiet.

"Which means they'd have a problem with it."

She moved her hair to her other shoulder, freeing up the space around her neck and collarbone, where her sweater had fallen to the side, teasing me with the softness of her skin.

The delicateness.

Both triggered such strong memories in my head.

"My brothers are extremely protective of me. Neither of them is a fan of your family, so I don't think they'd be thrilled. But they also love me and want me to be happy, even while they're being overprotective." She stalled. "What I'm trying to say is that opinions can be changed, Cooper. Different ideas can be accepted, it just takes time."

"You're telling me their opinion wouldn't stop you?"

Her brows rose. "No, it wouldn't stop me."

I was getting in deeper than I'd intended.

I needed to back up.

"Do you want to know why?" she asked.

Fuck.

I did.

But I didn't.

"No." I shook my head.

"I'm going to tell you anyway. I'm—"

Her voice cut off when the bartender delivered my next round and said, "Would you like another?" to Rowan.

"Please," she replied.

"Your food should be out in a few minutes," he told us before he left again.

I downed what was left in my glass, set the empty on the bar top, and as I was about to change the subject, she whispered, "Cooper, look at me."

I didn't like it the last time she'd said that.

I didn't like it this time either.

"Rowan—"

"Don't try to argue. Just look at me."

When I did, the expression on her face penetrated straight through my damn chest.

"It wouldn't stop me because regardless of how much of an asshole you are to me, I'm wild about you. I can't even say I'm *still* wild about you. Still would imply I feel the same way now as I did before. And I don't." She glanced down for just a moment, and when our eyes reconnected, the emotion was intense as it stared back at me. "This—this feeling—it doesn't even compare to when I met you here the first time."

Her hand went to my leg. Not a place anywhere near my dick. This was a spot to ensure I was listening. "Why would I even bother saying this to you? Why would I put myself out there like this when you've reminded me endless times that we shouldn't be together? When you've repeatedly treated me as though you hate me?" She mashed her lips together, her chest rising so high. "Because I know you don't. Because I know you care about me. Because I know if the circumstances were different, we would be together." She scanned my pupils like before, but this sway between my left and right eyes was filled with tenderness rather than curiosity. "Tell me

I'm wrong."

I ground my teeth together, holding the new glass of bourbon like it was a gun.

Each time I exhaled, I heard the air move out of me, waiting for the relief to come.

It never did.

What it did instead was add to the tension, the build, where I was certain there was no break.

"Rowan…"

"You don't lie. Remember that."

I wanted to chuckle. That was my go-to defense mechanism. My way of avoiding whatever I wanted to say. But it wasn't there in my chest, in my throat. I couldn't even force the sound through my mouth.

I chewed at my lip until I tasted the metallic flavor of blood. "You're not wrong."

"Then, why do you care what they think?"

My voice was raw and impatient as I hissed, "They're my family."

"Am I worth it?"

"Don't ask me that, Rowan."

She pushed her hand down harder. "Am I?"

"You're asking me to choose."

"I'm doing no such thing. I'm asking you, am. I. Worth. It?"

Before I could reply, she got off her stool and wedged herself between the two seats, sliding until she was standing between my legs with her arms resting on my shoulders.

I should have moved away, not allowing her this close, but it had been too long since I'd put my hands on her waist.

Since I'd gripped her with all my strength.

Since I'd felt her heat beneath my fingertips.

"All you'd have to do is have a conversation with them," she voiced. "Let the topic simmer and smooth out the bubbles when they arise—if they even do."

"But you're a partner. Are you forgetting that?"

"I've read over the bylaws. There's nothing in our corporate paperwork that says we can't have a relationship. So, please, don't use that as an excuse."

She was right.

Every reason I'd ever given her was an excuse.

I was sure there was a way to get my family on board. Hell, there was a chance it might not even be that difficult. I didn't know. I just knew that work had been the one constant in my life. The one area where I knew what to expect, where I didn't have to worry about any games or emotions. Where I could lay it all out there. And now, Rowan was part of that space, and with that came pressure and expectations.

What if we didn't work out?

What if things ended badly?

What if we could no longer work together?

Her hands moved to my face, cupping both cheeks. "You're spiraling, and you don't have to. We're right here, right now—nowhere else." She pressed her thumbs against the sides of my mouth. "You know what Sky said? The reason you're so mean to me is because you're in love with me. Is that true?"

That word hit me like I was driving ninety straight into a brick wall. "Neither of us knows what that word means."

Her hands dropped from my face. "Cooper—"

"Two cheeseburgers with caramelized onions, mushrooms, and swiss," the bartender said, setting the plates on the bar top, "and fries with truffle oil. Is there anything else I can get either of you?"

"Ketchup," Rowan replied. "Loads of it." Her eyes stayed on me as she spoke, and once the bartender was off to get her loads of ketchup, she said to me, "Maybe you're right about not knowing that word. But what I do know is that I want to share many more cheeseburgers like this one with you. And I want to keep coming back to Lake Louise with you. And as much as I hate arguing with you about everything, I would take bickering every single day over silence. I hate your silence, Cooper. It means you don't have the desire to fight back, and it's your fight that I crave."

This wasn't what I'd expected for tonight.

Shit, I hadn't expected this conversation at all.

Or to feel affected by her admission.

Or to have my feelings challenged.

"I've been holding this in," she went on. "It's not getting me anywhere, except more frustrated. I'm tired of going in circles. Not a single one of those loops has brought us closer." She let out the smallest sigh. "I hope this will."

"You're putting it all out there. Unafraid."

"Don't mistake this for confidence. That's not what you're hearing. I just know that if I don't tell you how I feel, I'm going to regret it." One of her hands moved to my chest, the spot right above my heart. "And I think you will too." Her face was suddenly closer to mine. "If you want this, if you want me, then you have to make this right."

I took a moment before I said, "What do you want me to do?"

"I want you to fight for me, Cooper. The same way I've fought for you."

Chapter Twenty

Rowan

"I want you to fight for me, Cooper. The same way I've fought for you."

My pulse was racing like I'd just sprinted a mile. My insides tingly. My hand a little unsteady as I released his face and rested those fingers on his shoulder. My other hand, which was holding his chest, moved to the opposite side of his neck, and I searched his eyes, waiting for a response.

I could have pushed off this conversation, postponing it a few weeks, even months, accumulating hundreds of arguments under our belt and more assholeness, letting the tension come to a roaring peak.

But why?

Just to prolong what I wanted to say to him? To hope that during the extended period of time, his feelings—the ones I believed he had—would grow stronger?

Screw that.

There was something inside me that couldn't wait.

That needed him to know where I stood.

What I wanted.

What I knew to be true.

That I saw right through his bullshit behavior.

And after I confessed, he didn't push me away. He didn't tell me I was wrong.

He just stared into my eyes and gripped my waist as the emotion ran through his face.

The silence between us built, and so did the angst, the tiny sparks that ignited within me increasing to bolts of electricity while the seconds ticked.

And then, out of nowhere, as though he couldn't handle it anymore, he whispered, "I need something." His fingers spread like a fan, and I swore his large hands covered both of my sides and most of my stomach. "I need to kiss you."

Intimacy was Cooper's love language.

That was when I felt more than just passion. What came through his fingers, his mouth, his body was deep, more fulfilling, far more powerful than anything I'd ever felt before.

I wanted to experience that again.

I wanted it to own me.

Just because he didn't have words didn't mean he wasn't giving me an answer. This was the way he was choosing to reply, and I'd take it.

Because it was a language I also spoke.

"Why are you even asking?" I questioned.

The smallest smile widened across his lips. "I'm not. I'm warning you."

Once that warning met the air, I was hit with the heat from his mouth as it pressed against mine, followed by his hands surrounding my face, holding me close, keeping us aligned.

Together.

Locked.

I didn't just feel the dominance in his lips as they melded to mine or the wetness of his tongue as it slid in. I felt the warmth of his skin and the strength of his fingers. I tasted his familiar flavor and inhaled his unique scent, ones that I'd missed so much.

As my eyes stayed shut, my body fell against his, and I listened to what his mouth was telling me, absorbing the way his kiss penetrated my bones and muscles.

I heard his unspoken words.

And I felt his affection in the way his lips enclosed mine, in his fingertips, in every exhale that breezed across my skin.

If I'd had even the slightest bit of doubt, it was gone.

Cooper Spade didn't just want me.

He needed me.

And when he pulled back, his gaze taking me in, every thought I had was confirmed in his expression.

"Rowan…"

I knew the look that followed. It was one that told me he wanted more.

That made two of us.

But not tonight.

This moment was the finale of the evening. A memory that would end with the most perfect kiss.

While his hands dropped from my face, mine rose from his shoulders and cupped his handsome cheeks, his prickly scruff tickling my palms. It was then, as I held him near me, that I gave him one final glance.

I wasn't analyzing. I'd done plenty of that already.

I wasn't memorizing. I could draw Cooper with my eyes closed even though I wasn't an artist.

I was silently telling him that I'd heard him.

That I understood.

And that I was ready to see his fight.

But just as that thought began to leave my mind, scattering into pieces that were the size of dust, it was replaced with another. One that I hadn't even considered until now.

"How long have you been at the bar?" I asked.

He didn't immediately reply, but when he did, he said, "About ten or fifteen minutes."

"Did you stop somewhere before you came here?" I focused on his eyes. "A door of a suite perhaps? Maybe one that you didn't knock on, but you were there long enough to make noise?"

He took his time licking his lips. "Maybe…"

So, I hadn't been hearing things.

That was Cooper outside my room, his weight shifting just enough to make the floor creak, putting the right amount of pressure against my door to cause the air to crack.

There was a reason he'd halted at my door. That he got close enough to press a part of himself against it. That he hadn't been ready to give in to his vulnerability and knock.

What he didn't realize—or maybe he did—was that his lips had just told me everything he would have said outside my door.

"Thought so." I swiped his mouth with my thumb, and I took a step back, moving out from between his legs to stand in front of my barstool.

When the bartender had delivered our food, I'd asked for ketchup, which he'd brought in a small metal bowl, delivering it without me even realizing.

I set that bowl on top of the fries, and lifted my plate, smiling at Cooper as I said, "Enjoy your dinner."

"You're leaving?"

"I'm going to my room."

He tried to reach for me, but I wasn't close enough. "You're going to make me eat alone?"

"I thought you were going to drink your dinner?" I winked,

reminding him that the only reason he had a burger and fries was because I'd ordered them for him.

"Yeah, well, I thought I was going to be down here alone"—his eyes narrowed—"and that certainly didn't happen."

I grinned even harder. "I'll leave you with those thoughts, then."

"Hello, Miss Cole," a woman said the moment the elevator doors slid open and I stepped onto the executive-level floor of Spade corporate headquarters. "I'm Kathleen, the executive assistant to Jo, Macon, Cooper, and Brady. It's lovely to meet you." She held out her hand.

"And you," I replied, shaking her fingers. "Please call me Rowan."

"Rowan, I feel as though I should officially welcome you to the company, but since it's a merger, I'm not sure what the appropriate protocol is." As she released me, she clasped her fingers together. "I guess I'll just say I'm excited to be working with your assistant, Trista, to make sure the seven partners have everything they need."

"I'm excited as well." Now that the news had been announced across both companies and the two teams were preparing for the merger, I wasn't going to let Kathleen or any of the employees know that the seven of us were still at war, and I was nervous as hell about it. "As for Trista, you're going to love her, she's fabulous."

"I can see that. In our little interaction, she's been so kind."

I glanced around the large, beautifully designed space. "This is my first time here. Probably my last, too, since we'll be moving into our new building soon."

"I was over there just the other day." She smiled as she pulled at the bottom of her suit coat. "I can't get over how pretty it is.

Bright and open. I'm really looking forward to the new vibe."

"Me too."

A semi-lie, but one worth telling.

She pointed toward the double doors behind her. "Everyone's waiting in the conference room, so I won't keep you any longer."

"Everyone?"

"Jo, Macon, Brady, even Walter." She began walking toward the doors. "Walter happened to swing by the office today. When he heard about the meeting, well, I assume he just couldn't resist."

When we'd returned yesterday afternoon from Lake Louise, Cooper had set up this meeting and only mentioned the architect was attending. He'd said nothing about the rest of his family joining us.

What was I about to walk into?

And why hadn't he said anything about the others?

"Just this way," she said as we moved through the double doors, entering a long, well-decorated hallway. "Can I grab you anything to drink? Coffee? Water? Sparkling water?"

I shifted the large bag that hung over my shoulder to position it in front of me. "I brought some water with me, thank you."

We passed a few doors, and she paused outside one that was closed. "All right, then." Her fingers gripped the large metal handle. "Everyone is in here. Please let me know if I can be of any assistance. And it was great to meet you, Miss Cole—Rowan." She grinned.

I returned the gesture, and as she pulled the handle, opening the door, I stepped inside, the murmur immediately turning to silence.

Multiple sets of eyes hit me at once, their gazes not exactly warm or fuzzy.

Instead of a conference room, I felt like I was standing on a stage.

Naked.

And everyone was gawking at every flaw on my body.

The only thing that brought me back to the moment was Cooper's voice as he said, "Rowan, welcome. Please come take a seat."

I needed him to give me more calm than that, but it was a solid start.

Enough to get my feet moving and my hand to lift in the air and wave. "Good morning, everyone. It's nice to see you all." I searched the space until my eyes landed on Cooper. "Thanks for the welcome."

He nodded, and I noticed that today's scruff was just slightly longer than yesterday's.

His suit was darker than the last one he'd worn.

His sexiness, of course, was right on point.

My goodness.

"It's great to have you here, Rowan." Walter's voice was bold and boisterous. "I hope you don't mind that I'm joining you."

I gave him my warmest smile. "Not at all, Mr. Spade. It's nice to see you."

Cooper and Brady sat at both heads, Jo was across from her father, Macon next to her, and the architect was sitting on Walter's side of the table, so I slid in between Cooper and Jo. I gave her a quick smile before I turned toward Cooper.

Since the merger meeting at the Daltons' law firm, every time we were around Cooper's family, his presence was cold and standoffish. But there was something different about him today. It was his eyes, the way they looked at me. The way he kept them narrow and focused on mine.

"Now that you're here, let's explain to the group what's going on." He glanced toward the others, but the movement wasn't natural. It was almost like he had to force himself to look away from me. "My hope is that by the end of this meeting, one of us will have some insight into what we should do and what steps we should take from here."

Cooper was holding a remote, and after hitting a few buttons, the TV in the back of the room showed pictures taken from several different angles of the lot, even aerial shots, with a digital rendering of a hotel-like structure.

"This is a mock-up that I threw together," the architect said. "It doesn't depict an east build-out, nor does it show the kind of design we're planning to construct. This will just give you an idea of the size of the hotel and how much of the land we'll take up once construction is finished."

I stole a quick glance at Cooper, grinning from the *east build-out* comment the architect had made.

He knew just what was making me smile.

And he reacted by shaking his head before he said, "The concern is the weight that the hotel is going to put on the soil and if it'll push the soil toward the shoreline, threatening erosion to the point where it's unsafe to build. Now, we don't have any data or proof that this will be the case, we're just taking every precaution and coming up with a backup plan if this does happen."

"While I was at the property, I collected soil samples from different locations around the lot," the architect said. "If we'd like to send them in for testing, at least the samples have been taken."

Cooper ran his thumb across his lips. "I think we can all agree that's a place to start."

There was a collective agreement from everyone around the table.

I gripped the armrests and said, "I think it's also worth mentioning that I've reached out to the governing officials in Alberta to discuss our concerns with them. I left a message, but so far, I haven't received a call back."

"A good step two," Walter said to me.

I reached inside my bag, grabbing the map I'd tucked in there before I left my house. "And possibly a step three." I stood, pushing my chair back to give myself enough room to spread the large paper over the table, finding myself much closer to Cooper in the process. "As you can see, this is a standard map of the lake."

"Clearly," Brady said, his voice dripping with sarcasm. "Why don't you tell us something we don't know?"

I ignored him and continued, "I've highlighted all the hotels that hug the lake. Those are in yellow. The ones that I've also circled in orange are hotels that are more comparable to ours in size. Now, we do intend to build the largest structure, so nothing like ours currently exists there, but at least these will give us something to go on."

"Except they give us nothing to go on," Brady said. "Because none of them are nearly as large as ours will be."

"Yes, that's what I did say," I countered.

Brady hadn't bothered with a tie, the top two buttons of his shirt undone, spreading a bit wider as he crossed his arms. "So, isn't this example of yours a waste of our time?"

He'd gone head-to-head with Rhett. Apparently, now, it was my turn.

I didn't mind. Men like Brady didn't scare me.

I smiled. "No, I don't believe it is. If none of these hotels are experiencing any issues with erosion, then we know the lot can hold their amount of weight. Rather than look for an entirely new piece of land and sell this one, our backup plan could be to build a hotel equal in size as one of those."

Brady's brows furrowed. "Which isn't what we want to do."

"You mean, what *you* don't want to do," I pressed. "You can't say *we* because I was never asked that question." I looked at Cooper, appreciating the amusement on his face now more than ever. "Correct me if I'm wrong, but this is a Cole and Spade project now, yes?"

Cooper instantly replied, "Yes."

"Then, like I was saying," I continued, "if we downsize here, on our current lot, and only take up half the land"—I placed my palm over the east side—"we can portion off the unused side and sell it. Before any of you say, *What about the lost revenue, going from twenty-two stories to fifteen?* We can make those fifteen floors suite-only."

I pointed just southeast on the map, where I'd drawn a purple square. "Right here, there's another lot for sale. This area is downtown Banff, about a forty-ish-minute drive from Lake Louise. It receives a huge amount of tourism, and it's an extremely popular ski destination. If we build a smaller hotel where we intended, we could build another one here. That's two—one on the lake and another in the middle of downtown with just enough space in between. We can go with completely different styles of design and offer different amenities. We could even go with an entirely different feel if that's what *we*"—I glared at Brady—"decide to do."

I pulled my hands back and brought my chair in closer, my arm brushing with Cooper's as I took a seat. "I would have run these ideas by you, but they came to me in the middle of the night when I couldn't sleep, and I didn't want to call and wake you."

Cooper raised his hands. I wasn't sure what he was going to do with them until I realized he was slapping them together, clapping at me. "Rowan... I'm fucking impressed."

A response that surprised me.

Especially when it came with a smile too.

"That makes two of us," Walter replied.

"And three," Jo added.

"You put in some good work," Macon added.

I squeezed Cooper's shoulder, silently thanking him. "I have one final suggestion," I offered. "Rhett isn't a soil expert, but he's a general contractor. He obtained his license because he thought it was an important skill to have with all the building Cole International has done over the years. I'm not saying we shouldn't consult the governing officials of Alberta or send in the soil for testing—all of that should certainly take place. But I also think it's worth discussing this with Rhett. He's going to look at this from a perspective that I'm assuming none of us have."

"Then, why wouldn't you bring him today?" Brady asked.

"Because—"

"I told her not to," Cooper said, interrupting me. "I didn't want this to turn into an argument between the Coles and the Spades, which, given the way you're treating Rowan, Brady, I can see that's exactly what would have happened if Rhett had walked through the door with her."

The room turned quiet again.

Cooper hadn't asked me not to bring Rhett; he hadn't even known I wanted us to consult with Rhett.

He'd given his brother a little fib.

But it was one that showed he had my back.

And it was that praise, that realization, that was singing inside my head.

Cooper turned his chair to face me. "I think talking to Rhett is an excellent idea. I'll reach out to him personally and set up a meeting for the three of us."

I felt the warmth move over my face as I whispered, "Perfect."

Chapter Twenty-One

COOPER

"What the fuck was that?" Brady asked me as I returned to the conference room after walking Rowan to the elevator.

I took the seat I'd been sitting in before, noticing the three vacant spots where Walter, Rowan, and the architect had been during our meeting. Macon, Jo, and Brady were now the only ones left.

And based on Brady's reaction the second I'd come through the door, I knew a talk was coming. I'd also gotten a text from him on my way back from the elevator that told me to return to the conference room.

Something was definitely up.

"What was what?" I questioned.

He swiveled forward and placed both forearms on the table. "You know exactly what I'm talking about."

The way I'd chimed in on his conversation with Rowan when they were discussing Rhett. The way I'd come at him when he'd been coming at Rowan.

I was just tired of the banter; it wasn't needed.

She'd held her own—there was no doubt about that—but it had gotten to the point where I wanted to step in and shut that motherfucker up.

"Because I stood up for her—is that your issue? Because she happened to be right?" I sighed, letting him know what I thought of this. "Come on, Brady. You were lighter on her than you are with her brothers, but your intentions were obvious to everyone in this fucking room. You just wanted to fight." I pushed myself higher in the seat and squared off my shoulders. "Let's be honest here. If I'd been the one who presented those ideas, you wouldn't have said shit. In fact, you probably would have clapped."

He shook his head, like he was disgusted. "She presented nothing special."

"And this is where I'm going to have to disagree with you." Macon looked from me to Brady. "Given the circumstances, she came up with some solid options. More than our own fucking brother came up with."

"Truth," I joked.

"That doesn't mean I like the Coles," Macon continued. "But Rowan proved herself today, and it's only fair to give her credit for that."

"Let's cut the bullshit, shall we?" Jo voiced. "This isn't about the options she came up with and presented. She could have solved every issue the Spades ever had, and we'd still have an issue with her. And if I'm being completely transparent with you guys, I don't like that about us or myself. We need to grow up." Jo linked her hands together and placed them on the table. "Rowan seems nice. Dedicated. Knowledgeable. And she isn't afraid to put Brady in his place, and I commend her for that."

"Fuck off," Brady groaned.

"She's all of those things," I said.

Brady leaned further into the table, his eyes squinting as he stared at me. "Why the hell are you so pro-Cole right now?"

I dragged my teeth over my bottom lip. "I'm not."

"Then, you're pro-Rowan," he clarified. "What, did you get fucking sweet on her while the two of you were in Canada this week?"

The second I showed any kind of softness, Brady would start digging. I had to choose my words carefully.

"Are you forgetting that before Walter and Ray gave us this company, I was told I had to partner with Rowan on the Lake Louise build-out?" I leaned back in my chair. "I could do that in one of two ways. I could fight her on everything and make things miserable for myself." Which I'd done very well. "Or we could somehow come together for the sake of the company and build the best hotel possible. Just like Jo said, I needed to grow up, and I'd be a goddamn idiot not to take the latter."

Brady continued to stare at me. "Do me a favor, brother. Look at Jo."

"What?"

"You heard me. Look at Jo," Brady repeated.

I glanced toward my cousin, unsure where he was going with this.

And then I heard, "Macon, do you see what I'm seeing?" from Brady.

I looked back at my older brother, trying to figure out what he meant. When I couldn't, I shifted my gaze to Macon and finally said to him, "Tell me you don't know what the hell he's talking about either."

"Oh, I know just what he's saying." A cockiness grew over Macon's face, which he then directed at Brady and said, "When Cooper looks at Jo—or probably any woman for that matter— he has a different expression on his face. But the second Rowan walked into the conference room this morning, he lit up like a fucking Christmas tree. He couldn't take his eyes off her the whole meeting."

They'd seen right through me.

Fuck me.

There was a vibration in my pocket. Hoping this would give me a break from this conversation, I took out my phone and read the text on the screen.

Rowan: *Thank you for today. I don't think I said that before I left. But I want you to know I appreciate you.*

"It's her, isn't it?" I heard.

I slipped the phone back into my pocket and replied to Brady, "Who?"

"Rowan," Brady said. "Because that smile is on your face again. The one Macon was just talking about. You had it when she walked in this morning, and it stayed until she left, reappearing when you just looked at your phone. But you know when it really peaked? When she grabbed your shoulder." He smiled at me, something my brother rarely did. "Yeah, you thought we missed that. We didn't." He pounded his fist on the table. "Why don't you tell us what this is really about, Cooper?"

"Jesus Christ," I groaned.

"Don't look at me," Jo said the moment I did. "Even though I noticed, too, I wasn't going to say a word about it until I could talk to you privately."

My hand immediately shot up and pressed against my forehead, swiping backward across my hair, only stopping when I reached my neck.

The conversation I'd had with Rowan at the bar had been eating away at me. Although it wasn't really much of a chat since she did all the talking and I mostly just listened. But it had been that moment when some of this shit really hit home. When she made me question how I'd been handling things. When I started to contemplate if I could somehow make this work.

Because, deep down, that was what I wanted.

I'd known that since I'd first met her in the bar before Christmas.

The only things that had changed during that time was that I'd found out she was a Cole and she'd become one of our partners.

But every day since I had found out who she was, I asked myself the same questions.

Do I want her?

Do I want this?

And every day, those answers were yes.

I just needed to give in, something I wasn't good at, and to find a way to make this work, which I knew was going to take some time and finessing.

This—here—was the first step.

"I'm going to tell you something that's going to blow all of your fucking minds." I filled my lungs, holding the air inside, feeling my chest pound. "You know the woman I met in Canada, who I spent all of Christmas with?"

"You mean the one you texted us about?" Macon asked.

I nodded. "That was Rowan."

"Shut the fuck up," Macon blurted out.

"I didn't know at the time that she was a Cole." I gripped the back of my neck, squeezing the muscle. "She never gave me her last name, and I didn't know Ray's daughter's name, so I wouldn't have made the connection."

Brady's head tilted. "But she knew who you were, didn't she?"

"Yes, she did."

"That was her first mistake," he hissed. "Be done with her."

"Hold on a second," Jo offered. "Can you blame her? If things were going well between you two—and it sounds like they were while you were in Canada—then she wasn't about to drop the Cole bomb and ruin it. At least I wouldn't have despite how wrong that is."

Brady glared at Jo and then at me. "When did she tell you?"

"When she walked into the Daltons' conference room. I about fucking lost it. But then I was able to piece together why she'd gone MIA after Canada. Why she hadn't wanted to give me her number. It all made sense—she hadn't wanted to tell me who she was." My hand dropped, and I grabbed the armrest. "It doesn't matter. None of that is even the point to this—"

"Oh, it's more than one point, it's two," Brady said. "Point one, she's a Cole. Point two, she's now a partner."

"Please don't tell me you're going to pull the partner card," Jo said to him. "I'm married to our attorney, and Macon's in a relationship with one of our senior-level employees. Even if we had a no-fraternization policy, which we don't, the two of you met and became something before the companies merged, which means the policy wouldn't apply to you. Since we don't have that policy, it's a moot point." Jo clicked the pen she was holding, like the boss that she was. "And, Brady, each of the points you just tried to make, well, in my opinion, they can be overlooked."

Brady pointed his thumb at Jo. "She's Team Cole too. What the fuck?"

"Why does there have to be sides?" she asked. "Can't we all just stop this fighting? I'm so tired of it."

"I am too," I agreed.

"Do any of you even know why we hate them so much?" Macon questioned. "I mean, how it all started?"

"No," I replied. "And I've been wondering the same damn thing. Aside from all the bullshit we've gone through with them over the years, the shady shit that went down behind our backs. The lost properties, the questionable marketing. Why have we grown up hating this family?" I loosened my tie, pulling the Windsor knot a few inches from my throat. "I don't recall a single memory where Dad or Uncle Walter ever mentioned their history with the Coles or when all this bullshit even began."

The room turned quiet.

"Do her brothers know about you and Rowan?" Macon asked.

"Nah." I took out my phone and set it on the table. "There was no reason to tell them anything since once I found out who she was"—I whistled out some air—"I pushed her as far away as I could."

"Don't tell me that's what you're still doing," Jo said softly.

I looked at my cousin and said nothing.

"Because by the way you were gazing at her, it certainly appeared like something was happening between you two," Jo continued.

Brady pushed back his chair, but didn't get up. "Wait. Is Jo right? Are you fucking dating her?"

"I'm figuring shit out." My eyes left his to glance at each of their faces. "Do any of you have a problem with that?"

"Yeah, me." My oldest brother was wearing such a scowl. "I don't know how I feel about it."

My hand left the armrest, and my arms crossed over my chest. "You can feel whatever you want. But it's not going to change how I feel about her."

"You're honestly telling me you really like her?" Brady pushed.

I wouldn't be able to take this moment back. Once the words were spoken, I couldn't edit them.

But I knew the way I'd been feeling lately; the fucking monster that had been digging into my chest had everything to do with wanting to be with her and feeling like I couldn't.

With that came anger. The lack of patience that was even worse than normal. A grumpiness that roared every time she was in my presence.

And then the night at the bar, everything changed.

She instantly brought a calm through my body.

She grounded me.

She made me consider opening the door when I'd done everything I could to keep it locked.

Fuck, I'd even gone as far as almost knocking on it.

Right before my hand touched down on the wood, I questioned if I could make it work. If I could settle the situation in my head because of the war between our families.

I didn't know if I could.

That was why I'd walked away from her room. Forced myself to get in the elevator and go downstairs.

But while we were in the bar and she stood between my legs with her hands on my shoulders, I'd realized something important.

It didn't fucking matter.

What mattered was us.

"Yes," I replied. "I'm telling you that I really like her."

"How do you think her brothers are going to react?" Jo asked carefully. "I'm worried that Rhett is going to try to eat you up and spit out your bones."

"Cooper's fucked because that's exactly what Rhett's going to do," Brady offered.

I shrugged. "Let him try."

Brady reached up and gripped the top of his chair. "That's all you're going to say? Our families somehow, someway have to be civil enough that we can run a business together. And you're about to light all the shit on fire."

I held my phone and leaned into the table. "I'm not lighting shit on fire. This war existed long before I had feelings for Rowan. What I'm going to do is get to the root of the problem and tackle it from there." I had no idea how, but I would. "And you're just going to have to play nice, Brady, and realize that the Coles aren't our enemy. They're three people who are going to double, if not triple, the billions we have in the bank."

I got up, tired of this conversation, and I walked to my office, closing my door behind me and taking a seat at my desk. My computer monitor showed there were over two hundred emails I needed to read and probably at least half I needed to reply to. There were folders overflowing the corner of my desk, papers I needed to look at and process. I had a meeting in an hour I needed to prep for.

But instead of handling any of it, I unlocked my phone and replied to Rowan's text.

Me: *I know you can hold your own, but I wanted you to see a little fight in me.*

Rowan: *Real talk: it was hot.*

Me: *It wasn't exactly honest, but, shit, I'd had enough of him.*

Rowan: *I'm the only one who will ever know, and that truth has been vaulted.*

Me: *You know…in a couple of weeks, I'll be able to walk down the hall to see you.*

Rowan: *A move you're looking forward to?*

Me: *Yes.*

Rowan: *You get more interesting by the second, Mr. Spade.*

Me: *I'm not done. You're about to see a whole lot more.*

Rowan: *I'm ready…*

Chapter Twenty-Two

ROWAN

"I told you I wasn't done," Cooper said once I opened my front door, "and that you were about to see a whole lot more."

A visit that hadn't been planned, taking me completely by surprise when, seconds ago, he'd called from my gate to let him in. With the two bags he was holding in his hands, I assumed he'd come straight from the grocery store, telling me this was going to be more than just a pop-in.

"Yes, you did. I just didn't expect it to happen so soon." But, man, I was so happy it had. I held the side of the door, blocking the entrance. "What if I wasn't home?"

"But you are."

"What if I hated surprises?"

"You don't."

I tugged at my lip, trying to hide the excitement on my face. "What if I wasn't hungry?"

He chuckled. "Then, I would have one fucking incredible dinner all by myself."

The cool air was turning his ears and the tip of his nose red, a look that was adorable on a man who was far too sexy to ever be described as adorable.

As he stood in front of me, wearing jeans that hugged him in a way that wasn't tight but showed off his muscular legs, his jacket open revealing a dark blue shirt underneath that played up the color of his eyes, I was trying to keep myself tamed.

But, my God, this dreamy alpha brought everything out in me.

More than just passion.

Tingles.

A smile that was growing by the second.

He made me feel...

"And what if I already ate?" I challenged.

"You don't eat this early." He shifted his weight. "And if I was to guess, you got home from work about an hour ago"—his eyes dipped down my body—"and immediately changed into the comfortable clothes you have on." His stare unhurriedly lifted, and every inch it rose was making it harder for me to breathe. "You poured yourself a glass of wine, and you were sitting in front of your computer, catching up on some emails, thinking about what you were in the mood to eat, but you didn't do anything about it. Then, I showed up."

"What, do you have some hidden camera on me?"

His smile was so handsome and charming; my bare toes drove into the hardwood floor beneath them to stay grounded.

"I know you better than you think I do, Rowan."

My arm rose to the highest part of the door that I could reach. "Why are you really here, Cooper?"

"I didn't like the way Brady spoke to you in the conference room this morning, and then I spent all day thinking about you. Sure, I could have called. I could have asked you to come out and grab something to eat with me. But I asked my private chef, Klark, to talk me through a step-by-step process of how to prepare short ribs with pappardelle instead, and I took my ass to the store." The softest smile made its way to his lips. "Now, I'm here."

"You've never cooked that before?"

"I don't cook. Not even for myself."

"But you're cooking for me…"

First, there had been the talk in the bar in Lake Louise. Then, there had been the meeting in his conference room where he had my back and the text exchange that followed. And now, he was here, doing this.

This was the man I'd originally met over Christmas.

I'd just never thought I'd ever see this version of him again.

My arm dropped, and I opened the door wide enough for him to come in.

"I can't explain why I wanted to cook for you. For a man who barely knows his way around his own kitchen, this is a bit of a stretch for me. But, shit, I want to do it." He took a step closer, our bodies now inches apart, his face slowly leaning down toward mine.

"Here's what else I can tell you. I want to make this dinner for you, and under no circumstances will anything else happen between us this evening." He moved both bags into one hand, holding my chin with the other. "I'm not going to strip your clothes off. I'm not going to lift you onto the counter and lick your pussy. I'm not going to carry you into your bedroom and fuck you for hours." He swiped my lips with his thumb. "Tonight is going to be different, Rowan."

If I'd thought it was hard to breathe before, I was positive, at this point, I couldn't draw in a single bit of air.

But where my lungs were tight, the rest of my body was experiencing something so opposite. A looseness that almost made me wobbly.

Cooper had always shown his affection through touch and

intimacy. He was suddenly taking that out of the equation. He was…courting me.

Spending time with me.

Telling me, through his actions, that he wanted more and was willing to take those steps.

And because of that, this overwhelming feeling rose through my body.

I didn't know what it was.

I didn't know what it was called.

I didn't even know how to describe it.

All I could do was take it and feel it—everywhere.

"All right, then," I whispered. "Show me how it's going to be different."

His lips landed on the side of my face, pressing into my cheek.

It was there that I felt him breathe me in.

That I felt the heat of his mouth.

That I felt the hardness of his body as we became aligned.

And it was that moment that showed me how well we fit together.

Not pieces of a puzzle—those edges were far too rounded. We were like jagged blades, his pointy spikes filling my hollow grooves.

"Bring me inside, Rowan."

As his lips left me, I swallowed, trying to encourage my body to move, gradually peeling myself off the side of the door, and I walked into my foyer, waiting for him to follow before I closed the door behind him.

He'd been here before, so he knew where to carry the groceries, and that was where he headed. Instead of joining him in the kitchen, I went to the bar, taking a tumbler off the shelf and filling it halfway with bourbon, bringing it into the kitchen, where he was setting all the ingredients on the counter.

"Looks like I really nailed that description." He nodded toward the end of the island, at my laptop and wine, where I'd been sitting before he came over.

I winked at him. "You did." I closed the screen and moved the laptop out of the way, but I held the wine and took a sip. "I was following up with the governing officials of Alberta. They finally got back to me."

"Any good news?" He began opening cabinets, eventually finding where I kept my pots and pans, and he took out a cast iron skillet.

"I explained our concerns, and they're going to investigate. It didn't sound like it was something they'd ever encountered. I'm not sure if that's a good thing or a bad thing."

He set the skillet on the gas range, placed a large pot next to it, and turned on the oven. "It means that whatever decision we go with has to be the right one, or we're fucked. Bringing it to their attention will put all the eyes on us."

I winced. "Oops."

He laughed. "No, you did the right thing. We always want to take the proper steps when it comes to building. Sometimes, the officials—in any county, state, or even country—just need to feel included. It doesn't hurt to butter them up a little. Sounds like you did that, and you'll end up doing a lot more of it."

I twirled the wineglass over the counter. "My positive deed for the day...you had one yourself, I hear."

After he opened the package of meat, he glanced up through his long golden-brown lashes. "You're talking about my phone call with Rhett?"

"*Mmhmm.*"

"Whoa, that dude is fucking feisty." He shook his head. "Once we made our way through some strong-ass banter, he said he needed to see the land in person. I had our assistants schedule a trip for the three of us. We leave in less than a week."

"So I've been told." I reached across the counter, putting my hand on his. "Thank you. You could have had me make that call… and you didn't."

"I'm not going to hide from the motherfucker. I'm also not going to tell him what's going on between us." He ran his teeth over his lip. "I'll leave that up to you."

"Fair enough." I sighed. "But the real question is, are we going to survive the Rhett and Brady shitstorms that'll rain down the second they find out about us?"

He laughed again. "Have I told you how fucking sexy it was to see you go head-to-head with my brother?" Without waiting for a reply, he continued, "I want you to know, I didn't chime in because I thought you needed help. I chimed in because the asshole wasn't going to stop. When he sniffs out blood, he goes right for the kill, and I wasn't going to listen to another second of it."

I watched him open a few drawers until he found my spices and he added garlic and other seasoning to the meat.

"I don't stop either, Cooper. Haven't you realized that about me yet? Like the other night in Canada, that wasn't the first time I'd brought up that topic. It was just the first time you responded to it the way I wanted you to." I grinned.

"*Mmm*, yes. And I love that about you."

"Honestly, Brady and Rhett are almost the same person, so I know how to deal with them and keep them from showing their fangs. But I appreciate you stepping in. It shows me you have my back, and *that* is sexy as hell."

He washed his hands and added water to the large pot, prepping it with salt for the pasta. "About that shitstorm… I told them."

I was about to pour myself a refill but froze. "Told who what?"

"My family." He added heat underneath the skillet, and the gas began to hiss. "After you left, I told them you're the same woman I met in Canada over Christmas—they had known I met someone there I liked, they just hadn't known it was you. Now, they do."

I rubbed my lips together, like I was wearing lip gloss but I wasn't. "And how exactly did you explain our situation?"

"I told them we're figuring things out." He turned around, letting the meat cook behind him, to lock eyes with me. "And that I really like you."

I felt my lids widen. "Wow."

"Too much?"

"No." My head shook. "The perfect amount." I took a moment before I continued, "How did they take it?"

"Are you sure you want to hear?"

My heart began to pound. "Yes. No. But yes."

"Macon is so easygoing. He doesn't have love for the Coles quite yet, but he doesn't have a problem with us." He took out the bag of fresh pappardelle. "As for Jo, she gave you several compliments, she likes you. And she gets it better than anyone, probably due to the way her relationship started with Jenner—a story I'll tell you someday."

A story I couldn't wait to hear.

It was no coincidence he'd left the best for last.

"And Brady?" I exhaled. "I'm sure he had plenty to say."

He placed the few veggies he'd brought on a cutting board and found a knife to chop them with. "Nothing will ever please him. I stopped trying a long time ago. It's just who he is, and I've accepted that. Still, I saw no reason to hide what's going on from any of them."

He had known Brady was going to give him an earful, and he'd still gone through with it. And what that showed me was that he wanted more.

He wanted...

I stared at him in awe. "You're that sure of...us? Huh?"

His actions were enough; I just wanted the words too.

He came closer, and when he reached me, he cupped my cheeks, tilting my chin until I was fully facing him. "I think you know that if I wasn't, I wouldn't have said anything to them. I also wouldn't be here right now."

I one million percent knew that.

But I still had questions.

"Why, Cooper? What caused this change?"

"It's not the remarkable answer that you're probably looking for."

I scanned his eyes. "I just want the truth. I don't care what that looks or sounds like."

He pressed his nose against mine, his eyelids closing. "I kept telling myself that once you withheld your identity, there was no turning back, but that was only an excuse. And then I kept telling myself that you're a partner, and that was an excuse. And then I harped on you being a Cole, which became another excuse." He pulled away to gaze at me, his hands staying in place. "I was afraid that if we got together, it would add even more tension between the families, and it would jeopardize the future of the company. But then I realized, that kind of weight isn't on me. You and I, we don't have that kind of power, and it's not our responsibility to hold things together. It takes all of us to do that, and if the company implodes, it certainly won't be because I'm dating one of the partners." A streak of pain shot across his face, and I knew that was because he cared so much about this business. "Far bigger issues than that will be our breaking point—if we have one."

A realization that hadn't come easy for him.

Not when he had given his whole life to Spade Hotels. Not

when someone cared as much as he did about what his family thought.

"You know, your father and Walter gave zero fucks when they merged us. What they've both repeatedly said is that it's going to work out." His thumbs rubbed around my lips. "You and me, we're merging as well. Our situation is no different, so we should give zero fucks about what the others think."

I nodded. "That makes a lot of sense, Cooper."

"If anyone asks, I'm going to repeat what my uncle keeps saying and tell them it's all going to work out. But I can tell you right now, we're not going to take the blame for anything that happens. I don't care what any of them say, if something goes down, we're not at fault."

"Nothing is going to happen." Except for falling in love—a word that smacked me so hard that my lips pursed while my lungs exhaled. "But you're right—again."

"I don't know if this is going to be easy, Rowan. I don't know how they're going to react when they all find out and see us together or how much shit we're going to have to navigate—if any. But I don't care. I'm in this. All the way." He held me tighter. "And if it takes a fight beyond fighting for you, then I'm fucking ready."

Chapter Twenty-Three

COOPER

I hadn't planned on spending the night at Rowan's. I'd intended to just go over and cook us dinner, clean up, and hang out for a little while. But as we lay on her couch with a movie playing in the background, the bourbon and wine kicking in, we got to talking about work and Lake Louise, our individual goals for the merger and the future, and we ended up falling asleep. It was sometime in the middle of the night that we both woke at the same exact moment, and I lifted her off the couch and carried her into her bedroom, crawling in next to her.

My mental alarm had me rising a little after six. Since Rowan was still sleeping, I went into the kitchen and got some breakfast ready. Another meal I never typically cooked for myself. Klark always had something prepared that I just had to stick in the microwave.

But at her house, I fried up some eggs and toasted a few slices of bread and cut up the strawberries and pineapple I'd found in the fridge. I was just plating it all when I heard the sound of her bare feet stepping across the hardwood floor. When she rounded the corner of the kitchen, I noticed she'd added a cardigan to the outfit she'd fallen asleep in, and as she stopped at the base of the island, she pulled both sides of the sweater around her.

God, she was fucking beautiful in the morning. There was no makeup left on her face, and her hair was a little rowdy. Her eyes big and curious.

"I thought you'd left...like last time."

Last time.

It had been an asshole move to rush out of her house after I fucked her.

Not my proudest moment, especially considering where we were now.

I slid the egg onto her toast and set the frying pan in the sink, freeing up my hands so when I turned to her, I could pull her into my arms. "I wouldn't leave without kissing you goodbye."

Her face warmed with a smile. "I love that. But also, you'd better not." She wrapped her arms around my waist and gazed up at me. "I see that you cooked. Again. And given that last night's dinner was one of the best meals I'd ever had, I'm pretty excited to taste whatever you whipped up."

I held the sides of her face and gave her a gentle peck. "It was good, for sure, but you might be giving me a little too much credit."

"Stop. It was excellent."

I gave her another kiss, but I moved carefully. Putting my lips anywhere on Rowan triggered every fucking feeling in my body. There had been moments last night when I had to do everything in my power not to try to take things further. The only reason I hadn't was because I wanted her to know we could spend time together without me tearing her clothes off.

But, damn it, I'd wanted to.

And I was having a hell of a time fighting that want right now.

I needed to get my mind off how gorgeous she looked, how

tight her pussy would feel on my dick, how wet she would be after I licked her.

Fuck.

So, I asked, "What's your day look like?"

"I'm going to check in again with the Alberta officials and see if I can do some buttering up, like you suggested last night, and then I want to start going over some of the designs the architect sent. They look good, but I want to really dig in and add my own spin." She traced her fingers up my lower back. "I can't believe he threw together two options so quickly. It's one thing to have the full build-out ready since that was our original idea, but to have already put together something for the half-size project? Now, that's impressive."

"Well, you had an impressive, badass pitch."

She laughed. "I wouldn't call it a pitch. I just wanted to come in with a few ideas. You know, in case you decided to question my knowledge or ability again." She winked.

"I didn't..."

"You did. But I forgive you."

"And, look, you hit it out of the park."

"I'll do even better once I get to the bottom of this, and I—I mean, we—can really start planning." She grinned, letting me know the wording hadn't been a mistake, and she tightened her grip around me. "The land I found in downtown Banff needs a bit more of my attention. I want to see what I can find out about it. I know it's for sale, but I want to see if it's truly a viable option."

I pushed the hair off her face. "Has Jenner checked out the land?"

"I sent him the info yesterday afternoon. I copied you on all those emails—didn't you read them?"

I released her and reached for the plates, waiting for her arms to drop before I carried them to the table. During my second pass,

I brought the two mugs of coffee I'd made and sat across from her. "I didn't get through my email yesterday."

She took a sip of her coffee. "That's not like you."

"My brain was preoccupied, and my productivity was shit." I popped a strawberry into my mouth.

"Oh, yeah?" Her eyes narrowed. "With what?"

"You."

Her cheeks turned a light shade of pink as she pointed at her chest. "Me? What about me?"

"A little of everything."

She bit off the corner of her toast. "*Mmm*. Delicious." She finished chewing and added, "Now, tell me all the things, Cooper."

"All the things," I repeated.

Her eyes widened as she nodded.

"I don't know... I just couldn't get you out of my mind. I thought about what you'd said to me at the bar. The way you always look at me. How it felt when you touched me in the conference room. How I feel when I'm around you. That I can't seem to be able to get enough of you...like now, fuck, I don't even want to go to work."

"And again, that's not like you at all."

"No."

"Tell me something. What does it feel like?" Her voice was so light; it was just above a whisper.

"You mean inside my body?"

"Yes." She set her hands on the table. "I want to know if I'm feeling the same thing."

I glanced toward the window, a view of the Hollywood Hills outside, trying to find the right words that would describe this sensation. "It's like someone lit a match under my feet." My eyes locked with hers. "And from there, it's spread to every part of my body. A fire. But it's not a burning. It feels more like..."

"A tingling."

"Yeah," I agreed, really thinking about that word. "Exactly." I reached across the table until my hand was on hers. "I'm going to be honest, Rowan." As I paused, I took in her eyes, and I slowly took a breath. "I don't know what this feeling is called."

"I don't either."

"But I'll tell you something else… I don't want it to go away."

• • •

Me: *Any luck with the Alberta officials?*

Rowan: *You still haven't checked your email? Because the answer is waiting for you in your inbox.*

Me: *I just wanted an excuse to talk to you.*

Rowan: *You don't need an excuse, Cooper.*

Rowan: *Just like you didn't need an excuse to show up at my house…and stay the night.*

Me: *Best night of sleep I've had in a long time.*

Rowan: *Me too. I'm ready to do it again.*

Me: *Next time, I can't promise I'm going to keep my hands off you.*

Rowan: *I don't want you to…*

Chapter Twenty-Four

Rowan

Me: *Since you don't check your email, LOL, I thought I'd let you know that I did some digging. Jenner did too. The land in downtown Banff is a solid contender. It can give us everything we need should we need it.*

Cooper: *I heard the architect sent in the soil samples.*

Me: *So, you do check your email.*

Cooper: *I can't say my productivity has been any better today, but, yeah, I skimmed the messages that came in.*

Me: *What am I going to do with you?*

Cooper: *How about…what are you going to do to me?*

Me: *Ohhh, yesss. Tonight?*

Cooper: *Can't tonight. I'm going out with my brothers to catch up. It'll be a late one. I don't know what time I'd show up and what drunken state I'd be in. Rain check?*

Me: *And the Coles weren't invited to tag along? That's not very company culture-like of you.*

Me: *Kidding. Obviously.*

Cooper: *Sorry to say, I think it's going to be a long time* *before Rhett gets an invite to one of our Spade nights out.*

Me: *Sigh.*

Cooper: *We'll get there…*

Me: *Okay, Walter.*

Me: *You sound just like him.*

Cooper: *It's becoming my standard answer for everything lately.*

Me: *I think you're manifesting peace.*

Cooper: *I'm manifesting normalcy so when we all move in together, it's not hell.*

Me: *That too.*

• • •

Cooper: *Did you see the itinerary your assistant sent for our trip to Lake Louise?*

Me: *I've been in a meeting for the last hour and just saw it. I thought Rhett was flying there with us? And now, he's not coming until the day after we arrive. Let me talk to him and find out what's going on.*

Cooper: *I'm not complaining…*

Me: *Shush.*

Me: *He's going to be in Boston, working on another project, and he didn't know how long that was going to hold him up. So, yes, he's just going to meet us there the following day.*

Cooper: *That means I get you all to myself for an entire day and night in Canada.*

Me: *It does.*

Me: *What are you going to do with me?*

Cooper: *I have ideas.*

Me: *Which are?*

Cooper: *It's cute that you think I'd tell you.*

Me: *I'm positive I could get it out of you.*

Cooper: *How?*

Me: *Come on. I know your weakness, and it involves my mouth. It wouldn't be hard—getting it out of you, I mean. LOL.*

Cooper: *Are you talking naughty to me, Rowan?*

Me: *;)*

• • •

Me: *Have fun with your brothers tonight.*

Cooper: *You're sweet.*

Cooper: *I fully expect half the conversations to be about you.*

Me: *Because Brady just can't help himself. No offense, he's a dick.*

Cooper: *I can't help myself either. Am I also a dick?*

Me: *You were, yes. A giant one. Ha-ha.*

Me: *If it makes you feel any better, I'll be hanging with Sky, who's going to want to discuss the same thing. She's the only one I can talk to about you. I'm still waiting for the right time to tell my brothers—and, ugh, that time just hasn't presented itself yet.*

Cooper: *I get it. What are you going to tell Sky?*

Me: *That I've kinda fallen for you.*

Me: *And trust me, she already knows that, but she's going to hear it again.*

Cooper: *That feeling…it's there even when I'm not with you.*

Me: *Same.*

• • •

Cooper: *I'm sure you're asleep, but I just got home and wanted to say good night.*

. . .

Me: *Best message to wake up to. Did you have a blast last night?*

Cooper: *All I've got to say is that it's a good thing our offices haven't merged yet. You would have seen the result of some serious debauchery. Things weren't pretty this morning for any of us. I honestly can't believe we even made it in.*

Me: *Hungover?*

Cooper: *Half dead.*

Me: *But I want to see that. I want to see every side of you.*

Cooper: *God, that's sexy.*

. . .

Cooper: *I don't like that it's been two sleeps since I've seen you.*

Me: *I almost slept at the office last night. This merger is creating more work than I anticipated. Are things as stressful over there as they are here?*

Cooper: *It's been rough—I can't lie.*

Me: *I'd kill for rough. It's been brutal.*

Cooper: *Let me take you out tonight and get your mind off it. I promise to keep you so occupied that you won't remember you even have a job.*

Me: *I want that. So much. But I'm going to be here until at least ten. And then I need to go home and pack because I won't have time to do it tomorrow night. It's my niece's birthday, and it's a whole thing.*

Cooper: *Ridge's daughter?*

Me: *Our little Daisy, yes.*

Cooper: *That means I won't see you until our flight to Banff.*

Me: *Miss me?*

Cooper: *Fuck yes.*

Me: *Good.*

Chapter Twenty-Five

COOPER

I helped Rowan into the backseat of the SUV and slid in beside her, immediately putting my arm around her shoulders, my lips against the side of her head. That apple and cedarwood scent—fuck, I couldn't get enough of it.

"Now that dinner's done, there are a few things we can do," I said to her, the vehicle still parked, the driver waiting for his next instruction. "I know you've been stressed, and I'm sure you're exhausted, so I didn't want to make our night as busy as I made our day, but there are two ideas I came up with."

"Getting pampered was extra tough," she joked, referring to the masseuse I'd hired to fly with us to Banff so she could give Rowan a ninety-minute massage during the flight.

Once we had checked into the hotel, a bubble bath followed before we ate lunch in front of the fireplace in my suite. The afternoon was spent driving to downtown Banff so we could check out the property she'd found that would hold our second location, should we need one. And after coming back and getting ready, dinner had been at the town's highest-rated steak house.

"Today honestly couldn't have been more perfect, Cooper." She rubbed her stomach over her jacket. "And now, I'm so stuffed."

"Good." I gave her a quick kiss. "As for the options, one is to go ice-skating. There's a rink about fifteen minutes from here, and we can go check it out. Or we can go back to the hotel and get a nightcap at the bar and call it an early-ish evening—"

"I want that." She put her mitten-covered hand on my cheek. "It's been far too many nights since you last stayed at my house. Rhett arrives tomorrow. Let's soak in every second we have left." She lowered her voice as she added, "Alone."

"You read my fucking mind." I leaned toward the front seat. "You can take us back to the hotel. Thank you."

As the driver pulled away from the restaurant, Rowan rested her head on my shoulder. "So, interesting tidbit: I've never been ice-skating."

"Really?"

"Sounds funny now that I say it out loud. It's something I probably should have done by now."

I kissed the top of her head. "You hate the cold. If you loved it, then, yes, it would sound funny that you hadn't gone."

She glanced up at me. "I'm guessing you've been? And you're probably really good?"

"I played a little hockey back in the day." I smiled.

"You did?"

"All throughout high school. I wasn't looking to play at a college level, so I stopped after my senior year, and I've only been on skates a few times since."

She straightened her head, shifting in her seat to turn toward me. "Why didn't you want to continue playing?"

I sighed. "My father asked me that same question on fucking repeat."

"I'm sorry—"

"Nah, I don't mean it that way. I mean, he just didn't understand my reasoning. He pushed hard and was disappointed when I turned down the offers that came in." I stole a quick glance out the window. "Being a college athlete is a ton of work. I knew that because I was friends with several guys a few years older than me in high school who accepted scholarships, and when they came home on break, they'd tell me all about it." I rubbed my hand over my pants to warm it up before I slid those fingers around her neck. "Back then, I didn't want that level of commitment, not when I'd worked all through high school at Spade Hotels. I just needed a break. I was looking to have fun and enjoy every last second of freedom until I graduated and went to work full-time for the company."

"I get it." She nodded. "So, did you have as much fun as you'd hoped?"

"*Yesss*," I hissed with a laugh. "I probably took it to the extreme." Four years I wasn't going to get into because I didn't think she'd want to hear about the women and the parties and the fucking mayhem. "Did you play any sports, growing up?"

"I didn't. I'm really not much of an athlete. If a ball comes flying at me, I duck. I make no effort to catch it because, one, I won't be able to, and, two, I'll end up hurting myself in some way."

I spread my fingers across her neck, rubbing the base of her jaw. "I'll make sure not to plan anything sports-related for us."

"Unless it's skiing, please don't, thank *youuu*." She giggled. "But I totally get why you didn't want to play at a college level, and I disagree with your dad. Kids need to be kids at that age, and there's nothing wrong with wanting that." She paused. "My dad was just as much of a hard-ass if it makes you feel any better."

"I had a feeling we grew up similarly."

"You know, he always treated me the same as the boys, but I felt like—even now—he expected more from me than them. My brothers wanted to be part of the company from day one. It wasn't that I didn't, I worried what it would be like to work for my father. If the expectations would tarnish the pedestal that I'd put Cole International on."

"But you finally caved."

"Not before I could prove to myself that I could be a success without my father's help. I needed that first." I could feel her take a deep breath. "Without that achievement, I wouldn't have ever joined, I don't think."

"Do you miss what was yours?"

"*Ohhh*, good question." She took a moment to continue. "I miss the ladies who worked for me and the customers. I miss traveling to Europe to meet with the designers and then styling the different pieces I bought there, which I only did for a handful of my regulars."

"It fulfilled you." My voice was quiet.

"It absolutely did."

"Are you getting that same feeling from the hotel business?"

"It's funny, when I joined Cole International, the first project I was going to spearhead myself was Lake Louise. That was going to be my baby. I hadn't been that excited about work in a long time. And my father was giving me all the control, so I could do things any way I wanted as long as I maintained the Cole branding." She glanced down. "I know you thought the same would be true for you, that Walter was giving you the build-out and that hotel was going to be yours. I'm sorry we're in this situation. I know it's not what either of us wanted."

I lifted her face until it was pointed at me. "Do you feel like I took the hotel away from you?"

Her hand went to my leg, her eyes now holding mine, even in the dark. "Took it away from me? Definitely not. Teaching me how to compromise and see things the Spade way? Yes."

My hand slid up to her cheek, my fingers sinking into her hair. "I promise we'll make it work in a way where we'll both be happy."

She nodded. "I believe that, and I promise that however this project turns out, whether it's one building or two or if we don't even end up here and we decide to do construction somewhere else, I'll work with you, not against you. I want this hotel to be something we both love."

Before she could say another word, I pressed my lips against hers.

Damn, this woman was perfect. Right down to the way she tasted. The sweetness on her tongue made every part of me throb.

I'd been thinking about this night for the last week. The chance to finally spend time with her.

And so far, it had gone just the way I'd wanted it to.

I pulled my lips away as the SUV came to a stop in front of our hotel. I opened the backseat door, climbed out, and helped her onto the ground, thanking the driver before I led her inside. My hand stayed on her lower back as I walked her to the bar, locating two seats on the far side.

As she reached her stool, Rowan slipped off her jacket, revealing the sexiest emerald-colored dress underneath, one I'd been staring at all through dinner.

One I couldn't fucking wait to strip off her body.

"You have no idea what you're doing to me right now," I growled in her ear.

She smiled as she placed the coat on the back of her stool, along with her purse. "You like green, huh?"

"I like you."

"What if I were wearing red?"

"It wouldn't make a bit of a difference. Any color, style, fabric—at the end of the night, it's all going to end up on the floor."

She laughed, and when the bartender approached, she said,

"An extra-dirty martini, shaken really, really well, please."

"So, there are ice chips on top," I added, which was the only way to make a martini.

"You got it," the bartender replied. "Regular or blue cheese olives?"

"Regular," she requested.

"And for you?" he asked me.

I'd been in the mood for bourbon, but, shit, that martini sounded good.

"I'll have the same," I told him.

I turned toward her, keeping my jacket on because I didn't intend for us to stay down here long.

And because every fucking second we were in this bar, my dick was growing harder.

"There's something about this bar that I just love." She scanned the entire area before her eyes returned to me. "I don't know if it's the shape or the way it's laid out. How the drinks are always so good or if it's even the decor."

I slipped my arm around the back of her. "It's none of those things."

"No?"

I pointed across the bar. "It's because that spot right there is where you met me." I waited for her eyes to return. "That's why you love it."

"The start of…so much."

"Listen"—I leaned into her neck, the dress low-cut so her whole throat was revealed, along with her collarbone and chest, and aside from the thin straps on her shoulders, her arms were bare—"if it had been easy, it wouldn't feel as good as it does now."

"You're saying I wouldn't want you as badly?"

I kissed right below her ear and leaned back. "I'm saying it was worth the fight."

"I hope you're not done fighting, mister. I'd say you still have a long way to go." She winked.

"Is that so?"

"*Mmhmm.*" She picked up the martini the bartender had just placed down and waited for me to lift mine before she continued, "To Lake Louise. Without this magical place, there would be no us."

"Us…"

"Don't even tell me that word scares you."

I shook my head. "Not even close." I clinked my glass against hers and took a drink.

Just as I was setting it back on the bar top, my pocket vibrated. I'd silenced my phone for the evening, only calls from my short Favorites list could get through. I reached inside, took it out of my pocket, and saw Jo's name on the screen.

She knew where I was and who I was with.

The call had to be important.

"I have to take this," I said to Rowan. "Give me just a few minutes, and I'll be back."

"No problem."

I stepped away from the bar and moved toward the lobby, holding the phone to my face. "Jo, what's up?"

"Are you alone?"

I leaned against a pillar that ran from the floor to the ceiling and faced the bar. The view was of Rowan's back, her hair dangling halfway toward her ass, her arms resting on the bar top, where her fingers were wrapped around the thin stem of the glass.

God, even this angle was fucking gorgeous.

"I am now, yes," I replied.

"I want to talk to you about something that I found out tonight."

"All right."

"Shit, Cooper, this is heavy. I don't even know where to start."

Heavy?

I focused on Rowan. "Start at the beginning but keep it quick. Rowan is waiting for me."

"I need you to promise you won't hang up with me and tell her anything we've just talked about."

My brows rose. "What do you mean, Jo?"

"I mean, what I'm about to tell you is serious. Like, super serious, Cooper. I need to know that you'll keep it between us. I'm not even telling Brady or Macon. Just you."

What the fuck was she talking about?

Why was she only telling me?

And why the hell couldn't I say anything to Rowan?

"Go on. You have my word."

A few seconds ticked by before she said, "I was at my dad's house tonight, having dinner with him. It was just the two of us, and we were almost two bottles deep. I'm positive that's the only reason we began talking about the Coles. Not work-wise. I'm talking about as people. Who they are outside the walls of the office. I'm also positive that the wine is the only reason Dad opened up to me. You know him. He's a vault with no door. He doesn't overshare. He doesn't even gossip."

"I know."

"But this had to be eating at him, and he clearly had to get it out. Because, out of nowhere, a look came over his face, and suddenly, he was getting emotional."

The back of my head hit the pillar. "Walter…got emotional?"

"Yep."

"Over what?"

"Ray…"

"What the fuck are you about to tell me, Jo?"

Chapter Twenty-Six

ROWAN

"Is everything okay?" I asked Cooper as he rejoined me at the bar.

He'd been gone for probably close to ten minutes. And during that time, my stare had swept the entire bar and as much of the lobby as I could see, finding him halfway between both areas, his back pressed against one of the extravagant pillars with the most serious expression on his face.

"Yeah, yeah." He picked up his martini and took a drink. That one sip must not have satisfied him enough because he shot back all the vodka that was left in the glass. "I apologize for being gone so long."

Something inside me caused me to say, "Do you want to talk about it?"

He set the empty down and turned toward me, his demeanor suddenly much more laid-back, his shoulders relaxing and lowering. "Talk about what?"

"Whatever that phone call was about."

I wasn't sure if he was upset, but I could definitely tell he was attempting to calm himself down. Whatever had brewed—or was still brewing—I wanted to help with.

He chuckled first and then held my cheek as he kissed my forehead. "All's good." He tucked the hair away from my face as he stared at me. "Since we got on the plane this morning, everything has been perfect."

I nodded. "Agreed." I wasn't sure if I should push harder to get him to discuss things. I decided to tread carefully and said, "If you want to talk about it, I'm here to listen."

He held me a little tighter, the look on his face shifting to pure dominance. "What I want is to get you up to my suite."

And what I wanted, aside from his attention and the way he was going to make my body feel, was just a bit of vulnerability.

There were moments when he was inside of me that I felt Cooper at his rawest.

I wanted to feel that tonight.

I wanted to see it.

I wanted to know that he was okay after whatever had just gone down during that phone call.

I smiled. "How long do I have to wait?"

"*Mmm.*" He moved in closer, but didn't kiss me. "You don't."

I rubbed my hand over his thigh. "Then, let's go now."

He called over the bartender and said, "I'll charge these drinks to my room."

The bartender produced a bill that Cooper signed, and the moment the leather billfold was closed, the pen no longer in his hand, he stood. He took my jacket and purse off the back of my chair and held out his hand for me to take. With our fingers clasped, I got up, his grip then moving to my lower back as we walked through the lobby toward the elevator.

I could feel the neediness in the way he held me. How his fingers rose to the spot on my back that wasn't covered by the dress, thirsty in the way they circled that area, possessively lowering to my ass.

A feeling that told me the moment I stepped into his room, I'd be naked.

I went inside the elevator and turned at the back wall, meeting his face the second he pressed the button for our floor.

"I'm surprised you're not stopping the elevator so you can have me right now," I joked.

"I thought about it."

"And?"

He nodded upward. "There's a camera in the corner up there. There's not a chance that I'd let security or someone at the front desk see any part of your body." His hands went to my waist, his mouth to my neck.

His kisses weren't just passionate; they showed control.

"Not willing to share me..." I exhaled.

"I don't share what's mine, Rowan." He kissed up the side of my neck to my ear, sucking the lobe before he added, "Which means there isn't a motherfucker in this world who's going to see what's underneath that dress. That's only for me."

There were different levels of ownership, and this one was so hot.

My head leaned back into the wall, and I moaned.

"It's been far too long since I've tasted your pussy. I think I need to remind her just how much she's mine."

I didn't know how, but he was holding some of my weight, my frame feeling so tiny within his muscular arms.

"I can't fucking wait to taste her, Rowan."

As his words hit me, I couldn't breathe.

I couldn't think beyond the image of his mouth between my legs.

That was the only thing I could focus on, aside from the fact that this elevator needed to hurry, the doors needed to open, and I needed to get inside his room.

"Do you want that?" He exhaled against my ear. "Do you want me to lick your cunt until you come?"

If there were words, I didn't have them.

I couldn't even attempt to form a single syllable.

Between the way his air was hitting my bare skin and his lips pressed against me and the presence of his body so close to mine, I was gone.

So, all I could do was moan again. "*Mmm.*"

"It's a good fucking thing you're not going to have to wait much longer," he whispered. "I don't think either of us could handle that."

Just as he finished speaking, the doors opened.

So did my eyelids, which I hadn't even realized were closed.

His hand clasped around mine, and we rushed out of the elevator and down the hallway until we arrived at his room.

"Hold these for just a second." He set my jacket and purse in my arms while he grabbed his wallet from his pocket, removing the room key from inside.

While he scooped the jacket and purse from my arms, I slid my hand around the back of his neck. "Kiss me." I took in his eyes. "I need your lips. Now."

I didn't know what had come over me.

What had caused me to be so demanding.

What had made me keep him in this hallway rather than go into his room.

But this need was pulsing so hard and so fast inside me that I couldn't go another second without feeling his lips on mine.

Without any hesitation, he slammed our mouths together, aligning our bodies, holding me against the wall, where all I could feel was the hardness behind me and in front of me.

He kissed me like we'd just said our vows.

Like there was nothing more important than locking our lips.

Like he could stand here all night, giving me everything I'd ever wanted.

I never understood the concept of time being frozen.

I'd only experienced the opposite. Where life seemed to move too fast. Where I hung on to each second, desperate to make it last longer.

But here, in this hallway, I finally understood.

Because everything had completely melted away.

It was just us.

Our lust.

Passion.

Desire.

Oh God.

The thought that within the next few minutes, he was going to inhale every inch of my skin.

I couldn't wait—

"What the fuck?!" I heard, yelled in the angriest roar, immediately cutting off my thoughts.

What the...*fuck*?

Before I could react—or even think—Cooper and I were suddenly pulled apart; the sensation of him leaving me was like a suction cup being peeled off a flat surface.

The sound, the movement, the speed in which he left me all made my eyes fly open.

Once they did, my heart sank.

My entire body stiffened as I processed exactly what I was seeing.

Time was no longer frozen.

It couldn't be. Not when Rhett was standing in front of Cooper, snarling as he looked at him, his position telling me that he'd pulled Cooper away from me, and now, his arm was raised, and his fist was flying through the air.

"No!" I screamed as my brother attempted to punch Cooper in the face.

Cooper dodged Rhett's flying fist, and having a feeling that Cooper was going to retaliate by throwing his own punch, I moved in between the men. I spread my arms wide, keeping Cooper behind me.

"Rhett, stop it right now!"

"You want me to fucking stop?" My brother was trying to reach past me, attempting to get his hands on Cooper, but I wouldn't let him, swatting his hand away every time he tried.

But Rhett was only half the battle.

I was also wrangling with Cooper, who was trying to move around me, doing what he could to get his hands on Rhett.

I wasn't going to allow any of it.

Not even when Cooper said, "Get out of my way, Rowan." His voice was calm but extremely sharp and dripping with ice. "I'm going to fucking kill your brother."

"Kill me?" Rhett shouted back. "Your hands were all over my fucking sister. So were your lips. I'm the one who's about to kill you." He attempted a side move, which I blocked. "Who the hell do you think you are, Spade?" He was moving like he was in a boxing ring, his feet quick, his concentration directed on his enemy. "How dare you touch her!"

"He's my boyfriend." I put my hand on Rhett's chest, hoping the contact would settle him, but he didn't even look at me. Not even when I added, "That's who he is."

"Rowan, I don't need you to protect me." Cooper was doing everything but lifting me, yet nothing was getting me out of the way. I was far too determined. If I stayed in the middle, I knew neither side would throw a punch. "If your brother wants to fight,

I'll gladly give him the beating he needs. It's about time I kicked his ass."

Both men were panting, pushing against me to get to the other.

"No!" I looked over my shoulder and then at Rhett. "Neither of you are fighting—do you hear me?"

"I'm going to rip his fucking face off," Rhett promised.

"Both of you, stop!" I lifted my hand off Rhett's chest and waved it in front of his face, getting his eyes to focus on me. "You're not hearing me. I'm telling you Cooper is my boyfriend. You're not going to do anything to him—do you understand?"

It was as though the words had finally hit him.

Which was confirmed when a whole new level of rage rolled across his face. "He's...*what*?"

"My boyfriend." I paused. "It's been going on since my very first trip to Canada." A statement that wasn't fully accurate, but minor details didn't matter now. "I didn't tell you because I felt like I couldn't." I took a breath. "But I wanted to, and I've needed to, and I've just been waiting for the right time when you, Ridge, and I were all face-to-face because I wasn't going to have this conversation over text."

He shook his head, the movement almost violent. "I don't believe you. You're just bullshitting me." He avoided Cooper's eyes. "You wouldn't date him. You wouldn't do that to our family."

Rhett's protectiveness of me caused him to be a ticking time bomb that was going to detonate at any second. Because I didn't know how he was analyzing any of this, I wanted to make it clear that what he had seen wasn't our first kiss. That Cooper and I were far more than a one-night stand. That we were actually something.

I felt that would hold much more weight than anything else I could say.

But that wasn't enough. So, I tried to add, "Rhett, I care about him—"

"Fuck you." He was pointing at Cooper. "It's one thing to play dirty, but to go after my sister? That makes you a fucking slimeball—you know that?" He stared him down. "That's so low... even for a Spade."

"You can call me whatever you want, but don't pretend to know how I feel about her or go and throw accusations around that aren't true," Cooper said. "You know nothing, Rhett—about us or the situation. But what I can tell you is that whether you approve of us or not, that won't change a thing." His hand went to my stomach. "She's mine."

Rhett's stare dipped to Cooper's hand and lifted back up to his face. "You're lucky she's standing between us. If she weren't, you wouldn't be walking out of this hotel alive." He shoved his hands through the sides of his hair, and that was when he finally looked at me. "This is un-fucking-believable." His top lip lifted, like he was about to snarl. "Rowan, tell me this is all a lie. That you're not with him—"

"I'm with him, Rhett. And I'm telling you, I really care about him."

Rhett was breathing heavily, and I could hear his fury in every exhale. "Wow. You're better than I thought you were, Spade. Better than I ever gave you credit for. This is some serious mindfuckery."

He clapped his hands together several times. "You really outdid yourself by going all out to fuck my family, didn't you?"

His fingers then balled into a fist. "Why? For what? So you could piss on the enemy? Because you somehow thought this would give you the upper hand? So you could go around saying you fucked a Cole? Why, Cooper? Explain this to me because I don't understand why you would do this—"

"Because I love her," Cooper said, his hand tightening on me. "That's the reason I did this. There is no other explanation."

Cooper's response slapped me.

It then slipped inside my body and shot straight down to my toes.

He loved me.

A word neither of us knew the meaning of.

But was that still true?

Wasn't I showing Rhett how much I loved this man?

"You love her." Rhett was looking at him, like he'd repeated a statement in a language he didn't understand. "This has nothing to do with love." His gaze lowered to mine. "The quicker you realize that, Rowan, the better." He hissed out a mouthful of air. "I'm leaving. I'm going back to LA right now." He placed his hand on my arm. "And you're coming with me."

"Take your fucking hand off her right now!" Cooper blasted through the air.

"She's my sister—"

"I don't give a fuck," Cooper followed up with.

"I'd never hurt her," Rhett said.

"I don't believe a fucking word you say."

Rhett's hand dropped from my arm.

Oh God.

I needed to take a stance. More so than I'd already done. Something that would show Rhett that Cooper's feelings weren't one-sided.

That my feelings were just as strong as his, and my brother was going to have to learn to accept that.

I wasn't going to abandon my man just because Rhett told me to.

My brother had put me in this situation. He was forcing me to choose a side.

And there wasn't anything wrong with the one I was picking.

Now that Rhett's hands were free but balled into fists, he snapped, "Rowan, let's go."

"I'm staying right here." I hugged my stomach. "I'm not leaving Cooper."

Rhett's eyes didn't widen; they narrowed. "You're fucking kidding me, right? You're going to stay here with this motherfucker who's only going to use you and hurt you—"

"Rhett, you need to stop speaking," Cooper warned. "Right fucking now."

"You don't care about her," Rhett barked. "I don't give a shit what you say; it's all a lie. You're after one thing. I just hope to hell my sister realizes that before it's too late—"

"Stop!" I flattened my hand in the air. "Enough!"

These men knew nothing about one another. Everything at this point was just based on speculation, so there was no way Rhett knew what Cooper's real intentions were.

But I was done hearing it.

"Rhett, listen to me," I started. "You need to put all of this aside and remember why you're here." I let that statement sink in as much as it could. "This company needs your help. Cooper and I need your help. Can you please put your opinion aside and stay here in Lake Louise? We'll all get some rest, and we'll meet in the morning, and we'll go to the land to figure out how to build this hotel."

My brother laughed. It wasn't the kind of chuckle I always heard from Cooper.

This sound was nefarious.

"You're fucking delusional." He walked over to where he'd left his suitcase, and he wrapped his fingers around the handle. "I'm going to ask you one more time. Are you coming with me?"

I stepped back until I felt Cooper's body fully against mine. My fingers then reached for his, melding them together while he continued to press his palm over my stomach, stretching his hand as wide as it would go. "I'm staying right here."

His look should have filled me with dread.

But it didn't.

"You're making a mistake, Rowan. One you're soon going to regret."

"Because I care about him?"

"Because he's going to fucking destroy you." When he pointed this time, the tip of his finger was directed at the both of us. "Mark my words."

He turned around and walked down the hallway, disappearing at the bend.

Once he was gone, I swallowed the acid that had quickly risen to my throat, and gradually faced Cooper.

My body weakened.

My chest heaved.

I tried to find something to say, and the only thing that left my lips was a sob.

Cooper's hands immediately went to my cheeks. "Baby, it's okay. I promise, it's okay."

"Why did he do this?" My voice wasn't any louder than a whisper. "Why did he make me choose?"

He scanned my eyes, back and forth, taking my emotion as it began to pour out of me. "He's wrong, Rowan. About everything." He leaned his face down and pressed our noses together. "I know, in your heart, you know I'm not going to hurt you."

I didn't just believe that.

I felt it.

I trusted it.

"Tell me you're not going to listen to him." He pulled back a few inches to connect our stares. "Tell me you're not going to let that bastard tear us apart."

My head shook. "I won't. I can't." A tear rimmed my lid for only a second before he caught it. "Because I'm…in love with you."

· · ·

Me: *I've called you three times, Rhett. Please call me back.*

Me: *We need to talk about this.*

Me: *Please come to your senses and at least have a discussion with me. We're adults. Why aren't you acting like one?*

Me: *There's no reason to hate the Spades anymore. They're a part of us now. You need to put this feud behind us—for the sake of the company and for me.*

Me: *Rhett, I love him too.*

· · ·

Rhett: *I will never accept this. Not ever.*

Chapter Twenty-Seven

COOPER

Rowan and I stood by the lake, a few feet apart, staring at the general contractor while he assessed the land. Since Rhett couldn't put his anger aside, his fucking panties far too knotted and wadded up his ass, my assistant had found us someone else.

But the disappointment was clear on Rowan's face. She wanted her brother here. She wanted him to support us and the company.

She wanted our relationship to be accepted.

Goddamn it, I wanted that too.

But I wasn't going to get on my fucking knees and beg that bastard for acceptance. Shit, that was the last thing I was going to do. So, if that meant going with a different contractor, so be it.

What I couldn't handle was how last night had affected my girl. How the moment we left the hallway and got inside my room, she stripped off her dress and climbed into bed and went right to sleep.

Except I knew she wasn't sleeping.

She was breathing too hard and too fast.

She just didn't want to talk. She didn't want to dissect what had happened. She didn't want to open up about her feelings even though she'd told me she was falling in love with me just minutes before.

Rowan Cole was in love.

With me.

Words I hadn't expected. Feelings I hadn't anticipated.

Yet here we were, and things were messy as hell.

The Spades would come around. They already were. I just had to deal with the random shit that Brady gave me. But he could toss as much as he wanted my way; I'd handle it.

As for the Coles, that was an entirely different story. A story that Rowan didn't even know about. The only reason I did was because Jo had called and told me.

Fuck.

There was so much going on behind the scenes that went far beyond us.

That was going to make things extra heavy.

And they were things I couldn't stop.

Couldn't control.

Couldn't protect her from.

What I could do was be here when she needed me—and she would—and ensure that Rhett wasn't going to ruin things between Rowan and me.

That motherfucker was unpredictable, unhinged, and rowdy as hell. If he thought he could change the future I had with his sister, he had another thing coming to him.

He was allowed to have an opinion. I didn't have to agree with that opinion. But the moment he fucked with my relationship—if it ever came to that—was when I'd interfere.

Rhett Cole wasn't someone I was afraid of.

In fact, I would happily put that fucker in his place.

But that had nothing to do with what was happening right

here, right now, and the look on Rowan's face.

While the contractor began to measure the soil, I put my hand on her waist. She was on her phone, focused on whatever was on the screen, and she slowly glanced up at me.

"You want to talk about it?" I asked.

She'd spoken similar words to me last night when I returned to the bar after my conversation with Jo. A discussion I wasn't able to have with Rowan, which was why I hadn't said anything. But Rowan could talk about what was bothering her. She could express how she was feeling. And getting it out would only help since it certainly couldn't make things worse.

"I'm just so upset with Rhett," she said softly. She tucked her hair behind her ear. "The way he acted, the things he said, the accusations that made no sense. He doesn't even know you, Cooper. Why would he say such things?"

"He wasn't listening to you. He doesn't know the timeline of us. And I'm sure he's well aware of my reputation when it comes to women." I tightened my grip on her hip. "And in some roundabout, fucked-up way, he's just looking out for you." When I released air, it came out so hot that it almost whistled. "I don't like what he said, but if that was his way of trying to protect you, then a small part of me can understand."

Her head shook as she glanced up at the sky and took a long, deep breath. "It's none of his business."

"You'd protect him. I know you would."

Her eyes locked with mine. "Are you really sticking up for him?"

"Fuck no. I hate that motherfucker—I'm sorry, but I do." I pulled back my thoughts, taming my voice before I continued, "However, I'm capable of seeing both sides of a situation, and his, as much as I can't stand it, makes sense. I don't think I'd want my little sister, if I had one, to date someone like me either."

"Were you really...*that* bad?"

I sighed. "Listen, I've hidden nothing from you. I was straight up and honest the night we met at the bar. I didn't know what the fuck this feeling was until it happened with you. So, yeah, things hadn't exactly been pretty. Meaning I'd worked my way around LA a bit—"

"I honestly don't need to hear any more."

"Fair." I paused. "But I don't know if he was even referring to my reputation or if he was just being an asshole because I'm a Spade."

"With him, anything is possible."

"Have you heard from him?"

She shoved her phone into the pocket of her jacket. "He replied to one of my texts, and all it did was make me angrier and more hurt. I don't even know which one I am at this point."

"Probably a lot of both."

She put her other hand in her pocket, keeping both hidden and away. "What if this never gets better? And we're constantly at war? What would that even look like as a company, never mind a couple?"

I'd thought about that while we both lay in bed last night.

The outcome of this merger—not just as a brand, but Rowan and me too.

It would certainly make things complicated if the Coles were never able to accept us. If every time we were in Rhett's presence, he acted the way he had last night.

But after my chat with Jo, something told me things were about to change within the Cole family. Maybe they would calm. Maybe they would be more accepting.

Maybe things, like my relationship with Rowan, would be put into perspective.

I didn't know...it was just a hunch.

"Let's not focus on the what-ifs." I pulled her closer. "Rhett just found out—and by found out, he busted us in the hallway while I was all over you. Jarring, I'm sure, for him. Give him some time. It's still fresh and extremely new to him. He might need a minute, and that's all right."

Her eyes turned more emotional. "He told me he would never accept us, Cooper."

"He's a hotheaded prick. I'm not surprised he said that." Jesus, I really needed to stop talking shit about her brother in front of her, but, hell, I couldn't help myself. "Once he's had a few days to process and he sees us together more, he'll relax."

"Rhett doesn't relax." She swallowed. "He gets even."

"So does Brady." I smiled. "Can you imagine the two of them assigned to the next build-out?"

She laughed, and, damn, it was a sound I needed to hear.

"No"—her eyes widened—"I cannot. And I don't want that to ever happen."

"If I was to bet, it won't happen again after us."

She studied my face. "Because we're failing?"

"Because if the seven of us want to get along and work together, I think it's best that we're all given separate tasks to manage. Whether that's departments or build-outs or whatever, we just need equal ground."

"Oh, yes. I agree."

I lifted my hands to her face, taking a quick peek at the contractor before I gazed back at Rowan. "I don't want you inside your head, where this is all eating at you. There's enough stress with the merger and what's going on here at Lake Louise and..." All the other factors she didn't know about yet, but instead of saying that, I squeezed her harder. "I just want you to focus on what we can control." I moved our faces closer together. "That's us, Rowan. We can control what happens between you and me.

That's where I want your mind." I rubbed my thumb over her lip, the gloss causing my skin to stick to hers. "No more going to bed, pretending to be asleep. Do you know how fucking torturous that was for me—when I knew you didn't want to talk, and you were naked within inches of me, and all I wanted to do was put my mouth all over your body and make you forget the night had ever happened?" I tilted her face up. "But what I didn't know was if that would upset you more, so I let you keep your back to me, and I watched your shoulder rise every time you took a breath, and I observed you, waiting for the moment you turned over."

"And I never did."

My thumbs moved to the center of her cheeks. "No, you didn't."

"You could have rolled me over."

I gave her a light kiss. "Don't tell me that now."

"I'm just telling you, in the future, if it happens again, roll me toward you. Force me to talk—or don't—but please at least touch me. I want that, Cooper. I need that." She slid her hand out of her pocket and put it on my chest. "I've learned a lot about you, and one thing I know is that you're the most intimate and passionate when we're both naked. Dare I even say, the most loving. So, being with you in that way is something I'll always want. Whether I'm upset, angry, or in the mood to strangle my brother, it doesn't matter. I just want to feel that with you."

And what I felt from her made my fucking dick hard.

I scanned her eyes before my hand lowered to her chin. "You have no idea what you're doing to me right now."

"I think I do."

"No." I mashed my lips together. "You couldn't possibly."

There were so many thoughts running through my head; I couldn't compartmentalize any of them. "I'm about to do something that you're either going to love or fucking hate me for."

She laughed. "What?"

I took another glance at the contractor, who was making his way over to us. "You're going to find out soon." My hands dropped from her face, and I turned toward the guy. "Do you have good news for us?"

"Yes, and no." He held out his tablet, showing us the screen and the photos he'd taken of the land. "The back end of the lot can handle the weight. There's no question about that. It's the front end I'm really concerned about." He flipped to the next picture, which was the shoreline. "You mentioned the soil is being tested. That's a good start. But I'm going to recommend that if you want to build a hotel as large as we spoke about, then you're going to have to stabilize the ground, and that means"—he pointed at a spot about fifteen feet from where we stood—"starting there and digging twenty, maybe thirty feet down. I'd have to run the numbers, there's a chance it could be even more. But from there, you'd have to build a foundation and possibly even a new seawall. And that seawall might have to be rebuilt every five or so years—I don't know, that's something I can't predict. But I can tell you that you're gambling with the weight."

"Will the foundation hold?" I asked.

He shrugged. "It should. Do I know for sure? Absolutely not. When it comes to nature, there are just too many factors at play. And here, you're also dealing with water, and that makes things even more temperamental."

"If it were you, what would you do?" Rowan asked him.

He hugged the tablet against his chest. "I like money too much to gamble. If I knew there was a chance I was going to lose hundreds of millions over something environmental, I wouldn't even consider it."

I wasn't surprised by anything he said. I'd had a feeling this was going to be the result.

And last night, while I'd watched Rowan fake sleep, I'd confirmed plan B in my head.

"And a hotel in the normal size that we discussed, as in the same height and weight that already exists around the lake, that's doable, yes?" I asked.

"I don't see that being a problem at all." He glanced toward the water and back. "I'm going to write this all up in a report. Do you have any questions for me?"

I didn't want his presence to be here any longer than it needed to be.

"I think we're good," I told him.

He adjusted the top of his coat. "Your assistant gave me your information. I'll email everything over in the next few days."

He shook my hand and Rowan's, and then turned to walk to his car.

"What are we going to do?" she asked me the second he was gone.

I couldn't hide the smile on my face. "We're going to get well acquainted with the snow."

It took a moment before her brows shot up. "We're...*what*?"

"Don't move," I instructed, and I pointed at the ground so she knew I meant for her to stay still.

Once I was sure she would, I went to the SUV that was parked at the base of the lot, where the driver was waiting for us behind the wheel. He rolled down his window as I approached, stalling just long enough for me to say, "We're not going to need a ride back. Thank you for waiting."

"You sure?"

I started walking back toward Rowan and looked over my shoulder to reply, "Yeah, I'm sure. Thanks."

As I headed in her direction, I heard the tires crunching over the snow and the sound of the engine revving as he hit the road.

By the time I reached her, confusion owned her face.

"I'm lost," she said, searching my eyes for an answer. "You sent the driver home. How are we going to get back—"

"Come with me." I grabbed her hand and walked her toward the water. "I promise, in a few minutes, you're going to be even more lost."

We took a few steps before she said, "You're such a puzzle, Mr. Spade."

I chuckled, glancing at her just as we reached the edge of the trees that bordered our land, separating us from the neighboring building. Trees that would be knocked down as soon as we started building.

But now, I was happy as hell they existed.

"I think you know exactly what's on my mind, Rowan."

"Wait." Although she continued to walk, I saw and felt her hesitation. "Here?"

"Yes."

She squeezed my hand. "In the snow?"

"Yes." I nodded toward the small clearing up ahead. "But don't worry, I'm not going to put you on the snow. I know how much you hate it."

"You're relentless…"

"Nah, baby, I'm just fucking hungry, and the only thing that will satisfy me is your pussy." I took her through the opening and stopped in front of the medium-sized boulder, my hands going to her waist, holding the button that I was about to unhook. "It's been too long since I've eaten. I can't wait any longer to taste you."

"You're not serious." She was smiling.

I pulled the button through the hole and unzipped her pants, lowering them, along with her panties, giving myself just enough room to fit my face in between. Then, I took off my jacket and set it across the top of the boulder. "Sit."

"You do realize it's freezing outside, don't you?"

"You won't feel the cold in a few seconds." I pointed at the rock. "Sit."

"Yes, sir."

I laughed again. "I wouldn't play with that word, I might start liking it."

"If that's all it takes to get you to eat me, I'll say it every day."

I lowered myself to the base of the rock, placing my hands on the inside of her thighs, my face against the entrance of her pussy, where I positioned my nose and took a long inhale. And as I stared up her body, I said, "You don't have to say anything to get me to go down on you, Rowan. I dream about licking your cunt. And if I got to do it every day, it would be just as much for me as it would be for you."

Her hand dived into my hair. "If I wasn't already in love with you, that would have sealed the deal."

"Does this seal it even stronger?" I stuck my tongue out and focused just on her clit, softly licking the very top, giving her only the tip of my tongue.

"*Yesss,*" she moaned.

But as I picked up speed, I gave her even more, sinking a finger into her wetness, arching it upward toward her G-spot. That was the area I circled, and with my tongue, I flattened it to give her extra friction.

Additional pressure.

And within a few laps, I increased the momentum, shifting horizontally and vertically so she was getting pleasure from every angle.

"Oh my God." She was yanking my hair so hard; I was positive she was loosening strands.

I didn't care.

I wanted to feel her come.

I wanted to taste it.

To hear it.

I wanted the inside of her thighs so wet that my scruff was sliding over it.

"Cooper!"

I licked harder, driving my finger into the deepest part of her, and when I felt her clit harden and the slight rock of her hips, telling me she was on the verge, I upped everything I was doing.

The speed.

The intensity.

And my ears were suddenly filled with the sounds of, "*Ahhh*," as she screamed. Her legs caved inward; her stomach shuddered even though it was covered in her jacket. "Cooper! Fuck!"

I could feel the ripples.

The peak that she reached.

And I could taste the cum as it dripped out of her.

Fuck me, it was everything I'd wanted, the flavor I was after, the sounds I needed, the sight I'd been dying to see.

Rowan Cole.

She was perfect.

And she was mine.

As her body began to recover, easing through the final waves, I slowed my movements, licking until there was only stillness.

I moved back several inches, taking in her whole face and the satisfaction that filled it. "I guess I need to call us a car." I smiled right before I ran my tongue over my lips to get every drop of her off them. "Unless you want me to do that again…"

She didn't reply.

She just directed my face right back into her pussy, and the second my tongue swiped her, she immediately moaned again.

Chapter Twenty-Eight

Rowan

It was one thing to see the dynamic of the Spade brothers, their different personalities on display when they interacted with one another, conversations that were full of sarcasm and humor and dominance. Cooper always stood out. The combination of his looks and power was electrifying to watch. But it was something entirely different to observe Cooper lead a discussion with the vendors who were interested in opening within what would now be our Lake Louise and downtown Banff hotels. He had such a way with words, a type of charm that was impossible to ignore.

And the Westons, like me, were positively captivated by him.

Since we'd made the official decision to move forward with the two properties, instead of gambling on the one, we were looking to fill the commercial spots within each hotel. Cooper and I had spent the last two weeks meeting with different vendors.

According to my man, we'd saved the best for last.

The Weston family—owners of Charred, the nationwide high-end steak house, and Musik, their newly launched club that had opened in Macon's Kauai hotel—were sitting around our new conference room table. Considering they already had steak houses in many of the Spade hotels, they were a shoo-in.

But for the last thirty minutes, while discussing the details of the steak house, they'd been debating which of the two properties should house the restaurant. So far, there was no solution. Walker, Colson, Beck, Hart, and Eden—the five founders and siblings—couldn't come to a decision.

Cooper hadn't been able to help either.

But I had an idea.

While Walker and Colson flipped through the digital designs of both properties for what felt like the hundredth time, the other three looking at the blueprints, I interjected and said, "May I offer a suggestion?"

All eyes immediately shifted toward me.

This was my first time really speaking out during the meeting. Cooper had been in control up until this point, his descriptions like art, his tone a whole mood.

This family listened to him.

So, whatever I offered needed to be on point. I wasn't automatically going to receive their trust by default. I had to earn it.

And I would.

"The last time I was in Denver," I began, "I dined at Toro, which I'm going to get to in a second. First, I want to know why it's your only fish restaurant and raw bar."

Ironically, during my first work trip to visit our Denver hotel, I'd met up with some college friends, and they'd taken me to Toro for dinner. At the time, the significance of that restaurant obviously hadn't registered, but as I was researching the Westons last night, I had been pleasantly surprised to find out I'd not only eaten there, but I'd also loved it.

Walker—who reminded me of Cooper in so many ways,

especially his charm and alpha-ness—placed his arms on the table and turned his head toward me. "We've looked for additional markets that would accept our newest concept. We don't want to open in Manhattan or Miami or even LA. There's too much competition in the seafood market. We want to build where the restaurant will earn a well-deserved reputation and not get lost in a sea of others."

"But you chose Denver," I said. "Which is a large metro market with thousands of restaurants."

Walker glanced at Beck, an NHL player who, according to Cooper, had less of an active role in their company and was more of their financial backer.

"Although it's a destination city, it's also a foodie town," Beck replied. "We didn't want to pick a spot like Las Vegas where ninety-five percent of the diners are vacationers. We wanted a spot where we could grow a loyal following. In the nine months since the restaurant opened, Denver has been nothing short of a success."

I felt Cooper's eyes on me as I replied, "It's one of the best meals I've ever had. Easily Michelin-worthy. That's just the food. The interior, vibe, ambiance—it was all amazing. And I think it would be the perfect addition to downtown Banff." Before any of them could reply, I added, "Hear me out. Sure, it's a destination with a tiny population of residents, but it's an extremely popular destination. Also, there's nothing currently like it in Banff. You'd be a staple. A landmark, so to speak."

I lifted my tablet off the table and pointed the screen at them. "Here's a list of the current restaurants in that area." I circled the air around the bottom of the tablet. "As you can see here, there are only two fish restaurants, neither offering anything raw, and the price points are extremely different in comparison to your Denver menu. We're talking a thirty to forty percent increase. Of course, we're also talking three stars to five stars." I smiled. "What I'm saying is, this town needs a restaurant like Toro."

I set the tablet down, taking in each of their faces, trying to determine how they were accepting my news. "My recommendation is to put Charred at the Lake Louise hotel. The area has a more traditional feel, which will work extremely well with that kind of cuisine. That market just feels more steak to me. Deep, bold, jammy wines and dark decor. The scent of leather and caramelized onions and garlic greeting you at the entrance."

I paused as I gazed toward Cooper, his stare telling me he wanted to devour me on top of this table.

I must be doing good.

"For downtown Banff," I went on, "I'd go with Toro. It's a more contemporary crowd. You can fill the space with bright colors and futuristic designs. A menu that satisfies a younger palate with eclectic cocktails and a slew of raw options."

I had one last thought, hoping it would answer their questions before they even asked them. "Now, you're probably wondering why I would suggest a seafood restaurant for the mountains and steak on the water. Seems as though it should be the opposite, am I right?" I shook my head, tucking my hair back before it made its way into my eyes. "Seafood eaters want to hear the words *fresh*, whereas meat eaters want to hear *aged*. Banff is closer to the airport. There's nothing like hearing a server say that the oysters are flown in every day, that the fish is fresh and never frozen. You could use that in your marketing. I assume it would be just as easy to get the seafood to Lake Louise, but it's going to satisfy your guests' ears, I promise."

"Now, that's a very interesting idea," Eden said, breaking the few seconds of silence that had passed.

She was a tough one. I could tell that the moment she'd shaken my hand at the start of this meeting, her grip as tight and strong as any of her brothers. It wasn't easy to be the only woman in a group of five, I imagined, along with working with them full-time.

I couldn't even wrap my head around the idea of having two more Rhetts.

Rhett...*shit.*

I checked my watch, wondering what was taking him so long to come in. Ridge had stopped by toward the start of our meeting to introduce himself to the Westons. Since they had done so much business with the Spades prior to our merger, it was inevitable he'd be working with them too. But so far, Rhett hadn't made the effort to even walk down the hallway to meet them even though he had said he would.

"To be honest," Eden continued, "that isn't something we ever even considered when we talked about building a restaurant in one of your two hotels."

"It's not something we ever even thought about," Walker said, correcting her.

I glanced between her and Walker. "But would you consider it?"

Eden turned toward Hart, a dark curl sticking to her gloss that she quickly moved away. "What do you think?" she asked him.

Hart's green eyes were so deep that they rivaled Macon's. "I think it's something we should consider. This would give us an entirely different audience to test. We know the concept works in a metro city with a high population of residents. But a vacation spot that flourishes in both winter and summer seasons could be exactly what we've been looking for."

"A double build-out in locations that are roughly forty minutes apart. Whoa. That's ballsy," Colson said. Colson's voice was assertive, but his posture was as laid-back as could be, reclining in the chair so far that it looked like he was watching a game. "We'd be investing a significant amount of money in a small radius.

Something we've never done before."

"Neither have we," I told him. I then glanced around the table to connect eyes with everyone, making sure they understood the significance and weight of my statement. "Cole International nor Spade Hotels has ever built resorts this close together. It's not a model we believe in. With the type of hotels we construct, we don't want our properties to compete against themselves, putting our guests in a position where they have to choose between two of our resorts. But in this case, we believe the risk is worth it." I clasped my hands together. "Close, yes, but locations that offer completely different experiences. Just like your restaurants would."

Walker shook his head, the overhead light catching the darkness of his locks with ends that had a haze of gray. "You know, we came here with a semi-plan. Charred would go in one. Myself, I was leaning toward downtown Banff, but I don't think that's the case anymore. You've given us a lot to think about, Rowan."

I smiled. "I'm happy to hear that."

"Let's go back to the office and discuss things?" Beck said to the group. When he looked at Cooper and me, he said, "We'll have an answer to you in the next couple of days."

"Doing business on a game day—I like it," Cooper said to him.

Beck laughed. "I have no choice, someone's got to keep this crew in line." He pointed at his siblings before his hand returned to his lap.

"My brothers and I will be at the arena tonight," Cooper voiced. "We expect a win against Dallas."

"You and everyone else." Beck laughed. "How much did you put on the game?"

Cooper whistled as he exhaled. "Far too fucking much."

Beck pushed back his chair and stood. "When you win—and you will—I'm going to negotiate a better rate on the square footage you're going to be charging us for the two restaurants. Remember that while you're kicking back in your box seats tonight, buddy."

Cooper walked around to Beck's side of the table and clasped his hand on Beck's shoulder. "I'd be disappointed if you didn't put up a fight."

Cooper shook his hand and then said a few words to each of the siblings as they made their way toward the door.

I did the same, starting with Eden. "It was really lovely to meet you," I told her.

"And you," she replied. "When we heard about this merger, we weren't sure what to think, but after today, I can speak for my brothers when I say we're really looking forward to this new partnership."

"I appreciate that," I told her.

I said my goodbyes to her brothers, and the door finally shut, leaving Cooper and me alone in the conference room. He positioned himself by the door, blocking me from leaving, facing me as he leaned against the wall.

He eyed me up and down before he said, "Two restaurants? I sure as fuck didn't see that coming."

"What can I say? I'm good under pressure." I winked.

"Bullshit. You had that up your sleeve the whole time, you were just waiting for the right moment to drop it."

I laughed. "Maybe." I crossed my arms, feeling the pull of my suit jacket.

"I've got to say, it was sexy as fuck, and I'm slightly jealous it wasn't something I thought of."

"We both know the other vendors we interviewed are more than adequate, but they're not the Westons. Their following is as loyal as ours, and there's no one better to fill those spaces, so why stop at one when we can have two?"

He nodded, like he was listening to music, his hands rising to clap. "You did something fucking epic today, partner."

"Partner?"

"I would have called you baby, but I didn't think it had the right level of clout."

I moved in a few inches closer, yet still kept enough distance that if anyone came in, it wouldn't look questionable. Not that it would matter; both families knew about our relationship, and this conference room was located on the executive floor of our new office space, a build-out that had been fast-tracked so we could all move in immediately. Aside from our assistants, only a Spade or a Cole or Jo would be walking in, and none of them would be surprised by what they saw.

But when we'd moved in, one of the conversations I'd had with Cooper was office etiquette. Here, I wanted to keep things professional. This entire building was a space meant for work, and that was what we needed to focus on.

Outside this building was an entirely different story.

So far, Cooper had only broken that rule once. It was a night we both worked late, and he came into my office and locked the door. Of course, once I finally peeled myself off the top of the desk, I reminded him that was something that would never happen again. And when he'd nodded in agreement, I had known he was full of shit.

He wanted me.

Office rules weren't going to change that.

"I'm so disappointed in Rhett," I said, shifting gears. "I don't care if he's upset with me and he wants to murder you, he should have done the right thing and introduced himself to the Westons. Talk about a lack of decency." I sighed. "I don't know what his problem is. But I'm over it."

"Are you going to talk to him about it?"

I nodded. "Right now." I shifted my tablet in my hand. "Swing by my office before you leave for the game."

"You're going to Sky's after work?"

My head tilted back as I sang, "I cannot wait. PJs, wine, and a massive bitch session." I looked at him again. "Everything I need and more."

"Don't show me your neck." His stare dropped to the area I'd just exposed. "Not with how badly I want to fucking kiss you right now and how it's taking everything in me not to lock the door."

And that was my cue to leave.

My teeth found my bottom lip and bit down before I replied, "You wouldn't dare."

"I wouldn't? Don't goad me, Rowan. You'll find yourself naked in less than ten seconds."

I poked his chest and moved around him toward the door, his hand grazing my waist as I passed him. "Ten seconds?" I looked at him over my shoulder. "I'm disappointed in you, Spade. I thought you could do it much quicker than that." I hurried out before he had a chance to reply and went down the hallway, stopping in front of Rhett's doorway.

I was hoping I wouldn't find him inside. That an appointment had taken him out of the building and that was why he hadn't come into the conference room.

But, damn it, he was in there.

As I closed the door behind me, he briefly looked up from his monitor. The moment he saw it was me, he returned his gaze to the screen.

"What do you want?" he barked.

I took a seat in the chair in front of his desk. "For starters, how about a solid reason why you didn't show up to my meeting?"

He crossed his arms. "You're not my mother, Rowan. I don't have to give you shit."

"You're right. I'm not. But you're acting like a child, which is the reason I'm treating you like one." I kept my voice calm even though he was testing every bit of patience I had. "You're a partner, Rhett. Just because you're one of seven doesn't mean you can do whatever you want, whenever you want. We're one company now, so things like attending meetings with vendors you haven't yet met would be a great way to show your support." I exhaled so loud that my chest ached. "You're not putting the company first. Instead, you're acting like a selfish prick."

"*Fuuuck*," he growled. "You just won't stop, will you?"

"Stop doing what?" A surge of adrenaline shot through my body. I just wanted my brother on board. Whatever was making him act this way, I wanted to shake it out of him. "I love you. I would do absolutely anything for you. It kills me that you're treating me this way—"

"Then, you shouldn't have fucked a Spade."

That was it. I'd reached my limit.

"A Spade? That's all you've got?" I leaned forward until I was gripping the edge of his desk. "You've fucked half this town, and have I ever said two words about it? No. Who you sleep with is none of my business. Just like who I sleep with is none of yours." I squeezed the wood between my fingers. "But the man I'm with isn't just any man, he's your business partner. Someone you'll be working with until the day you retire. Someone who is no longer your enemy. So, get over it, Rhett, and get it to-fucking-gether. Stop thinking about yourself and start thinking about your family and how this attitude you're giving everyone is tearing us apart. You're the only one who has an issue with this—"

"The only one?" he challenged. "We both know that's a lie."

"If you're talking about Ridge or Dad, you're wrong. I've discussed this with both of them. In fact, Dad gave me his blessing." My eyelids narrowed. "My happiness is what matters to him. I hate that you can't see it that way."

I'd had a conversation with Ridge and Dad as soon as I got

back from Canada, knowing Rhett was probably going to tell them what had gone down when he caught Cooper and me in the hallway and I wanted them to hear my side of things. Dad wasn't thrilled that I'd been dishonest with Cooper and hidden my last name, but he certainly wasn't upset that I was dating a Spade.

If anything, he was ecstatic.

A reaction that had somewhat shocked me.

"I'm talking about Brady."

"Brady…" I pushed myself away from his desk. "At least he's not acting like an asshole to Cooper and me, unlike someone else I know."

I stood, knowing I wasn't going to get anywhere with him. My hope deflated like a popped balloon, and I moved over to the door.

"You've always been someone who fights the current. Normally, I stand by your side with my arms around you, holding you in the water and helping you tread. But there's only so much I can do, and I'm tired. I'm burned out. And I'm defeated." My voice softened with each word. "Rhett, I'm sorry to say, but in this case, I'm going to let you drown."

"Girl, you'd better slow down, or you're going to be asleep in an hour," Sky said as she picked up the bottle of wine to pour me a refill. "You know wine makes you extra tired, and that's not happening tonight. We have Chinese food on the way and some incredible desserts to devour, and I rented the *Barbie* movie because everyone at work said I needed to watch it, so, sorry, you're watching it with me." She aimed the bottle at the edge of my glass. "Look at tonight like a marathon, not a sprint."

Tonight wasn't either.

This was what I called survival mode.

I was spread across her couch in yoga pants and a T-shirt, fuzzy socks, with my hair in a high, messy bun.

Attire I'd been dreaming about since I'd left the office.

"We'll do it all, I promise," I replied. "It's just…been a day."

My eyes closed, and I attempted to fill my lungs.

Just breathe.

That was what every meme, doctor, and online article said to do when you were on the verge of a panic attack.

Except I couldn't breathe.

Everything was tight.

Everything hurt, even my body.

Everything was swirling in my head, moving so fast I couldn't grasp a single thought.

"What's going on, babe?" she whispered.

I felt the glass get heavier, and several seconds later, I heard the bottle being set on the table.

Sky's hand then went to my head, playing with the hairs that had fallen from my elastic. "Talk to me, Row."

I slowly turned my head toward my best friend, my eyes gradually opening. "I'd much rather talk about you."

"About me? And my boring-ass day? How I busted my client trying to cheat the IRS out of thousands in taxes by attempting to manipulate his books?" She rolled her eyes. "Trust me, whatever you're about to say is much more interesting than any of that."

"It isn't. *Trust me.*"

"Now, you're just lying. Speak, woman. Before I do something silly, like grab your phone and call Cooper and ask him what's going on with you." Her face turned stern before I could say a word. "And don't think I wouldn't. You know I'd do anything to get my bestie to purge when I know she needs to more than anything."

I didn't deserve her.

And I was positive there was no one better in this world than her.

"I know you're stressed," she continued. "I've been hearing it slowly eat away at you during our calls and get worse every day. I kinda had a feeling you were reaching a breaking point."

My hand went to her arm, holding it like it was Cooper's hand. "I'm close. Closer than I've ever been."

"Is it Rhett?"

I nodded. "He's a giant dick, and we had it out today. Or we semi had it out. He didn't say much, which you know makes me even angrier." I bared my teeth and scrunched up my face. "But Rhett is only a portion of it. There's Brady, too, Cooper's brother, who isn't a fan of us either. And then there's the Canadian project, going from one hotel to two, doubling the amount of work that needs to be done. For the past week, I've stayed at the office past ten o'clock at night every evening, and I'm there before six every morning." I stopped to guzzle more wine.

"You're tired."

I nodded.

"More like exhausted," she clarified.

I nodded again.

"And you don't know which end is up."

"It's affecting me, Sky. Everything aches—and I mean, everything." I released her for just a second to push on the middle of my chest. I hadn't bothered with a bra when I changed into these clothes, but my boobs still felt constricted. How did my brother have such an effect on me that no matter what I did, I just couldn't get comfy. "And then, on top of it all, there's the boutiques."

A topic I hadn't discussed with anyone.

Hardly even myself.

"The...*what*?"

"Last week, the woman I'd sold my business to reached out

and asked me to buy it back. An even swap for what she'd paid me for it." I lifted my hand to my neck, circling to the back where it met my shoulders. "She wanted to give me first dibs before she sought another buyer." My hand lowered to my stomach, rubbing the unsettled rumbles. "I guess it's too much for her."

Her eyes widened as she stared at me. "Have you considered it?"

"I don't know."

"But you do know."

I pushed my head further into the cushion. "Maybe it was a mistake, joining the company. Maybe it would make things easier for Cooper and me. Maybe my brother would hate me a little less—"

"Please stop this nonsense. You love what you're doing, and you're good at it. And you love working with Cooper. And Rhett will come around. He's just being ridiculous, and Rhett has a tendency of being ridiculous when he's taken off guard and things don't go his way." Since my hand had finally returned to her arm, she put her fingers on top of mine. "Tell me you're going to stay right where you are—and I'm not saying that as your accountant, who would like to inform you that it'll be a tax nightmare to buy the business back. I'm saying that as your best friend."

I had to make a decision fairly quickly. The buyer had mentioned she'd give me a week to think about it, two tops.

I was at the nine-day mark.

Purchasing the boutiques back would be a whole new change of pace. It would be bailing on my family, the Spades, and Jo.

Part of me thought it would be easier for everyone.

Part of me thought it was the worst thing I could ever do.

"I need to ponder it a bit more," I admitted. "My head is so cloudy, I can't think straight."

"It's because you're on your period. Day two always makes things extra cloudy, extra irritable, and *extra* stabby."

"My...period?"

"Our cycles are in sync, so, yes, you should be on day two."
She sighed. "Shit, the stress has caused you to be late, hasn't it?"
When I didn't respond, she continued, "I'm not surprised. It's wild
what stress can do to our bodies." She nodded toward my face.
"Your period is coming though. You have the whopping zit on
your forehead to prove it." She winced. "You couldn't cover that
sucker up even if you tried, which means there's no doubt you'll
have it by morning."

"Fuck me, that's probably why the desire to beat Rhett's ass
is stronger than normal." I groaned. "See what this is all doing to
me? What he's doing to me? Even my period is sending me a sign.
A sign that I should buy back—"

"Your period is telling you that you need to put yourself first,
and you haven't done that in a while." She squeezed my fingers. "If
you're going to work late, then you need to go for a walk during
lunch and move your body. You need to take melatonin before
bed, so you actually get some solid rest. And you need to book
yourself a ninety-minute massage for this weekend, so you can
unplug and reset." She rested her elbow on the cushion next to
my head and turned completely toward me. "Listen to me, Row.
You're not Superwoman. There's a lot happening in your life, and
you're doing an incredible job, juggling it all, but you're holding
everything in, and look at you—you're kind of a mess, and I say
that with all the love."

I laughed. "No. You're right."

"You can't fix things with Rhett—that's now on him. You can't
work twenty-four hours a day. You can't make Brady adore you.
And you can't buy back a business that no longer serves you. This
is who you are now." She cupped my chin. "This is the path you're
supposed to be on, Row, and for the love of God, stop questioning
it."

Chapter Twenty-Nine

Cooper

What the fuck?

That was one of the many thoughts that pounded through my head as I read the email that had just come through my inbox. With each word that my eyes scanned, my teeth ground a little more, my jaw locked, my fingers clenched into a fist.

I was squeezing the damn mouse so hard that the fucking plastic top cracked.

The sender was, no surprise, Rhett fucking Cole.

If he weren't Rowan's brother, I would have strangled the motherfucker by now.

And this email was the last straw, which was something I would have said to his face, but when my assistant had come in about an hour ago to deliver another cup of coffee, he'd rushed past my open door with his bag and jacket.

Man, he had balls to send the entire executive team this email, an outline of why Rowan and I were idiots to purchase the land in downtown Banff, how the contractor we'd hired—the contractor who had replaced Rhett because the asshole had bailed on us—was a moron and his findings were incorrect. According to Rhett, a special foundation could have been poured that would have held the weight of what we wanted to build and it would have strengthened the soil, allowing us to move forward with our original plan.

But it was an opinion that no longer mattered—that wasn't even relevant at this point.

Because Rhett knew it was impossible to revert back to our first concept.

We were now under contract with the Westons for Charred and Toro. We'd also signed with three additional restaurant brands to build Italian, Mediterranean, and Mexican eateries within the two hotels. Since the Coles used a different contractor than us, we had both working on bids for the properties. We'd submitted our blueprints to the governing officials of Alberta to begin the permitting process.

There was no backing out.

Rhett had sent that email in an attempt to get under my skin.

And it fucking worked.

Jesus Christ.

I rolled my chair back, getting my ass up, and I pulled open the door, walking down the hallway to Rowan's office. As I approached her doorway, her light was off, and she wasn't inside.

When the hell had she left?

She never took off before me. I always went to her office and forced her to shut down for the night, and she'd either come to my place for the evening or I'd go to hers.

I pulled my phone out from my pocket, checking the notifications, looking for a text from her that I'd missed.

And, fuck, there was one.

Rowan: *Leaving a little early. I came by to tell you, but you were in a meeting.*

Rowan didn't leave early ever.

Something was up.

I typed my reply as I walked back to my office.

Me: *Are you all right?*

Rowan: *Eh.*

Eh? What the hell is eh*?*

Had she gotten into an argument with Rhett? Was the tension he was creating becoming too much?

I knew shit was intense with the build-outs. We were doing double the work. Our vendors were blowing up our emails and calling relentlessly. The interior designer was inundating us with questions. We were working hard to incorporate a feel that represented both companies—something that had never been done before, so there was no baseline; we were creating our own. And this was the first time Rowan had ever worked on a build-out, so each step was completely new to her.

Still, she was handling it all like a boss.

Sure, she was stressed.

I saw it in her face. I felt it every time I touched her body.

But she wasn't one to complain, and she hadn't. In fact, she was the most positive woman I knew.

I needed to get to the bottom of whatever *eh* was.

I grabbed my things from my desk and called down to the valet, letting them know I needed my car. It was already parked by the door by the time I got downstairs. I tipped the attendant and drove out onto the street.

Eh.

A word I'd never heard Rowan use, and it was fucking eating at me as I drove to her house. I didn't want her to be upset. I didn't want her to be angry. Whatever emotions she was feeling, I wanted to take them from her and bury them.

Unless the *eh*…had to do with me?

I hadn't even considered that when I got behind the wheel and started heading for her place.

Had I fucked up?

Without even knowing it?

It was possible. This whole relationship thing was new to me, and I was learning as I went.

It was that worry that had me pulling into the high-end market a few blocks from her house, parking in a spot out front, and rushing inside. I didn't know what I was looking for. I just thought showing up with something would make whatever *eh* was better.

There were flowers by the entrance. Long stems of colorful petals that were bunched together and wrapped in a cone of plastic. I grabbed one and wandered through the store, looking to see if something else caught my attention.

If she was hungry, I was going to take her out. If she wanted to drink, she had a whole bar at her house.

The flowers were perfect.

I quickly paid for them and got back into my car. As I weaved up her street and turned into her entrance, I slowly pulled up to her gate, pressing the button that would notify her that I was here.

There was a camera staring right at me. She could see my face through an app on her phone and on any of the tablets in her house. Therefore, she didn't have to talk through the intercom and ask who I was.

What surprised me was that she didn't say anything before she opened the gate.

Not even a *hiii*, which was her typical greeting.

I parked in front of her garage, and as I was walking up to the front, she appeared in the doorway. She crossed both sides of her sweater, hiding her chest, one that she'd put on since she'd gotten home, along with the yoga pants and socks.

"Flowers?" Her voice was soft, almost breathy.

As I got closer, I noticed she'd also washed off her makeup.

A natural look that I fucking loved on her.

But what wasn't the norm was the color of her cheeks. They were flushed while her forehead and chin were pale, her eyes glossy.

I knew my baby well enough to know she was hurting.

Once she took the stems from my grip, my hands immediately went to her waist. "The *eh* in your text made me think you needed a smile." I dipped into her neck, gently kissing it. An unfamiliar sheen of sweat was on her skin. When I moved my face back, I asked, "What's wrong, Rowan?"

She held my stare for several seconds and brought the flowers up to her nose. "They smell amazing." She attempted a smile. "They're beautiful. Thank you."

"I went to your office to bitch about your brother, and you were gone."

She nodded. "Yeah…about that." Her hand dropped to her side, and her neck tilted back so she could look at me. "Wait, what about my brother? Did he do something?"

"You haven't read your email?"

"I…no."

She hadn't read her email.

Her skin was red, her eyes glossy, she'd left work early—every goddamn alarm was going off in my head.

This wasn't like her.

Rowan was usually the one who told me about the emails that came in, not the other way around, because she read them much sooner than me.

"Today has been"—she glanced behind her, into the foyer, as though someone were standing at her back, and then her eyes returned to me—"different." She swallowed. "Tell me about Rhett. At least I'm assuming you're talking about Rhett." Even though I was holding her, she took a few steps back, moving out of my grip.

I followed her. "The asshole sent us and the entire executive team his findings on the land in Lake Louise and how, in his opinion, we could have built the full-sized hotel that we originally planned."

Still walking, she paused halfway to the kitchen. "He sent us that info...*now*?"

"And felt the need to bash the contractor we'd hired, which we'd only done because your brother left us high and dry. Not to mention, the results of the soil testing contradict everything Rhett said in his email."

"I don't understand." When she shook her head, her hair got caught in her eyelashes. "He knows we've already purchased the land in downtown Banff and we've moved forward with the plans to build two hotels."

That summary alone made my blood pressure skyrocket.

"Why would he do that?" she asked.

I pushed the hair off each side of her face. "To make me irate. It worked."

Her gaze shifted between my eyes. Back and forth. Multiple times. "Cooper, when will this end?" Her tone was the softest it had been since I'd arrived.

I had the same question.

"I'm terrified it's not going to and then..." Her voice trailed off.

So, this was what was bothering her.

What was causing her to be so quiet, her skin to be flushed.

That bastard got to her as much as he got to me.

I needed to put a stop to this.

But first, I needed to get Rowan to relax.

I remembered one of the ways I'd done that in Canada. Fortunately, the bathtub in her en suite was even bigger than the one had been in my hotel room, and this one would easily fit both of us.

I held the sides of her face. "I'm going to fix this. I promise." My words bounced right off her; her eyes didn't change, and neither did the red in her skin. "But first, I want you to stay right here, okay? Don't move."

I took the flowers out of her hand and brought them into the kitchen. The first spot of counter I came to was the island, and that was where I set the arrangement, directly next to a small plastic bag. I wasn't sure why the bag was holding my focus, but I couldn't look away from it.

Not when the bag was wide open, revealing a box inside.

A box that...

Fuck.

It can't be.

I had to be seeing shit. I was sure of it.

But just to be positive, I reached into the bag, holding the stiff material, and I pulled it out to read the label.

Which I did again.

And again.

My gaze lowered to the brand.

The logo.

The fucking description.

"Cooper..." Rowan said from somewhere behind me.

I heard her.

But my feet wouldn't move, the wood beneath them like quicksand. The thumping had returned to my heart, the rate this time like I'd been sprinting, the words I wanted to say stuck in my throat.

"Cooper..."

I blinked hard, making sure my eyes weren't playing tricks on me.

And each time they opened, I saw the same thing.

The identical words from before.

The brand.

Logo.

Description.

"Look at me," she whispered.

She'd moved to the other side of the island, directly in front of me, the few feet of counter the only thing that separated us.

While squeezing the box with a strength that just wasn't necessary, I gradually looked up at her.

"Rowan…" Where her air seemed to be labored, I was having a hard time breathing at all. My thoughts were all over the place, my chest suddenly a fucking mess. "Is this the *eh*?"

She mashed her lips together as she stared at me.

And eventually, after it seemed like a million fucking minutes had passed, she nodded.

I set the pregnancy test on the counter and flattened my hands against the cool stone. "Baby…do you have something to tell me?"

Chapter Thirty

ROWAN

"Baby...do you have something to tell me?"

As I stared at Cooper, his question swirling through my head, I was positive I was going to throw up again. Which had happened at work this morning and a second time late this afternoon. In my mind, during each heave, I'd come up with a million reasons why I felt sick.

This morning was due to the wine I'd drunk the night before. My stomach was still upset—it had to be; that was why the coffee I'd had after lunch hadn't settled right, and it caused me to be ill again.

But those reasons didn't explain why I'd felt sick yesterday.

Or the day prior.

And now, there was a pregnancy test on the counter in my kitchen, sitting directly between Cooper and me, and he deserved an explanation.

"I don't know if I have something to tell you," I whispered. "I haven't taken a test yet." I nodded toward the box. "That's the first and only one I bought."

He moved around to my side of the island, turning my body until I faced him. His hands cupped the sides of my neck, a place on my body he didn't usually hold.

But as he did, his grip was gentler than it had ever been.

"Rowan, there must be a reason why you think you're pregnant."

Just breathe.

The saying I'd been repeating nonstop, and it had done nothing to help my anxiety. In fact, I was sure it was doing the exact opposite of what I needed.

Because I couldn't inhale.

I couldn't exhale.

I couldn't calm these nerves.

I was overtaken by nausea and tingles—not the kind that came from between my legs; these were like little fires igniting in my chest, sending flames toward my throat that closed my airway.

"I'm late." My eyes welled with tears, the emotion coming completely out of nowhere. Like it had yesterday. And the day before. Angst pouring right out of me like sweat from a run. "That's happened in the past, but it's never been this late."

He stroked underneath my ears. "You've been stressed. I'm sure that can do plenty of shit to your body." His voice was much calmer than I'd expected.

Except I hadn't expected anything.

I didn't anticipate Cooper coming over.

I was going to make myself some tea to soothe my stomach and take the test alone. If the result was negative, which I had a feeling it would be, I wouldn't say anything to him at all. There would be no reason to. The delay had been caused by stress, and my anxiety had created all these wild symptoms.

If it was positive, well, that was an entirely different story, and we would have a lot to talk about.

"Yes," I replied, "stress can definitely do that. I'm sure that's the case." I nodded, reconfirming that thought in my head. "But it might be worth mentioning that I haven't been feeling very well." I attempted to release the little air I had been holding in, and I ended up coughing from it. "I've gotten sick a bunch of times, and my breasts hurt. Like, they *really* hurt, Cooper."

His head shook as he processed, a look of concern coming through his expression. "Why didn't you tell me?"

"Because I didn't know if it was all in my mind or stress-induced or if it was really something much more. I couldn't take the unknown for a second longer. Plus, Sky's been hounding me to get a test—"

"You told Sky?" He searched my eyes. "And not me?"

I put one of my hands on top of his. "The conversation went down during our last girls' night. Our periods are in sync. And that's when I figured out I was late, and then when mine never came, the questions started."

He moved his face closer. "What upsets me the most, Rowan, is that you've been dealing with this worry or uncertainty—or whatever you want to call it—on your own. Or I guess with Sky when I should have been the one helping you through it."

"You're here now."

"I'm going to be honest with you." His stare deepened. "When I saw the pregnancy test, it tripped me up. I didn't know what the fuck to do. My body froze. I couldn't piece things together, everything was scattered. It took me a second to realize what I was even looking at."

"It's a lot. I know. I've had some time to put my brain there. You've had seconds. I get it. But what I keep telling myself is that I'm on the pill. Although it's not a hundred percent, I've been on it for a long time. I take it religiously. The chances are there, I suppose, but they're so slim."

His hands dropped from my neck, causing mine to fall, and he held my waist, lifting me onto the counter. He then moved in between my legs; our faces now aligned. "We haven't been very careful. We only used a handful of condoms over Christmas, and that doesn't dent all the times we've had sex. The chances are there—I'm sure of it."

He was right.

We hadn't really been careful at all.

But I didn't think that mattered. Not with being on the pill and having that layer of protection.

With each day that passed, still no period in sight, the signs were adding up far too quickly.

They could be nothing.

Or they could be everything.

My lungs expanded, my arms moved to his shoulders, my fingers shook so hard that I had to squeeze them into fists. "What if..." I trailed off, too anxious to fill in the rest of the words. "Should we even go there until we know?"

He rested his forehead against mine. "Listen to me. I've told you that I'm in love with you. Since I said that to you, those feelings have only grown." He put a few inches between us so he could lock eyes with mine. "I'm not going anywhere. Whatever happens, we're in this together. So, whether you have my baby in nine months or so, or in two years, or in five, my answer isn't going to change."

"Your answer," I started, but my throat was burning, my eyes dripping, my lips quivering, "is that you want this baby?"

He rubbed his thumb over my mouth. "Were you afraid that I didn't?"

"At this moment, Cooper, I'm afraid of everything."

Before I could say anything else or think or even react, he was wrapping his arms around me and pulling me against him.

Our chests collided, my breasts immediately screaming in pain, our faces in each other's neck, our lips pressed against the opposite skin.

I never understood the power of a hug.

Until now.

And I was positive, with everything I had, I never wanted him to let me go.

"Don't be afraid," he said. "I want you to give me those fears and let me hold them for you."

As my eyelids clamped shut, wetness began to soak in around me—through his shirt, coating my eyelashes, covering my mouth.

"But is being a father what you really want? Now?"

"Are you kidding." It wasn't a question. It was the most serious statement he'd made. "Of course it's what I want. Was it in my plan for it to happen now—if that's even the case? No. In the future? Absolutely. But now or then, it makes no difference. I want a child, Rowan. I want that baby to be a part of me. And holding it and loving it, I want that more than anything."

I finally exhaled.

But what came out felt like more than just air.

And relief.

And sadness.

What came out was energy that had been pent-up since Cooper had first kissed me in Lake Louise.

"I wish things were that perfect," I said softly. "Because they feel so incredibly complicated." The tears were coming down harder. "Our families, Cooper. Rhett. Brady—"

His hand went to the center of my stomach. "If you're pregnant, that'll be my baby in your belly, and I don't give a shit if they hate me or hate us. You and that baby would be the only things that matter."

The water from my eyes was falling onto my lips, and I did

nothing to stop it.

I couldn't.

"I almost quit," I blurted out.

His gaze intensified, like he was trying to search mine. "Quit what?"

"The woman who bought my boutiques reached out and told me she no longer wants them. They're too much for her, and she wants to sell them back to me for what she paid."

The hand that was on my neck tightened. "You didn't take her offer, did you?"

"I thought about it." I paused. "I wondered if I left our business, if things would get better with Rhett and Brady. I don't know about your brother, but mine is so bothered by us being together and seeing us interact. It's not helping our case. So, if I worked somewhere else—"

"Fuck no. That's not happening. I don't give a damn what Rhett and Brady like. It's not their call to make, and their opinion doesn't weigh enough to influence you to leave." He tilted my face up a bit more. "Do you hear me?"

I nodded.

"We'll figure this out, Rowan. We will."

It took me several seconds to say, "Something has to give."

He rubbed a circle over my navel. "It will. Trust me."

I linked my fingers behind his neck.

Exhaustion was taking over my body, but it wasn't settling my mind. What was happening in there was like a shooting range, and with each bullet, I kept missing the target.

"Why?" That was the only syllable I was able to release.

"Why what, baby?"

My thumbs dived into the sides of his hair. "Why do you love me?" When he began to wipe some of my tears, I added, "What was one of the things that made you fall for me?"

His lips parted, and a puff of air came from them, full of sage and burnt orange, scents that I'd grown to crave.

He took his time looking around my face, as though I were art, and underneath each layer of paint, he was seeing a piece of symbolism that he hadn't noticed before. "Even in your sleep, you reach for me. It could be the middle of the night, and in between your deep breaths, your foot will cross my ankle, or your hand will cling to my arm, or your fingers will intertwine with mine. When you showed me you need me in your dreams as much as you want me in your life, I knew I was in love." He pressed the softest kiss against my lips, his palm still rotating against that special spot.

"Rowan," he said once he separated us, "it's time to take that test."

Chapter Thirty-One

COOPER

I sat on Rowan's bed, my feet on the floor, my eyes on my leather Tom Ford cap-toe shoes. I was still wearing my suit, but when I'd brought her into the bedroom, I'd taken off my jacket and tie and unbuttoned the first few buttons of my shirt. While she was in the bathroom, taking the test, I waited out here. My brain in a completely different place than it had been when I drove to her house.

Eh.

A word that was almost laughable now. But a word that had been strong enough to get me into my car and bring my ass here. I hadn't even been aware that a drive had the potential of changing my whole fucking life.

A baby.

With Rowan.

I hadn't predicted this. Expected it. And despite everything I'd said to Rowan in the kitchen a few minutes ago, I was positive I wasn't ready for a baby. But she didn't need a man who would fall apart during moments when she felt she was at her weakest. She needed someone to hold her up. Someone who was there for her. Someone she could trust, count on, rely on, who would wipe the tears that fell and dry her face once they stopped.

Sure, inside, I was a fucking mess. Afraid. Fearful. Questioning if I could handle the responsibility, if this would change our relationship that was going so well, and if it would create strain on the love that was holding us together.

If I was prepared to take this on.

But would I ever be?

I remembered a conversation I'd had with Ford Dalton, during one of the times he'd had a few cocktails and turned transparent about his daughter. Being ready was one of the things he talked about. That, at the time, he hadn't been. That he hadn't known what the fuck he was doing, and it was a surprise he hadn't been prepared for.

But that surprise had turned into the biggest blessing of his life.

I believed that.

I saw Ridge at the office with Daisy, his daughter. How he held her tiny hand when they walked down the hallway. How she sat on his lap behind his desk, attempting to help her dad get some work done.

The way he looked at her.

The way he cared for her.

I could do that.

Even if it was something I'd wanted years down the road, with a wedding band on her finger, and one house instead of two. If the merger had taught me anything, it was that things didn't always go the way I'd originally planned. But when a new course had been chosen for us, what had come out of that was an even larger fleet of properties, partnering with a woman I'd fallen in love with, and an empire that was now worth double and more than we could have ever built on our own.

What would come out of this wasn't something I could dominate. All I could do was embrace it. Open my arms and accept that something much larger was in control.

So, when the handle of the bathroom door twisted, my ears picking up the sound of the metal, my head lifted to meet Rowan as she opened the door and walked out, her socked feet stepping across the hardwood floor. I straightened my back and spread my arms, and I wrapped them around her the second she was within reach.

"I haven't looked yet," she whispered.

Her free arm rested on my shoulder, and the other held the test off to the side, a strip of plastic I hadn't bothered to attempt to read as she made her way to me.

While I held her waist, I stared into her gorgeous face. Cheeks that were even more flushed than before. Eyes that were still glossy, rimmed in red from all the emotion she'd shed.

"It doesn't matter what it says, Rowan. My feelings for you aren't going to change."

Although I'd already promised her that, she needed to hear it again.

She needed to feel it in the way I held her.

"Cooper...I'm terrified."

Her vulnerability was one of her sexiest traits. The fact that she could say those words and not feel ashamed or bashful about speaking such a raw truth. That was what I wanted from her. That was what I wanted to be here for—to help her overcome that sensation.

To take the weight so she didn't have to bear it alone.

"Talk about it," I said. "Tell me why."

She glanced up at the ceiling, like she was trying to catch her breath. "It's almost double-sided. On one side, if I'm pregnant, we're going to be having a baby, and neither of us is ready for that. And if I'm not, then my anxiety is creating some scary things, and my body is revolting from all the nerves."

"If a baby is coming, then we're going to make ourselves ready." I backed that up with my grip, giving a strength she needed. "Whatever that looks like, Rowan, we'll make it happen. And if you're not pregnant, then we're going to focus on why your body is revolting and solve that problem."

I could take work off her plate and delegate many of her responsibilities.

The real issue here was how Rhett and her family were going to react to this news when things were already so fucking turbulent with them.

On top of that, there was something else. Something she didn't know about—or she would have told me—a bit of impending news that had the potential of pulling Rowan into the darkness.

A layer that would change things even more.

For her.

For everyone.

An unexpected divergent.

And something told me that when that news was finally shared, the dynamics between her immediate family would be much different.

I just didn't want that news to make things worse for her.

And I knew it would.

I gripped her tighter, moving my hands toward her navel. "One step at a time." I then lifted my arms and cupped her face, aiming her gaze at mine. "I love you. Know that." I squeezed. "Feel that."

"I do." She nuzzled into my hand. "And I love you too."

The movement was slow, steady, her fingers rising through my stretched arms, and she positioned the test between us, my stare on the window that showed the results.

A word that was as clear as day.

"Cooper…"

My eyes returned to hers, the emotion slowly seeping in, filling the beautiful emerald with pools of tears.

I was positive the same emotion was entering mine as well.

I didn't let my thoughts explode.

I kept my mind on track.

The here, the now, the way Rowan needed me, and my hands worked their way down until they were positioned at her waist to frame her stomach.

This was no longer just a part of her body.

This spot, this center, was now the home of my baby.

As she continued to stand in front of me, I pressed my lips against her belly, pushing against the flatness, knowing it was only a matter of time before it started to grow.

I would be here for that.

I would rub it.

Kiss it.

Talk to it.

The same way I was doing now.

Her hand went to my head, sliding through my locks as my mouth stayed glued to her. Whatever was inside, I needed it to feel my love.

"My baby," I whispered. I kept my lips there and looked up at her. "Our baby."

Chapter Thirty-Two

ROWAN

Even though I'd feared my anxiety had gotten out of control and the symptoms I was experiencing were a result of that, deep down—as much as I couldn't believe it—I had known I was pregnant. So, when I saw *pregnant* on the digital test that I'd taken with Cooper at home, every one of my fears was confirmed.

And maybe even a part of me, a small part, was relieved that it wasn't all in my head. That my body was acting this way because a baby was growing inside of it and that it wasn't stress or my nervous brain causing me to be sick.

An appointment with the OB-GYN confirmed, once again, everything we had already known to be true. But what sealed that truth was hearing the baby's heartbeat. That little pound, which sounded more like a chug, caused both of us to get misty-eyed.

We discussed with the doctor that when I hit my second trimester in a few weeks, we would find out the sex of the baby.

Cooper and I agreed; we didn't want to wait until the delivery to know what we were having. We wanted to finalize a name and have something to call our little one. We wanted to choose a color when it came to the design of the nursery.

Each night, while we lay in bed, him rubbing circles over my belly, we talked about what this pregnancy would look like, how we wanted the birth to take place in the hospital, how I was a firm believer in pain management when it came to the delivery. How I would continue to work until I was ready to stop with every intention of returning to my position once I felt comfortable enough to leave the baby.

We didn't want a gender reveal party. We wanted that moment to stay intimate, just like our entire relationship had been.

Of course, Sky would insist on a baby shower. Cooper said his mother would, too, and I knew mine would want to plan one, but there was plenty of time for that. We weren't even out of the first trimester yet.

And until we were beyond that fragile time frame, we weren't going to tell our families.

We wanted to stay in this perfect, happy bubble for as long as we could.

Since I wasn't showing, that made things easy to do.

But what was surfacing from my body was a need to nest. I wanted to look at the space in my home where our baby would eventually sleep. I wanted the sight of a crib. A rocking chair. A changing table and a custom closet.

And those were the things I tried to visualize as I stood in the doorway of my guest bedroom, looking at the space, trying to determine where everything would go.

"What are you doing, baby?" Cooper's arms surrounded me from the back, his hands pressed against my stomach, a warm, semi-rough cheek brushing mine before his lips made their way to my neck.

"Thinking. Planning. You know, all the things."

"What kind of things?"

"Crib things. A rocking chair thing."

"*Ohhh*. That."

I turned my neck to look at him. "You haven't thought about any of that?"

"Sure I have." His smile was mischievous. "Tell me how you're feeling."

"You mean since the last time you asked twenty minutes ago, right before you took that phone call, and I wandered in here?"

He laughed. "Pregnancy has made you even spicier." He kissed me.

"I'm exhausted," I said when I got my lips back. "I know I took a nap earlier, but I'm almost ready for another."

He lifted his hands to my shoulders. "Does anything hurt?"

"Everything. Just rub."

He began to massage from my neck to my biceps, working into the muscles, getting areas I hadn't even realized ached.

"*Yesss*."

"How about here?" He moved to my lower back.

"Oh my God. Whatever you do, do not stop."

He chuckled as he focused on my SI joints, and the looseness he was creating caused me to lean against his chest.

"Are you hungry?"

"You're always trying to feed me, Cooper."

He rose to my spine, tracing up to my neck and down to my tailbone. "I was feeding you before you were carrying my baby. Nothing has changed."

"While you were on your call, I snacked on some pineapple."

"You finished the one I just cut up, didn't you?"

"*Mmhmm*. I can't get enough. The tartness and coldness—it's everything."

"I know. It's your fourth one this week. All I want to do is have Klark make you these elaborate meals, and the only thing you want to eat is pineapple."

"It's all that sounds good to me. Damn you, first trimester."

His fingers climbed their way across my lower back. "Do you feel well enough to go out?"

"If you keep rubbing, I'll say yes to anything."

"Anything?"

I gently elbowed him. "If I don't fall asleep the second I hit the bed tonight, then, yes, anything."

He growled in my ear, his hands pushing harder, sliding to my hips and past my sides. "Come with me."

He held out his hand, waiting for me to grasp it, and he walked me through my house and out the door, locking it with his key.

When we were in the car, his hand settled on my thigh, heading out of my driveway, I asked, "What do you have up your sleeve, Spade?"

"What do you mean?"

"You're not taking me to dinner—you know I won't be able to eat without getting sick. You didn't give me time to grab my purse or phone. So, where are you taking me exactly?"

He lifted my hand to his lips, pecking the back of my knuckles. "I can't have you all to myself for a couple of hours?"

My eyelids narrowed. "I know you better than that."

"Enjoy the ride, Rowan. It's going to be a short one."

We weren't going in the direction of restaurants—that much I knew. We also weren't headed toward any shops. This was the area of town where our houses were located, and we were only getting deeper into the residential section.

But as he continued to weave through the Hollywood Hills, a thought came to me. My birthday was in a couple of days...he wouldn't.

He couldn't.

"For the record," I said, "if you're taking me to a surprise party or anything that even remotely looks like that, I will kill you."

"And give you that level of attention that you'd absolutely hate?" He grinned. "I wouldn't dare."

"But Sky would, and if the two of you are up to something—" I cut myself off when he pulled through an open gate, entering a driveway where he parked not far from the front door.

There was another car in front of us.

One I didn't recognize.

He turned off the engine and tilted his body so he faced me. "Let's talk about your thirtieth for a second."

I glanced from the house to his face. "We're going to talk about it here?"

"What do you want for your birthday?"

My hand went to my stomach. "I have everything I want." I sighed. "Okay, I lied. I would give anything to have the dirtiest martini and some sushi. And to stay twenty-nine because I just don't love the idea of turning thirty." I deflated into the seat. "Since none of that is possible, I swear I don't want anything."

"I'll drink one for you."

I rolled my eyes. "Of course you will. Dick." I winked.

He cupped my neck. "I've thought a lot about what I want to get you. What feels right, given the way our lives have recently changed. We haven't talked about the next steps of our relationship and what that looks like. I want to."

I studied his dark blue eyes. "You mean…marriage?"

"Yes."

"Cooper, we don't have to—"

"Hear me out." His thumb grazed my lips. "We're bringing a human into this world, and we're going to be that human's parents. I don't want you to feel like you're alone in this. That there's anything you have to do by yourself. I will be here, always."

"I know," I whispered, the emotion already nagging at me.

"But as I've been processing those thoughts, I can't help but wonder if you want to go into that delivery room with an engagement ring on your finger. Or a wedding band there instead." His stare deepened, and I swore I could feel it penetrate my chest. "I tried to put myself in your shoes. To consider what I would want if I were you." He shook his head. "I can't even attempt to go there and take a stab at what those hormones would make me want or feel."

I kissed the back of his thumb. "I'm relieved there's only one of us experiencing those hormones. Having both of us be this emotional and achy and needy would be over the top."

When we both stopped laughing, he said, "I want to give you what you want, Rowan."

"What I want..." I said in my softest voice, pondering that question as my words hit the air. "Here's the thing: a ring isn't going to change the way I feel about you or what's going to happen between us. We're still so new, Cooper, and we've created something that's about to rock our worlds. There's no reason to rush an engagement or marriage just because I'm pregnant. Besides, taking your name isn't going to make me love you more. You have me." My hand went to his. "I know I have you. That's enough." I leaned across the front seat to get closer to him. "But you know what I love? That you just asked that, that you would do anything to make me happy. That you left the decision up to me rather than proposing because you felt like it was the right thing or you felt obligated."

"When I put a ring on your finger, Rowan, it won't be because you're carrying my baby or out of an obligation. But because I want you to be my wife. And I would ask you that question right now and have zero regrets."

He'd shown a level of commitment that had taken me by storm.

But for what we were facing, for the times we had ahead of us,

I wanted to soak in the now.

I wanted to get to know our relationship more.

I wanted to fall in love with him again after he became a father.

"Our baby is so lucky to have you as their dad." I relished in his gaze. "You're going to put that peanut's needs first, just like you put mine. It takes an incredible man to do that, and that's another thing I love about you."

"You can keep the compliments coming."

I kissed him, needing to taste that cuteness and charm, and when I pulled back, I took a look at the stunning house that was in front of us.

Two stories. The prettiest white-and-sage exterior. Pristine landscaping.

"Why are we here?" I asked.

"We have a showing."

My neck whipped to the left to stare at him. "A...*what*?"

"It goes back to your birthday and what I thought about getting you. Jewelry? That's too simple. A car? You can buy fifty of those yourself. What you don't have is a home that belongs to us." He held my chin. "A house where we're going to raise our family. Where we'll sleep every night under a roof that we call home. Where I'll get to watch our child grow inside you. Where our baby will spend their first night when we bring them home from the hospital. You told me you have everything, but, Rowan, we don't have this."

The tears were present, and the first one dripped. "Cooper..."

"I called my realtor and had him pull a handful of houses that would meet our criteria. Things I knew you'd want, mixed in with my requirements. Once we view this house, he'll take us to the four others he picked. If none meet our needs, then we'll keep looking until we find one we love."

"A home." I could barely get the words out.

A place that was a piece of the three of us.

Where our baby would grow up.

We would never have to decide if we were staying at his house or mine.

We were meeting in the middle.

And that was exactly where I wanted to be.

I slipped my fingers across his cheek, holding a part of him that was as handsome and sexy as his eyes. "Both of these gifts"—I nodded toward the house and then glanced down at my stomach before meeting his stare again—"are the best things you could ever give me."

"I want to give you and our baby the world, Rowan."

Chapter Thirty-Three

COOPER

Rowan: *Headed to the interior designer's office in a few minutes. Since the realtor got back to me this morning and said he could get us into the new house, I'm going to bring her there so she can start taking measurements.*

Me: *I want shit ordered as soon as possible, so have her make mock-ups of each room immediately.*

Rowan: *Yes, sir. LOL.*

Me: *We're moving in 2 weeks, baby. I want the house perfect for you. We still have time to make it perfect for our little one.*

Me: *How are you feeling this morning?*

Rowan: *The doc wasn't kidding about the second trimester. Aside from being tired, I'm pretty good. The breakfast you made is staying put, and I even dug into some pineapple after you left for work. ;)*

Me: *Don't rush into the office. We have no meetings today. Take full advantage of that. Shit, take the day off.*

Rowan: *Not my style—you know that.*

Me: *Are you still good with me telling my family today?*

Rowan: *We're in the clear. No reason to hide it from them anymore.*

Me: *When you get to the office, we'll tell them together.*

Rowan: *Cooper, we've talked about this. You're going to tell your fam. I'm going to tell mine. I still think it's better that way.*

Me: *I was just seeing if you'd changed your mind.*

Rowan: *Have you seen Rhett this morning?*

Me: *We passed each other in the hallway. It was silent and uneventful.*

Rowan: *He dug at me in our family group text and said I'm never in the office anymore and I'm barely working. We've been to Canada five times in the last month. Just because I'm not at the office doesn't mean I'm not working. For him to even question my work ethic literally makes me bananas.*

Me: *I know that. Everyone knows that, I promise.*

Me: *Don't let him get under your skin.*

Rowan: *I'm about to get in the car. I'll call you on my way into the office.*

Me: *I love you.*

Rowan: *xo*

I set my phone down, still staring at the screen and her messages about Rhett, my blood fucking boiling. His comment was bullshit. He knew that Rowan was the most dedicated, hardworking executive we had on this team. He also knew that making that comment would piss her off.

He could have said far worse.

But the fact that he'd said anything at all, that was what got to me. That he had intentionally tried to hurt her. If he was teasing her, like big brothers often did, I could forgive that. But since the merger, Rhett had made things progressively worse, and I knew the moment he found out about this pregnancy, he was going to flip his shit.

I'd been putting off the inevitable, hoping things would repair themselves, wishing the motherfucker would come to his senses.

That obviously wasn't going to happen.

Discussing this with him wouldn't get me anywhere. He was too hotheaded.

I needed to go in the back way.

Which I would, but first, I had to tackle my own family.

I picked up my office line, hitting the button that would connect me to our assistant.

"Hi, Cooper. How can I help you?" Kathleen asked.

"Can you set up a meeting with my brothers and Jo? I want it to be today. As early as possible. And put us in the conference room, it has more room than my office."

"I'll work on that right now, and I'll text you the time."

"There's one more thing I need you to work on..."

"I now have to use our assistant to coordinate our schedules to get us all at the same place, at the same time," I said to my family as I walked into the conference room, where they were already seated around the table. "What the fuck happened to us? When did we get so busy?"

"Pre-merger, we were busy," Jo said, the exhaustion evident on her face. "Post—I don't even know what day it is."

I took a seat at the head. "We need an executive meeting to discuss more staffing. Of course, we have to include the Coles in that meeting. I'm sure they're drowning as much as we are. I know Rowan is at least." I set my hands on the table, linking my fingers. "I can't speak for the other two. I've only had a few exchanges with Ridge and nothing but dirty looks from Rhett, so I don't know how either of them feels about the workload."

"Ridge and I have had plenty of conversations," Macon said. "I can't believe I'm going to say this, but I actually like the dude."

"Nah, I can see that," I replied to him. "The couple of times we've talked, he's been cool."

"Rhett's a lost cause." Brady sighed.

The room turned silent.

"Listen, there's always one in every family who makes things a little more challenging," I told them. "Brady is our challenge." I gave my eldest brother a big, fat grin.

"Fuck off." Brady gave me the finger.

Jo straightened the collar of her jacket and looked at Brady. "You've been that way for as long as I can remember. We love you for it."

"Speak for yourself," Macon joked. "Brady's just all right in my opinion."

"Well, your opinion sucks," Jo countered.

"Someone is suddenly Team Brady now?" I teased my cousin.

"Why are we talking about me?" Brady shook his head. "Am I the reason you dragged our asses in here, or was it to gossip about the Coles, or do you have an actual purpose for this meeting? Because I have a shitload of things I need to do, and I really don't feel like spending all night at the office."

I chuckled. "Perfect example." I nodded toward Jo. "And you were actually leaning toward Team Brady."

Jo rolled her eyes.

"I brought you in here to tell you guys some news." I looked around at each of their faces.

Macon, taking in the silence, hovered his body over the edge of the table. "You bought her a ring, didn't you? That's what this is about."

"No." I glanced down, wondering what they were going to say to the next part. "Rowan and I are having a baby." I rubbed my lips together, waiting for their reactions. Just in case they needed more, I added, "She's pregnant."

Macon's response came immediately. With his hands flat on the table, he pushed up on them, semi-standing. "Before I freak out, this is a good thing, yeah?"

I chuckled. The question was certainly warranted. "Yeah, man. It's a really good thing."

"*Fuuuck* yeah!" Macon yelled. He got up and wrapped me in a man hug. "Congrats, brother. I'm going to be an uncle. Shit, I'm excited."

When he released me, Jo reached across the short distance between us and put her hand on my arm. "Oh, Cooper." Her eyes gleamed as she gazed at me. "I'm so, so thrilled for you and Rowan. Why isn't she here so I can congratulate her too?"

"She wanted me to tell you guys alone." I thought of how to phrase the next part. "She thought it would be better."

"Because of me," Brady said.

His voice sliced through the air.

I nodded. "Yes, you're one of the main reasons."

His arms stayed crossed, the same position they'd been in since he'd sat down.

"I know you're not pleased about us—"

"I'm over it, Cooper," he said, cutting me off, his arms finally dropping. "I've been over it. The fact that you keep tiptoeing around me is what I don't understand." I went to cut in, and he continued, "Do you think I'd be upset that you and your girl are going to bring another Spade into this world? Fuck no. I'm happy for you guys."

"But she's a Cole," I offered.

"And I'm a fucking adult." He pushed his chair back and crossed his legs. "I wasn't happy in the beginning. I was furious at Walter for this merger. We all were. I just let it eat at me for a lot longer than the rest of you." He exhaled loudly. "I haven't exactly warmed up to Rhett, Ridge, or Rowan, which is on me. I'm not against the idea. I just haven't bothered to make an effort."

"But you will?" Jo asked.

Brady seemed to really think about the question. "I'll consider it."

That was as strong of an answer as we would get from him.

But I could tell he wasn't done by the way he was eyeing me up.

"Are you going to marry her?" he asked.

"Yes." I turned my chair to get a better angle of my oldest brother. "We've talked about it. She knows how I feel and what I want. And it'll happen. We're just going slow—as slow as we can, given that we're going to be parents soon."

"Do you know what you're having?" Jo asked. "I have so much I want to buy that little nugget. I need to know if I'm buying pink things or blue things."

I smiled. "We find out in a couple of weeks."

"Dude, we're going to spoil the shit out of that kid," Macon said.

"How's Rowan feeling?" Jo asked.

"She just got through the first trimester, which kicked her ass. She was sick to her stomach. Tired all the time. Achy as hell. She's doing a lot better, but now, she's on the verge of showing, so I'm sure a whole new set of symptoms will be coming for us."

"How are you handling all of this?" Macon asked. "I mean, you went from zero to a million. You good?"

Another question that was well deserved, but my answer was ready and honest. "I'm definitely good. I'm just trying to give her everything she needs. I have the easy part when it comes to this."

Brady tapped his hand on the table. "Now, it makes sense why you got a new house. I'm assuming it's for all of you?"

"*Ahhh*," I breathed out. "At thirty years old, I'm finally saying goodbye to my bachelor pad." I grinned. "Instead of deciding on her place or mine, I thought fresh would be best."

"Good call," Brady replied.

"A fucking baby," Macon voiced softly. "I wasn't expecting that."

"Neither were we." I laughed. "I think it still shocks the hell out of us every day."

Macon's back straightened. "Does her family know?"

My head hung. "She plans to tell her parents soon now that we're past the twelve-week mark. Ridge probably as well. But I know she's afraid to tell Rhett."

"I'm going to give you a piece of advice," Brady said before the room had a chance to turn quiet. "You're the problem, so you need to fix that shit for her. Do it now before it spirals even further out of control."

"I'm already on it," I told them.

"Hi," Rowan said as I answered her call, her voice coming through the speakers of my car. "I'm just heading to the office now. The meeting with the designer went great. She took photos. Measurements. I think we're going to see mock-ups in just a few days—which, before you ask, is record timing."

I chuckled. "Excellent."

"Where are you? It sounds loud."

"I'm driving to Walter's."

"Now?" She paused. "*Ohhh*, you're going to tell him the news, aren't you?"

That, among several other things, but I wasn't going to mention any of that to her.

"Yes." I turned at the light, heading toward Beverly Hills. "I told Macon, Brady, and Jo about the baby this morning."

"Oh my God. *Annnd*?"

"Everyone is really happy for us. Even Brady, if you can believe it." I slowed at the red light.

"Honestly, I kinda can't." She became silent. "He seriously had positive things to say?"

"I know it's hard to process this, but things with him are going to be okay."

Air huffed through the speaker. "In other words, I can stop avoiding him in the hallway."

"Please don't do that anymore. Face him straight on. I promise that will get things moving much faster between you two. I know that puts things on you, but in this case, it's needed."

"I can be the alpha in this scenario. I don't mind." Her voice made me smile.

"He's not going to bear-hug you, like Macon probably will the next time he sees you, but I assure you, when it comes to Brady, you have nothing to worry about."

"Cooper…" Emotion was suddenly filling her tone. "I'm so relieved."

"Does that mean you'd be down for a family dinner tonight?"

She laughed. "Tonight? Really?"

"Jo and Jenner invited us over to their house to celebrate the news. She promises mocktails, whatever the fuck that is. Macon and Brooklyn are coming. Brady said he is too. I wouldn't be surprised if some of the Daltons pop over."

"I want to cry."

"It'd better be out of happiness."

"It is." She sniffed. "Oh God, I'm just suddenly so overwhelmed by all the love."

My grin grew as I pulled up to Walter's gate, hitting the code that would allow me to enter. "I'll call you on my way back to the office, baby."

"See you soon."

I hung up and parked off to the side of his driveway, an area designated just for his guests. While I was walking to the front door, Walter's housekeeper, Mary Sue, opened it. A woman who had been working for him since he'd divorced Jo's mom and bought this mansion.

"I saw you drive in," she said as she welcomed me. "It's nice to see you, Cooper."

"And you, Mary Sue." As I stepped into the foyer, my stomach growled from the scent. "Did you make cookies?"

She smiled, her cheeks like a paper fan with the way her wrinkles folded. "Chocolate chip, just took them out of the oven. I'll bring some into the study, along with milk." She patted my shoulder. "Hurry on. Your uncle is waiting for you."

I made my way through the house, passing through the wide hallways and boxy rooms, sconces on the wall leading me toward the back, where his study was located. Inside, the walls were aligned with hardcovers and antique art, the room filled with the scents of leather and a faint hint of cigar.

Walter's style was more old money than new money.

"Cooper," he said as I neared the couch where he was sitting. He didn't rise to shake my hand; he just extended his arm. "I was surprised to hear from Kathleen today, inquiring if I was free to meet."

"I'm surprised you're not out, golfing with my father."

He released my hand. "I was intrigued to hear what my nephew had to say and moved our tee-off time."

I took a seat on the couch across from him, the cushion beneath me not even sinking when I sat. "What I have to say is a conversation that's been long overdue."

"How so?"

I stayed silent as Mary Sue delivered a plate of cookies with three glasses of milk, shutting the door after she left.

When the lock clicked into place, I said, "Since the merger, today's the first day I can say that things feel back to normal between my brothers and me. Brady finally came around, but, Jesus Christ, it was a battle."

"I knew it was only a matter of time before it happened."

I rested my elbow on the armrest, loosening my tie. "You know, you've been saying that since day one."

"That's because I know my family. I know what they're capable of. And I was right."

"But the problem is, Walter, we don't know the Coles. We don't know why we were supposed to hate that family for all these years. We just heard you and my father bash them nonstop. In turn, we tore them apart because we felt if the Coles were that bad to you and Dad, we couldn't ever find anything redeeming in them." I gripped my neck, trying to keep the resentment out of my voice. "Had we known what they'd done to you, we could have made our own choice. We could have moved on much faster than we did—and even though we're past it, we still don't have much of a relationship with them."

"You mean the brothers. I'd say your relationship with Rowan is just fine."

I nodded. "You're correct."

"What are you asking for, Cooper?"

I took off my suit coat and rested it over the back of the couch, my arms pressed against my knees. "I want to know why you and Ray had it out for each other. What caused this whole goddamn mess in the first place. And I want to know why, out of nowhere, you wanted the companies to merge."

Walter crossed his legs, but never broke our stare. "Why does it matter? The past is in the past."

"I understand that your generation isn't the strongest communicators, but my generation doesn't have that problem. We overshare. And as partners, we have the right to know what instigated this." As I took a break, I scanned the room, remembering all the business chats that had gone down in this exact spot over the years. "Most importantly, when Rowan and I bring our baby into this world, we want support from both sides. I'm not confident that we'll get that from the Coles."

"I see." Walter's eyes narrowed. "Sounds like congratulations are in order."

"It is—"

There was noise at the door, the twisting of the handle, opening just enough for Ray to walk through.

"Gentlemen," he said as he shut the door behind him. He shook both of our hands, and he took a seat on the chair that was to the side of the couches.

I addressed him and said, "Thank you for joining us, Ray."

His hands had a slight shake to them as they lifted off his lap and settled on the armrests. "What did you want to talk to me about?"

I stared at the man with respect, frustration, and with sympathy. "There's a problem. I want to talk to you about it, and I want to know how you're going to fix it."

Chapter Thirty-Four

ROWAN

I came to a halt halfway between my father's kitchen and living room, my eyes widening, my face looking as startled as I felt.

What are they doing here?

Ridge and Rhett were plopped on the large sectional in the living room, a beer in their hands. Ridge busied himself while he looked at his phone, whereas Rhett glared right at me.

When I'd reached out to my dad last night, I'd told him that I needed to speak to him alone. This was the time he'd asked me to come over to talk.

Had he forgotten that I'd specifically said I needed to chat with him privately?

Or had he just completely ignored my request?

Regardless, there was no way I could have that talk with him now. Not with Rhett in the room. Which was another topic I'd planned to bring up once I told Dad I was pregnant.

Since that discussion wasn't going to happen today and I wasn't in the right mindset for what I assumed would be a volatile family reunion, I turned to head back into the kitchen to say goodbye to

Dad. Just as I did, holding the glass of water he'd previously been pouring when I came in, he walked toward me.

"I know what you wanted," he said in a low voice, a few feet separating us. "Please understand, this is what I wanted. And it's very important, Rowan."

Wasn't it important that he honored my wishes? Instead of disregarding what I'd asked for?

When I didn't respond, he moved past me and took a seat on the couch, tapping the spot beside him. "Come sit, Rowan."

I couldn't believe my ears.

I couldn't believe what I was seeing.

A talk—was that what he wanted? A conversation that would only frustrate us, and we'd circle the drain until one—or all—of us left?

As much as I wanted resolution—and, my God, I did—I couldn't handle any blowouts today.

I just didn't have it in me.

I wrapped my arms around my stomach and said, "Dad—"

"Please." He set his water on the small table next to the couch. "I've asked your brothers here and told them I need them to listen. Now, I'm asking the same of you." He nodded toward the kitchen. "If a drink will make you feel better, then go grab yourself one, like your brothers have."

If I could, I would.

The thought of a dirty martini made my mouth water.

But since I couldn't have anything stronger than a mocktail, I attempted to fill my lungs and sat beside my father, my brothers spaced out across the sectional with several cushions between them.

I glanced at my siblings. "I can't remember the last time the four of us got together like this."

"It's been too long," Ridge said.

I nodded. "I agree."

And the thought gutted me.

That we'd gotten to this place. That Rhett's feelings were so strong.

That things felt so broken.

"Where's Daisy?" I asked Ridge. "I'm dying for one of her hugs."

"With Mom," Ridge replied.

"I asked Ridge not to bring her because the four of us need to have a serious talk," Dad said. "It's difficult for me to say this, but I realize I've made a huge mistake, and I want to apologize."

I couldn't recall a single time in my life when my father had apologized for anything.

His tone, his choice of words—I was shocked.

I turned my body to face him. "What are you talking about, Dad?"

"The merger," he replied. "I gave you little to no explanation. One day, it was business as usual. The next, you're finding out we're partnering with a family you've despised your entire life." He sighed. "That's my fault. I'm to blame for this."

Rhett laughed. "And you decide to say this to us now? Not then? Not when it mattered most? So, for all this time, you've dragged us through something none of us wanted without giving us any explanation—"

"Yes," my father said, cutting him off. "That's precisely what I did, and I just apologized for it. I told you I made a mistake. I'm owning up to it."

I put my hand on my dad's leg. "Why don't you tell us how it all transpired? Maybe if we understand the how and the why, we'll deal with it better as a family." As I spoke, I looked directly at Rhett.

He was fuming. Even his cheeks were red.

His anger was boiling, and I knew that was from his unanswered questions.

I felt it too. We just let things affect us differently.

"I'll get to that," my father said. "First, I want to explain my history with Walter Spade, something I've also never told you before." He lifted the glass of water and took a sip. "Walter and I used to work together at a swanky Beverly Hills hotel. We were eighteen years old, alternating between bellhop and valet. If you can believe it, Walter was my very best friend."

Rhett hissed out some air. "No, I can't believe it."

"Until we were twenty-one, we were practically inseparable. During our lunch and dinner breaks, we'd talk about our goal of buying a hotel together. We both lived at home, and we saved every dollar we made to get us to that goal. Except a month after my twenty-first birthday, everything changed." When he shifted in his seat, a look came across his face that told me he was in pain.

"Archie, one of our regulars, was checking in, and I was his favorite bellhop. I was bringing up his luggage, and we got to talking, which we did every time he came to the hotel, as often as once a month. But this conversation turned more personal, and he asked what I wanted my life to look like in ten years." He gazed toward the windows, a view that overlooked the large pool out back. "I told him I wanted to own not one, but two hotels by the time I was thirty. And he asked how I was going to make that happen." A small grin came across his face. "So, I told him the pact I'd made with Walter, who he knew because Walter and I worked the same shifts." Still holding the water, he returned it to the table. "He told me about his business and how it had started with a partner, a good friend of his, and how it had destroyed their friendship, and he'd eventually bought out his friend. And he warned me that this would happen with Walter."

"I remember you mentioning Archie before," I offered. "Isn't he the one who left you the collection of cars when he passed, and that helped fund your second hotel?"

Dad nodded. "That's the one."

"I know the history of Cole International," Ridge said, "so I know you listened to his advice. Why?"

"Why?" my father repeated, linking his fingers. "What I learned by working in those two departments is that there's a big difference between having money and wanting money. That man had money. He'd done something right to earn it. So, when he spoke, I listened. Over the next six months, he called me regularly and became my mentor, and at some point, he offered to help me finance my first hotel."

"Why would he do that?" I asked. "What would he get out of it? Unless you gave him a cut?"

"I didn't." Dad pulled at his sleeves. "The man's wife had died a year before, and they had no children. I'm assuming, although I can't confirm, that he looked at me like a son. And just like I'd help any of you, he helped me. But there was one stipulation."

"Let me guess," Rhett offered. "Walter couldn't be a part of the deal."

Dad nodded. "The offer was me, or the deal was off the table."

"And you took the deal," Ridge added.

It wasn't a smile that covered my dad's face, more like he was recognizing he'd made the right decision. "Without any hesitation, shame, or regret." He let those words sink in. "Needless to say, Walter didn't take the news kindly. I was getting the opportunity the two of us had dreamed of, and he felt betrayed. But unless Walter and I got a backer, we'd never be able to afford the hotel or get approved for the financing. We both secretly knew that. Our aspirations were just so big, we didn't let it tarnish that vision." He bobbed his head. "That's why, when the offer came in, I knew I had to bite."

"And that's when the best friends became enemies," I said softly.

"Immediately," he told me. "Walter became jealous and bitter—I don't blame him. He ended up partnering with his brother, and that's when the games started. A ruthless competition that spanned over thirty years." When Dad pushed up a sleeve, I saw dark purple bruises on his skin, and before I could ask what they were, he said, "I wasn't innocent in all this, and I don't claim to be. I played that game just as hard as he did. We were rivals, and things got dirty. Was it wrong?" He shrugged. "Who knows at this point? We all did wrong. But had I not taken that deal, Cole International wouldn't have existed. The three of you wouldn't have been employed by the family business. I know for certain I wouldn't have had the life I've created." His eyes softened. "Or any of the life that I have left."

His choice of words made me say, "Dad—"

"Why didn't you tell us?" Ridge asked, interrupting me. "Why did you keep that to yourself for all these years?"

"Because it never mattered before. All you needed to know was that the Spades were a competing brand and the Coles didn't come in second place. The backstory was pointless chatter."

"But it mattered once we merged." Rhett's voice was sharp. "And even then, you didn't explain it to us."

"My priorities have been a little jaded lately, son."

I glanced at my brothers, who were so fixed on my father that nothing could pull their stares away.

"What are you saying, Dad?" Ridge asked.

He bent his leg, crossing it over the other one. "What you should be asking is, why did the merger take place?" His head lowered. "Since you haven't asked, I'm going to answer that for you." He took a breath, and it seemed almost labored.

"You know, I never envisioned what the end would look like.

Would it be a hundred hotels? A certain revenue? A specific age that I'd reach? I didn't know, and I never felt like it was enough, so I just kept going. Until I couldn't anymore." He'd been gazing at his lap, and he finally looked up. "It started with a pain in my stomach that I ignored for as long as I could."

"Dad..." A sense of dread came over me. It was so thick that my hand went to my throat, trying to help me breathe, the anxiety bringing me to that all-familiar edge.

"You said nothing about this," Ridge told him. "We had no idea you weren't feeling well."

My arm slipped around my father's shoulders as he said, "I saw one doctor after the next, not trusting any of their opinions. I thought they were just a bunch of fucking scam artists who wanted to hook me up to a machine and fill me with poison. For what? To make the pain feel only a small percent better? That's all they could promise me."

A wave of dizziness came over me, and it came on so hard and fast that I squeezed his shoulder to hold on.

Poison.

Pain.

Machine.

It couldn't be...

"I wanted an option that wasn't available for just anyone, something all the money in the world could buy. So, while you thought I was vacationing in France and Germany over the last few weeks, I was seeing specialists."

My hand left his shoulder and flattened against my stomach. "Please tell me they can help."

My eyes were already filling with tears. My chest was so tight that it felt like it was about to shatter.

"It's a good thing that, very early on in my diagnosis, I saw the writing on the wall. I knew what I was facing, and that was when I went to my old friend Walter," he said. "I intended to sell him the business. That would give the three of you more money than you'd ever need and far fewer headaches than if you continued to run this business together." He rubbed his hands as though they were cold. "Cole International was my dream. A dream that I forced on the three of you. So, I thought to myself, if I wasn't here, would they still want it? And when I couldn't answer that question, I knew I had to talk to Walter."

"Dad, how sick are you?" Ridge asked. "Are you—"

"Meeting Walter went differently than I'd planned," Dad continued as though Ridge had never asked about his health. "He told me he was on the verge of retiring, and handing both of our fleets to his three nephews and his daughter would be far too much. Handling the Spade hotels was one thing, handling all of ours, too, would be quite the task for only four executives. That's when we came up with the idea of merging. With the seven of you, we believed you could handle all the properties and you would dominate the hotel industry in a way we'd never been able to achieve individually."

"Dad—"

He put his hand up to stop me from speaking and continued, "We knew it would be rocky. There were a lot of personalities at play. We also knew that you would put your opinions aside and do what was best for the business.

"Considering we're not too far into the merger, the numbers are proving that you're running one hell of a business." He glanced at each of our faces. "As for the way you're treating each other, that needs a lot of work." A calm but needed grin spread across his lips. "But everything Walter and I wanted years ago is coming true, and we're enjoying our friendship again."

When the room was silent for a few seconds, Rhett pushed himself to the end of the couch. His legs spread, his arms resting on his thighs. "Dad, you're glazing over the most important part of this. Are you better? Worse? What's going on with your health?"

Dad took his time answering. "Nothing good, I'm afraid." The sadness in his eyes was evident as he looked at me and then shifted to my brothers. "I'm terminal."

That word made my entire body shiver, tremors that just wouldn't stop.

I was fighting a sudden wave of nausea, a pounding in my chest that had a rhythm I'd never felt before. "What does that mean?"

His hand went to my arm, his fingers icy as they held me. "I have less than a year to live."

"*Nooo!*" My hands covered my face as the scream shot from my lips. "This can't be right. There has to be something they can do—"

"There isn't." His hand was now on my back, rubbing circles.

"Fuck," Ridge groaned.

"Dad..." Rhett voiced in a tone I hadn't heard from him in a long time.

"They've tried everything. They've run every test. Nothing will kill this cancer. At best, they just want to keep me comfortable. That's what the seventh doctor told me last week, after I didn't believe the sixth one that I'd met with prior." His hand stilled on my back.

"I didn't give up hope, that was why I didn't tell you. Why I didn't want to make my illness the reason for this merger even if it was. And I needed some time to come to terms with every doctor telling me the same thing. That's why you're just finding out now." He focused on Ridge. "I don't want to be a patient." He then stared at Rhett. "I don't want you to look at me like I'm sick and incapable." And then he glanced at me. "What's keeping me going is the three of you and my Daisy. However much time I have left, that's how I want to spend it. With the four of you."

The emotion was taking over.

I could barely process what I was hearing or the reality of what I was facing.

The thought that, one day soon, my father would no longer be here.

It sounded like hope and love were the only things that were keeping him going.

As wrong as this timing was, I wanted to give him more of both.

"It's the five of us now, Dad." I felt every eye in the room turn toward me. With my hand on my stomach, I moved it in a circle. "I'm pregnant. Almost sixteen weeks."

"You're what?"

My gaze shifted to Rhett, who'd just blurted out those two words. "It's true." I then took in my father's face. "So, while you're fighting for the four of us"—the knot in my throat grew so large that I didn't know if it would ever shrink—"fight for this baby, too."

"You're pregnant." Dad's eyes seemed to elongate, his head moving in a way that told me the news was everything he had wanted to hear. "Now, I know why..." He put his hand on top of mine even though there wasn't any movement in my belly.

"What are you saying, Dad?" I asked.

"Never mind." He waved his fingers across the air.

"I wanted to tell you all. I just didn't know if the news would be accepted." I focused on Rhett. "The thought of you tearing apart this pregnancy because I'm having this baby with a Spade is something I can't handle." My throat constricted. "Especially now."

Just breathe.

I followed the saying.

I repeated the words.

"It's time to move on, son." Dad was speaking directly to Rhett. "It's my fault you feel the way you do. I ingrained those feelings in you at a young age, and you're just as competitive as your old man. You want the best, and the Spades were getting in your way. I can't fault you for that, but what I can tell you and show you"—he pointed at his chest—"is that life is too short."

Dad's hand went to the back of my head, holding it. "When I'm gone, your sister and her beautiful baby, your brother and Daisy, and your mother are all you're going to have left. So, if you're going to be angry with someone, be angry with me. Not the Spades. Not your sister. And not her unborn child."

I found Dad's fingers and clasped them within mine. "I l-love y-you." I fixed my gaze on Rhett. "And I-I love y-you." I wiped my eyes. "I feel like I-I've lost my b-brother, and now, I'm l-losing my dad, and it's—" My voice cut off as my father wrapped his arms around me.

The emotion had only partly come through, and now, it was racking my body, my breath coming out in pants. My muscles spasming, my stomach churning.

The pain was one thing. But the fear of losing someone I loved was entirely different, and it caused the angst to rock through me.

The feeling didn't shed from my body. It poured out like a dam had been lifted.

And while I felt the warmth of my dad's embrace, there was suddenly a whole new set of strength that moved around me.

That held me.

That wrapped his tight arms across my body, hands that landed on my stomach below.

I tried to see through the tears, knowing they were Ridge's, so I didn't know why I was bothering to look.

But when I saw the tattoo on his thumb, the tiny lion with the long mane, I found myself crying even harder.

"Rh-Rhett," I whispered, which was as loud as I could get, "don't ever let me go again."

Chapter Thirty-Five

Cooper

"How's your dad?" I asked Rowan when she walked into the kitchen after a visit with her father, closing my laptop and setting it on the table to focus solely on her.

She placed her purse on the counter as she made her way into the living room and sighed before she said, "Ornery."

She'd dressed in what had become my favorite getup. Yoga pants and a tank, a sweater hanging at her sides. What the outfit also showed, aside from her incredible curves, was the small bump she was finally sporting.

I couldn't get enough of it.

Every time she was within reach, I would rub it. Like I was planning to do now as I waved her over.

As she neared the chair I was sitting in, I captured her, and as I wrapped my arms around her, I pressed my face to her belly.

"What do you mean, ornery?"

"When I dote on him, he kicks me out." She rested her hands on top of my head. "Which is why I'm home. He literally told me to leave." She groaned. "His housekeeper can do everything for him, and he doesn't bitch. I offered to get him a drink when he started coughing, and by the way he reacted, you'd have thought I was committing a sin."

I kissed the center of her stomach, rubbing my scruff against it. "To him, baby, you are. He doesn't want to be a patient. He told you this. And when you ask him every five minutes if he's okay, that drives him wild."

"What would make you think I was doing that?"

"I know you." I smiled. "In fact, you were probably asking him every three minutes."

She rolled her eyes. "I can't help it, Cooper. I'm pregnant. I want to dote on him. I want to make sure he's okay. I have this motherly instinct that's hormonally pulsing through me. And when I see my father needs something, I want to get it for him. When he looks like he's in discomfort—or even if he doesn't—I'm going to ask."

I smiled. "Then, you're just going to keep getting kicked out."

She bared her teeth. "Ugh, I should bite you."

"Just don't be disappointed or upset when it happens." I laughed. "Were your brothers there?"

She ran her hand over my cheek. "Rhett was. Ridge had stopped by earlier with Daisy, but I missed them."

"Rhett's not leaving his side, is he?"

She shook her head. "He's taking it the hardest. I mean, we're all a mess—you know that, you see that. But Rhett and Dad are so similar. I'm worried about him. Hell, I'm worried about the both of them. It's consuming me."

Since the news broke, Rhett's change had been the biggest. Witnessing the way he was processing his father's illness wasn't easy to see. Not even knowing him that well, I could tell how badly he was hurting. All three of Ray's kids had been greatly affected. But the only positive that had come out of this was that Rhett was becoming an easier person to be around. There was still a lot of improvement needed, but at least the two of us were talking. We could have conversations without wanting to fight, where he wasn't fucking snarling at me. He'd even offered me a congratulations on the baby and shook my hand.

One day, we'd probably be friends. It was just going to take time.

Going to Walter and Ray was the best thing I'd done. Even though, at the time, I hadn't known why there was so much beef between the families, I knew Ray was the one who would have to fix what was happening within his. And I knew once he told them about his illness—something I'd learned from Jo because Walter had had too much wine and spilled the news—I had a strong feeling the dynamics were going to change.

And they had.

"Nothing is going to happen to Rhett," I promised her. "I know you've got him, and I know you'll coddle him as much as he'll let you, but I've got him too."

Her other hand joined my face, cupping both sides. "What would I do without you?"

"You won't ever have to know."

Her eyes suddenly widened, and at first, I thought she was reacting to what I'd just said, but then she grabbed my hand out of nowhere and placed it where my lips had been kissing her belly.

"Cooper, feel." Her hand went on top of mine, moving it around until she found the spot she was looking for. She pushed on the back of my palm, holding it tightly against her. "Did you feel that?"

There was a slight patter, like rain hitting the windshield.

"The baby..."

She nodded. "That's the first time I've felt anything like that."

"Is it a kick?"

"I think so."

I pulled my hand away and put my face there instead, my eyes closing, listening for the movement, any beat I could hear inside. "How could I love something so much and not even be able to hold it yet?" I turned my face to look up at her.

"Because it's a part of you." Her hand was now in my hair, running through my locks. "This is what love is—what it looks like, feels like." She took a breath. "This is fulfillment, Cooper."

"With the baby."

She searched my eyes. "And with us."

I remembered the conversation we'd had at the bar when she told me she'd never experienced love before. She'd mentioned that it was something she learned from her previous job when she worked the floor and saw the way couples interacted.

"Words that cause a smile," I said softly, repeating the statement she'd said back then almost verbatim. "A look of complete contentment and security. The comfort in certain acts— easy ones, like holding someone's hand."

"You listened to me," she whispered.

I winked. "I tend to do that a lot."

"God, I love you." Her hand went to her stomach. "And I love you."

I gave her belly one more kiss, and I stood, clasping my fingers with hers. "Come with me."

I walked her outside onto the patio, taking a seat on one of the couches in front of the fireplace.

Our new home had a different view of the Hills than the previous houses we'd lived in. The lot here was much larger, higher up, the scenery vast and open to the hills of homes.

With my arm around her shoulders, I reached into my pocket and pulled out the small box, setting it on her lap.

"What's this?"

I took in her profile, and, God, she was fucking gorgeous. Pregnancy had done nothing but enhance her features, making them more prominent. Everything on her face was richer—the color of her eyes, skin tone, even the way she moved her mouth and kissed me.

I held the back of her neck, rubbing across a spot that caused her to melt the moment I began to massage it. "We've had the results for almost a week. You've been extremely patient, and I know that wasn't easy. Never once have you asked when I'm going to give them to you."

A request I'd made when we went in for the last ultrasound, which revealed our baby's sex. I told the doctor to put the findings in an envelope rather than voice it out loud. And I'd told Rowan that I was going to do something special with the results. Since we still didn't want a party and we wanted to keep it only between us, that didn't mean I was going to allow the moment to escape without making it memorable.

"It's the gender of our baby," I told her.

"In this box?"

I laughed, knowing what I'd said sounded a little strange. "Yes."

She carefully pulled at the wrapping paper until the velvet box was bare, her hands positioned along the top and bottom, and she looked at me. "I can't believe we're finally finding out what we're having."

We'd chosen a name for each gender, both having an extremely special meaning to this family. Once we knew the sex, we'd continue to keep the name to ourselves until the baby was here, not even revealing it at the baby shower that was coming up in a few months.

We had our reasoning for keeping it private, and when the time came, everyone would understand why.

"Show me what's inside the belly that I love." I nodded toward the box. "Open it."

She gave me a kiss, her lips mashing against mine. The sweetness of her scent, the apples and cedarwood, was only getting stronger throughout her pregnancy.

When she pulled away, she carefully lifted the lid. "Oh my God. Oh my God!" With the box balancing on her lap, she covered her mouth with her hands.

Inside was a band of diamonds that I'd designed, the stones in multiple shapes as they spread across the platinum setting. Of course, I didn't know if those diamonds would be in pink or blue; the answer was in the envelope I'd handed to the jeweler, and the rest had been up to him at that point.

The color that stared back at me made my heart fucking pound and my lips pull into the widest smile.

"Cooper…" she breathed, the emotion thick in her voice as I lifted the ring out of the box and slid it over the appropriate finger on her right hand. When she looked at me, the tears were already starting to fall. "It's so beautiful." She threw her arms around my neck. "Just like our baby girl is going to be."

Chapter Thirty-Six

ROWAN

"We just landed," I said to my father, holding the phone to my ear as I climbed into the backseat of the SUV. "How's everything going?"

"You mean since you last checked in? Which was—"

"Just over three hours ago," Rhett voiced, cutting my father off, proving that Dad had me on speakerphone. "He's fine. We're both fine. Go have a good time. You have nothing to worry about."

Except I had everything to worry about. Dad was declining a little more every day. He was now using a walker to get around. If Cooper hadn't insisted on taking a babymoon, then I would have been sitting right next to Rhett, driving them both wild.

"Stop it, you two. You know I have to ask." I sighed. "I'll be back in four days and—"

"You're going to check in at least three times a day while you're gone, we know," Rhett said. "Do us a favor, at least try to spend some time with Cooper. That is why you're in Canada, isn't it?"

I looked at Cooper as he got in on the other side of the backseat and rolled my eyes. "Yes...*sir*."

That was one of the reasons we were here.

The other was to sign a lease on the house that Cooper had found us to rent, which we'd be moving into about six months after the baby was born. That was when the build-out on the two hotels would start, and we'd be relocating here until construction was done.

Cooper had wanted to go somewhere tropical for the babymoon.

But Banff was close, and I really wanted to see the house before I got too far into my third trimester and my doctor wouldn't let me fly anymore.

"You're missing the pie my housekeeper just made," Dad said. "It's peach. Delicious."

"And are you eating it?" I asked.

Dad's appetite was diminishing. The doctor just wanted him to eat and get in as many calories as possible. His housekeeper's desserts were the one thing he craved, so she baked for him every day.

And when I was there, I sampled.

I blamed her for all the baby weight I'd gained.

"He's devouring it," Rhett said.

"Good," I replied. The driver took us past the tarmac and onto the road, heading toward the rental. "I'll give you guys a call in a little bit. Dad, have another slice of pie, if you can."

"*Gooo*," Rhett replied. "I've got him. Stop worrying."

I smiled. "Love you guys."

"Love you," they said in unison, and I hung up.

"Everything all right over there?" Cooper asked, moving closer to put his arm around me.

"As well as they can be, I suppose." I set my phone on my lap, but as it vibrated, I lifted it to check the screen. "Even his voice is becoming weaker. What if he's not—"

"Don't." He pressed his lips to my temple. "I know what you're going to say, and that's not going to happen. He's fighting like hell to be here for when our baby is born. You see that every time you go over there. Focus on that, Rowan. The moment we get to set our little girl in his arms—that's what I want you thinking about."

I nodded.

Because if I said anything, the tears would come, and I didn't want to cry.

I'd done so much of that lately.

"What does Sky want?" he asked, his lips no longer on my temple, his head nodding toward my phone.

I'd forgotten that it had vibrated and that was the reason I was holding it.

Sky: *Peonies or lilies?*

Me: *You mean, in general or...*

Sky: *Your mom and I are in a full debate over the centerpieces for the baby shower. So, peonies or lilies?*

Me: *Peonies.*

Sky: *I'm always right. Don't worry, I won't say that to your mom. LOL.*

Sky: *I want you to know, I've been trying to get my niece's name out of her. She's either the best liar ever or she really doesn't know it.*

Me: *Girl, if Mom knew the name, so would you.*

Sky: *If that hadn't been your answer...murder.*

Me: *LOLOLOL.*

Sky: *How's Dad today? I'm sure you've talked to him no less than three times already.*

Me: *Actually, only two—shocker, I know. Today's pie flavor is peach. Hopefully, he'll be on his second slice soon.*

Sky: *Love you.*

Me: *I love you way more.*

"You're lucky to have her," Cooper said the moment I put my phone away, a conversation he'd been reading as I typed.

My friendship with Sky was something I never took for granted. It was a blessing I was thankful for every day of my life.

I stared at my man. "In ways I can't even describe." I nuzzled his face and then glanced out the passenger window. "I love it here."

"I know you do." He pulled me in tighter. "Which is shocking, considering how much you hate the weather, but I know this town's significance is much more important to you than the temperature. And just think, you're going to get to spend a shitload of time here pretty soon."

I glanced at him again. "Let's not rush that thought."

He nodded. "I know, baby." He pressed his lips against mine. "I know what that means, and I'm not ready for it either."

We weren't talking about the baby.

We were talking about the passing of my father. There was no way he had that much time left in him.

"Look," he whispered, "we're here."

I turned just in time to see the gate lift and the SUV pull up the driveway, stopping in front of the house. I blinked several times, taking in the exterior, the cozy but contemporary architecture, the well-maintained landscaping.

It was stunning.

But it wasn't the house we'd rented—at least not the one in all the pictures.

"Whose home is this?" I asked, but he was already out of the backseat, coming around to open my door. I clasped his hand, and he helped me out. "Cooper, where are we?" I asked since I wasn't sure he'd heard my last question.

"What do you mean?"

The smirk on his face told me he was up to something,

especially as we approached the front door and he hit several buttons on the keypad, the door unlocking and opening.

"I mean, this isn't..." My voice trailed off as I stepped inside, my neck immediately tilting back as I took in the tall ceilings that were decorated with beams. "My God, this is gorgeous."

"The place you picked was cute." His hand left my back and linked with my fingers. "But if we're going to have a nanny living with us because you plan on working while you're here, then we need a house much larger than the one you chose." He squeezed my fingers as our eyes locked. "Let me show you around."

I laughed as we headed into the kitchen. "You're unbelievable."

"Why?"

"I picked out a twenty-five-hundred-square-foot home, which is plenty big for three adults and a baby. You trump that with probably around, I'm guessing, five thousand square feet. With more rooms and extras than we'll ever need."

He stopped in the center of the kitchen, a room designed in white and cream and stainless steel, wrapped in a modern farmhouse feel. "You're saying you don't like it?"

"I *looove* it."

"I knew you would."

I released his hand to hold his arm. "Show me more."

He led me through the large, comfortable living room with its oversized couch and fireplace, the beams continuing throughout, past an office, dining room, the decorations becoming more intimate as we entered the primary suite.

"Wow." I left his arm to walk to the whole wall of windows, spanning the entire back of the bedroom, the view of the Rocky Mountains absolutely spectacular. "Cooper, I'm not going to hate waking up here every morning."

His arms surrounded me, his hands clutching my stomach.

"It's so pretty, it almost doesn't even look real."

"There's still a lot of house to show you. Four bedrooms upstairs. A gym. Theater room. Wait until you see the pool and guesthouse."

I slowly turned around to face him. "A guesthouse?"

"For the nanny."

My head tilted. "You don't want her to live upstairs in one of those bedrooms?"

"I want my wife to feel comfortable walking around naked if that's what she decides to do." He leaned into my neck, kissing just below my ear. "I want to be able to taste you on every counter in this house whenever I want." He straightened his back, towering over me again. "I realize she's going to be here all the time, but her having her own space will give us some needed privacy."

Wife was a title he'd been using more often when the two of us were alone.

A title that didn't come with a ring or marriage.

It didn't have to.

In my mind, I was already married to Cooper.

But that wasn't the reason I was grinning.

"It's going to be a while before we move in here, correct?" I confirmed.

His eyes narrowed. "Correct."

"So, you're telling me there aren't any tenants who are renting it in the interim."

He chuckled. "Why are you asking that?"

I glanced to my right, confirming what I'd seen when we first walked in. "Because there are some awfully familiar paper cranes and a wooden bear on the nightstand. Unless you're going to tell me the owner or tenant has the very same ones that we gifted to each other?"

He surrounded my face with both of his hands. "You don't miss a thing."

"You bought this house, didn't you, Cooper?"

"You love Banff." He swiped my cheek with his thumb. "We're going to be spending a lot of time here. Why not make it feel like home?"

"You got me a house in my favorite town. You even brought those gifts, which you know mean everything to me, to decorate the nightstand with. How do I even thank you for this?" I kissed him, fingering the bottom of his shirt.

"It's our favorite town, and you're giving me a baby. I don't need a thank-you."

I peeked over my shoulder at the view. "You know, it does make sense that our daughter should fall in love with the place where she was conceived."

"A detail she doesn't need to know for a *very* long time."

He'd reminded me how lucky I was to have Sky in my life. But I felt the same about my relationship with Cooper.

The way he put me and the baby first.

The way he supported us.

And loved us.

I giggled as I took a glance at the big, wonderful, fluffy bed. "If we now own this home, then that's our bed, right?"

"It is." He traced my lips with the pad of his finger. "Why are you asking?"

"I think you know why." I slipped my hand beneath the bottom of his shirt, running my palm over his abs.

"Is there something you want to do on that bed, Rowan?"

"I want you to fuck me." I pulled his shirt over his head, dropping it on the carpet, getting straight to work on his belt, button, zipper, and when those were unhooked and lowered, his jeans fell to his ankles. "Now."

"Do you know what I want to do?" He bent down to take off his shoes, socks, jeans, and stood back up in just his boxer briefs.

Cooper had been giving since the day we'd met. But since I'd started carrying his baby, his mouth couldn't get enough of me.

"You want to lick me."

He growled, "I always want to fucking lick you."

One of his arms went to my back, another slid behind my knees, and I was suddenly in the air. He no longer carried me from the front—he didn't want to put the pressure on my belly. And even with my heavy stomach, he still made me feel tiny in his arms while he crossed the carpet, setting me on the edge of the mattress.

The moment I was sitting, he got to work on my clothes, stripping every piece from my body until I was naked, and that was when he got on his knees, separating my legs, his head getting lost between them.

I could no longer watch what he was doing. I was too big to see past my bump.

But I could feel.

And since getting pregnant, that sensation had only been heightened. My entire body tingly, sensitive, and throbbing for him.

"Cooper..." I exhaled as he kissed up my thighs.

His tongue swirled across each inch that he pecked, getting closer to the spot that was craving him.

"I can smell how wet you are. Fuck, I can't wait to taste you."

I gripped the end of the bed, holding my legs apart, moaning in anticipation.

But he wasn't there yet.

He was taking his time. Pressing his mouth against the top of my leg and the inside, moving to the other thigh before he licked my entrance.

"*Yesss*." He flicked the same place again. And again. "Just as fucking wet as I knew you'd be."

I squeezed the comforter into my palms. "You're teasing me."

"No, baby, I'm teasing myself. I want it as much as you."

"Cooper, I—" I gasped as he moved to my clit. The place on my body that was screaming for him. It felt like a fire was brewing and his tongue was smothering the flames. "Oh. My. God."

It was almost too much—if that was even possible at this moment.

Because even though he was focused on my pussy, lapping the top while fingering the bottom, I didn't just feel it there.

I felt it in my nipples.

My throat.

My mouth.

"*Ahhh.*" My head fell back, my eyes squinting. I didn't have to focus. I didn't have to search. Whatever he was doing to me was bringing me right there. "Cooper!"

I was heading toward the peak. I didn't run. This was more of a delicious, incredible crawl as the tip of his tongue slapped across me horizontally several times prior to him sucking my clit into his mouth. While he held it with his teeth, giving pressure to each side, he used his tongue to add friction to the front. And when he released it, he resumed his previous speed.

"Fuck!" I yelled.

But that wasn't the only thing that was leading me. His finger was aimed toward my stomach, hitting that spot deep inside, circling it, using the same pressure as his tongue.

"Yes!" I cried.

My body rocked forward.

My knees fell inward.

"Cooper, *yesss!*"

The most intense blast shot through me, keeping me right there, like I was suspended in the air, and that lasted for at least a couple of seconds before the shudders set in.

"Fuck yes. Let me taste that cum."

Even the wiggles, as they racked my body, were wilder than I had been prepared for. These weren't waves. These were crests that had me holding on with all my strength while he drained the orgasm from my body.

He didn't stop. He just went softer, slower.

Until I completely stilled.

"Damn," I whispered. "You just ate me like you needed that orgasm for yourself."

"I did."

"My God, you're hot."

When he surfaced, my wetness was all over his lips, and as he licked it off, he slid out of his boxer briefs and moved me higher on the bed until my head was on a pillow.

Our options were somewhat limited with my belly, but what I really enjoyed was spooning. He knew that was where I was the most comfortable, and he immediately got in behind me, raising my leg over his, his hand going to my breast once we were locked in place.

"God, I fucking love you pregnant," he hissed as he entered me. "You're so tight, damn it, and you have no idea how wet you are right now."

He didn't slam as he thrust inside. That had changed since the addition of the belly.

Instead, he was gentle with his strokes. With the way he squeezed my nipple. How he flicked my clit with his thumb.

It was as though he was worried about the both of us and caring for the both of us at the same time.

But I begged, "More," because I needed a bit of roughness.

I needed his power.

I needed to feel his dominance.

"Just like that," I breathed. "Don't stop."

When it came to sex, Cooper paid attention to my entire body.

He aroused places that didn't necessarily cry for his focus, like my thighs, knees, and arms. But when his fingers or lips grazed one of those spots, it made me realize how much I was tuned into him.

How he had all of me.

How every part of my skin was just as desperate for him.

"You're getting tighter." He kissed the back of my neck. "I can feel how close you are."

Even his voice sent shivers through my core.

I reached behind my head and gripped his hair, trying to meet him in the middle each time he reared back and pressed in. "Harder."

"If I go harder, you're going to make me come."

"Then, make us come together." I drove my nails into his scalp, and while his pace picked up, I still demanded, "Faster."

"You're fucking naughty—you know that?"

I released my lip, something I hadn't realized I'd been biting. "Show me how naughty I am, Cooper."

My words hit a trigger because the moment they left my mouth, he instantly amped things up—from the way he drove into me to the way he touched my clit.

He was using all of me to bring me to that place.

"Fuck!" he roared.

As our bodies rubbed against each other, his flesh turned hot, and his breath swished all the way to my nipples. I could feel the short hairs on his lower stomach as they scratched my back, the prickly ones that hit my ass every time he plunged in.

I swore those hints of masculinity were a combination that helped bring me toward the edge.

Because within a few more pumps, I was shouting, "*Ahhh*," and my body was full-on building.

"You're even tighter," he grunted. "Fuck me."

This time, I wasn't dragged toward the peak.

I shot straight there.

And while I was frozen in that place, he plunged in even harder, his movements turning sharp, possessive, his breathing coming out in deep exhales. "Rowan!"

That was when I knew he was giving me exactly what I wanted.

"Just what I've been dying to hear." My body was starting to come down, the bursts less intense, the shudders slowing. But even through his strength, I could feel the wetness. How each stroke created more. "You're filling me."

"*Mmm.* Yes. *Fuuuck.*"

His comedown was as gradual as mine, and when he finally settled behind me, our rising chests the only movement, I released his hair, combing through the strands that I'd pulled.

Silence only ticked for a few seconds until I heard, "Are you okay?"

After each of our intimate moments, he always asked now.

I understood.

I was just as protective.

"Of course," I whispered.

His hand went to my chin, guiding it until I was looking at him. "Then, kiss me."

"My insatiable man." I smiled.

"That was for you." He aligned our mouths. "This is for our baby."

Epilogue

Cooper

"She has your eyes."

Rowan's voice was like a song against my ears as I lay with her in the hospital bed, our baby wrapped in her arms, positioned in front of us so we could take in every feature.

Features we'd been staring at nonstop.

Remembering every second.

Loving endlessly.

Healing from the whirlwind of the last twenty-four hours.

Rowan's contractions had brought us right to the hospital, where she had the baby seven hours later. In that delivery room, I held her hand and the back of her thigh, and talked her through one of the most challenging moments of her life. Even with the help of an epidural, labor wasn't easy on her mentally or physically.

I had been a nervous mess; it had been so hard to see her go through that.

But that woman was my fucking hero.

And her determination and strength gave me the most

amazing gift.

My daughter.

A perfect, beautiful little princess with the biggest blue eyes and pudgy cheeks, a tiny sloped nose and thick, pouty lips.

A face as gorgeous as her mother's with a set of lungs like mine.

"And she has your nose," I told her, running my finger down our baby's nose, her skin so soft that I was afraid I'd hurt it. "How is she ours? How in the hell did we make something so flawless? And how am I already thinking of all the men I'm going to kill if they even look in her direction a hundred years from now?"

Rowan laughed. "She got the best of both of us." She adjusted the blanket. "I mean, look at these toes. I've literally never seen anything cuter."

I kissed both of her feet as they lay still, our little one fast asleep, minutes after Rowan finished feeding her.

"And the hair." I lifted her hat just enough to see the dark locks. "She definitely got your color." I moved the fabric down again and put a finger under her chin. "I love you so much, it hurts."

"I couldn't have said it more perfectly."

I turned to the woman who would soon become my wife. *That* I was sure of. And I kissed her forehead, holding my lips there, breathing her in. She didn't even smell like the hospital. She smelled like the woman I'd fallen for—apples and cedarwood.

"The way you fought in that delivery room was nothing short of amazing. I hope you know that."

"I focused on your voice, and you got me through it. I couldn't have done it without you."

I didn't know about that.

The woman lying next to me had courage and a toughness like I'd never witnessed before. I didn't know a single dude in my life who could have survived that labor.

Myself included.

But knowing I had been there for her, that I'd helped even in the smallest way, meant a lot.

"And now, we have her," I whispered.

"*Annnd* she already owns you."

"Is it that obvious?"

Rowan grinned. "When I woke up from the little nap I took, the two of you were sitting on the chair, her tiny head resting on your bare chest. That's an image I'll never forget."

"I don't want to let her go. I want to protect her from everything."

Her eyes gleamed while she stared at me. "You're the father I knew you'd be. Seeing that side of you, watching you hold our little girl... Cooper, I can't explain it, but that's a kind of love I wasn't ready for."

"Baby..." I said softly, my lips on Rowan's forehead, making sure she knew I was addressing her and not the one in her arms.

There was a vibration in my pocket, a notification that could only come through by one of my Favorites since everyone else was silenced.

I took out my phone, and there was a text from Rhett on the screen. I showed the message to Rowan.

Her eyes instantly filled. "Yes," she said, responding to Rhett's text, "tell them to come up."

"You're sure you're ready?"

I didn't care what anyone in this family wanted.

I cared what Rowan wanted and what was best for her.

"I'm ready."

I replied to the message and kissed Rowan's cheek, carefully lifting myself out of the bed. I walked to the door and stood at the entrance, waiting for the familiar faces to appear in the hallway.

Rowan and I had talked about this. She was extremely specific about what she wanted, how the visit was going to go down in two waves. She had her reasoning, and I backed it fully.

Daisy, Rowan's mom, my brothers, my parents, Jo, Jenner, and Walter would visit second.

First up were Ridge, Rhett, and Ray, and they were making their way toward the room.

Ridge had his phone in his hand, ready to capture the pictures Rowan had requested. And Rhett was behind his dad, pushing Ray's wheelchair.

In the last few months, Ray had progressively gotten worse. In fact, once this introduction was over, Rhett would have to take Ray straight home and help him into bed. We knew Ray was on borrowed time, now requiring oxygen around the clock, with tubes buried in his nose and his frail arms hovering on the armrests, his face gaunt, his eyes hollow.

Rhett pushed him next to the bed, and once the chair was locked in place, Rhett took a spot next to his sister, his hand on her shoulder, admiring the baby in her arms.

"Dad…" The tears were deep within Rowan's eyes even though she was trying so hard not to shed them. "I'm so happy you're here."

Ray slowly lifted his hand and clasped Rowan's. "My l-little girl"—he stopped to take a few breaths—"is a m-mother now."

When Rowan's head bounced, a tear finally fell. "I want you to meet her."

I lifted the baby from her arms, waiting for Ray to position his in a way that would hold the weight of our daughter. And even when I placed her down, I knelt beside him, staying close and ready in case she became too much.

Rowan's face dampened as she looked at her dad, her fingers locked with Rhett's, while Ridge stood at the foot of the bed, his phone aimed at the group, snapping pictures from every angle.

"My g-goodness," Ray said. "Isn't s-she the most b-beautiful baby?"

"Her name is Rayner, Dad."

Ray looked up, the emotion heavy on his face. "Rayner…"

"She's named after her grandfather. One of the most amazing men I know."

• • •

Turn the page to start reading an excerpt from the next book in the series, *The Sinner.*

Prologue

BRADY

Commercial airlines weren't for people who had billions worth of assets. But since my younger brother had booked our private jet before I had the chance to reserve it, that was exactly what I'd been stuck with, waiting for my flight to take off to Edinburgh to look at property for a new hotel. It didn't matter that I was stretched out in my own pod or that I'd been greeted with a glass of scotch when I'd stepped into first class or that a five-course meal was being offered during the seven-hour flight.

I was fucking pissed.

I didn't want to people—my family would say that was because I was a grumpy asshole, I referred to it as being selective. I didn't want a three-hour layover at JFK that I'd just barely recovered from since LAX didn't have a direct flight. I didn't want to deal with the crowd during the chaos of embarking and at baggage claim and locating my driver when they'd normally be parked directly outside the plane.

Macon had already gotten an earful when I found out he and his girlfriend were taking the plane to Hawaii to visit her family. But the conversation I'd had with him a few days ago over this wasn't enough. He needed a verbal whipping because there was no reason he couldn't be on a commercial flight, and I could be the one flying in luxury across the Atlantic.

I pulled out my phone, getting ready to send him a scalding text, when Dominick's name came across the screen. I connected the call and held my cell up to my face. "Tell me something good."

Like myself, Dominick was the oldest Dalton, a group of lawyers my family not only did business with regularly, but we were extremely good friends with. And since Jenner, Dominick's brother, had married my cousin Jo, the Daltons were basically family now.

"As opposed to something bad?" He chuckled.

"Listen, not even a down pillow and a foot massage could make me a happy man right now."

"We both know there's only one thing that makes you happy and you're not getting it on that flight."

Pussy.

There was nothing else that could turn this day around.

But there wasn't anyone in this first-class cabin or in the flight crew who was hot enough to even make my dick hard. So far, during this entire trip, there was only one woman who had the power to do that. A flight attendant I'd seen earlier when I was coming out of the airline's lounge to go to my gate. A blonde, far too fucking beautiful for her own good with a body to die for. And just when I'd gotten a solid look at her, she had disappeared into the sea of passengers.

I breathed in, wishing it was the scent of the blonde's cunt rather than the bullshit recycled air that came through the vents. "You're right. Fuck me."

"I hoped to catch you before you took off. Glad I did. You're gone for just a couple of days, yeah?"

"Long enough to make an offer on a piece of land or purchase an existing hotel that we're going to gut and make our own."

Now that the Spades had merged with the Coles, our biggest competitor in the hospitality space, and the elders of both companies had retired, the seven of us—my two brothers, my cousin Jo, the three Coles, and me—were running the business. Together, we'd decided that Edinburgh was the next location to house one of our five-star resorts and I would be spearheading the project. The six others were an opinionated group, but I'd made it clear when I left LA that this was *my* hotel. They picked the city, I chose everything else, and I gave zero fucks about what any of them thought going forward.

"Do I dare guess that you're taking a commercial flight back home?"

"Fuck off, Dominick."

He laughed as I drained my last sip of scotch, setting the glass a little too hard on the small table beside me. The tumbler wasn't out of my hands for more than a few seconds when a flight attendant, carrying a glass of amber liquid, started making her way over to me.

Not just any flight attendant.

The goddamn blonde I'd seen earlier at the airport, a woman so fucking gorgeous, my cock was throbbing inside my pants.

Man, wasn't that some luck.

Things hadn't gone my way when Macon had scored the jet out from under me, but things were changing. Because it certainly wasn't a coincidence that the flight attendant I'd gotten a semi over earlier wasn't just on my flight, but was assigned to the first class cabin.

Now that I was much closer to her, unlike when we were in

the airport, I could take my time gazing at every inch of that face and body. Her long hair was curled around her cheeks, like I'd circled the locks around my fist and caused kinks in the strands. Her eyes were the deepest, most piercing blue. She had on a uniform, consisting of a light blue button-down, knee-length skirt, and blazer, leaving everything up to my imagination, and my imagination was wandering to a far-off, naked land. But what I could see from here was the outline of one perfect, extremely sexy body, with tits that were perky and hips that were so enticing I wanted her legs straddling me. My stare bounced from her full lips to her nipples, so hard that I could see their outline through her shirt.

Damn it, she was a fucking dime.

She stopped at the entrance of my pod. "Mr. Spade, I thought you could use a refill."

Hearing her say my name made my pre-cum bead at the tip.

She took my empty and replaced it with the glass she was holding, her fingers clutched around the girth, like it was my dick. "Oh"—her hand covered her mouth when I turned my face, showing her that I was on the phone—"I'm sorry, I didn't realize you were busy. Excuse me—"

"What's your name?"

She was trained to smile, but what came across her mouth wasn't fake. It also wasn't forced. I could tell we were mutually satisfied with what we were looking at.

This was going to be fun.

"Lily."

Lily.

Oh. I liked that.

And I liked having only inches between us, the nearness giving me hints of her fruity scent.

I lifted the drink in the air, moving it toward my chest. "How about you come back in a few minutes, Lily, and bring me another one of these."

In addition to her grin, she gave me a fluttering of her lashes before she walked away.

"*Fuuuck*," I groaned to Dominick. "Things are about to turn around, my man."

"You're telling me you're going to hit that mid-flight?"

I would have hit it in the airport, but she'd taken off before I had the opportunity to speak to her.

This was my second chance.

I watched Lily's ass as she made her way toward the galley at the front of the plane, cheeks that had just the right amount of padding and thickness. "Brother, I'm going to taste her before dinner is even served."

Acknowledgments

Nina Grinstead, it doesn't matter if you're running a fever, coughing up a lung, in the middle of date night, or traveling to Europe—you're always there for me. For my stories. For these characters who are a part of you just as much as they're a part of me. You're Team B forever, moving mountains, encouraging me in every way to make my dreams come true. To many more framed text messages on my wall. I love you. To the moon and back.

Jovana Shirley, how do we not live in the same state so we can attend every concert together and have weekly cocktails? One day, hopefully very soon, those drinks are going to happen, and I'll get to tell you in person how much I appreciate everything that you do for me. It goes beyond the words you edit—I hope you know that. Like I always say, I can never do this without you. Love you so, so hard.

Ratula Roy, at the end of every book, I'm always saying, "Never again," about a certain challenge that tried to break me in the story. And every time, you help me address that challenge. You inspire me to face it head-on. And you help me cross it. That's a friend. You don't give up on me, and you never let me fail. When I'm dropping every ball, you're juggling in the background. When I'm guzzling wine, you're sending me virtual cheers. You are incredible. I love you more than love—and I'll never stop saying that to you.

Hang Le, my unicorn, you are just incredible in every way.

Judy Zweifel, as always, thank you for being so wonderful to work with and for taking such good care of my words. <3

Vicki Valente, you've been the most wonderful addition to my team. Thank you for all your hard work. I appreciate you so much.

Nikki Terrill, my soul sister. Every tear, vent, virtual hug, life chaos, workout—you've been there through it all. I could never do this without you, and I would never want to. Love you hard.

Pang and Jan, working with the two of you is one of the best parts of my job. Love you both so much. And, Pang, you have literally blown me away with the special edition layouts. I can't get over what you've created and designed for me. I'm so, so lucky to have you.

Sarah Symonds, one more down, my friend. I've lost count of how many books you've helped me through. I just know that having you in my life, on this journey, and in my corner makes me a better person. Love you.

Brittney Sahin, another book that I survived because of you. I swear, you keep me going in ways you don't even understand. Love you, B, and I love us.

Kimmi Street, my sister from another mister. Thank you from the bottom of my heart. You saved me. You inspired me. You kept me standing in so many different ways. I love you more than love.

Extra-special love goes to Valentine PR, my ARC team, my Bookstagram team, Rachel Baldwin, Valentine Grinstead, Kelley Beckham, Sarah Norris, Kim Cermak, and Christine Miller.

Mom and Dad, thanks for your unwavering belief in me and your constant encouragement. It means more than you'll ever know.

Brian, my words could never dent the love I feel for you. Trust me when I say, I love you more.

My Midnighters, you are such a supportive, loving, motivating group. Thanks for being such an inspiration, for holding my hand when I need it, and for always begging for more words. I love you all.

To all the influencers who read, review, share, post, TikTok—Thank you, thank you, thank you will never be enough. You do so much for our writing community, and we're so appreciative.

To my readers—I cherish each and every one of you. I'm so grateful for all the love you show my books, for taking the time to reach out to me, and for your passion and enthusiasm when it comes to my stories. I love, love, love you.

About the Author

USA Today best-selling author Marni Mann knew she was going to be a writer since middle school. While other girls her age were daydreaming about teenage pop stars, Marni was fantasizing about penning her first novel. She crafts sexy, titillating stories that weave together her love of darkness, mystery, passion, and human emotions. A New Englander at heart, she now lives with her husband in Sarasota, Florida. When she's not nose deep in her laptop, working on her next novel, she's scouring for chocolate, sipping wine, traveling, boating, or devouring fabulous books.

Printed in the USA
CPSIA information can be obtained
at www.ICGtesting.com
LVHW091155110424
777081LV00003B/231